A Taste of Honey

A Taste of Honey

JAMI ALDEN

APHRODISIA
KENSINGTON BOOKS
http://www.kensingtonbooks.com

KENSINGTON BOOKS are published by

Kensington Publishing Corp.
850 Third Avenue
New York, NY 10022

ISBN-13: 978-0-7582-1574-1
ISBN-10: 0-7582-1574-6

First Trade Paperback Printing: April 2007

10 9 8 7 6 5 4 3 2 1

Printed in the United States of America

CONTENTS

Stripping It Down

I

The other day my friend—let's call her Sue—came crying to me about the latest disaster in her already-pockmarked love life. He was perfect, she sobbed. Smart. Cute. Employed. (Trust me, that's a new one for her.) On their first date they met for brunch and talked for hours. On their second date he showed up with flowers and took her to the hot new restaurant she mentioned wanting to try.

And afterward he took her back to his ultramodern loft and banged the hell out of her.

You know what happened next, don't you girls?

He said he'd call. Of course, he didn't.

The dog.

But don't be so quick to put this doggie down.

The way I see it, it's not his fault. It's hers.

Of course, loving and supportive friend that I am, I didn't tell her so.

But really, when are the Sues of the world going to grow up and stop taking it so hard when the boys they bang merely act as expected?

The flowers, the restaurant? Unoriginal moves to get us in the sack. And once they do, they're off, sniffing another ass like any good dog would.

You know me, I'm not saying don't give them what they want—assuming you get what you want too.

But if you're going to be like Sue and spend the morning after crying over your used condom, save yourself the heartache (and your friends the earache) and stay home with your pocket rocket.

> *—Excerpt from "Stripping it Down: A Modern Girl's Adventures in Dating" by C. Teaser, from online magazine Bustout.com*

"Come on, Kit, it's your turn."

Kit Loughlin winced and took another sip of her chardonnay as eleven pairs of eyes gave her their undivided attention. Why did these types of gatherings always degenerate into this?

"Really, there's not much to tell," she protested.

Not that she had any qualms about discussing her sex life, given that she mined it (and embellished it) regularly on a twice-weekly basis for "Stripping It Down."

But telling all under a pseudonym was one thing. Baring all at her best friend Elizabeth's coed bachelorette party was another.

"Come on," Nicole, another bridesmaid, urged. "Everyone else has revealed the sordid details of their first time. You have to go."

Once again she fought the urge to smack Sabrina, the bridesmaid whose stupid idea this game had been in the first place. Why would anyone in her right mind think it was a good idea for a soon-to-be-wed bride and groom to reveal the details of their past sexual encounters? In front of a crowd, no less.

Yet both the bride, Elizabeth, and the groom, Michael, had jumped in with gusto, eagerly regaling their friends with stories of backseat groping and awkward penetration.

Kit had been hoping to skip her turn, purposely removing herself from the giant sectional that dominated the living room of the Mexican villa to take up a post by one of the windows overlooking the beach.

Everyone else had told their story. Now she was trapped.

She ignored a particularly piercing pair of green eyes that seemed intent on boring a hole straight through her.

"C'mon, Kit, don't be such a prude," Elizabeth prodded with a tipsy giggle.

Easy for her to say. When Elizabeth described her first time, she didn't have the distinct pleasure of having the other party in the room staring at her.

Jake Donovan watched her, one dark eyebrow arched, smirking in a way that made her want to smack it off his face. God, if she had known Jake would be joining them on their hedonistic weekend to Cabo, Kit never would have come.

"Yeah," Jake rumbled in a voice that after twelve years still had the power to send waves of heat down her spine, "we all want to know."

She glared at him, six foot four of gorgeous sprawled on the couch in casual arrogance, the perfect genetic blend of his Italian mother and Irish father, with strong, masculine features and green eyes that stood out against his naturally dark skin.

He wasn't even her type—not anymore anyway—in his yuppie uniform of golf shirt and khaki shorts.

She went for artsy, rocker types. Guys who wore Gucci and Prada and product in their hair. Not stuffy venture capitalists with their dark hair cut conservatively short and their all-American ex-football-player brawn draped in the latest corporate logo wear. She met enough of those through her day job as a business reporter for the *San Francisco Tribune*.

But she couldn't discount the way his eyes glowed against his tan or that his abdomen had none of the softness she'd come to associate with men of his ilk. Unlike his three younger brothers, Jake had left their little town of Donner Lake and never returned, eschewing his father's construction business for an MBA. But even though he didn't do anything close to manual labor, his biceps strained the sleeves of his golf shirt, veins visible along the swell as he took a sip of Pacifico and grinned.

So he went to the gym in between making millions as a venture capitalist. He still had no right to look so smug. Especially given what she knew about his prowess in the sack.

Or lack thereof.

"Really, there's not much to tell," she repeated, casually taking a seat on the arm of the overstuffed armchair occupied by Michael's brother, Dave. "It was over so quickly I barely remember it myself."

Jake sat up straighter.

Got your attention, eh, big boy? Suddenly she relished the chance to let Jake know exactly what she thought of his stick-it-in-and-come technique. "It was all very typical, really," she continued. "I was seventeen, and the guy was a friend of my brother's—a few years older, of course, so I'd had lots of time to build up a big, hard crush on him."

All the women in the room affected sympathetic smiles.

"So one night, he shows up at our house looking for my brother. It was summer vacation, and he and my parents had already gone to the city for the weekend." Everyone ooohed. Except for Jake. He was staring at her quizzically, as though he himself didn't know exactly where this was going.

"And this guy, who was totally drunk—although I was too stupid to realize it at the time—tells me some sob story about having a big fight with his girlfriend." She rolled her eyes and took another drink of wine, relishing the way Jake was shifting uncomfortably.

"The next thing I know, he's kissing me, and of course, having the giant crush on him that I do, I don't stop to think that perhaps this is not the best idea." Pausing for maximum impact, she said, "Five rather painful and awkward minutes later, I was watching his bare ass disappear out the front door."

Even the guys winced at that one.

"What happened after that?"

Kit snorted. "Like you have to ask? He got back together with his girlfriend and never talked to me again."

Jake was glaring at her now, his acre-wide shoulders so tight she could see the outline of his muscles straining against the soft cotton of his shirt. She met his glare head on, daring him to dispute any part of her story.

She reached for the bottle of chardonnay and tipped the last of it into her glass. "I'll go get more wine," she said, eager for an excuse to escape the room and Jake's frosty green stare.

She ran down to the wine cellar on shaky legs, praying she wouldn't do a header down the stone staircase. Her pink strappy stiletto sandals certainly didn't help matters. Warning herself to calm down before she broke something, she took the last three steps with extra care and leaned against the cool stone wall of the corridor.

She'd managed to keep it together ever since Jake showed up yesterday morning. After the stunned shock wore off, she'd retreated behind her usual brash friendliness, never hinting that she and Jake were more than casual acquaintances who had gone to high school a few years apart in the same tiny California mountain town.

Leave it to some stupid party game to dredge up twelve-year-old memories best left dead and buried.

What was the fascination with the first time, anyway? For Kit, it had been nothing more than an uncomfortable tearing of a flap of skin and a necessary death of any romantic illusions she might have fallen victim to.

She should be grateful to Jake for that at least. Who knew what kind of asinine things she might have done by now in the name of love?

Taking a deep breath, she shoved uncomfortable thoughts of Jake out of her head and admired the veritable treasure trove of vino that surrounded her. She had to give her best friend's fiancé credit. When Michael took his friends on vacation, he did it in style. The villa he'd rented had eight bedrooms, a full staff, and an infinity pool overlooking Land's End.

Kit was contemplating a bottle of ninety-one pinot noir when she sensed the warmth of another body behind her.

A big, tan hand wrapped around her hip, and hot breath grazed her neck. "Interesting story you told up there, Kit. Funny, I don't remember it going exactly the way you described."

Her whole body stiffened and she struggled not to melt back into his chest. Reaching casually for the bottle, she said, "I think I included all the pertinent details."

"And made up a few. I did put my pants on before I left. Not that you'd know, since you ran upstairs crying and locked yourself in your bedroom."

She turned around, stepping back in an attempt to put more space between them. Her bare back met the cool foil of dozens of bottles. He was so tall she had to tip her head back to see his face. "Considering your performance, can you blame a girl for crying?"

His full, firm lips compressed in a tight line, and he braced his arms on either side of her shoulders. "I never apologized for that night, Kit. It didn't go the way I wanted—"

Kit ducked under his arm and darted over to the refrigerator that housed the whites. "Don't get yourself all worked up over an awkward hump on my parents' couch." Ugh, the last thing she wanted to do was rehash their one brief, clumsy encounter. She'd spent twelve years burying the stupid, idealistic seventeen-year-old she'd been, and she had no interest in resurrecting her tonight.

"Now come on, Kitty Kat," he said, and she winced at the use of her childhood nickname, "the least you can do is let me make it up to you."

Jake's serious, apologetic expression melted away, replaced with a crooked—damn her hormones for noticing—sexy smile and a hot, lustful gleam in his gaze.

Kit's jaw nearly dropped at his arrogance. She may have gotten over the trauma of that night twelve years ago, but she certainly hadn't forgiven him. And she definitely wasn't interested in having him "make it up to her."

"Trust me, I'm over it."

He moved in until she had no choice but to rest her hips against the top of the minifridge. "You're not just a little bit interested in finding out what tricks I may have learned in the last decade?" He glanced meaningfully down at the deeply plunging front of her silk halter top. She didn't need to look down to know that her nipples were two hard points outlined against the flimsy peach fabric.

Reaching out with one finger, he traced the neckline of her top to where it ended almost at her navel. "Cold?"

She would have said yes, but even she wasn't that much of a liar.

He stepped closer, his hair-roughened knee brushing the inside of her thigh. The ragged hem of her denim micro-mini slid up another two inches.

A thick, dark lock fell across his forehead as he bent close enough for her to feel the heat of his breath on her cheek. Her heart rate picked up, and she wondered vaguely if he could see it beating against the bare sun-kissed skin of her chest. How was it, after all this time, he still had the power to transform her into a weak-kneed adolescent?

"You had your shot," she whispered, her lips so close to his she could almost taste him, "and you failed miserably. I'm not big on second chances."

He leaned forward, and the moist heat of his mouth against her collarbone sent a pulse of heat straight to her groin. "I think," he murmured as his tongue flicked along the sensitive cords of her neck, "in this case," his lips closed over her right earlobe and Kit told herself she would get up and move in two seconds but God she loved having her ears sucked, "you should make an exception."

Before she could breathe, his mouth closed over hers, lips molding and shaping as his tongue flicked against the seam.

Hot damn, he had learned some new tricks.

She kept her fists clenched firmly at her sides but couldn't stop herself from parting her lips, just a little, for one tiny bit of a taste. He pressed his advantage, plunging his tongue inside, licking and sucking until she had no choice but to fist her hands in his hair and wrap her legs around his hips.

"God, I've been dying to touch you," he groaned into her mouth. "From the second I saw you, acting so cool. Burning so hot underneath."

As though to prove himself right, he shoved his hand between her thighs and pulled aside the now-drenched strip of lace covering her mound. He uttered a low grumble of satisfaction as his fingers met smooth flesh, already slippery wet from just one kiss.

Some sane, rational corner of her brain sent out frantic signals, warning her to stop this before it went too far—as though it hadn't already.

Which were promptly drowned out as he nosed aside the gathered neckline of her top and sucked one hard, rosy nipple deep into his mouth.

She tossed her head back and moaned as a thick, blunt finger stroked against her clit. She clenched her fingers in the fabric of his shirt, wanting to tear it off but not having the presence of mind to do so. Spreading her legs wide to give him better access, she rocked her pelvis against his hand, shuddering when he sank two fingers in to the last knuckle.

"Mmm," she moaned as he twisted his fingers inside her, his thumb jumping into the mix to give her clit some much-needed attention. One, two strokes against the slippery bud and she was gone, the walls of her vagina clamping down in an orgasm so intense her screams echoed off the stone-lined ceiling.

He kissed her softly, quieting her, pressing his palm against her sex until the last tremors of her climax faded away.

Like a slap in the face, Kit suddenly became aware of her position. Legs sprawled wide on top of a minifridge, one boob hanging out of her halter, and Jake Donovan's hand once again in her pants.

Hopping off the fridge before he could catch her, she hitched her top back over her shoulder and smoothed her skirt back down her hips. She glanced at her watch. "Wow. You made me come inside of five minutes. You *have* improved."

He grinned and made a move to grab her. "I could make you come with both hands tied behind my back."

She had to get the hell out of that cellar before she begged for a live demonstration. "You've proven your point well enough." She haphazardly grabbed a few bottles of wine from the shelves. Arms full, she flashed him what she hoped passed for a sly, sophisticated smile and said, "Thanks. I needed that." She half ran back up the stairs, ignoring his shout of protest. *See how you like being left high and dry, cowboy.*

2

Thanks, I needed that. Jake couldn't help but grin at Kit's parting words.

As cool and casual as if he'd served her a drink. But despite her nonchalance, she hadn't been able to disguise the postorgasmic flush that crept all the way up her plunging neckline to her cheeks or the way her hands had trembled as they reached out to grab the bottles of wine.

She'd studiously ignored him as everyone loaded up into a van and headed into town for the evening's festivities, and she was careful to seat herself so she had a window on one side and a bridesmaid on the other, ruining his chances of copping a feel in the dark taxi.

Now he leaned against the bar of the crowded dance club, watching Kit bump and grind with Sabrina as Gwen Stefani sang about feeling hellagood. Dark hair rippling around her shoulders, hips swirling and thrusting to the beat, Kit was sex personified.

Every male eye in the club was drawn to her like bees to honey. And damned if she didn't know it.

The little tease.

She licked her lips in an exaggerated gesture and glanced in his direction, pinning him with her cool, mocking gaze for a split second before lowering her lids in a look of mock ecstasy.

His cock thickened against the confines of his slacks as he remembered what she *really* looked like when she came. How she strained against his hand, her tight, slick cunt gripping his fingers as she tossed her head back, plush mouth opening around her throaty cry.

She'd left him aching in the wine cellar, practically light-headed as every drop of blood in his body seemed to throb insistently in his cock, demanding satisfaction. He'd taken a quick, freezing shower before the group headed out to the nightclub, promising his dick imminent satisfaction even as it wilted to semi-hard.

Watching her, he took a pull from his bottle of Pacifico, imagining as he lifted his hand to his face that he could still smell her rich, spicy scent on his fingers. The mere memory was enough to bring his erection back to full attention. Dammit, at thirty-four he was supposed to have better control over himself than this.

But his reaction to Kit was no more manageable than it had been twelve years ago. From the moment he'd walked into the villa and seen her out by the pool, every nerve ending had been on high alert. Normally, he wasn't a big believer in fate or divine intervention. But seeing her silky curves barely restrained by a tiny black bikini, laid out before him like a sensual buffet, he'd sworn he felt the hand of God.

He finally had a chance to make up for the way he'd so badly bungled things when he'd been an idiot twenty-two-year-old, raging with hormones and completely lacking in good sense or self-control.

He and his girlfriend—he could barely remember her face now—had fought, and when he'd found Kit, home by herself for the night, he'd stupidly accepted her invitation to hang out and watch TV. Two years earlier Kit had morphed from an awkward, skinny teenager to long-legged sexpot seemingly overnight, and he'd been struggling to keep his hands off her ever since. But as his best friend Charlie's little sister, Kit had been strictly off limits.

But Kit had purposely tempted him, sitting oh-so casually close, close enough that her smooth, tan thighs, left bare by ridiculously short denim cutoffs, brushed against his legs as she shifted on the couch. Next, her white button-down shirt had come off in deference to the heat, even though the air conditioning had been set high enough to make her nipples poke out like little bullets against the thin fabric of her tank top.

What had really done him in, though, were her eyes. Grayish blue, thickly lashed, bright against her summer-tanned skin. Arresting, knowing, seemingly full of sensual awareness that no seventeen-year-old girl could have.

He'd wanted nothing more than to push her down on the couch and give her exactly what she was asking for, begging for. But she'd been off limits, untouchable, and he'd fought the impulse with every sinew in his ragingly horny body.

He would have succeeded, if she hadn't pinned him with that look. The same look she'd given him five seconds ago. A knowing, almost mocking look that said she knew exactly what he wanted and dared him to take it.

He'd love to blame what happened next on being drunk. But contrary to Kit's story, he hadn't had enough to be even mildly buzzed, much less the sloppy inebriate she'd described. He'd fallen victim to lust, pure and simple, barely able to get inside her before he exploded with the force of a soda bottle that had gone through a spin cycle. It was still one of the most sexually humiliating episodes of his life. By that time, he'd had plenty of experience, thought he'd known how to control himself and hold out until the girl he was with was satisfied.

Only to have whatever expertise he possessed fly out the door when he finally succumbed to the temptation of Kit.

No question he'd blown it—in more ways than one. On that they vehemently agreed. She hadn't exaggerated his performance or lack thereof. Afterward, she'd transformed from sexy, knowing woman into an innocent young girl who'd just experienced an awkward, unskilled, and uncomfortable introduction to sexual intercourse. Guilt had curdled in his stomach as she ran from the room, tears streaming down her face.

Idiot that he was, he'd convinced himself that she would never want to hear from him again. By the time he'd extricated his head from his ass and realized that she probably would have appreciated at least a phone call, months had passed, and when he saw her again over Christmas break she was dating some little tattooed punk who played guitar and whined about corporate control of America.

The music changed to Prince's "Cream," and Kit moved behind Sabrina, sliding her hand across the other woman's abdomen as they swung their hips in tandem. Some jackass in a tank top tried to move up behind Kit and get in on the action. The women smoothly danced away, dashing the poor slob's hope of ending up as the creamy center of a Kit–Sabrina sandwich.

"Maybe they'll start making out soon." Dave, the groom's brother, gestured toward the women with an exaggerated leer.

Jake drained his beer, placing the bottle on the bar behind him. "Don't count on it." The only person Kit would be making out with tonight was him.

* * *

"We should start kissing. That'll really make their night," Sabrina said over her shoulder as Kit let her hands hover dangerously over Sabrina's breasts.

Kit laughed and tossed her head back. Guys were so easy. Give them a whiff of girl-on-girl action and they were convinced you were going to reenact the double-ended dildo scene from *Where the Boys Aren't, Volume 6.*

All the boys were watching now, waiting to see how far they would take it, hoping with every inch of their hard little dicks that Kit would actually slide her hand into Sabrina's top, that Sabrina would turn around and slip Kit some tongue.

Though she hated to admit it, Kit only cared about holding the attention of one pair of gleaming green eyes. Keeping her lids lowered, she snuck another glance at the bar, her rhythm faltering when she found the space formerly occupied by Jake's broad shoulders now filled by two nearly identical bleached blondes.

Suddenly a large, proprietary hand slid around her hip to flatten across her stomach. She didn't even have to turn around to know it was Jake. Even in the crowded dance club, she could pick up his scent, soapy clean with a hint of his own special musk. Without a word he pulled her back against him. The rigid length of his erection grinding rhythmically against her ass let her know her dance floor antics had been effective.

What she hadn't counted on was her own swift response. Sure, he'd gotten the best of her in the wine cellar, but she'd written it off as a result of not having had sex since her last "friend with benefits" had done the unthinkable and actually wanted an exclusive relationship. She'd had to cut all ties and hadn't found a suitable replacement in the last six months.

Tonight, she'd only meant to tease and torment Jake, give him a taste of what he wanted but couldn't have. Now she wasn't so sure she'd be able to stick with that game plan. The memory of her gut-wrenching orgasm pulsed through her, her nerve endings dancing along her skin with no more than his hand caressing her stomach and his cock grinding against her rear. His broad palm slid up until his long fingers brushed the undersides of her breasts, barely covered by the thin silk of her top.

She was vaguely aware of Sabrina raising a knowing eyebrow as she moved over to dance with one of the other groomsmen.

Without thinking she raised one arm, hooking it around his neck as she pressed back against the hard wall of his chest. Hot breath caressed her neck before his teeth latched gently on her earlobe. The throbbing beat of the music echoed between her legs, and she knew she wouldn't be able to hold him off, not when he was so good at noticing and exploiting her weakness.

"Let's go," he whispered gruffly, taking her hand and tugging her toward the edge of the floor.

She wasn't *that* easy. "What makes you think I want to go anywhere with you?" she replied, breaking his hold and shimmying away.

A mocking smile curved his full, sensuous mouth. "Wasn't that what your little show was all about? Driving me crazy until I take you home and prove to you exactly how good it could be between us?" To emphasize his point, he shoved his thigh between hers until the firm muscles pressed deliciously against her already-wet sex. "What happened earlier was just a taste, Kit. Don't lie and tell me you don't want the whole feast."

She moaned as his mouth pressed hot and wet against her throat, wishing she had it in her to be a vindictive tease and leave him unsatisfied, aching for her body.

But her body wouldn't let her play games, and she was too smart to pass up an opportunity for what she instinctively knew would be the best sex of her life. Jake was right. She wanted him. Wanted to feel his hands and mouth all over her bare skin. Wanted to see if his cock was as long and thick and hard as she remembered. Wanted to see if he'd finally learned how to use it.

And why not? She was a practical, modern woman who believed in casual sex as long as her pleasure was assured and no strings were attached. What could be more string free than a hot vacation fling with a guy who lived on the opposite side of the country? And this time she'd have the satisfaction of leaving *him* without so much as a good-bye.

Decision made, she grabbed his hand and led him toward the door. "Let's hope you haven't oversold yourself, cowboy."

"Baby, I'm gonna give you the ride of your life."

Outside, downtown Cabo San Lucas rang with the sounds of traffic and boisterous tourists. Jake hustled her into a taxi van's back row, and in rapid Spanish he gave the driver the villa's address and negotiated a rate.

Hidden by several rows of seats, Kit had no modesty when he pulled her into his arms, capturing her mouth in a rough, lusty kiss. Opening wide, she sucked him hard, sliding her tongue against his, exploring the hot, moist recesses of his mouth. Her breath tightened in quick pants as he tugged her blouse aside and settled a hand over her bare breast, kneading, plumping the soft flesh before grazing his thumb over the rock-hard tip.

Muffled sounds of pleasure stuck in her throat. She couldn't ever remember being so aroused, dying to feel his naked skin against her own, wanting to absorb every hard inch of him inside her. She unbuttoned his shirt with shaky hands, exploring the rippling muscles of his chest and abs. He was leaner now than he'd been at twenty-two, not as bulked up as he'd been when he played football for UCLA. The sprinkling of dark hair had grown thicker as well, teasing and tickling her fingers, reminding her that the muscles that shifted and bulged under her hands belonged to a man, not a boy.

Speaking of which . . .

She nipped at his bottom lip and slid her hand lower, over his fly, until her palm pressed flat against a rock-hard column of flesh. The taxi took a sharp curve, sending them sliding across the bench seat until Kit lay halfway across Jake's chest. He took the opportunity to reach under her skirt and cup the bare cheeks of her ass, while she seized the chance to unzip his fly and reach greedily inside the waistband of his boxers.

Hot pulsing flesh filled her hand to overflowing. Her fingers closed around him, measuring him from root to tip, and they exchanged soft groans into each other's mouths. He was huge, long and so thick her fingers barely closed around him. It had hurt like a beast when he'd taken her virginity. But now she couldn't wait to feel his enormous cock sliding inside her, stretching her walls, driving harder and deeper than any man ever had.

She traced her thumb over the ripe head, spreading the slippery beads of moisture forming at the tip. Her own sex wept in response. Unable to control herself, she reached down and pulled up her skirt, climbing fully onto his lap. She couldn't wait, her pussy aching for his invasion. God, this was going to be good.

If anyone had told her twelve years ago that someday she'd be having sex with Jake Donovan in a Mexican taxicab, she would have called that person insane.

Pulling her thong aside, she slid herself over him, teasing his cock with the hot kiss of her body, letting the bulbous head slip and slide along her drenched slit. She eased over him until she held the very tip of him inside . . .

The taxi jerked abruptly to a stop, and Kit dazedly realized they'd reached the villa. With quick, efficient motions Jake straightened her skirt and shifted her off him, then gingerly tucked his mammoth erection back into his pants. With one last, hard kiss he helped her down from the van and paid the driver as though he hadn't been millimeters away from ramming nine thick inches into her pussy in the back of the man's cab.

Kit waited impatiently by the door, pretending not to see the driver's leer. Like they were the first couple to engage in hot and heavy foreplay. Jake strode over, pinning her against the door as he reached for the knob and turned.

And turned again. He swore softly.

"What is it?" Kit was busy licking and nibbling her way down the strip of flesh exposed by Jake's still unbuttoned shirt. He tasted insanely good, salty and warm.

"I don't suppose you have a key?"

She groaned and leaned her head back against the door. "I didn't take one." There were only four keys to the villa, and when they went out they all made sure they had designated male and female keyholders. Unfortunately, tonight Kit wasn't one of them, and apparently neither was Jake. "What time does the housekeeper leave?"

Jake looked at his watch. "Two hours ago."

He bent over and picked up the welcome mat, then inspected all the potted plants placed around the entry for a hidden key. Watching the way his ass muscles flexed against the soft khaki fabric of his slacks, Kit knew she was mere seconds away from pushing him down and having him right there on the slate-tiled patio.

He straightened, running a frustrated hand through his thick, dark hair. Eyes glittering with lust, he muttered, "There has to be a way in here."

"Through the back," Kit said. All they had to do was scale the wall that surrounded the villa. The house had several sets of sliding glass doors leading out to the huge patio and pool area. One of them was bound to be unlocked.

With a little grunting and shoving, Jake managed to boost Kit over the six-foot wall before hoisting himself over. Holding hands and giggling like idiots, they ran across the patio. But Jake stopped her before she reached the first set of doors.

"Doesn't that look inviting?"

She turned to find him looking at the pool. Wisps of steam rose in curly tendrils off the surface. The patio lights were off, the only illumination generated from the nearly full moon bouncing its silvery light off the dark water. A smile curved her mouth, and renewed heat pulsed low in her belly. "I could get into a little skinny dipping."

He pulled her to the side of the pool and quickly stripped off her top. Kit arched her back and moaned up to the sky as he paused to suck each nipple as it peaked in the cool night air. Her legs trembled at the hot, wet pull of his lips, her sex fluttering and contracting as it ached for more direct attention.

His hands settled at the snap of her skirt. "I like this thing," he said as he slid the zipper inch by agonizing inch. "Kinda reminds me of those sexy little shorts you wore that first time—"

Her whole body tensed. She didn't want to think of that night right now, didn't want to think about the last time she let uncontrollable desire get the best of her. Her fingers pressed against his lips. "I'd rather not revisit unpleasant memories."

She caught the quick hint of a frown across his features, but he hid it quickly as he slid her skirt and thong off, leaving them to pool around her feet.

"In that case," he said as his shirt slid off his massive shoulders, "I better get down to creating some new ones."

3

Damn, the woman knew how to hold a grudge. But the sting Jake felt at Kit's reminder of just how unpleasant she found the memories of their first time quickly faded at the sight of her in the moonlight, fully nude except for her stiletto-heeled sandals.

With her long legs and soft curves, sex radiated from her pores like a perfume, sending pulses of electricity straight to his groin. His cock was so hard he actually hurt.

In the clear moonlight he could make out the sculpted lines of her cheekbones, the dark sweep of lashes over her blue eyes, the full curve of her lips. Her dark hair swung forward over her shoulders, playing peekaboo with tight, dark nipples.

His hands followed his gaze, tracing the taut, smooth plane of her abdomen, coming to rest just above what he'd felt before but hadn't seen. Her pubic hair was a dark, neatly trimmed patch over plump, smooth lips. Her breath caught as he combed his fingertips through the silky tuft of hair, inching his way down but not touching the hot, silky flesh that lay below.

He was afraid if he touched her he wouldn't be able to stop

himself from pushing her onto a nearby lounge chair and shoving his cock as hard and high in her as he could possibly go. His hands trembled at the remembered feel of her soft pussy lips closing over him, stretching over the broad head of his penis as she straddled him in the cab. If the driver hadn't stopped, he knew he would have lost control, would have fucked her hard and fast until he exploded inside her, ruining his chances of proving he'd learned anything about self-control in the past twelve years.

So instead of dipping his fingers into the juicy folds of her sex, he knelt in front of her and removed her lethal-looking sandals before shedding his slacks and underwear. Taking her hand, he led her into the pool.

He pulled her against him until her breasts nuzzled his chest like warm little peaches, reveling in the sensation of cool water and warm skin. He kissed her, tongue plunging rough and deep, just the way he wanted to drive inside her. He couldn't believe after all these years he was here with her again, touching her, tasting her. She tasted so good, like vodka and sin, her wet mouth open and eager under his. One taste and he regressed back to that horny twenty-two-year-old, shaking with lust and overwhelmed by the reality of touching the woman who had fueled his most carnal fantasies.

Greedily his hands roamed her skin, fingers sinking into giving flesh as he kneaded and caressed. He wished he had a lifetime to spend exploring every sweet inch of her. Kit gave as good as she got, her hands sliding cool and wet down his back, legs floating up to wrap around his waist. He threw his head back, clenching his jaw hard enough to crack a molar. Hot, slick flesh teased the length of his cock, plump lips spreading to cradle him as she rocked her hips and groaned. He backed her up against the smooth tiles that lined the sides of the pool. One thrust, and he could be inside her.

"No," he panted, "not yet."

Water closed over his head as he sank to his knees, drowning out everything but the taste and feel of her. Eyes closed, he spread her pussy lips with his thumbs, nuzzling between her legs until he felt the tense bud of her clit against his face. Cool water and hot flesh filled his mouth as he pulled her clit between his lips, sucking and flicking until her hips twitched and he heard the muffled sounds of her moans distorted by the water. A loud buzz hummed in his ears, and it occurred to him that he might pass out soon from lack of air.

Surfacing, he sucked in a deep breath and lifted her hips onto the tile ledge. She drew her knees up, resting her heels on the edge to give him unimpeded access to her perfect pink cunt. He parted the smooth lips with his thumbs, lapped roughly at the hard knot of flesh, and circled it with his tongue, sucking it hard between his lips as her pelvis rocked and bucked against his face. Every sigh, every moan, every guttural purr she uttered made his dick throb until he was so hard he feared he might burst out of his skin.

"Oh God, oh, Jake," she moaned. Another rush of liquid heat bathed his tongue, and he knew she was close. The first faint flutters of her orgasm gripped his fingers as they slid inside, clamping down harder as the full force of climax hit her.

Kit stared up at the bright night sky as the last pulses shuddered through her. Taking several deep, fortifying breaths, she risked a look at Jake. His dark head was still between her thighs as he rained soft, soothing kisses on the smooth inner curves. Tender kisses. Loving kisses, even.

Oh Christ, she might be in really big trouble.

She could never remember responding to a lover like she did to Jake. Then again, she'd never had a lover treat her like Jake did.

Her last partner was exactly the type she liked. She told him what she wanted and he listened, bringing her efficiently to satisfaction before finding his own.

But he hadn't looked at her like she was the most beautiful woman he'd ever seen. He hadn't run his hands over her skin like he wanted to memorize every inch of her. He hadn't buried his head between her legs and licked and savored her pussy like it was the most succulent, exquisite fruit he'd ever tasted.

And he sure as hell had never made her come so hard that her vision blurred and her body felt like it was wracked by thousands of tiny electrical currents.

She heard the sound of water splashing, and her stomach muscles jerked as Jake held his dripping body over hers. Bracing himself with his hands, he came down over her and kissed her with a tenderness that almost made her want to cry.

Crap. What was wrong with her? This was Jake, the man who'd so rudely introduced her to the world of slam bam thank you ma'am. To give him credit he'd proven—twice now—that he could make her come. Really, really hard. But still. It was just an orgasm.

The smartest move would be to get up and leave before she fell victim to this weird hormonal anomaly. But her brain had ceded all control to the area between her legs that still throbbed and ached to feel all of Jake buried deep inside her.

And to think men got a bad rap for being controlled by their dicks.

She draped a lazy hand around his neck and slid her fingers into the wet silk of his hair. Then he was gone, water splashing as he levered himself out of the pool. She could barely summon the energy to turn her head to watch him dig around the pockets of his pants.

Moonlight cast silvery shadows on the muscles of his back and shoulders, illuminating the drops of water cascading down his long, strong legs. A renewed jolt of energy rushed through her as he turned, his cock jutting out in stark relief. Though she couldn't see his eyes, she could feel him watching her as he rolled on a condom with slow deliberation. Stroking himself, reminding her that in a few moments the whole of that outrageously hard length would be buried deep inside her.

She rolled to her knees as he walked toward her, reaching for him as he got close. He brushed her hands away, slipping back into the water and pulling her in with him. The cool tile was hard on her back as he pulled her close for a rough kiss. He lifted her leg over his hip, burrowing the tip of his erection against her. "I can't be gentle," he murmured. "I've waited too many years to have you again."

Waited years? What did he mean by—

The thought was abruptly cut off by the sudden, swift presence of him shoving inside her. Even though she was wetter, readier, than she'd ever been, the sheer size of him caught her off guard. Stretching tight slick flesh, pressing deep, and just when she thought she couldn't take any more he drove in another inch.

Her mouth opened wide on a silent scream of pleasured pain, her startled gasps swallowed by his mouth as he pumped inside her with his cock and his tongue. Towering over her by several inches, he surrounded her, dominated her. She'd never felt so invaded, so claimed. She wasn't sure she liked it. But her body did.

She felt herself easing, softening around him, relaxing to take him deep with every surge of his hips. "Oh, Kit," he groaned, the helpless note in his voice perfectly matching the way she felt. Suddenly he pulled out, ignoring her embarrassing wail of protest as he spun her around to face the edge of the pool.

Gripping her hips so hard it should have hurt, he thrust in

from behind, whispering all the while how beautiful she was, how hot and tight her pussy felt around him. Whispers that faded into groans as his hands reached around to cup her breasts, pinching her nipples hard enough to make her yell as she pulsed and clenched around him. His hips pumped faster now, short shallow strokes interspersed with long deep plunges as he gasped and heaved behind her.

Bracing her hands on the tile wall, Kit pushed against him, working herself on his swollen shaft, pushing him so deep she felt him at the base of her spine. Her climax hovered around the edges of every stroke, knotting and tightening low in her belly. Suddenly he stiffened behind her, a low roar bellowing from his chest as he jerked heavily inside her.

The tight walls of her pussy clamped down in response, clenching around him as her own orgasm pulsed through her core with such force she might have drowned if he hadn't been holding her up.

He cradled her against him as he nuzzled his mouth against her neck. Though she wasn't one for postcoital cuddling, Kit allowed herself to enjoy his tender affection. He was preventing her from drowning after all.

"Aw, shit," he muttered.

Not exactly what she was expecting him to say.

Abruptly he pulled out and levered out of the pool as she gradually became aware of what he must have heard. Motors running. Doors slamming. Drunken laughter. "C'mon, unless you want to be tonight's late-night entertainment."

Kit considered herself adventurous when it came to sex, but she had no desire to be caught in the act by ten of her closest friends. Hurrying as much as possible on sex-weakened legs, Kit awkwardly heaved herself up and onto the patio.

Jake gathered up their clothes and wrapped her in an over-size pool towel before tucking one around his hips. Pulling her over to a set of sliding glass doors away from the main entry, he whispered a quick prayer, followed by a sigh of relief when the door slid open without protest.

Someone cranked up the stereo as they padded down the dark hallway.

How was she supposed to get to her room unnoticed when she had to cut through the living room? The hall light snapped on, and heavy footsteps echoed against the tiles. Grabbing her arm, Jake pulled her into a bedroom, dimly lit by a single lamp on the heavy wooden bedside table.

His bedroom, she quickly concluded when she saw the shirt he'd been wearing earlier carelessly tossed across the foot of the queen-size bed.

Grinning like a son of a bitch, he tumbled her back on the mattress and flung her towel across the room. "Guess you'll have to hide out in here."

"Morning."

Kit's eyes flew open in horror at the sound of Jake's sexy, sleep-roughened voice in her ear.

How could she have possibly stayed the entire night in his room?

First rule of casual sex, never sleep over. It implied a certain level of intimacy and always resulted in an awkward morning after. Not that she hadn't tried to leave. After their second round, Jake had done what any normal man does after climax and had rolled over and started snoring. She'd even waited a good ten minutes to make sure he was really out.

But the second her feet hit the floor his hand had closed around her wrist. "Where do you think you're going?" he'd asked. "I'm not done with you yet."

And he'd tucked her underneath him and slid inside her as though he hadn't already come twice in the space of two hours.

Afterward, she'd been so exhausted, like an idiot *she'd* rolled over and fallen asleep.

God, she hoped she hadn't snored or drooled. Nothing like the harsh light of day to take the polish off a lover. She risked a look over her shoulder.

Of course, Jake *would* look perfect. Instead of looking like a sleepy slob, he looked gorgeous with his dark hair sticking straight up and beard stubble darkening his jaw. Sexy and relaxed in way that made a girl dream of long Sunday mornings spent cuddling and making love and pretending that the rest of the world didn't exist.

The moronic, naïve, seventeen-year-old that lurked inside her was making her presence known. Making love? As if! She needed to get the heck out of there.

"Mmm, don't leave," he cajoled, rubbing a very impressive—and tempting—morning erection against the inner curve of her thigh. She glanced at the clock, relief mingling with disappointment as she remembered the spa treatments the girls had scheduled for today.

"Gotta go," she said briskly, forcing herself from the all too cozy bed and scrambling into her clothes. "We have spa appointments, and besides"—she tossed him a naughty glance over one shoulder—"I'm sore."

His green eyes sparked with wicked heat. "Sure you don't want me to kiss it and make it better?"

While the idiot seventeen-year-old inside Kit pleaded with her to stay, the Kit who was older and knew better waved him off and got out of the room while she still could.

Monday morning, Kit woke up and cursed, finding herself in the same place she'd been yesterday morning: Jake's bed.

Dammit.

No matter how hard she fought it, she hadn't been able to

keep herself from falling asleep burrowed up against his over-size chest and sleeping like a dead woman all the way through to morning. This morning she hadn't even noticed when he got up. But he must have been up for a while since his side of the bed was cold. Thank God for small favors. She didn't think she could fake immunity from his sexy morning-after self just now.

Yesterday after the women had returned from getting buffed, oiled, and polished within an inch of their lives, she'd been determined to keep a little distance. The last thing she wanted was to start acting all couple-y and give everyone the wrong impression.

Yet somehow she'd spent the evening glued to his side before they retired shortly after dinner.

She sighed and rolled over, silently reprimanding herself for once again falling prey to Jake Donovan's considerable charms. And despite Kit's attempts to stifle her with neglect and copious amounts of alcohol, that ridiculous teenage girl who had so foolishly imagined herself in love with Jake so many years ago kept clamoring for attention. Going on and on about how this had to be fate, bringing them together like this, her agenda fueled by Jake's constant attention and considerable sexual skill. *Look at the way he stares at you when he thinks you're not looking*, teenage-idiot Kit crowed. *Listen to the way he laughs at your jokes. Isn't it nice to be with a guy who actually gets your sense of humor?*

And talk about gorgeous . . . You have to admit after all these years it's fun to be with a guy who's so big and strong and . . . dominant.

Kit conceded that point. For years the guys she hooked up with tended to the slender, wiry side, the exact opposite of Jake's six foot four of imposing brawn. At an athletic five seven, she wasn't particularly petite herself, and she had to admit it was kinda fun feeling almost dainty in bed.

But so what? So he was still incredibly hot, and his sexual technique had improved by several orders of magnitude. Jake, she reminded herself firmly, was still the original dog that had crushed the romantic spirit of her seventeen-year-old self, screwing her literally and figuratively without so much as a follow-up phone call. And she was no longer an innocent girl in the throes of a wicked crush, but a grown woman who knew better than to put much stock in a handful of orgasms.

Once they got on their flights this afternoon—he to Boston, she to San Francisco—the last two days would fade to a vague memory of hot sex under the Mexican moon.

Not bothering to hunt for her clothes, Kit snatched up one of Jake's XXL T-shirts and pulled it over her head. It hung past her knees, providing plenty of coverage for her walk of shame back to her own room. She tried not to notice the masculine soap and sandalwood scent that clung to the soft cotton as she padded down the hall. Nevertheless, she couldn't ignore the fierce pulse beat that picked up between her thighs at the thought of nuzzling her nose into the naked skin of his chest, the silky underside of his arm, his hair-roughened inner thigh . . .

As she crept across the living room, thankful that she'd yet to encounter any other guests, she picked up the low rumble of his voice coming from the kitchen. She didn't mean to eavesdrop, and wouldn't have even stopped if she hadn't heard her name.

She crept into the adjoining dining room, and from her vantage next to the china hutch she could hear them clearly without being seen.

"She's one hot piece of ass." Kit was pretty sure that was Dave, her least favorite of the groomsmen. Unfortunately he was also the groom's brother, so he had to be included in the wedding party. He'd struck Kit as an overgrown frat boy trying to perpetually relive the glory days of the Sigma Chi house, so she wasn't surprised or particularly offended to hear his assessment of her. "Is she as wild as she looks? I bet she's a screamer."

Kit tensed, bracing herself for Jake's contribution to the locker room talk, telling herself she didn't give a crap what he had to say.

"If you say one more word about her, I'm going to take this spatula and shove it straight up your ass." Even more shocking than his words was his tone: low and lethal and definitely not messing around.

"Hey man," Dave's voice sounded garbled, like someone was choking him, "I was only kidding. It's not like I'm talking about your wife or anything—"

Jake's next words stunned her. "As far as you or anyone else in this house are concerned, Kit is mine, got that? And if you so much as look at her again before we leave today, I'll feed you your own testicles."

Kit's shoe slid from her nerveless fingers, its impact unnaturally loud in the tiled, high-ceilinged room.

"What the—"

Crap! She made a mad dash across the dining room and down the hall to the room she hadn't slept in for the past two nights.

How dare he be so possessive, she fumed. *Kit is mine.* Whatever! She wasn't anyone's, thank you very much, and one weekend of—albeit fantastically amazing—sex was not about to change that.

Especially when it involved Jake Donovan. Did he really think, after all these years and the way he had treated her, he could waltz back into her life and give her a few mind-blowing orgasms, and she'd allow herself to be dragged back to his cave?

Fat chance. It was time Jake got his own bitter taste of reality.

4

What is it about an old flame that really gets our engines revved? Why is it that some guys make us come back for more, even when they don't deserve it? Me, I'm not one to offer up second chances. Yet I spent the most incredible sun- and sex-soaked weekend of my life with a guy who, based on his past performance, never should have gotten within an inch of my panties again in this lifetime. But boy had this dog learned some new tricks— enough to make this girl howl . . .

Kit groaned in frustration as a knock sounded at her door. Who could possibly be here at nine P.M. on a Tuesday night? Maybe if she pretended not to be home, whomever it was would go away. One thing she did not need right now was an interruption. Not only did earnings reports start tomorrow, but also in less than twelve hours she had a deadline on another article in her ongoing investigation into local biotech companies that had fudged clinical study data on pharmaceuticals they were developing.

She clicked on a URL and pulled up yet another article on the fun things various drugs could do to one's liver, dreaming wistfully of the day when she could write things like "Stripping It Down" and get paid enough to leave the dry, clinical world of business reporting.

The pounding at her door continued. It was probably her neighbor Margot from across the hall wanting to watch TV since Kit had cable and Margot didn't. She slid her bare feet into the red fuzzy scuffs under her desk and shuffled over to the door.

"You can come in," she grumbled as she flung open the door without bothering to look through the peephole, "but you have to keep quiet."

"If I remember correctly, last time I saw you, you were the one making most of the noise."

Kit stepped back in shock at the sight of Jake Donovan in her doorway, a take-no-prisoner's grin stretched across his unfairly handsome face.

"What the hell are you doing here?" she snapped before she could stop herself. She thought for a split second she was hallucinating. In the week since she'd returned from Cabo, Jake had never been far from her thoughts. Especially when she'd written the last two installments of "Stripping It Down," during which she'd revisited every delicious moment she'd spent at the mercy of Jake's sexual potency.

Ignoring her question, he pushed his way past her and into her apartment without an invitation. Closing the door behind them, he caught her chin in one hand and tilted it up to meet his kiss. "I never did get to kiss you good-bye," he said as he released her, licking his lips as though savoring her taste.

She felt a wash of shame across her cheeks. After she'd heard his outburst in the villa's kitchen, she'd quickly packed her stuff and asked one of the maids to call her a taxi. After sneaking out the back entrance, she'd left for the airport without so much as a good-bye to anyone. Especially not Jake.

Not the best form, she conceded, and definitely not the move of a woman who was as nonchalant about Jake as Kit told herself she was. But Jake was getting ideas, as evidenced by his outburst to Dave, and at the time Kit could think of nothing but getting far, far away before he foolishly tried to make something out of their meaningless weekend fling.

And the fact that he was in her apartment, unannounced and uninvited, a mere week later warned her that Jake might not have taken their weekend as casually as she would have liked. "You flew across the country just to kiss me good-bye? Should I worry that I have a stalker on my hands?"

Jake chuckled and walked into the living room, tossing his suit jacket across the back of the couch as though he did it every day. As he loosened the knot of his tie, she couldn't help admiring the way his shoulders strained the brushed cotton of his button-down shirt, the way his suit pants draped over the tight muscles of his butt. He leaned his weight against the back of her putty-colored sofa, heat crackling from his eyes as they scanned her from her messy ponytail to her ratty red slippers.

She fought the urge to cringe. Of course, Jake would be dressed like a GQ wet dream while she had to answer the door in a threadbare T-shirt she'd picked up for free at a conference somewhere and a pair of ancient boxer shorts. Not that she cared what he thought of how she looked—she wasn't sure she wanted him here at all, and the less desirable he found her the less likely this situation would get complicated.

Never mind the fact that her nipples had risen up like bullets at the first flick of those cool green eyes.

"Don't worry, Kit," he said, "I won't be boiling any bunnies.

My firm is working on a deal out here and they want me in the San Francisco office for the next month or so."

That sounded reasonable enough. She had, of course, Googled Jake the minute she got home and knew that his firm did have an office in San Francisco and had invested in several local technology companies.

What an idiot. As if he would actually fly all the way from Boston to see her, regardless of how phenomenal the sex had been. She didn't know what was scarier—the initial thought that he *had* taken their weekend too seriously or that she was actually disappointed he was there only for business.

"I called your brother to get your info," he continued, "and figured I'd stop by." He pushed up from the couch and walked slowly toward her, not stopping until he stood mere inches away.

"You could have called first," she said, folding her arms across her chest to hide her body's intense reaction.

"After the way you left"—he slid his hand up and around to cup her neck—"I wasn't sure you'd agree to see me."

She licked her lips nervously, clenching her hands around her biceps as she fought the urge to sweep his feet out from under him and knock him to the floor. "You didn't think I'd want to see you?"

His teeth flashed whitely against his tan skin. "I knew you wanted to see me," he said, "but I didn't know if you'd agree."

He leaned closer, until she could feel his warm breath across her lips. "Pretty sure of yourself, aren't you?" she murmured, her lips brushing his chin as she couldn't stop herself from rising up on tiptoe and leaning in.

Grasping her ponytail in his hand, he pulled her head back, teasing her lips open with his tongue before thrusting inside. Her arms uncrossed and coiled around his neck, pulling him close as she opened her mouth wide for his invasion.

He groaned and sank into her, sucking and biting at her lips like a starving man. Heat pooled between her thighs until all she could think about was getting him naked and inside her as quickly as possible.

Still, she couldn't let him win so easily. Jerking her head from his grasp, she said, "So that's it? No flowers, no dinner? You were in town and thought you'd look me up for a booty call? I wonder what Charlie would think about you treating his baby sister like this."

Jake slid a proprietary hand up the back of her shirt, his splayed fingers sending hot shivers down her spine. The other wrapped around her hip, drawing her close enough to feel the heat of his erection through the fabric of his pants. "You want me to work for it, Kit? Dinner? Flowers? I'll do whatever you want." He kissed her hard, leaving her lips swollen and throbbing. "But I spent the whole flight like this," he growled, pulling her hand down to his fly so she could feel for herself how hard and huge he was, "thinking about how soon I could get inside you."

It was too much. She didn't want to hear the want, the *need* in his voice, scaring her even as it sent a gush of liquid heat pulsing between her thighs.

"I'll play any game you want," he whispered as his tongue trailed down the sensitive cords of her neck, "but I thought at this point we could be honest with each other."

Relief, mixed with disappointment, coursed through her. Kit focused on relief. Clearly whatever possessive feelings he had for her had faded, and all he wanted from her was sex. Why beat around the bush pretending to date when all he wanted was some good old-fashioned, no-strings-attached sex like they'd had in Mexico?

Because that was exactly what she wanted too.

Liar.

But Kit ruthlessly silenced the voice that tried to tell her she wanted more.

Instead she grabbed Jake by the tie and pulled him into her bedroom, where they stripped each other with frenzied efficiency, pausing to kiss and lick each new patch of skin as it was revealed. Backing him up against the edge of the mattress she pushed him down, following after him until she landed sprawled naked across his milewide chest. Like a cat in heat she rubbed herself against the lightly furred wall of his chest, hissing as his hands covered her bare breasts, palms rasping against the sensitive points of her nipples.

His cock was hot and throbbing against her belly, and she positioned herself over him so she could slide her dripping slit along the rock-hard flesh. Big hands cupped her ass, grinding her against him until she was on the verge of orgasm from that brief contact.

Not yet. She pulled away slightly, leaning down to trace her tongue between his pecs as something he said in that wine cellar tickled at the back of her brain.

With one hand she guided his hands up to the wrought iron rails of her bed frame, while the other slid open the drawer of her bedside table. In only a few seconds she managed to locate what she wanted.

The cold snap of metal sounded unnaturally loud in her tiny bedroom, and Jake's eyes flew open as he found himself handcuffed firmly to her headboard.

His biceps bulged deliciously as he tested the bonds, and finding himself firmly tethered, he relaxed back against the pillows.

Knees spread on either side of his torso, Kit sat back, surveying him like a conquering Amazon claiming her prize.

"I'm at your mercy." He smiled.

"You certainly are." Leaning forward until her breasts just

brushed his face, she moaned as he obediently turned his head so he could tongue first one, then the other nipple into his mouth. She sat back again, and his mouth released a hard point with an audible pop. "Whatever shall I do with you?"

"I could make some suggestions, but since you're the one who wanted to play power games, I think it should be up to you."

She wondered what Jake would say if she admitted this was the first time she'd used the handcuffs. A gag gift from a girl's night out, the pink fur-lined novelty item had rested unused in her bedside drawer for the past two years. As sexually liberated as she liked to think she was, she'd never had the urge to tie a man down and had certainly never trusted one to do the same to her.

But Jake was so cocky, so sure of himself, she couldn't resist the temptation to put his skills to the test. "You told me in Mexico," she said, gently raking her nails down the skin of his chest, "that you could make me come with both hands tied behind your back." A film of sweat erupted on his skin, and she felt the tip of his cock jerk against the back of her thigh. "Let's see how you do with both hands tied to my bed."

A slow, sexy smile spread across his face, and she could tell by the flutters low in her belly that he wouldn't have to try all that hard. Licking his lips in anticipation, he whispered, "Climb on up, Kitty Kat."

She settled herself over him, knees on either side of his ears. Her breath caught, eyes closing as he nuzzled her labia apart. Her fingers wrapped around his where they gripped the headboard, a soft moan pushing through her lips as his tongue made a soft foray. Flicking and swirling, he teased and taunted her clit with soft brushing strokes, then abandoned it to trace the drenched seam of her lips, pushing his way into her hot core in a soft tongue fuck.

Her hips rocked to meet the soft thrusts, her sounds of pleasure giving way to frustration as he kept his strokes light, brushing, never settling into a firm rhythm that would drive her to orgasm.

Proving that just because he was tied up didn't mean he was powerless.

"Damn you, stop teasing," she said between clenched teeth.

He laughed softly, the vibration sending shuddery pulses against her aching flesh. She sighed as his mouth opened over her clit, drawing the tight kernel between his lips and lashing it with firm strokes of his tongue. He feasted on her with hungry sucks of his lips, lapping and plunging against her.

Within moments she felt the familiar tightening in her core as her orgasm bloomed low in her belly. His mouth's relentless assault drove her over the edge, his tongue driving inside her quivering cunt as she trembled and pulsed against his face.

Hot tingles spread down her arms and legs as she slid herself down his body, coming to rest with her head against his chest. "I guess you weren't lying."

He lifted his head off the pillow and leaned forward to press a kiss to the top of her head. "I hate it when people exaggerate their abilities, so I try never to do it myself."

Kit sighed and squirmed against him, jerked out of her sleepy postcoital lassitude by the insistent prodding of his erection against her ass, reminding her that she might be well satisfied, but he was still very much aroused and raring to go. It would serve him right if she left him unsatisfied and tied to her bed, but she couldn't bring herself to do it after he'd done such a good job of getting her off.

True, she had a petty vindictive streak and she didn't know if she'd ever be through with Jake, but to leave him hard and aching seemed outrageously unfair.

Not to mention a horrible waste of a perfectly good erection.

She nibbled and sucked her way down his torso, loving the salty taste of his skin, the musky scent of aroused male teasing her nostrils. Her tongue traced the narrow line of hair that bisected a perfect six-pack, skittered around his navel, and stopped just short of the rigid shaft jutting up and tapping insistently against his belly button.

A bead of pre-come pearled on the tip. His cock jumped against her tongue as she lapped it off. Every muscle stood out in tight relief as she punished him with the same teasing licks, the soft, kitten-like laps he'd used to torment her. A vein stood out starkly along his shaft, throbbing double time as he strained against her firm hold.

Finally she took him into her mouth, and his thrilled groan was enough to send a bolt of renewed want straight to her core. He was so big she could barely fit her lips around him, her mouth stretched around the tip of his cock as she struggled to take him deeper. Grasping him in her hand, she worked him in short, tight strokes as her tongue swirled against the silky smooth head. His hips moved restively, and she could tell he was fighting the urge to thrust into her mouth.

As much as she loved the taste and feel of his cock in her mouth, it wasn't enough for her either. Her pussy wept and throbbed, aching to feel the thick stretch of him sinking inside her.

"Where are you going?" His voice held the strain of a man pushed to the brink of his endurance.

She leaned over and took his mouth in a deep, tongue-thrusting kiss but didn't answer as she pushed herself off the bed and sauntered away. When she pulled away his expression was wary. He was actually worried that she wouldn't come back. Did the cheap thrill she got from that make her a sadist?

5

For a minute Jake thought he might actually cry with relief when, instead of leaving him with the world's worst case of blue balls, Kit reappeared with a naughty smile and a condom in one hand.

She paused in the doorway, unabashed in her nudity, looking so beautiful and sexy he thought his heart might burst. "You didn't really think I was going to leave you."

"I don't know what to expect from you." He jerked against the handcuffs for emphasis.

Somewhere in the midst of their frenzy, her hair had fallen out of its ponytail, and the thick brown strands tickled his cheeks as she kissed him. "Lucky for you," she murmured against his lips, "I'm not done with you yet."

Jake had used the time she'd spent rummaging in the bathroom for a condom to pull himself together, but his control nearly shattered at the feel of her smooth hand against his raging hard-on. Instead of the delicious feel of her fingers as she covered him in latex, he focused on random details of her room: how her dresser was nicked and obviously used; the framed Ansel Adams black and whites that seemed too calm for the vibrant, badass image she seemed to cultivate.

But then she was sliding herself over him, the tight walls of her body gripping him so tight he feared he was going to come right then and there. He clenched his teeth, holding himself back with every sinew in his body as she began to move over him, her back arched, tawny pink nipples jutting out in hard little points until his mouth watered to taste them. He tried to lift himself off the bed, the movement hampered by the handcuffs. "Let me loose," he said, "I need to touch you."

"What if I don't want to?" she said breathlessly, bracing her hands on his chest as she started a slow, lazy pace.

Bracing his feet on the bed, Jake drove his hips hard, high enough so he knew she'd feel him against her spine. "Unlock the goddamned handcuffs," he growled, barely recognizing the almost savage tone of his own voice. He thrust again, eliciting a keening moan from between Kit's kiss-bruised lips.

She leaned over and retrieved the key from the bedside table, and in seconds he was free. His hands immediately moved to grasp her hips, holding her still for his slow, deep thrusts as he held a nipple captive between his teeth. *Such a little tease,* he thought affectionately. Trying to act so tough, leaving him without a good-bye in Mexico and pulling her little dominatrix act on him tonight. Whether she was willing to admit it or not, she was as powerless over this thing between them as he was.

Now it was the perfect time for a little demonstration.

Kit gasped in surprise as, in one movement, Jake flipped her onto her back and captured her wrists above her head. So enthralled by the feel of him buried impossibly deep inside her, she didn't register the metallic click until she tried to reach her hands up to cradle his head.

Goddamn him! "Let me go." She struggled and bucked against him, but that only served to shove his cock more firmly inside her as her clit ground against his pubic bone. He swallowed her angry sounds of protest with his mouth. She retaliated by biting his lip hard enough to taste blood.

He jerked back, incredulous as he touched his tongue to the wound. She couldn't decide who was more shocked by her savagery.

She watched him warily as he hung frozen above her, still buried so deep she could feel his pulse inside her body. Then a scared little shiver skittered through her as a positively evil smile spread across his face. "Don't start games you don't want to play, Kit."

She didn't have time to wonder what he meant. She was too horrified by the fact he was rummaging through her nightstand drawer while she lay pinned and helpless to do anything about it. Her journal was in there, along with private mementos and . . .

"You naughty girl, Kitty Kat." She immediately recognized the small cylindrical object in his hand, along with its telltale hum.

She jerked and moaned as he passed the tip of the vibrator over her nipples, the jolt causing her cunt to spasm around his cock. Unaccountably embarrassed to have him find her sex toy, modest though it may be, she strove for bravado. "Most guys are intimidated by a vibrator. Think they can't match up."

"This little guy?" He held up the white toy, not more than five inches long and an inch and a half in diameter. Deliberately, he slid out of her until just the head of his erection lodged inside her body. He drove himself back in with excruciating leisure. "I don't think I have anything to feel threatened by."

"It's not the size of your boat," she said, the high, thready tone of her voice betraying her.

His slow, steady strokes kept her from finishing the rest of the saying.

Coming up on his knees, he draped her legs over his hips and moved in steady, measured thrusts until she was a moaning, writhing mess who could barely remember that the world existed beyond his cock. Without breaking his pace he traced the vibrator down her belly, resting it just above her mons. Her clit pulsed at the indirect stimulation, and she let out a harsh cry.

Then he froze, halting his thrusts and moving the vibrator away. Her eyes snapped open and he hung above her, braced on one trembling arm as sweat dripped from his forehead to sizzle on her chest. "Damn it, don't stop," she demanded, but there was a pleading tone in her voice too. She squirmed against him, sure if she could get some leverage she could end this torture for them both.

But he held her hips pinned to the bed, forcing her to stay still before bringing her to the brink again, and a third time, until finally the need to climax had become a physical pain.

"Please," she begged helplessly, hating him for doing this to her, hating herself for being so weak. "You're killing me."

Immediately he came down on top of her, cradling her face in his hands as he whispered his apology. "I'm sorry, baby," he murmured against the flushed skin of her cheek. "I'll make it all better."

Sliding his hands behind her knees, he pressed her legs back against her chest. He slid the vibrator against the outside of her labia, as though realizing that her clit was too painfully sensitive for such direct stimulation. Within seconds she came, squeezing her eyes shut as every muscle in her body seized in ecstasy.

She was vaguely aware of his shout and the feel of him jerking inside her.

She'd be lucky if the neighbors didn't call the police, what with all the yelling and caterwauling.

Jake nuzzled his face into her neck and murmured something, and for a horrified second Kit was afraid she was going to cry. "Unlock me," she said through gritted teeth.

He fumbled for the key and released her from the handcuffs. Kit immediately jumped from the bed and grabbed her robe. She didn't like the way she felt, shaky and vulnerable and exposed. Didn't like the way Jake could burst into her apartment, into her life, and start chipping away at the wall she'd spent the past twelve years building around herself.

She needed to be alone, regroup, and put this thing with Jake in its proper perspective.

"You need to go," she said curtly.

His dark eyebrows raised in surprise, but he didn't budge from her bed.

"I mean it. I have a deadline and I've already wasted enough time with you."

"I had a really long flight and I'm just going to sleep. You won't even know I'm here."

Ha! Like she could possibly relax enough to focus knowing that Mr. Universe and his wonderdick were sprawled out in her bedroom.

"No way. Didn't your company book you in a hotel or something? I'm sure you'll be much more comfortable there." As she spoke she flung his pants, boxers, and shirt at him. He swore when she tossed his belt at him and the buckle caught him on the forehead.

"I get the point," he grumbled, rising from the bed. Kit turned her back, knowing if she allowed her eyes to feast on his lean, naked body, she'd end up right back in that bed with him, and deadline be damned.

Needing to get away, she waited for him in the living room, holding out his suit jacket when he emerged, blessedly, clothed.

"You're sure I can't stay?"

"Do you need cab fare?" She did her best to banish the slightly nauseating guilt at the hurt, angry look in his green eyes.

But then the hurt was gone, as a self-sure, slightly amused smile teased at the corners of his full lips. Before she could react, he pulled her into his arms. Instead of the fierce kiss she expected, she felt the soft press of his mouth against her forehead, her cheek, and finally her mouth. "Good night, Kit," he whispered. "I'll call you."

She stared blankly at the door for a good five minutes after he left. She felt completely discombobulated. On the surface, her life was exactly the same, but it seemed like it had been taken apart piece by piece and put back together slightly askew, until nothing looked or felt quite right.

The e-mail program on her computer jarred her out of her daze.

What was wrong with her? It was just sex. *With Jake Donovan,* little seventeen-year-old Kit whispered dreamily.

Like that made a difference. He was just another man, albeit one with more skill in the bedroom than any other she'd ever encountered. Nothing for her to get all bent out of shape about.

Still, it was probably best not to see him for the rest of the time he was in town.

She went into the kitchen and made a fresh pot of coffee since she still had hours of work ahead of her. Good thing too since she doubted she'd get any sleep.

But as she sat down at her keyboard, fully prepared to begin the next installment of how evil drug-discovery companies were willing to put patients' lives in danger to pump up the stock a few more points, she found herself instead clicking on her "Stripping It Down" folder.

Inspired, she began to type.

Girls, you'll never believe who showed up at my door, like a poor, pathetic puppy begging me for more . . .

6

Two days later, and still no call.

Kit wasn't surprised, or upset, she told herself firmly.

Sure, that's why you check your home voice mail twenty times a day and have asked the IT manager if there's something wrong with the e-mail server.

Okay, maybe she was a little upset, but only because the sex with Jake was so beyond anything she'd ever experienced before, and she wanted more. It was that simple.

Thankfully, writing her column for Bustout.com had helped her put her latest evening with Jake in proper perspective.

The article she was working on blurred on her computer screen, and she rubbed her eyes. As a business reporter, she hated earning report time, listening in on endless shareholder calls, and attempting to put her own unique spin on why a particular company did or did not hit their revenue goal this quarter.

Her stomach jumped as her cell phone buzzed on her desk, and she reminded herself that Jake didn't have that number.

It was Tina, the editor in chief at Bustout.com. "Kit, have you seen your numbers this week?"

"I've been so busy here I haven't even had time to go to the site." Bustout had a handy Web program that not only tracked how many people accessed the column but also showed how many times a reader e-mailed the article to a friend.

Kit glanced over her shoulder to make sure no one was lurking in her cube door before she logged into the site. "Holy crap!"

"I know," Tina crowed. "Your last two columns have had fifty percent more readers. And check out your e-mail forwards."

Kit's heart skipped a beat. Her past two columns had been forwarded to no less than five thousand readers.

"You should see the feedback we're getting. Your stories about this guy from your past—readers totally love them."

Kit clicked on a link and logged into her C. Teaser e-mail account, created especially for her column fans to e-mail their thoughts.

Kit's grin grew wider as she scrolled down the list of messages with headings like "You're Hilarious" and "You are my Idol." Her grin wobbled a bit as she reached the end of the page. "You're a Ball Busting Bitch," she read aloud.

"Okay, not everyone loves it," Tina conceded, "but it's provoking a strong reaction, which is just as good."

"Kit, aren't you supposed to be covering the Smith and Downing conference?" her boss snapped irritably.

Kit fumbled for her mouse and closed the Bustout.com window before Tom could see. It was a given that most of the staff writers for the *Tribune* moonlighted and freelanced, but nothing could get you in hot water with Tom faster than if he thought you were writing for someone else on his time. Checking the clock she realized she did indeed have to get a move on if she wanted to make it to the conference in time for the keynote.

She pasted on an enthusiastic smile and gave Tom a thumbs-up as she started gathering her things. "I have to go," she muttered to Tina.

"Day job, I know. We're all waiting eagerly for the next installment of C. Teaser's blast from the past. Keep writing the way you are, and pretty soon you'll be able to leave the high-tech geeks and investment bankers behind."

Kit powered down her laptop, tucked it into her briefcase, and slung the case over her shoulder. Grabbing her purse, she did a quick check around her desk to make sure she hadn't left anything. She was meeting Elizabeth and Michael, the ecstatic bride- and groom-to-be, near the hotel where the conference was being held, and she didn't want to have to come back to the office. She scooted around Tom, taking care not to brush up against his pot belly as he partially blocked the exit from her cube.

He didn't like her, never had. And she knew exactly why. Because she didn't care about this job, not really. To her it was a means of paying the bills so she could write things she was really interested in. Yet she was talented enough to fulfill her reporter duties with relatively minimal effort and she never made noise about getting promoted to a byline or columnist slot at the paper. So Tom put up with her less-than-enthusiastic attitude in order to retain a reliable workhorse.

She glanced up just as she was squeezing by him and caught him looking down the front of her tailored button-front shirt. She nonchalantly held her briefcase up to her front so that when he casually tried to lean in he hit leather instead of her breasts.

Tom didn't like her attitude, but it didn't stop him from perving out on her.

She mulled over Tina's news as she walked to the conference. Readers were going crazy over "Stripping It Down." The thought made her giddy.

But what was she supposed to do now that her source of inspiration didn't seem inclined to come sniffing around anymore?

Was she going to have to admit to her readers that she, C. Teaser, man-eater extraordinaire, had experienced the all-too-common hump and dump?

It was either that or chase Jake down herself—something, as a rule, she never did.

The mere thought left a bitter taste in her mouth. In her world, men were dogs, and she was the cat, and they chased her. *You're Hilarious. You're my Idol.* Her readers' e-mails scrolled through her mind. Somehow she had to get Jake back in her bed.

Kit was deathly afraid that this once—purely for the sake of her career—she would have to break her own rules.

Jake fought the urge to toss Kit over his shoulder like a caveman as she walked into the Redwood Room. It had been two days since he'd seen her, and he'd barely resisted the nearly overwhelming impulse to call her or drop by her apartment unannounced. It was pure, dumb luck that Michael had e-mailed today to check in. When Michael found out that Jake was in town, he'd immediately invited Jake to join him and his fiancée, Elizabeth, for drinks with Kit.

Now he had the perfect, innocent excuse to see her, all without having to make a call. He'd planned on giving it one more day, instinctively knowing that if he came on too strong, too fast, she would turn tail and run, just like she had in Mexico. Kit had been freaked out the other night, even though she'd tried to hide it behind her tough chick bravado. He recognized her fear because he felt it himself.

Hell, the fact that he'd actually convinced the partners at his firm that he should work out of the San Francisco office for the next month made him break out into a cold sweat. Sure, he had legitimate business out here, but nothing he couldn't get done back in Boston.

He wondered what Kit would do if he admitted he was here on his own dime, that his only goal in visiting San Francisco was to prove to her that what they'd started in Mexico was real.

She'd run so fast she'd leave skid marks. Which was exactly why he'd gone dark for the last two days, to give her time to calm down, give her fear a chance to turn to irritation as she wondered why he hadn't called yet.

As a rule, he despised playing games with women. Jake prided himself on being straight with the women he dated. If he said he was going to call, he did. If he didn't think there was any potential, he said so, as tactfully as possible.

But he knew if he was straight with Kit and actually admitted that he thought she—Christ, it sounded disgustingly sappy in his own head—was "the one," she'd reinforce that wall she'd built around her to the point he'd never get through.

Served him right, he supposed, since he was the one who'd broken her heart by clumsily taking her virginity and never calling again. The fact that he'd wounded her so that even now, years later, the scar hadn't completely healed was evidence that she'd cared deeply about him. Ironically her fear offered the only evidence that he wasn't completely insane in his quest to win her heart.

Kit was scanning the room for their party, and Jake took the opportunity to watch her unobserved. Today she was wearing a suit, and she looked like the prototypical businesswoman fantasy come to life. Though the brown fabric was cut conservatively, the fitted jacket skimmed her curves, and her white button-front shirt was open at the neck, barely hinting at a perfectly tasteful amount of cleavage. Her skirt ended just above the knee and showed off the long line of her nicely toned calves.

His mouth watered as he remembered skimming his lips up the smoothly muscled length as it rested on his shoulder.

She spotted them where they occupied a leather sofa in the back of the bar. He watched her wide gray-blue eyes register recognition, surprise at his presence, and finally pleasure that she couldn't quite disguise at seeing him there. He didn't even realize he'd been anxious until he saw that little smile. Even in his anticipation, he'd been worried that she'd still be too freaked out to let him get close again.

He took pure, animal pleasure in watching her as she walked toward them with an easy, unhurried stride.

Elizabeth, seated in the middle of the two men, pointedly shoved over closer to Michael so Kit would have no choice but to sit pressed up against Jake. Jake slid toward the end of the couch, giving Kit just enough room to slide her hips in. As she sat her scent filled his nostrils, a fresh mix of perfume and shampoo that made him want to release her thick brown hair from its clip and bury his face in the curve of her neck.

"Fancy meeting you here," she said as she sat. The feel of her warm weight settling against him was enough to bring his cock to instant, aching attention. The way her tits bounced as she shimmied out of her jacket didn't help. Kit sat back, caught him watching, and raised a knowing eyebrow.

"Hope you don't mind that I invited Jake along," Michael said as he motioned the waitress over.

Kit ran her tongue deliberately over the plump, glossy curve of her lips. "I don't mind at all."

Jake grinned back and stretched his arm along the back of the couch, lust pounding through his veins when he felt her casually rest her palm on his thigh.

Patience. Pretty soon he would have Kit right where he wanted her.

I've got him right where I want him. Kit couldn't believe her good luck. Saved from having to chase Jake down in the interest of good column fodder! If it wouldn't have earned her a slap from Elizabeth, she'd lean over and kiss Michael in gratitude.

She'd been a little worried when she'd seen him, unable to completely suppress the insecure teenager who still lurked inside. What if he really had no interest in seeing her again? Men were easy enough, and she was confident that she'd be able to get him to sleep with her again at the very least. But the idea of having to work at it didn't sit right with her.

But given the way Jake was eyeing her the way a lion eyes a steak, she had nothing to worry about.

And, Kit admitted, she was equally eager to have him drag her off and pin her against the closest flat surface.

The next hour seemed interminable as they sipped their drinks and talked about Elizabeth and Michael's upcoming nuptials. A month and a half away, the wedding had Elizabeth wired so tight it was a wonder she didn't spontaneously combust. No wonder she was pounding the wine like it was water.

"Kit, you're one of my besht—best friends," Elizabeth slurred. "I really love you, you know?"

Oh no. Elizabeth had crossed the line from happily tipsy to "I love you, man" drunk.

"I love you too," Kit said gently, returning her friend's sloppy hug and pulling a face at Michael over her shoulder.

"But I worry about you," Elizabeth continued, grabbing her wineglass and not seeming to notice when she missed her mouth completely and spilled down her chin. She looked at the napkins Kit handed her as though she was not sure what to do with them.

Jake chuckled behind her, and Kit shot him a glare over her shoulder.

"I don't know why you would worry about me," Kit said to Elizabeth.

"Becaushe you need to find love, Kit. Everyone needs love."

Oh God, here we go. "There is nothing wrong with my love life," she said, though she recognized the futility of arguing with a woman who'd eaten nothing but lettuce all day in an effort to fit into her designer wedding dress and then consumed an entire bottle of chardonnay.

"You have all these men, Kit, like that Max, Mort—"

"Matt?" Kit supplied.

"Yeah, that one with all the tattoos?" Elizabeth scowled at the memory. "Dint like 'im." She belched a little, and Kit could feel Jake shaking with suppressed laughter. "Stupid tortured writer type."

Kit sighed but couldn't deny Elizabeth's assessment of poor maligned Matt.

"Shee, you have these men, Kit, but you don't have love. Don't you want to find someone to love, someone you can get sherious about—"

"Okay little matchmaker," Michael broke in, "let's get you home." He pulled Elizabeth to her feet and mouthed, "Sorry," silently to Kit over her head. Kit waved his apology away. The poor woman was planning a ridiculously lavish wedding for nearly four hundred people while running her own interior design business. It was enough to drive any woman to drink.

"Like my Mikey," Elizabeth said dreamily as Michael got her to her feet, supporting her with one arm wrapped around her waist. "Don't you want a man just like my Mikey?"

Frankly, no, Kit thought as she took in Mike's dirty blond, slightly thinning hair; his medium frame with shoulders that were showing the first signs of corporate slump; and a midsection that hadn't revealed an ab muscle in a decade. But Elizabeth adored him and he treated her like a queen, so maybe there was something to that.

"So tell me more about these men Elizabeth mentioned," Jake said as they sat back down and watched Michael guide his inebriated fiancée to the door. "I didn't know I was among legions."

Though he tried to keep his tone light, the derisive edge was unmistakable. "Typical sexist response," she said, pinning him with a look of disgust. "Not that it's any of your business, but you're not 'one among legions,' as you so charmingly put it." The way he said it conjured up an image of her lying naked and spread-eagled on her bed, pushing a guy off her even as she yelled, "Next."

Is that what he thought of her? So what if he did. She didn't give a crap.

"How many?" he said tightly, taking a big gulp of his vodka tonic as though bracing himself.

"Total? Or just this week?" A frisson of unease trickled through her veins as she met his icy green glare. His question didn't deserve an answer, yet she heard herself say, "More than can be counted on one hand, but fewer than can be counted on both." She took a hearty sip of cabernet and waited for his reaction.

"Total, or just this week?" he mocked.

"What about you?" she shot back. "Big stud like you, I'm sure you've had your share of tail. If I recall correctly, all four of you Donovan boys were notorious along the north shore." Their little town was right outside Lake Tahoe, near some of the best skiing and mountain sports in the country. As such, there was always a steady inflow of tourists, and Kit could feel her smile harden as she remembered all the stories she'd heard about Jake and some ski bunny or other.

A dark flush stained his cheekbones, evident even in the dim light of the bar.

"Yeah, that's what I thought," she said, telling herself she couldn't care less about Jake's lovers that came before or after her.

So why did the thought of him with another woman cause the wine to curdle in her gut?

Chalking it up to drinking on an empty stomach, Kit firmly reminded herself of her purpose. Taunting Jake about his sexual past and luring him into a combative conversation about sexual double standards was not going to help her write her columns.

Luckily he seemed equally eager to change the conversation's course. But not in the direction she would have liked. "So do you want to find love, Kit?"

Maybe I already have. The thought barely had time to register before she thrust it away. They had to get off this track, fast, before she said something she really regretted. Turning to face him, she set her wineglass on the table and slid her palm slowly up his thigh. Steely muscles jumped through the fabric, the heat of his skin coursing through her fingers. "Not tonight," she whispered. "Tonight I'll settle for good, old-fashioned lust."

The distraction was effective—for both of them. A hot pulse of said lust surged between her legs as Jake pulled her face close for a greedy, tongue-thrusting kiss. One hand traced the bare skin of her calf, up over her thigh, traveling upward to squeeze the curve of her ass in his big, broad palm.

For several minutes they made out on the couch like two crazed teenagers in the back of a bus. It was only as Kit's hand trailed down his abs toward his waistband that Jake seemed to come to his senses.

Lucky for her, since she'd been about to get them both arrested for lewd conduct.

Grabbing her briefcase in one hand and her in the other, Jake steered her out onto the street. The cold air brought her partially back to her senses. Even at this relatively late hour, this part of the city was crowded with the shoppers and diners that frequented San Francisco's Union Square neighborhood.

Kit cursed. They needed a cab, now. She barely recognized the sex-crazed woman who seemed to take over her body whenever Jake so much as laid a finger on her, but if she didn't get him inside her, and soon, her entire body was going to burst into flame.

Jake tugged at her arm, hurrying her along. She prayed his hotel was close.

Apparently Jake had another destination in mind. After a block or so, he yanked her into an alley between two buildings, dropped her briefcase, and unceremoniously pinned her up against a cold brick wall.

His mouth met hers with bruising force. "I can't wait," he muttered between his tongue's luscious forays. "I have to get inside of you."

Wet heat surged between her thighs, her pussy clenching in anticipation. Still . . . "What if someone sees us?"

"Don't tell me," he whispered as he bit and sucked at her neck, "an experienced, sophisticated"—she moaned as his hand clamped firmly over her mound—"woman like you would let a little thing like getting caught stop her." His fingers yanked the crotch of her thong aside and sank into her hot, willing folds. "I didn't think so," he said, pumping his fingers in and out, finding her more than ready.

Big hands shoved her skirt up around her hips. Kit yanked open his belt and tugged on his fly, groaning when his rock-hard cock surged against her hands.

"You make me so hard," he whispered, thrusting against her fist as he fumbled in his back pocket for his wallet. "It's only been two days, but I feel like I've been missing you for years."

She pulled him closer until the tip of his shaft brushed against her slick, wet core. His hand shoved hers aside to roll on a condom. "Are you always this prepared?"

He lifted her with a husky chuckle, pinning her firmly against the wall and hooking one leg up over his elbow. "If I was lucky enough to see you again," his voice hitched on a groan as he sank all the way in, "I wanted to be ready." He ground hard against her, pulled almost all the way out as her greedy inner muscles quivered and grasped to keep him buried deep.

Kit started to come as he shoved back inside. The back of her head ground against the rough brick wall; her leg gripped his hip as she struggled to press herself against him more firmly. A high, keening wail erupted from her throat, and Jake's hand came up to cover her mouth. She writhed and squirmed against him as he thrust in hard, heavy strokes, grinding the base of his shaft against her clit, making her orgasm go on and on.

He came with a softly hissed curse, replacing his hand with his lips to take her mouth in a surprisingly tender kiss.

Kit barely felt him pull out and straighten her skirt, slowly becoming aware of her surroundings. Holy crap, she'd just had sex in public—in an alley, for God's sake! Never in her life had she so completely lost control, especially when it came to sex. She watched Jake ditch the condom in a nearby dumpster and zip up his fly.

This was insane. The whole encounter had taken less than five minutes, and other than a couple of rumpled shirtfronts, their clothing had barely been disturbed.

With shaky hands she twisted her hair back up into a knot and secured it with her clip. Jake picked up her briefcase, and she wrapped her shaky fingers around the handle of her purse. She'd dropped it at some point during their ten-second foreplay.

He slid his hand around her waist and nuzzled his face

against her neck. "I want to get you home and get you naked," he murmured.

Unbelievably, her nipples immediately went rock hard and her pussy clenched in primitive response.

Kit chose not to dwell on her disturbing, overwhelming response to Jake and instead focused on the fact that if she could keep him around for the next month, "Stripping It Down" would have ample source material.

7

Jake went home with Kit that night and never left. Three weeks later he sat at her kitchen table drinking coffee in his boxers and eating his Cheerios as though he owned the place.

She eyed him over the Entertainment section of the paper, still not entirely sure how this had all happened.

First his toothbrush had appeared next to hers. Next, his razor took up permanent residence on her sink. Soon after, he'd started bringing a spare change of clothing, until finally, Sunday afternoon he'd arrived with his suitcase and asked her for a spare key.

Like an idiot she'd given him one.

Other items had followed. Instead of being used as a receptacle for nail polish and leftover takeout, her refrigerator now contained a wide variety of fruits and vegetables, milk, and beer. Even as it gave her pause, Kit had to admit it was nice to wake up and always have milk for her coffee.

Still, just because Jake was acting like a live-in boyfriend didn't actually make him one. After all, he was leaving in a little over a week to return to Boston, at which point she fully expected him to end their affair. Because despite his proprietary move into her apartment and into her life, he'd said nothing about wanting a commitment beyond what they currently had.

Which is more than fine with me, she reminded herself firmly. Though she would miss the sight of him half-naked in her kitchen.

Unable to resist, she moved behind him, sliding her fingers through the dusting of black curls covering his world-class chest. He tilted his head back and she kissed him, the taste of hot coffee and hotter man nearly bringing her to her knees.

Though she'd never admit it, there was something to this full-time boyfriend thing.

Not that she thought of Jake that way. Unfortunately, despite Kit's assertions to the contrary, Elizabeth had started referring to them as a unit, inviting them out as a pair, even going so far as to change Kit's hotel reservation for the wedding so she and Jake could stay together.

Even her editor at Bustout had gotten on the bandwagon. "What does your boyfriend think of these columns?" she'd asked Kit just last week.

"He doesn't," Kit had replied, "because he doesn't know about them. Besides, he's not my boyfriend," she'd said tersely, "he's research."

"Damn, you're cold." Tina laughed. "I almost feel sorry for the poor guy. Whatever he is, try to get him to stick around for a while, because thanks to you, the site's never been more popular."

At the time, Kit had been surprised not to feel the expected elation at her column's popularity. It was true though; her column—and consequently Bustout.com—had experienced a surge in readership over the past three weeks. And Kit had even received e-mails from her friends with copies of her own column, exclaiming over this hilarious, clever column that she just had to read.

Instead she'd been brooding over what Tina said. She tried to convince herself that C. Teaser was just a façade, a persona she put on for the entertainment of women everywhere. But when she thought about how she was using Jake for material, she wondered if that cold, calculating man-eater was the real Kit after all.

As she felt Jake's hands reach up to stroke her forearms, she tried to banish the guilt that snuck up on her more and more frequently these days. As though to remind herself not to get foolishly caught up in the haze of great sex and warm emotions Jake awoke in her, she had taken on a particularly harsh tone in "Stripping It Down" in the past couple of weeks. She'd purposely made Jake out to be a sex-hungry, pussy-whipped idiot held firmly in her thrall.

Which was so far from the wickedly intelligent, funny, charismatic, not to mention drop-dead gorgeous man that he was.

She buried her face in his hair as a voice whispered, not for the first time, that she was on the verge of completely screwing up her relationship with the one man she could spend the rest of her life with.

She banished the thought before it could take root, reminding herself of her purpose. She was with Jake only to further her writing career. And if she got some great sex and nice dinners out of the deal, hey, she'd take the perks.

"Ouch," Jake winced, tugging her hands away from his chest.

Kit didn't realize she'd been unconsciously digging her nails into his skin. She muttered an apology and made to move away, but he grabbed her wrists, staying her. "What are you doing tonight after work?"

"I was planning on working on a freelance project." Truth

was, the latest edition of "Stripping It Down" was due tomorrow, and she hadn't been able to come up with anything good.

"Any chance you could join me for a work dinner?"

Kit stiffened and straightened. Going out together with their mutual friends was one thing. In her world, at least, you brought a date to work functions only when you were ready to admit to the world you were using the "BF GF" words. Which was why in the three years she'd worked at the *Tribune*, she'd never had a date to the holiday party.

"I don't know if that's such a good idea," she hedged. "I mean I'm not, we're not," she stammered. Crap. The last thing she wanted was to get roped into one of those "state of the relationship" talks.

Jake managed to completely distract her simply by standing up. He was so much taller that her braless breasts were pressed against his abs, and against her stomach she could feel the bulge in his boxers stirring in interest. Her body responded like Pavlov's dog, even though he'd woken her up this morning with his tongue buried between her legs.

"It's not a big deal, Kit. Everyone else is bringing their wives and girlfriends, and I'll stick out as the odd guy if I go alone. Don't read anything into it."

His green eyes were bright with amusement, and she saw nothing in them to make her doubt his assertion that this was nothing more than a casual favor to him.

Damn, if she really wanted a relationship with him, her heart might actually break right now.

"Fine," she agreed, resigning herself to a long evening with stuffy venture capitalists and their trophy wives and girlfriends. "Tell me when and where."

Surprisingly, the dinner wasn't nearly as hellish as Kit had feared. Jake's surprised delight at seeing her hadn't hurt. After taking in her tight navy turtleneck sweater, chocolate brown pencil skirt, and knee-high chocolate suede boots, he'd pressed a kiss to her ear and murmured, "You look great."

Which made her glad she hadn't gone with the deep V-neck blouse and red ankle-strap fuck me pumps she'd been tempted to wear just to shake things up.

It was clear Jake was the baby in his firm, as most of the West Coast partners—the "younger crowd," Jake had assured her—were at least five years older than Jake's thirty-four. She couldn't help but be a little awed by his undeniable success at such a comparatively young age. Not that it surprised her. Even back in high school, Jake had exuded that certain something, like a pheromone, something that assured the world that he would never be average.

It was what had made her fall in love with him in the first place. What kind of a moron had she been, thinking he would find her equally special?

The thought drew her up short. Since when did she succumb to feminine insecurity? Besides, the woman she was now was twelve years and miles away from caring about whether any man—Jake Donovan included—found her "special."

Still, she was enjoying the solicitous boyfriend act he was putting on, holding her hand under the table, making sure her wineglass was full, smiling admiringly as she spoke intelligently about many of the companies the firm had invested in. It was rare that her business-reporting background felt like a social asset. Most of her friends weren't particularly interested in tech trends and the latest CEO shake-ups.

The only black mark on the evening was the fiancée of one of the other partners, a shrill, skinny woman around Kit's age. Once Amy, a junior PR exec, had heard Kit was a business reporter, she'd immediately launched into a list of her clients and all the reasons Kit should write feature stories on each and every one one of them.

That is, when she wasn't drooling over Jake like she wanted to spread death by chocolate icing over his body and lick him clean.

"You must work out," Amy said to Jake, her eyes flickering hungrily over him from across the table. Her fiancé, a stocky dark-haired man with a thick neck and well-developed paunch, didn't seem to notice.

Jake smiled uneasily. "I get to the gym when I can."

"Come on," Amy said, fluttering her eyelashes as though a grasshopper had just landed on her eyeball, "you don't get a body like that with occasional trips to the gym. What's your secret?"

Kit's fingers tightened around the stem of her wineglass. Of course she wasn't jealous. She never let herself care enough to be jealous. But she did believe in a code of conduct among single women. In Kit's world, one did not flirt with another woman's date.

The wicked devil who'd urged Kit to dress like a slut made another appearance on her shoulder. Leaning over the table, Kit said in a low voice so the rest of the table couldn't hear, "I'm very demanding. I keep him in shape with our marathon fuck sessions."

Amy's mouth sagged open, and her fiancé, who'd apparently been paying attention to the whole exchange, laughed so hard he shot wine out of his nose.

Almost immediately Kit wished she could take it back. It was a special talent of hers, having a few glasses of wine and making some scathing or inappropriate remark. In situations like this, her internal editor clicked off and she forgot that not everyone thought she was funny, even if she found herself hilarious.

For all that she tried to convince herself she didn't care, she didn't want to embarrass Jake in front of his coworkers.

Kit turned to Jake, almost afraid of what she'd see. There was no shock, anger, or even embarrassment on his face. His expression was one of smug pride that said he was the luckiest man in the room and he damn well knew it. "What can I say," he said, sliding a hand across her shoulders. "If she put out a workout DVD she'd be richer than that Tae Bo guy."

Oh. My. God. She froze in shock, wineglass halfway to her lips. *He gets me. This man who I've written off as the first and worst dog in my life understands me better than anyone I've ever met.* She felt like she was falling headfirst into the mischievous warmth of his eyes. *Not only that, he's actually charmed by me.* A panicky feeling swelled in her chest, and she was saved from having to analyze this new, terrifying revelation by the announcement that after-dinner drinks were now being served in the bar.

She caught Jake's hand before he could follow the others. "Come with me," she said, tugging him down the hallway toward the restrooms. She was suddenly edgy, restless, compelled to show him that she felt . . . something. Something she was in no way prepared to put into words.

She pulled him into the women's restroom and shoved him into the handicapped stall.

"Kit, we shouldn't—"

Pushing his back against the door, she sank to her knees and ripped open his fly. "Don't tell me," she whispered, pulling his pants and boxers below his hips, "that an experienced, sophisticated man such as yourself would let something like getting caught stop him."

He laughed softly to hear his words thrown in his face, the sound morphing into a moan as she grasped his pulsing erection in her fist and ran her tongue down its entire length. Grasping him around the base, she rasped her tongue along the underside, lavishing special attention on the spot just below the velvety plum-shaped head. He tasted so good, like salty man skin and earthy musk. The feel of him throbbing against her tongue made her thighs squeeze against the aching pulse of her sex.

Big hands threaded in her hair, guiding her motion as she sucked him as deep as she could, feeling him against the back of her throat, fingers coming up to tease his sac. In the past three weeks she'd come to know his body as well as she knew her own, knew exactly how to touch him to bring him to immediate, explosive release.

Now she used every trick in the book, trying to convey without words that despite all her efforts to the contrary, she'd actually come to care, that he was amazing in so many ways, that this month with him had brought her more happiness than she'd ever thought possible.

His groans echoed off the tile as her fingers cradled his balls and her fist pumped him hard and fast. Her lips sucked and teased the head, and just when she knew he was on the very brink, she sucked him deep, relaxing her throat muscles as he exploded into her mouth. She milked him of every last drop of come, kissing the tip one last time before tucking him back in his boxers.

Jake pulled her gently to her feet and closed his mouth over hers, groaning into her mouth as his hand started to draw her skirt up her thighs. She gently brushed him off.

"Don't you want me to?"

She pressed a finger against his lips, unable to stifle the tiniest of moans when he sucked it into his mouth. "That was all for you."

His slow, crooked smile was worthy of a toothpaste ad. "I need to know what I did to deserve it, so I can do it every day for the rest of my life."

Even though she knew he didn't really mean anything by it,

she was stunned that his use of the phrase "the rest of my life" in relation to her didn't send her into a tailspin of panic.

Kit woke up early the next morning to check her e-mail. For the first time ever, seeing all the praise for "Stripping It Down" didn't fill her with thrilled pride. Instead she felt a little nauseated. Last night she'd been forced to acknowledge that what she and Jake shared was special, beautiful even, and it wasn't right for her to denigrate it for the sake of entertainment.

She comforted herself with the knowledge that, at the very least, neither Jake nor any of her friends knew of her bitchy alter ego, and if she stopped now Jake would never know how she'd used their relationship to boost her column's readership.

As though reading her mind, Tina called at that very moment. "Kit, I'm sorry it's so early, but you'll never guess what happened." Even through the phone, Kit could hear Tina quivering with excitement like a Chihuahua.

Kit cut her off. "Actually I'm glad you called. I need some help brainstorming column ideas. I have to stop writing about Jake."

Tina was completely silent for several moments. "No, Kit, you can't stop now. That's why I called. An editor from Hardin Publishing just called me. She got a hold of your column and wanted to know if we—that is, you and Bustout—would be interested in putting together a collection of columns for a 'Stripping It Down' book."

The handset slid from her numb fingers.

"Kit? Are you there?"

Kit fumbled on the floor for the phone. "A book? Are you serious?"

"Not only that," Tina said, "she said she has a friend at *Bella* magazine who might be interested in buying the rights and giving you a monthly spot."

A monthly column in a national magazine? And a book? This was better than she'd ever dreamed.

"I'd hate to lose you," Tina was chattering, "but if they buy the rights we can expand the editorial staff. The only thing is"—Kit braced herself for the catch—"she wants to see more. She really likes the work you've done in the six months that you've been writing for us, but she thinks the last month's worth has been really stellar, and she wants to be sure you can keep writing at that level."

Kit squeezed her eyes shut as her stomach clenched. The last month. The Jake Chronicles, as she'd started calling them in her head.

She looked at the door of the bedroom, behind which he slept in blissful ignorance, having no clue that to thousands of readers, he was the anonymous, brainless dick attached to a body being sorely used and abused by one C. Teaser.

He'll never know. That's why you came up with the pseudonym in the first place.

But how was she going to keep the truth from him once she had a book published?

You know damn well he'll be gone and out of your life long before it ever hits the shelves.

That thought stopped her cold. But who was she trying to kid? Jake was leaving soon, and the fact that she'd come to care for him was irrelevant. She certainly wasn't about to sacrifice her career for him.

"Tell her to keep reading," Kit said. "Tell her the next week's column should be my best ever."

8

Jake glanced up as his e-mail whistled, relieved to have an excuse to stop reading the business plan spread out on his desk. Normally he could skim through these things in five minutes and absorb all the pertinent details. Lately his concentration was shot, and he knew exactly who to blame.

He clicked open the message from Michael, a forward of some column he'd found on the Web. Michael had added his own forward, *Makes you glad we caught a couple of the nice ones, huh?*

Jake usually ignored the jokes and things forwarded by his friends, but he found himself immediately engaged by the author's lacerating wit and undeniable flair for humor. He read the column with a combination of amusement and horror. Entitled "Stripping It Down" and written by a woman with the oh-so appropriate moniker C. Teaser, it was like an extra-harsh version of *Sex and the City*. This C. Teaser apparently had some schmuck by the short and curlies, leading him around by his dick until she tired of him, which, she assured her readers, would happen very soon.

Whoever the guy was, Jake felt sorry for the poor sap.

Oh, like you're one to talk.

He shook his head. Four weeks. Four weeks in San Francisco chasing Kit around and he wasn't any closer to having any sort of permanent relationship with her. Christ almighty. He had sex with her every night, had essentially moved into her apartment, and he was still afraid that if he referred to her as his girlfriend she'd run for the hills.

What an ass. For a guy who had a reputation for aggression, who was known for his ability to turn a no into a yes, he sure was acting like a pussy.

Of course, he'd never in his life faced the possibility of a rejection that had the potential to make or break the rest of his life.

Makes you glad we caught one of the nice ones. Honestly, Jake wasn't sure he had. After all this time, he still didn't know what to make of Kit. Sure, the sex was amazing, explosive, and while he was inside her he knew she wasn't holding anything back, knew that she was giving him everything she had.

And afterward she'd look at him, and for a few brief seconds there was no wariness, no distance, no wall in place to keep him from seeing what she really felt. And in those seconds he was sure she loved him as much as he loved her.

But inevitably the wall went up. She'd roll out of bed to take a shower or catch up on work. Anything to distance herself from the intimacy they'd just shared. Then he'd wake up in the morning with her nestled up against him like she couldn't get close enough.

This is bullshit, he thought angrily as he picked up the phone. He had to go back to Boston in a week, and by this time he'd fully expected to be planning a permanent move here to San Francisco, or hers to Boston. He'd even gone ring shopping the other day. But he, Jake Donovan, the guy who never let anyone or anything keep him from getting exactly what he wanted, had chickened out. Holding the three-carat diamond solitaire in his hand, he'd imagined proposing to Kit. And instead of immeasurable joy, maybe even a few happy tears, he'd imagined her eyes widening in horror as she gently patted his hand and told him that, while she appreciated the gesture, she simply didn't feel "that way" about him.

And like a wimp he'd handed back the ring that would look perfect on her slim, long-fingered hand and skulked out of the store.

Frowning, he picked up his phone and punched in Kit's number. Enough of this crap. He was sick of pussyfooting around trying to manipulate her into giving him what he wanted. Tonight they were going to sit down and have a good, long talk, and he was going to show some balls and actually admit how he felt. No more game playing. No more pretending that this was nothing but sex simply to keep her in her comfort zone. Tonight he was going to make Kit face some hard truths about the true state of their relationship.

And if she hit the ground running? At least he'd know he tried, but the mere thought of her dumping him pinched like an icy fist in his gut.

Kit answered on the second ring.

"Meet me for dinner tonight," he said curtly. "We have some things we need to discuss."

He was met with silence. Maybe he should have tried for a friendlier tone.

"I can't," she replied. "I have other plans."

"Other plans?" It stuck in his craw that after all this time, he still had to make plans with her in advance, that she didn't check in with him before making plans on her own like she would if they were actually a real couple.

Until now, he had purposely avoided questioning her, not wanting to cramp her style or give her reason to bolt. He had no such reservations now. "What kind of plans? Why didn't you check with me?"

"I didn't realize I had to check in with you, Daddy," she said, sarcasm oozing through the phone lines.

"What plans?" he repeated.

She paused. "A work thing," she said finally.

In the month he'd been here, she'd remarked several times that unlike his own job, she was grateful that her job at the *Tribune* required almost no work-based socialization. "A work thing," he said skeptically.

"It's for a freelance project, something I've been working on." Her voice was uncharacteristically flustered.

"Fine. I'll see you back at your apartment." He hung up, glaring at the phone as though it were her face. Something wasn't adding up. She'd been acting evasive for the past week. Just last week he'd gone to her office to invite her to lunch, only to find that she was out. When he'd asked her about it later she'd told him she was out with a friend. Two nights she'd arrived home late, offering sketchy details about where she'd been. And more than once he'd interrupted her working at home, only to have her immediately close whatever she was working on before he could see.

Was it possible she was seeing someone else? The mere thought of another man's hands on her, touching her, caressing her, having unbridled access to her smooth, tan skin and silky wet warmth, made him want to puke. Jake, who'd never been jealous over a woman in his life, struggled to contain the rage that surged at the mere thought of another man so much as looking at the woman he'd claimed as his.

Kit slowly unlocked the dead bolt of her front door. It was past midnight and she prayed Jake was asleep as she tiptoed into the room. Her head throbbed with a combination of guilt and frustration. She'd spent the last several hours with Tina and the editor from Hardin Publishing, who had flown out from New York specifically to go over the book deal she was putting together for Kit.

But instead of feeling elated over her soon-to-be-skyrocketing career, she felt ill. For the past week she'd walked around feeling like venomous snakes were nibbling her insides. In addition to her regular columns, she'd written several extra pieces for the book, all about Jake. She'd cried as she'd sent the most recent one last night, in which she'd written the biggest lie of her career.

My little puppy is returning home soon, and I can hardly wait. Don't get me wrong. I'm a big fan of regular sex, and this little doggie's no slouch. But lately he's been hanging on my bra straps, and I'm starting to feel a little . . . constricted.

The truth was, she was dreading Jake's departure but didn't know what to do about it. He hadn't mentioned anything about what would happen once he went home to Boston, and she'd been so busy and so consumed with guilt that she hadn't been able to work up the courage to bring it up herself.

Still, she was pretty good at reading people, and every look, every act, every touch told her Jake cared. Any uncertainty about their relationship was entirely her fault. She was the one putting it at risk with her skittish, and lately sneaky, behavior.

And judging by his tone earlier today, he was obviously irritated, suspicious of her sudden spate of meetings and plans that had nothing to do with him.

What was she going to do? Though she'd vowed not to let whatever it was she and Jake had interfere with this amazing career opportunity, she could no longer deny that she cared for him. Deeply.

Somehow, that naïve, unrealistic, idealistic teenager had taken over, reminding her of all the reasons she'd fallen in love with Jake then, and why she really, really liked him now.

Yet if they did get serious, what would she tell him? She couldn't keep her book and her new column a secret forever. What could she say? "Oh, by the way, Jake, I write this really mean-spirited column and I've completely exploited our sex life and made you look like a complete boob. And you better get used to it because I'll probably have to mock the most amazing relationship I've ever had for the foreseeable future."

For a woman who prided herself on avoiding male-related complications, she'd somehow managed to land herself in a huge, freaking mess.

Kit didn't turn on the light as she entered her apartment, hoping she could sneak in and slide into bed next to Jake and pretend for a few more hours that she hadn't completely screwed up her life.

The lamp clicked on, and she shrieked and dropped her purse. Jake sat in her overstuffed leather club chair, a glass in his hand.

"A little late, isn't it?" he asked in a voice so cold she expected to see icicles forming off the tip of her nose.

Cornered, she struggled for her usual bravado. "You've been sitting here in the dark like some modern-day Mr. Rochester? How very gothic of you."

He pushed himself up, tossing back the last of whatever

liquor remained in his glass before setting the glass down on the side table. "Where were you, Kit?" He walked toward her slowly, and she got the uncomfortable sensation that she was being stalked.

"I told you, I had a meeting," she snapped. At least that much was true, and she hoped he didn't press for details. She could bullshit over the phone, no problem, and had no compunction about embellishing for effect, but she had a really hard time maintaining her poker face when caught in a bald-faced lie.

Finally he was so close she could smell the familiar musk and sandalwood scent of his skin, mixed with the smoky aroma of scotch on his breath. She wanted to lick the taste off his lips, but his demeanor didn't exactly encourage affection.

"Are you cheating on me?"

She took a step back, stunned. Part of her was so relieved that he wasn't pressing her for details about her meeting that she nearly laughed. But that urge was overtaken by irritation. What kind of person did he think she was? Did he really think she could have him living in her apartment, have crazy, unrestrained sex with him every single day, all while fooling around with someone else?

She ignored the little whisper that said he had a right to be suspicious, given the way she'd been scurrying around lately.

Instead, she did what she always did and copped an attitude. "Cheating? Cheating would imply we have some sort of exclusive relationship," she pointed out dryly, "which we don't. But if you want to know if I'm screwing anyone else, the answer is no."

Kit's body language—head and shoulders back, arms crossed firmly over her breasts, one dark eyebrow raised imperiously—screamed "Don't touch," but Jake grabbed her by her shoulders and pulled her firmly against him. Relief coursed through him. Kit was still hiding something from him—of that he had no doubt—but it wasn't another man. She'd been a terrible liar as a kid, something that hadn't changed in the past twelve years. He knew she wasn't lying about being with somebody else.

So what was it, then?

He pushed the question aside. Now wasn't the time to care.

After all his patience, maneuvering, and attempts to manipulate, it had come down to this. He was going to have to bare his soul. Tell Kit that he'd fallen head over heels all over again in Mexico, and he'd come out to San Francisco with some ridiculous scheme to get her to fall in love with him. And pray that she didn't either laugh in his face or run screaming for the door.

"Kit, I have to go back to Boston soon," he began. Her blue-gray eyes were unreadable as he fumbled for what to say next.

"And?" Her hands had dropped to her sides, and though she didn't pull away from him, she didn't embrace him back either.

"Fuck it," he muttered, releasing her to plow frustrated hands through his hair, "no reason to beat around the bush."

She regarded him warily, and no wonder, since he'd started to pace and was muttering to himself like he was some kind of psycho.

"Jake, I know what you're going to say, and—"

"I love you, Kit."

His stomach dropped to somewhere around ankle level when he was met with stunned silence.

Finally she managed to croak out, "What?"

"I love you," he repeated, cradling her face in his hands, seeing the raw panic in her eyes. "I didn't come out to San Francisco for business, Kit. I came out for you. I fell in love with you in Mexico—hell, I think I loved you when you were still in high school. But when I saw you in Mexico last month, I just knew. I knew you were it. I know I hurt you a long time ago. I acted like a complete jackass, and I'd do anything if I could go back and change what happened. But that was years ago, and this is now. And I've tried to be patient, tried to give you space to figure it out on your own, but I'm running out of time, and I love you, Kit." He stopped to take a breath, feeling a faint tremor course through his entire body.

Or was it her? Her hands, as she lifted them to cover his, were shaking too, and in her eyes he saw naked vulnerability and fear. And underneath it, some fierce emotion that sent the first tendrils of hope radiating out from his chest. "This is it, Kit," he said, keeping his gaze locked on hers, "no more games, just the truth. I'm laying it all out, and I need you to do the same."

9

Kit gripped his hands for dear life, trying to stop the uncontrollable shaking of her body.

He loves me. He LOVES me!!!!

Joy poured through her veins. Jake Donovan didn't merely like her, didn't simply care for her, he loved her. And he'd fabricated an excuse to live in San Francisco for a month to prove it. To be with her.

Joy was immediately replaced by panic at the way he was looking at her, his killer green eyes so full of hope, fear, and expectation.

What did Kit know of love? She'd spent her entire adult life killing every tender emotion, every romantic impulse that smacked of the idiot girl who'd been used and tossed aside years ago.

But she cradled his face in her hands, stroking his cheeks with her fingers, loving the way his day-old beard rasped against her skin. Despite all her efforts, she realized, she loved him too. She opened her mouth but couldn't force the words past the lump in her throat, even though she knew how much he wanted to hear them.

Frustrated tears blurred her eyes. *Stupid jerk. Why can't you just say it? I love you. Three words, three easy syllables.* Her mouth opened but no words came out.

"It's okay," he whispered against her mouth, tongue stealing out to trace her parted lips. "You don't have to say it back tonight. But tell me you care. Tell me you'll give us a chance."

Kit kissed him back fiercely, trying to convey in that one caress all the emotion she felt but couldn't bring herself to put into words. She pulled away and buried her face in the warm skin of his neck, breathing him in, feeling his big body surrounding her as he wrapped her in his arms. "For so long I've been afraid to let myself love anyone," she whispered. "But I think with you I'm finally ready to risk it."

It may not have been "I love you too," but it was something, and tonight it was apparently enough for Jake. Tilting Kit's chin up he said, "I'll never let you regret it." His eyes were so full of love and desire Kit felt a fresh onslaught of tears and cursed herself for being so damn girly.

They made their way to her bedroom, stopping often to kiss, leaving a trail of discarded clothing across her living room. Closing the door, Jake paused in front of the full-length mirror mounted to the back. In the dim light cast by her bedside lamp their skin looked sleek and golden, and the sight of Jake's ropy arm wrapped around her front, his big hand splayed proprietarily across her stomach, sent a fresh wave of moisture between her legs.

"You're so gorgeous," he whispered, and she saw his lips tickle the side of her neck at the same instant she felt the soft tickle of his breath. "The most beautiful woman I've ever seen."

Both arms slid around her now, pulling her back firmly

against his front, and she saw her throat arch back as she felt the hard, insistent prod of his cock against the small of her back. Both of them watched, mesmerized by the sight of his palms sliding lightly down her stomach, over her hips, down the fronts of her thighs, until Kit was practically quivering in his arms.

His hands on her skin were the most erotic thing she'd ever seen, and in that second she understood what drove normal people to make their own home videos. And they said women didn't get off on visual stimulation . . .

Licking her lips in anticipation, Kit arched her back as Jake's hands slid teasingly up toward her breasts, pausing to trace the soft undersides. Moaning in frustration, Kit covered his hand with hers, watched herself place his palm over her breast and guide his hand to pinch one hard, honey brown nipple. Her breath hissed and her eyes dropped closed as he pulled at the tip, his mouth tracing a wet path along her neck and shoulder.

"That's it, Kitty Kat, show me how you want me to touch you. Show me all the ways I can make you feel good."

As far as she could tell, Jake had pretty much figured all of them out, but if he wanted instruction, who was she to refuse?

She pulled his other hand up to cover her neglected breast, sighing as he kneaded plump flesh and rolled her nipples between his fingers. "Kiss me," she whispered, tilting her head back against his shoulder. He bent his head and opened his mouth over hers, his tongue licking inside as though he couldn't get enough of her taste.

Releasing her mouth, he closed his lips over one earlobe, and another jolt of lust shot straight to her core. He nibbled and sucked the peachy flesh as his fingers rasped and tweaked her nipples, and Kit wondered, as she watched his hard, male hands claiming her body, if she was about to come with nothing more than his hands on her tits and his lips on her ear.

Wet heat pounded between her thighs. Grabbing his wrist she tugged his hand down to cover her neatly trimmed thatch of pubic hair. She shuddered, watching his fingers disappear into her moist heat, feeling strong, thick fingers stroke against the plump, slippery flesh of her pussy.

She watched herself, that wild woman in the mirror, her eyes heavy lidded, mouth slack with lust as she thrust her hips forward, trying to urge his hand harder against her. Two fingers worked between her legs, glistening with her juices, circling and rubbing the tight bud of her clit, sliding down to plunge inside.

"Yes, Kit," he growled against her neck. "Come for me."

His fingers pressed more firmly, and her eyes drifted closed as she felt the first sharp tug of her orgasm.

"Open your eyes," he said. "I want you to see yourself, how beautiful you are when you fall apart."

She did, and what she saw almost made her freeze. Her face, her whole body, was unguarded, vulnerable as she strained against him, letting him see the naked emotion in her eyes as she shuddered and convulsed.

Before the tremors faded Jake scooped her up and carried her the short distance to the bed, coming down over her so his weight was supported on his elbows. "You're so damned sexy," he said, rubbing the hot, hard length of his erection against the sweat-slicked skin of her belly. "Sexy and beautiful and amazing."

She wrapped her legs and arms around him, rubbing her hands up and down his back as she tried to touch every inch of smooth skin and hard muscle.

He pulled away long enough to slide on a condom, and she spread her thighs wide in welcome. Grasping his cock, she pulled him against her, urging him to slide hard and deep inside her pussy.

Eyes squeezed shut, head thrown back, Jake drove in, not stopping until he was buried to the hilt.

Electric shocks shot through every limb as Kit felt that thrust to the very bottom of her soul.

Cradling her head in his hands, Jake held her pinned with his fierce gaze. "I love you, Kit." He pulled almost all the way out, then slid slowly, deliberately, back in. "I'm not going to live without you. Do you understand me?" He punctuated his question with a rough circling of his hips, making her arch and strain as her greedy inner muscles clamped down around his thick shaft. "You're mine now, Kit. You've always been mine."

Her only reply was a low moan as her palms slid down to grip the hard muscles of his buttocks, pressing him even deeper inside. She wanted to swallow him whole, absorb him into her skin. Make him hers as much as she was his.

They rolled and twisted on the bed, trading who was on top, giggling as they got tangled up in the bedsheets. Eventually Kit found herself facing Jake on his lap, rocking against him in a slow, steady rhythm as his hands cupped her ass. He ground against her, holding himself impossibly deep as he swallowed her rising moans in his mouth. Curly chest hair rasped her nipples as she rode him, arms looped around his shoulders as she held him tight. Almost without warning her climax gripped her, pulsing through her in long waves as Jake held her close, whispering he loved her, kissing away the tears that leaked out of the corners of her eyes.

He buried his face in her neck, whispering a soft "yes" as he came.

Hours later, Kit lay snuggled up against Jake, unable to sleep. Even though she was physically and mentally exhausted, something ate at her conscience, refusing to allow her to escape into sleep.

Guilt.

For all the amazing sex she and Jake had had over the past month, this was different. Having Jake on top of her, inside her, knowing that he loved her . . . Now she understood what all those sappy morons meant when they talked about a spiritual connection.

Unbidden, Elizabeth's drunken question echoed in her head. *Don't you want to find love, Kit?* God help her, she did, and lucky girl that she was, she'd found it with Jake.

Slipping out of bed, she grabbed her robe and went into the living room, silently closing the door behind her. She knew what she had to do. She had to come clean, both with her readers and with Jake, and pray that he forgave her when she told him the truth about her man-eating alter ego.

Maybe if she put it into writing, it would be easier for everyone to take. She switched on her laptop and began to type.

Well girls, it's time for me to fess up. Time to let the world know that I, C. Teaser, invulnerable, unshakeable user of unsuspecting males, have done the unthinkable.

I've fallen in love.

Crazy, balls out, no holds barred, would move myself to the ass end of the planet and shave my head if he asked it kind of love.

I'm even thinking about popping out a couple of gorgeous, green-eyed, black-haired babies. You know how vain I am. The fact that I would even contemplate the risk to my hard-won flat abs should tell you something.

But alas, it's true. I'm afraid I haven't been entirely truthful with you over these last few weeks. Remember the little stray hound who came begging so sweetly? He's really a prince in disguise and he swept me off my feet . . .

Two hours later, eyes gritty and a little nauseated from lack of sleep, Kit sent the column to Tina and stumbled off to bed. She fell into bed, exhausted, smiling as Jake murmured in his sleep and spooned her from behind. As she drifted off she whispered a little prayer to the gods of newfound love, asking them to help Jake forgive her when she confessed the entire mess in the morning.

Jake was awakened by the harsh clanging of metal and the rumble of a truck engine that vibrated Kit's entire apartment building. God, he hated garbage day. He squinted at the clock. Five forty-five.

Kit didn't budge. Not surprising, since he'd felt her get up sometime around two. He'd promptly fallen back to sleep but had awakened briefly again when she'd slipped back into bed around four. Her bouts of insomnia had increased lately.

I'll just have to do more to tire her out, he thought with a grin.

The grayish morning light caught the side of her face. He loved watching her sleep, the way her full lips parted slightly as she crushed the side of her face into the pillow. Sometimes, like now, a little furrow appeared between her dark brows, as though she had worries she couldn't escape, even in sleep.

With a sigh of regret he slipped out of bed and left her undisturbed. As much as he wanted to roll her to her back and wake her by sinking between her legs, it was obvious she needed the rest.

He slipped on a pair of boxers, grinning to himself as he let himself out of the bedroom. He couldn't remember ever feeling this happy, this . . . peaceful. Though he hadn't really been conscious of it, the entire time he'd been in San Francisco, a subtle tension had weighed on his shoulders as he struggled to keep a balance between pushing Kit into a relationship without over-whelming her with the force of his emotions.

Last night had changed all that. She loved him, he was sure of it. She might not have been able to say it, but he felt it in every touch, every kiss, the way she wrapped her arms and legs around him in an almost desperate grip. The words would come eventually. What mattered was that they were going to be together. Bone-deep warmth surged through him as he imag-ined their life together. The words would come soon enough. All that mattered was Kit was finally his.

Steely morning light cast the living room in shadows, and he could hear the hum of Kit's computer in the otherwise silent apartment. He quickly fixed himself coffee and sat down at her desk to check his e-mail. As he clicked open a browser window and logged into his remote e-mail client, he noticed Kit's e-mail was still up. He glanced quickly at her in-box, then looked away.

Jake still had the nagging feeling that Kit was keeping some-thing from him, but snooping was not the way to ease his mind. How could he keep her hard-won trust if he went searching through her correspondence?

He was working his way through his messages when a mes-sage for Kit flashed on the screen. Reflexively Jake glanced at it.

The message was from someone named Tina, the subject line "Your Latest C. Teaser Column."

C. Teaser . . . something about that name bugged him. Now he remembered. That column Michael had sent him, where the funny, bitchy woman made fun of the majorly pussy-whipped guy she was dating.

A burning ache settled into the pit of his stomach. Why would someone e-mail Kit about C. Teaser?

Almost involuntarily, he read Tina's message.

Kit, your latest column was genius! One of the funniest ever. I still haven't read the one you wrote this morning (you must be getting tired of your sex slave if you're up at 2 A.M. writing instead of gettin' down!) but if it's anything like the last one, you should be signing a book contract by the end of the week.

Unable to stop himself, Jake searched through Kit's Sent folder and pulled up twenty editions of "Stripping It Down." With every word he read, the gnawing sickness grew until his whole body throbbed with hurt and rage as he realized what Kit really thought of him, of their relationship.

While he'd been falling in love, she'd thought of him as a sex toy and used him as fodder to entertain her readers. While he'd been entertaining visions of their future together, she'd been glorying in leading him around by his dick, waiting for the moment she could let him down hard as payback for the way he'd treated her twelve years ago.

He didn't bother reading the column she'd written at two o'clock this morning. He already knew what it said. No doubt she'd ridiculed his love, laughed at how thoroughly she'd duped him, and figuratively rubbed her hands as she anticipated how, very soon, she would grind his heart into a fine powder.

No wonder she hadn't been able to tell him she loved him.

Hot, humiliated tears burned his eyes, and he thought for a second he might barf all over her keyboard.

He had to get out of her apartment.

Grabbing his pants from where he'd dropped them last night on the living room rug, he hopped his way into them and slammed open the bedroom door. He saw her jolt awake in the corner of his eye but couldn't bring himself to look at her. If he did, he was afraid he'd strangle her, or worse, start crying like a chick and beg her to tell him none of it was true.

Tugging his suitcase out of the closet, he started throwing his clothes inside, yanking open the dresser drawer he'd claimed and shoving in shirts, underwear, and socks. Suits, pants, dress shirts were pulled from hangers and piled on top.

"Jake, what are you doing?" Kit asked. The mere sound of her low, sleep-husky voice nearly brought him to his knees.

How could he have been so wrong? How could he not have seen her for the cold-hearted bitch she really was?

He looked at her, reclining in the bed, un-self-conscious as the sheet slipped down to reveal gorgeous breasts he'd spent a good part of last night worshipping with his lips and tongue. Despite the stabbing pain in his heart, his cock sprang to eager attention. He had his answer.

"I'm leaving," he said, stuffing his running shoes into the corner of the suitcase. "Isn't that what you wanted, Kit?" He paused, staring at her hard. "Or do you prefer to go by C. Teaser, since that seems to be what you truly are?"

She swallowed audibly as all the color drained from her face. Her mouth opened but nothing came out.

At least she had the grace to look ashamed even if she didn't bother to defend herself.

She clutched the sheet to her chest, looking so vulnerable that for a moment he was ready to forget everything and believe it had all been a big, harmless joke.

But phrases he'd read drifted through his mind, cutting words that had the unmistakable ring of Kit's ruthless sense of humor. *Lately he's been hanging on my bra straps... Some might say I'm taking advantage, but why should I turn down the chance for a little pleasure along with a side of revenge?*

He shook his head, filled with disgust for both of them. "You got me, Kit, you got me real good. You wanted revenge, you have it. Congratulations. If I hurt you even half this much the first time we slept together, I'm surprised you lived through it."

"No, Jake, you don't understand—" She babbled something about the column, a book deal, being pressured into writing more about him even though she didn't mean it.

He continued as though she hadn't spoken. "I thought we were past what happened, Kit, but apparently you're still the same hurt little girl who wants to blame everything on me so you don't have to admit that you had as much hand in what happened as I did. I may have screwed up royally afterward, but you wanted it as much as I did."

"That's not true," she sputtered, "you came on to me—"

"We both know that's a lie." He laughed harshly. "And it's pathetic that you're still trying to convince yourself it's not. Almost as pathetic as the fact that you use what happened as an excuse to push people away, to never let anyone get close enough to have anything real with you."

"I loved you," she burst out, "and you tossed me away like a dirty sock! How was I ever supposed to trust anyone after that?"

"Jesus Christ, Kit, it was twelve years ago." He pulled on a shirt and zipped up his suitcase. "Past time for you to get over it and grow the fuck up."

10

The slamming of her front door echoed through the apartment. Kit wrapped her arms around her knees, still attempting to process what had just happened. She felt like she'd fallen asleep and woken up in some alternate universe, one in which everything had gone horribly, horribly wrong.

Numb, she managed to drag herself out of bed. Pulling on a robe, she wandered out into the living room wondering just what in the hell she was supposed to do now. The smell of coffee permeated the room. Coffee Jake had made before he stormed out in a fury like she'd never seen.

Her laptop was on, her e-mail in-box displayed for anyone to see. A burst of righteous anger hit her. How dare Jake snoop in personal e-mail! But even in her head the words sounded hollow. She could blame Jake all she wanted, but she was the one who'd kept things hidden, the one who'd mocked and ridiculed every moment they'd shared. Sick with grief and guilt, Kit let the tears roll unchecked down her face, stunned by the depth of her pain as she thought of the things Jake had read, how betrayed he must have felt.

More betrayed than she'd felt when he'd taken her virginity and left without so much as a good-bye.

His accusations rang in her head. *You're still the same hurt little girl who wants to blame everything on me so you don't have to admit that you had as much hand in what happened as I did . . . you use what happened as an excuse to push people away . . .*

She stumbled over to the coffeepot, poured a cup, and sank limply into a chair at her kitchen table. Staring blankly at the window over her sink, she let herself really remember that night. Jake was right. All these years she'd blamed everything on him. Painted him as an unrepentant seducer of virgins, a user who'd taken what he wanted without any regard whatsoever.

Now she allowed herself to remember that night, remembered what she'd tried so desperately to block out. How love struck she'd been by Jake, her older brother's gorgeous best friend. How much she'd wanted him to notice her, to see her, not as a little girl, but as a woman. A sexual, desirable woman. The eagerness and fear that had coursed through her when he'd appeared on her doorstep. The way she'd employed every amateur seduction technique in her pitiful arsenal, convinced that this was her big chance to prove to Jake that she loved him, that they were meant to be together.

He may have kissed her, but she'd made the first move. Rubbing up against him on the couch. Taking off her shirt so he was sure to see there was no bra under her paper-thin tank top. And she'd encouraged him to go further, shoving his hand up her shirt and down her shorts as she'd pulled at his clothing.

And yes, the actual sex had been painful, embarrassing, and disappointing. But what had really hurt was Jake's expression afterward. Instead of falling immediately, irrevocably in love after she'd given him the gift of her virginity, he'd looked embarrassed. Ashamed. As though he regretted what had just happened with every fiber of his being.

So instead of facing the situation like the adult she'd thought she'd been, she'd run up to her room and cried her eyes out into the belly of her teddy bear. And used the experience as an excuse to avoid love and intimacy and tears ever since.

It never occurred to her, until now, that Jake had been young too. In her eyes he'd always seemed so much older and mature. Maybe he was embarrassed and ashamed because he knew he'd botched her first time. Maybe he worried what his best friend would think about him doing his little sister on the sofa in the TV room.

And really, was it any wonder he'd never called her? What twenty-two-year-old man—boy, really—wanted to deal with a girl who'd run sobbing from the room after the first time they'd had sex?

She banged her forehead lightly on the kitchen table. God, she was such an idiot. An immature, emotionally handicapped idiot.

Maybe if she apologized . . . *You never chase after guys, remember?* But this was different. This was Jake. The first man she ever loved. The only man she ever loved. The man who, after all these years, proved to her that real love was possible.

Where's your pride? Are you really going to run after him and beg him to love you?

Pride? Hah! Pride had gotten her into this mess, and Kit considered it a small sacrifice if she could get Jake to love and trust her again. She didn't care what it took, what kind of blow her ego had to suffer. She had to get him back, had to make things right.

The question was, how?

*   *   *

A little over two weeks later, Kit still wasn't sure if what she was about to do was right. Or if it would work. One thing she was sure of, though, was that the intensity of her feelings for Jake hadn't changed. Sitting across from him at the rehearsal dinner at the Lighthouse Winery in Napa Valley, her heart felt like one giant, aching bruise.

He looked beautiful, his dark hair recently cut, gorgeous body set off perfectly in tan slacks and French blue button-down shirt. Kit wanted to think that the sharp cast to his features was due to the same inability to sleep and eat that had plagued her, but her usual confidence in her own appeal had faded considerably in the past two weeks.

She'd taken special care with her appearance tonight, carefully applying smoky eyeliner and pale lip gloss that made her mouth look like a ripe peach. Her coral print halter-neck dress was tastefully low cut, barely hinting at cleavage while leaving her arms and back bare. She could have been wearing a flour sack for all Jake seemed to care.

Jake sat across the large, round table, chatting up one of the other bridesmaids, his mouth quirked in a sly half smile at whatever she was saying. He'd managed to ignore her from the moment she walked into the room, as he had for the past two weeks, three days, and six hours.

To be fair Kit supposed he'd only actively ignored her for that first week or so. After several days of unreturned phone calls and unanswered e-mails she'd stopped trying, and instead geared herself up for confronting him here personally at Elizabeth and Michael's wedding.

But all of her personal pep talks and plans to run him down bodily if need be fled as he glanced up, met her gaze, and looked past her as though she were a particularly uninteresting houseplant.

She couldn't ever remember feeling this kind of utter dejection, fearing she was mere seconds away from bursting into tears and making a complete ass of herself.

She straightened her shoulders and did her best to ignore the knot of hopeless grief squeezing the life out of her. She'd come this far, and now was not the time to give up in despair. Once again she reminded herself that she was a strong woman who went after what she wanted, even if it meant beating the man she loved into submission if that's what it took to convince him.

That's what she'd do, she vowed. As soon she could get him alone.

Although with everyone from Grandpa Ed to fourth cousin twice removed getting up to give a toast, it could be awhile yet.

Kit's heart gave leap when, midway through dessert, Jake got up from the table. *It's now or never.* She whispered a little prayer, drained her wineglass for fortification, and grabbed her purse.

Weaving her way through the crowd, she made a beeline for the men's bathroom. Perhaps it was tacky to corner a man while he stood at the urinal, but good manners were the least of her worries.

She peaked inside the men's but found it empty. Frustrated, she started back toward the table when she saw a shadow moving across the courtyard outside. She slipped out the exit and jogged toward the figure, trying not to snap a heel in the cobblestones. "Jake," she called, and the figure froze.

She stopped ten feet away, unable to see his face in the shadows cast by the outdoor lights. But his body language all but screamed "Get away."

It took everything in her not to obey.

Instead she walked slowly toward him, until she was close enough to see his clenched jaw and cold glare. "Jake, please talk to me, just for a minute."

"I don't have anything left to say to you."

"Fine, listen then. Or better yet," she fumbled in her purse and extracted the sheet of paper she was looking for, "read."

He ignored her outstretched hand. "After what you did, you think I want to read anything you've put on paper?"

"Why won't you let me apologize?" she cried, nearly stamping her foot at his stubbornness.

He started to walk away, and she lunged at him, clinging to his back and refusing to let go. "Don't walk away from me."

He swore and choked as her forearms wrapped around his neck. "Fine. If I read this will you leave me alone?"

She nodded against his back.

Straightening his shirt, he snatched the paper out of her hand, and for a split second she was afraid he would rip it into tiny bits. Instead he brought it about two inches from his face. "Sorry." He smirked. "Can't read it. It's too dark."

"Auggh!" The Charlie Brown–like sound of frustration erupted from her throat, and Kit pulled him across the court-yard and through the first unlocked door she could find. Heavy and arched at the top, the door lead to the winery's barrel room, she realized as she flipped on a light. "Is this okay or do you need your reading glasses?"

He scowled but started to read the "Stripping It Down" column she'd written the morning he'd discovered her secret identity. The one where she'd confessed to the world that she'd fallen madly in love with Jake.

She held her breath as he read the first few lines. His eyes flicked up to meet hers, but his expression was remote, unreadable. No reaction at all to the fact she'd admitted she was in love with him.

He finished the page and handed it back to her. "I'm sure it will be great in your book" was all he said.

The sickly kernel of hope she'd nurtured for the past two weeks shriveled and died. He wasn't going to forgive her.

Taking the paper from his hand, she hung her head, sick with the knowledge that Jake Donovan had broken her heart, and this time she had no one but herself to blame.

Jake tried to keep his hand from shaking as he handed back the paper. He shoved his hands in his pockets, clenching them into tight fists as he fought the urge to pull her into his arms and tell her he forgave her, that she could write any damn thing she pleased about him.

I've fallen in love ...

He wanted to believe her so badly it was like a physical ache. But what if it was another lie? What if she was manipulating him to get more material?

Did he even care if she was?

Yes, he decided. His pride—at least what was left of it after he'd made a complete ass of himself and let her walk all over him—was the only thing keeping him going these days.

"There is no book," she said, followed by a soft sniffle.

Oh Christ, she was crying? Tough, take-no-crap Kit? The sound of her tears hit him like a hammer to the solar plexus. Then her words registered. "No book?"

She shook her head. "I told them I wouldn't include the columns about you, so they won't move forward with the book."

That made no sense. After he'd left San Francisco, Kit had sent him several e-mails trying to explain why she'd done what she'd done. Her explanation about the book hadn't improved his attitude, instead proving to him that she was willing to use people she cared about to further her career. That he remained anonymous didn't matter. How could he ever trust her when she could so easily exploit their relationship and twist it for public consumption?

Though he hadn't forgiven her, he understood how important this book was to her career. It was her big chance to break free of her boring job at the *Tribune* and have a career writing what she wanted.

She scrubbed her eyes with her fists and sniffed again. "I know it doesn't matter. It's still out there on the Bustout.com site, but I couldn't let them put it in the book. No matter how I tried to rationalize it, I couldn't do that to us." She paused and stared up at the ceiling in a futile effort to stop crying, before she continued in a trembling voice. "A magazine bought the rights to the column, so I'll still have that, but the stuff about you will never see the printed page, I promise."

Jake's mind reeled at this. After he'd read through all the columns, he'd been so sure Kit was a manipulative bitch, willing to do anything to further her career. Now it seemed she was willing to sacrifice it all. "Why?"

"Because I love you," she cried, sounding exasperated and none too happy about it.

He couldn't stop the flare of warmth that pulsed through him at hearing her say the words. Not exactly the way he'd hoped to hear them, but he'd take what he could get. "Let me get this straight. You gave up a chance to sell a book to protect me, even though only you and I will ever know those columns were about me?"

She shook her head. "You couldn't remain anonymous for long. The editor wanted to do a big publicity campaign, and people who knew about us would put two and two together. It wasn't worth hurting you more. And it wasn't fair to you, the way I used the column to get revenge for something I should have gotten over a long time ago."

Tears poured down her cheeks, her full pink lips trembling at the corners. She always tried so hard to be tough, unemotional, and now she didn't bother to hide her hurt and shame.

Or her love. He knew how hard it was for her to admit she cared, to lay herself on the line. Gone was her bravado and confidence. Kit was once again the naïve teenager waiting to have her heart crushed.

God knew he wasn't the man to do it. A slow smile spread across Jake's face as he pulled her into his arms, imagining those green-eyed, black-haired babies she'd mentioned in her column. She stiffened a moment, then melted against him, her body going boneless as she leaned into his chest and wrapped her arms around his waist, sighing like she'd found the one safe haven in the world.

She tilted her head back and looked at him with big, gray, mascara-smeared eyes. "Forgive me?"

Jake could barely speak past the lump in his own throat. "Yeah." It sounded like a croak. He kissed her, tasting salt and Kit, and it felt so good it almost hurt. His lips traced over her cheeks, forehead, even the tip of her red nose. "I want you to write your book, Kit." She started to shake her head. "It doesn't matter what you said, as long as I know the truth."

"Really?" she asked, her expression uncertain. "You're not going to do that thing where you say it's okay now but hold it over my head for the rest of our lives?"

He shook his head. "But the next time you write anything about me," he growled, backing her up against a wine barrel that was taller than he was, "it better be all about my enormous dick and how well I wield it."

Kit let out a watery giggle and threaded her fingers through his hair. "I have a deadline this week. You better refresh my memory."

To her delight, he wasted no time. His hands were everywhere, shoving inside the neckline of her dress to cup her breasts, sliding up her thighs to sink into the soft flesh of her ass, left bare by her thong underwear.

"God, I've missed you," Jake groaned, his hot, open mouth pressed against the sensitive inner curve of her breast. Kit felt a sharp tug at her neck as he undid the hook that held up the bodice. Her breath hissed out as he tongued a nipple into his mouth, sucking hard and starting a pulsebeat between her thighs.

He pulled away long enough to shove his pants and underwear down his hips and tugged hard on the crotch of her panties, shredding the silk fabric.

His fingers slipped and slid against the moist lips of her cunt, coaxing wetness and preparing her for his rough invasion. Hooking a leg over his hips he shoved his cock inside until he was buried as deep as he could possibly go.

She was pinned, helpless, unable to move as he held her there.

"You feel so good," he said, holding himself so still she could feel the pounding of his heart against her own, the faint tremors that wracked his body. "Tell me you love me again," he whispered.

"I love you." She clamped down on him, squeezing him from the inside, kneading his shaft and rocking against him. "I love you so much." Licking and sucking at his lips and tongue, she tasted his moans, tears squeezing out of the corners of her eyes as she realized how close she'd come to never being with him again. Never feeling his hands on her skin, never feeling him sinking so deep he felt like a part of her.

Never hearing him whisper "I love you" in that low, shaky voice.

Finally he began to move, short strokes deep inside her, his thick cock brushing against her G-spot with every tiny thrust. She came almost instantly, vaguely aware of his groans as he spurted hotly inside her.

For a long moment they held each other, leaning against the barrel as they regained their breath.

Eventually he pulled away, and they made their way across the courtyard to the bathrooms for a quick cleanup.

Though it was tempting to retreat to the hotel, they returned to the dining room where assorted friends and relatives were still making endless toasts.

Wrapping his arm around her waist, Jake pulled Kit against him and bent to whisper in her ear, "When we get married, promise me we won't do all those stupid speeches."

She licked her suddenly dry lips. "You want to marry me?"

His warm breath tickled her ear as he laughed. "How the hell am I going to keep tabs on you otherwise?"

Stunned, Kit leaned back against him, closing her eyes as the romantic, idealistic Kit she'd spent the last twelve years smothering had a big, triumphant belly laugh. *I told you so.*

Kit had to concede defeat. True love was possible. Not even a hard-headed, broken-hearted, wannabe cynic like C. Teaser could deny it.

A Taste of Sin

I

The aroma of fried fish and chips tinged by the subtle tang of spilled beer greeted Nick Donovan as he walked into Sullivan's pub.

He spotted his brothers, Mike and Tony, seated at their usual table in the corner, already working on a pitcher of Harp's Lager. A huge platter of fish and chips nearly covered the surface of the table, and his brothers were steadily shoving handfuls of food in their mouths in a manner that belied their lean builds. After a long hands-on day in their building and renovation business, they needed a few thousand calories just to keep upright. Nick was an hour late after staying to review a set of plans for yet another vacation home in their mountain town of Donner Lake, California, and his stomach rumbled in anticipation.

"Hey Mikey, Tony," he said, scraping another dinged wooden chair to the table. His brothers barely nodded, so focused were they on their feeding. Nick reached for a chip and nearly got his hand bitten off by Tony. He scanned the room for their regular waitress, his irritation growing when he couldn't find her. Dammit, he needed a fresh platter of fish and a tall Harp's Lager, stat.

"I still can't believe he's engaged," Mike said between mouthfuls of fried fish.

"No shit! And to Kit Loughlin, of all people."

Mike, Tony, and Nick were still reeling over their older brother Jake's phone call just the other night, announcing his engagement to Kit Loughlin. Kit had been in Tony's class in high school and Jake had been close with her older brother, but as far as they knew, Kit and Jake hadn't had much to do with each other back then. But a few months ago they'd coincidentally both been invited on a group trip to Mexico. Next thing Nick knew, Jake was moving Kit across the country to Boston.

"Wasn't Kit really close with Karen—" Tony broke off midsentence at Mike's steely glare. Nick's stomach clenched momentarily, then relaxed as Mike seemed willing to let Tony's comment slide.

Jake's engagement didn't come as a huge surprise, given he'd been living with Kit for several months now. But for a guy who'd been so seemingly content with his single status, Jake seemed in quite a hurry to make things legal.

"Mrs. Makwowsky flashed us her tits today," Tony said in an obvious attempt to change the subject. Nick knew Tony could barely tolerate the idea of his brother getting married. Not because Tony didn't like Kit, just that, like how watching a close friend die forced one to confront his own mortality, watching his brother settle down made Tony acknowledge that one day he'd have to give up his steady habit of ski bunnies and settle down.

"Did she actually whip them out?" Nick asked, going along with Tony's new thread of conversation.

"Nah," Tony said, wiping beer foam from his upper lip.

"But she decided she needed to take a swim when we were out by the pool."

"Swim? It barely hit seventy today," Nick interrupted. Still warm for the middle of October, but not exactly pool weather.

"And she just happened to be in a white bathing suit," Tony continued.

Mike chimed in, "The minute it got damp, you could see everything. And then she came up and talked to us about her plans for her gazebo, like nothing was wrong." Mike paused, ate another fry, and chewed thoughtfully. "You know, for a woman her age, her tits are actually not that bad. Kinda small-ish, but not sagging, with nice, big, nip—"

"Why doesn't it surprise me to find you guys talking about breasts?" Three pairs of eyes shot guiltily up at the laughing feminine voice, only to pause on the speaker's own very admirable rack. "You guys haven't changed since high school," she scolded, and plunked a platter of fish and a mug of beer in front of Nick.

Nick surreptitiously adjusted his fly as his dick acknowledged the owner of said breasts. Kelly "Jailbait" Sullivan. Back when he was in high school, she'd been the smartest girl in town—with the most spectacular set of hooters that God had seen fit to bestow on a woman.

Unfortunately, he'd seen fit to bestow them on her when she was only fourteen, the youngest high school junior in the class after she'd skipped middle school entirely. They'd all known each other since childhood, and their fathers were still close friends. Even though her prematurely ripe figure had tempted Nick beyond reason, he and his brothers had always maintained a protective, big-brother attitude toward her.

Mike and Tony jumped up and grabbed Kelly in bear hugs, swinging her around and rubbing her head like she was their favorite puppy. Her naturally fair peaches-and-cream complexion was slightly flushed when they let her go. She turned to Nick with a smile that made her thickly lashed blue eyes sparkle.

"Hey, Nick," she said, holding open her arms.

"Hey, Kelly," he said, pulling her against him for a brief hug. But it was long enough for him to catch the herbal scent that emanated from her dark curls and inhale the warm, sweet fragrance of her skin. He studiously kept his lower half away from hers. That's all he needed, for Kelly to feel his unexpected boner on her hip. Jesus, he hadn't had a pop-up like this since eighth grade.

"Have a beer with us, and tell us what it's like to be a big-time doctor," Mike said.

"Can't," Kelly replied, replacing their empty pitcher with a full one. "I'm working. I'm helping Dad out until he can come back full time."

Nick forced himself to concentrate on what she was saying. Now as he scanned her, taking yet another moment to admire those spectacular breasts housed snugly in a periwinkle blue sweater, he noticed that she had an apron emblazoned with "Sullivan's" tied around her waist.

He knew about Ryan Sullivan's recent knee surgery—he and his brothers had visited him in the hospital. But he'd had no idea Kelly, who had graduated from Harvard medical school five years ago at the ripe old age of twenty-one, would be home during her father's recovery.

"That's great, Kell," Tony said. "How long are you in town?"

Kelly pulled a rag from her apron and wiped a blob of ketchup from their table. Nick was momentarily mesmerized by the gentle sway of her breasts as she moved her arm in a rhythmic circular motion. Suddenly his brain was filled with a vision of her, naked and creamy on top of him, tits swaying as she rode his cock with abandon.

He shook his head slightly to clear his brain, frowning when he noticed that his brothers, too, were admiring the way she filled out her sweater.

"I don't know," Kelly was saying. "At least a couple of weeks, maybe as long as a month. It all depends on how Dad's recovery goes."

Great, Nick thought. *I'm condemned to a two- to four-week sentence of perpetual bonerhood.*

"We'll be seeing you around, then," Mike said.

Kelly grinned. "I certainly hope so." She turned and sashayed away, with three sets of eyes glued to her firm ass encased in sexy low-rise jeans.

"When the hell did Kelly Sullivan get hot?" Tony asked no one in particular.

"Yeah," Mike said. "Last time I saw her she was just a nerdy little college girl."

Nick frowned, not sure why he was so irritated at the idea of his brothers checking her out. "She was always cute."

"Not the last time I saw her," Tony said. "In fact, as I remember, she really didn't look so good."

"It was her mother's funeral, dumbass," Nick said, remembering the occasion a little over two years ago. "Anyone who's been crying for a week straight is going to look like hell." Kelly had been blotchy faced and puffy eyed, as had her sister, Karen.

At the time of her mother's death from brain cancer, Kelly had been in the second year of her residency. She'd left town immediately after the funeral and hadn't been home since. Which made her presence tonight, all lush curves and sweet smiles, even more surprising.

"Kelly? Cute?" Tony said. "Yeah, okay, maybe cute like a puppy is cute, or a kid sister."

"You just weren't looking hard enough," Nick said with more intensity than he'd intended.

Mike and Tony stared at him for several seconds, heads cocked, eyes narrowed. "Don't you dare tell me you messed around with Kelly Sullivan."

Even eleven years after the fact, Nick had no doubt that Mike and Tony would do their best to pummel him if they thought he'd taken advantage of sweet, shy, and at the time *way too young* Kelly Sullivan.

"Christ, no," Nick said vehemently. "She was fifteen." Jailbait. They graduated from high school at the same time, but Kelly had been just fifteen to his eighteen. As a rule, Nick dated older girls who had no problem getting naked in the back of his beat-up Ford Bronco. So when Kelly had started tutoring him in Geometry and English their senior year, Nick had never even considered putting the moves on her.

Okay, he'd considered it. Dreamed about it. Concocted elaborate fantasies about it. But he'd never acted on his lust, no matter how frustrated he was by the end of one of their tutoring sessions.

But now . . . He sneaked a look at her as he took another sip of beer. Now she was definitely old enough.

Kelly looked up, her lush, pink mouth forming a friendly smile when she met his eyes. Nick's face grew hot, whether from the fresh spurt of desire exploding in his gut or embarrassment at being caught staring, he wasn't sure. He glanced away, only to meet the speculative stares and matching raised eyebrows of his brothers.

"Thinking of finding out what you were missing?" Tony said with a sly grin.

Nick's soaring sexual desires landed with a thump. This was why he and his brothers didn't date women in their small, close-knit town. "Are you kidding me?" he said with a forced smile. "If Mom ever got wind that I was interested in Kelly Sullivan, she'd wet her pants with joy. The next thing you know, she'd have reserved the Elk's Club and measured Kelly for a wedding dress."

Mike and Tony went a little pale at the reminder of their mother's fervent—some would say manic—desire to marry her boys off, and raised their beers in salute. "And now that Jake's down, she'll be that much more anxious for us to pair-bond," Tony said glumly.

"Besides," Nick said, "Kelly's not the kind of girl for me." Mike and Tony nodded, mouths tightening in sympathetic grimaces. Though neither of them ever said it out loud, they knew Nick had taken his breakup with Ann hard and that the wounds she'd left had barely scabbed over after six months.

"Speaking of which," Tony said, "are you coming out with us Saturday night?"

Nick rubbed the back of his neck. "I don't know. I have some stuff I wanted to do around the house." In the past, he'd never passed up a chance to go out, have a little fun, get a little action. But since Ann had walked out on him, the prospect of picking up women for casual sex had struck him as more depressing than titillating. In the meantime, he kept busy renovating his house, erasing all of the changes Ann had made in the six months she'd lived there.

"Come on, man," Mike said, dragging the last few fries through the puddle of ketchup on his plate, "you have to get back in the saddle sometime. You haven't been out for months. It's time you put that bitch behind you and got back in the game."

"I'll think about it," Nick said. In his brothers' minds, the best way for him to get over his heartbreak was to go back to being the player he used to be.

Nick wondered what they would say if he admitted that Kelly's quick hug had incited more lust than he'd felt since Ann left him.

Too bad there wasn't a damn thing he was going to do about it.

Kelly took another order from a couple sitting at the bar, re-filling their glasses from the tap. Amazing how quickly it all came back. Even though it had been years since she'd worked her last shift at Sullivan's, she knew each beer by the feel of the tap handle, knew instinctively when a customer's food order would be ready and exactly where the Stoli sat on the shelf.

She'd arrived back in Donner Lake two days ago to get her dad settled after his knee surgery and marveled at how little things had changed. After four years of an emergency medicine residency in Boston, it was hard to get reaccustomed to the slow pace and wide-open spaces of the little mountain town where she grew up. Especially in October, when the summer rush was gone and the town awaited the first big snow, Donner Lake was like another planet compared to her real life.

It was different here, no doubt. But oddly comforting in a way she hadn't expected.

And exciting, too, now that she'd run into Nick Donovan. The minute he had walked in the door of the crowded pub, Kelly's nerve endings went on high alert to better detect and absorb every nuance of raw masculinity that emanated from his pores.

She looked over at his table again, mentally shaking her head. It seemed like a crime against nature that such perfect male specimens should come from the same family.

Kelly wasn't the only female in the room keeping tabs on their table. If nothing else, their size alone would have attracted attention. Nick, the tallest, stood just under six four with shoulders so broad he practically had to turn sideways to get through the doorway of Sullivan's. Mike was slightly shorter but had a bulkier, more muscular frame, while Tony was the smallest—relatively speaking since he was still a good seven inches taller than Kelly.

But it wasn't size that made every female patron at Sully's cast longing looks at the Donovan boys. It was because the Donovan boys, even with tartar sauce and ketchup smeared across their mouths, were absolutely, heart-stoppingly gorgeous.

With their thick black hair and sculpted features, anyone looking at them would be hard pressed to find a single flaw among the three faces. And if they did, it would surely only add to their allure. No doubt they'd inspired numerous female fantasies of a Donovan triple decker.

Mike with his hazel green eyes and air of quiet intensity. Tony with his deep chocolate gaze that could melt a woman into a puddle with a single glance.

And Nick.

Kelly sighed.

She hoped she hadn't come off as a complete dork. Even after all these years, one look from Nick and she dissolved into a puddle of insecurities. Her heart had pounded and she'd struggled for a light, casual tone as she'd approached their table. Lucky for her, he and his brothers had always been nice to her, even if she was a dork.

She had always wondered how someone as gorgeous and sought after as Nick managed to stay so damn nice. If anyone had the right to act like a cocky jerk when it came to women, it was Nick. But when women whispered and cast admiring glances, instead of preening and swaggering, Nick had always looked faintly bemused as though wondering what all the fuss was about.

To Kelly it was no mystery. Sure, he was hot—tall and burly with big, strong hands she could easily imagine sliding over her skin. But it was his eyes that really got her. Big, soulful pools of amber, promising a woman pleasure beyond anything she'd ever imagined. And he was so damn sweet, the kind of guy who could smash your heart into smithereens and you'd thank him all the same.

In the two years since she'd seen him he'd somehow managed to get even better looking, damn him. The clean lines of his cheeks and jaw were sharper and more defined, the intriguing laugh lines at the corners of his eyes deeper, his body harder and tighter.

All in all, her personal wet dream come to life.

Unbidden, the image of Nick straining over her, pumping high and hard inside of her, filled her head.

He was so big he completely stretched me out! I could barely walk for three days!

Vicki Jenkins's voice echoed in Kelly's head. Her cheeks flamed, and she gulped the glass of ice water she'd stashed behind the bar. Kelly had been fourteen, sitting alone on the bus as usual, trying to drown out Vicki's voice behind her as she checked over her homework. Her ears immediately pricked when she heard his name. Her crush on Nick had started her first day of freshman year when he'd helped unstick her jammed locker.

"I swear," Vicki was saying, "Nick Donovan has the biggest dick I've ever seen. It was so big he could barely get it all the way in."

"Did it hurt?" Kelly didn't recognize the other girl's voice.

"Oh God, no. He ate me out first. I was so wet when he finally fucked me it felt so unbelievably good."

At fourteen, Kelly had known the basics of sex, of course— had even read some D.H. Lawrence novels and had experienced the first tingles of arousal. But stretching? Eating out? Her naturally pale complexion had gone beet red as her mind struggled with Vicki's descriptions.

And from that moment, she'd never been able to look at Nick the same. At first he'd frightened her a little. When she'd started tutoring him their senior year, the prospect of spending several hours alone with him had made her extremely nervous. The night before their first tutoring session, she'd even had a nightmare where Nick was chasing her around his house sporting a baseball-bat-sized erection, screaming about how he was going to eat her.

But as the year went on, her nightmares were replaced by vivid fantasies until she could barely keep her focus on their work. She fought to keep her crush hidden as thoughts of him touching and kissing her naked body threatened to drive every coherent thought from her head.

But Nick had been either unaware of, or unwilling to act on, her attraction to him. Which, in hindsight, had definitely been for the best. Although at the time her fifteen-year-old self had been ready to throw herself off a building from his apparent indifference.

Despite the sudden appearance of ripe, womanly curves the summer just before her fifteenth birthday, Kelly had still been way too young for a guy like Nick to be fooling around with. Because even at age eighteen, not even out of high school yet, Nick had been a man, with a man's passion, a man's desires, not to mention a man's body.

Now, however, at twenty-six, Kelly wasn't an inexperienced virgin anymore. But she still couldn't help but wonder if she was finally ready to handle a man like Nick.

She scanned the room, letting her gaze fall on the Donovans' table. And was gratified to see Nick staring at her with his penetrating amber gaze. She smiled at him, oddly delighted when he looked away as though embarrassed.

Kelly hummed as she polished a glass.

Her heart skipped a beat when, fifteen minutes later, she

spotted Nick striding up to the bar, his hot amber gaze fixed on her. The thudding of her heart was matched by hot pulsing between her legs, and Kelly clenched her thighs together, as though somehow Nick might realize that under her jeans she was soaked just from looking at him.

She pasted a smile on her face and did her best to act nonchalant. "Do you guys need a refill? I can send Maggie over."

Nick smiled, a flash of perfect white teeth against his olive skin. "Nah, I need to close out our tab. We have an early start tomorrow."

She did her best to hide her disappointment, quickly tabulating their check and exchanging it for a handful of bills. Her hand shook a little as she handed him his change, and she spilled a handful of coins on the bar. *Klutz,* she silently berated herself.

Laughing nervously, she bent her head and snatched up the coins. Thick locks of hair fell forward into her face, and when she lifted her head, she saw Nick through a veil of near-black waves.

He reached out and tucked her hair behind her ears, and she nearly gasped as the callused tips of his fingers brushed the skin of her cheeks. The heat between her thighs intensified, and she suddenly worried that Nick could see her nipples, straining eagerly against the soft knit of her sweater.

But when she looked up at him he was staring directly into her face, taking in her flushed skin, seeming to focus on her mouth. Nervously she licked her lips and for a moment, she could have sworn he leaned in, licking his own lips, as though preparing to kiss her.

Instead he straightened abruptly, gave her a slightly strained smile, and thanked her. He tossed a few bills on the bar for a tip before leaving with Mike and Tony.

Kelly tried to convince herself she wasn't disappointed.

Yeah, right. Stupid to even let herself get all fired up. Guys like Nick didn't go for brainy nerds like Kelly, and it was a testament to how long she'd gone without sex that she could be so aroused by a friendly smile and a touch of his fingers.

Maggie, who had worked at Sullivan's for as long as Kelly could remember, must have noticed the lust in Kelly's gaze. "They are delicious, aren't they?" Maggie chuckled her raspy two-pack-a-day laugh.

Kelly turned a frown on Maggie. "I'm not—" If Maggie, a notorious gossip, thought there was anything going on between Kelly and Nick, it would be spread across town and all the way over into Nevada before morning.

Maggie waved away Kelly's lame protest. "A shame what that girl did to Nick, though."

Kelly bit her lip, not wanting to encourage Maggie but unable to resist taking the bait. "What girl?"

"Some girl from Stanford. A real piece of work. Came up here to study trees or some bullshit, acted like she was too good for us hicks who live here year-round. But she took a liking to Nicky, I'll tell you that, and he seemed pretty taken with her too."

"Are they still living together?" Kelly tried to keep her tone lightly curious but couldn't stop the knot of jealousy from forming in her stomach.

"No, the bitch left him this spring."

Kelly blew out a sigh of relief, which gave her pause. *Why should I care if Nick is single,* she scolded herself. She didn't stop to dwell on it as soon as she heard Maggie's next words.

"That girl thought she was too good for this town, too good for Nick."

"Too good for Nick? Nick's one of the best people I've ever known," Kelly blurted, too angry on Nick's behalf to be embarrassed about putting her heart on her sleeve.

"You're telling me, Kel," Maggie said, busying herself filling four pints of Guinness. "But you know, some people are suited for small-town life with a guy like Nick"—she paused and looked meaningfully at Kelly—"and some people aren't."

Kelly thought about her conversation with Maggie later that night as she watched the late show and tried to get tired enough to go to sleep. She couldn't imagine a woman ever dumping Nick once she had him. As far as she could remember, most girls, once they had their hands on him, dug their claws in deep in an attempt to keep him around.

Nick, he was a slippery one. He always managed to break free.

Maggie was right about one thing. Some people, like Kelly, weren't suited for life in this little mountain town with a guy like Nick. Not permanently, anyway.

At a very young age, it had become apparent that Kelly was, in a word, different. And when she read her parents' complete set of Encyclopedia Britannica by the age of five, it was clear they were going to have to do something with Kelly to keep that overactive brain of hers from getting her into trouble.

Since their school system didn't have a well-defined "gifted" program, her parents had decided to have Kelly skip several grades.

It might have been the best choice for her brain, but it was the worst possible option for the future of Kelly's social life.

Not only did she screw up the curve in all of her classes, but her classmates were busy dating and studying for their driving tests while Kelly was still asking Santa for Barbie's Dream House for Christmas.

Worse, her family hadn't known quite what to do with her. Her sister resented being known as "the geek freak"'s sister and to this day had a major chip on her shoulder about what she considered Kelly's special treatment during their childhood.

Even her parents seemed a little freaked out that two people of average intelligence could produce such a freakish level of genius. The one saving grace during her childhood was when Kelly's dad had let her work at Sullivan's. Technically she shouldn't have been serving beer at such a young age, but since her dad was a friend, the sheriff looked the other way. The patrons were amused and charmed by her, and Kelly had found friends, of sorts, and much-needed acceptance in some of the regulars.

But none of that mattered now. She was living in Donner Lake only for a few weeks and, in many ways, it was a relief after so many intense years of work and study. She had no doubt she'd be stir crazy and ready to get the hell out by the time she had to leave, but for now it was nice to come back to a place where people didn't worry much beyond the high school football team and whether this ski season would bring decent tourist traffic downtown.

For the time being, she was free from egotistical doctors, cranky nurses, and patients whose lives depended on her skills as an emergency room physician.

Her thoughts went back to Nick and the way he had touched her hair earlier tonight. Had he really been thinking about kissing her? Just the thought of Nick's lips moving over hers was enough to make her thighs clench. If only she'd had the nerve to grab him by the back of the neck and lay one on him.

She groaned and laid her head against the back of the couch. God, it had been so long since she'd had sex. And even then, she'd practically had to write Jared step-by-step instructions.

Which went to show that, for a man, locating the clitoris is only half the battle.

No doubt Nick would know exactly what to do.

Which got her thinking.

In high school, she'd never had a chance with Nick. But now she was older, she was available, and she was in town only for a brief time. According to Maggie, Nick wasn't looking for a commitment, and neither was Kelly. But with their parents such close friends, they'd have to be very careful to keep it quiet.

It might mean making the first move, which definitely wasn't her style. Then again, what did she have to lose? She was leaving in a few weeks anyway. The worst thing that could happen was he'd reject her.

Which, she conceded, would really, really suck. For more than ten years, Nick, in some version (Viking, Scottish Warrior, hunky EMT) had popped in and out of her fantasies, and he never said "no, thanks." Was her ego prepared for his rejection?

Stop being such a wimp! You always wait for guys to make the first move, and what has it gotten you?

Mediocre sex with men who would never measure up to her fantasies of Nick.

Pun intended.

Was she really going to let her ego ruin the one chance she had at making those fantasies come true?

2

No way was Nick getting within touching distance of Kelly Sullivan.

That's what he told himself early Thursday morning when his alarm woke him at 6:15. He sported a particularly intense case of morning wood, thanks to a vividly erotic dream. Just like last night, he'd arrived at Sullivan's to find Kelly working behind the bar. But instead of the jeans she'd worn last night, Dream Kelly was wearing a skirt. And when she bent over to reach for clean glasses, her naked ass had peeked out from under the hem.

In his dream, Nick had magically transported himself over the bar. His clothes conveniently disappeared as, without preamble, he pushed her skirt up to her waist and shoved his cock deep inside her wet, clenching heat.

It was so real, so vivid, he could smell her skin, the scent of her arousal, feel her soft ass cheeks rubbing against his abs with every thrust.

But her screams of pleasure grew ever more shrill and unpleasant. That's when Nick realized that the noise in his head wasn't Kelly's orgasmic cries, but rather the insistent BEEP BEEP BEEP of his alarm clock.

Sighing, he stepped under the scalding shower spray and quickly jerked himself off, closing his eyes and savoring the lingering images of his dream.

But dream or no, as far as he was concerned Kelly might as well come complete with a bright orange KEEP OUT sign.

So why, he asked himself later that evening, was he back at Sullivan's? He never came to Sullivan's on a Thursday. And yet here he was.

Kelly's dad, Ryan, was seated at a table near the bar, an aluminum cane perched conveniently nearby. He greeted Nick with a hearty wave and a broad smile on his ruddy face. His thick, dark hair was liberally peppered with gray, but it was easy to see where Kelly had gotten her Black Irish good looks.

"Nicky!" Ryan called. "Sit your ass down here and have a beer with me."

"You seem to be making a rapid recovery," Nick observed as he settled himself into a scuffed wooden chair.

"Oh, I'm doing pretty good. Kelly didn't want me to come out tonight, but Jesus, I'm getting stir crazy. For the past week I've seen nothing but the inside of my condo and the physical therapist's office."

Nick nodded sympathetically. Suddenly the short hairs at the back of his neck prickled. He turned his head, and sure enough, there was Kelly, balancing a tray of drinks on her shoulder. And, God help him, she was wearing a skirt.

Her face lit up in a wide smile when she spotted him. "Hey, Nick. I'll be over in just a second to take care of you."

Oh yeah, she could take care of him all right. Nick did his best to banish lustful thoughts of Kelly, at least for the moment.

It seemed bad form to be thinking filthy thoughts about a woman when you were sitting with her father.

Within minutes, she reappeared. Tonight she was wearing a Sullivan's T-shirt tucked into her denim miniskirt. Seated, Nick was nearly eye level with the full globes of her tits, straining against the soft cotton fabric.

"What can I do for you, Nick?" Her voice was low and slightly raspy.

"Now there's a question," he teased, instinctively flirting.

Roses bloomed on Kelly's cheeks, and her eyes traveled deliberately down his torso before coming to rest briefly on the bulge pressing against the fly of his jeans.

His balls tightened as he felt that look like a caress. There was no mistaking it, Kelly was as aware of him as he was of her. Last night, when he'd touched her cheek, a lightning bolt had jolted straight from his fingertips to his dick. He'd heard Kelly's gasp, seen her eyes dilate, her lips part. Trying to convince himself that he'd imagined her reaction, he'd beat a hasty retreat before he'd done something really stupid like haul her over the bar and stick his tongue down her throat.

As for his own gut-deep response—he put that down to the fact that he hadn't had sex since he'd come home to Ann's suitcase and her announcement that she was heading back to San Francisco.

Never mind the fact that he'd never gotten a hard-on simply by touching a woman's cheek. It was high school all over again, when just the barest brush of Kelly's arm against his had sent him into a death spiral of lust.

"How about a pint of Harp's and a basket of wings."

"Extra hot?" Kelly asked.

Nick licked his lips. "Absolutely."

Fortunately, Ryan didn't seem to notice the sexual tension that fairly vibrated between Nick and his daughter.

Kelly quickly returned with his beer, her breasts brushing lightly against his shoulder as she leaned over to place his drink. Even through the cotton of her T-shirt and the fabric of his shirt, he could feel the heat of her skin.

Forcing himself to focus on something other than the thought of Kelly's hot, bare skin against his, he turned his attention on Ryan. "You're a lucky man to have Kelly taking care of you."

"Oh, she's not taking care of me—that's what I pay for over at the Oaks." Ryan had moved into a condo in a nearby retirement community shortly after his wife's death. "After taking care of Connie—God rest her soul—I made sure I'd never put that burden on the girls." He smiled somewhat sadly up at Kelly, who moved behind him and rested her hands on his shoulders.

"Nope, Dad needs me here to take care of Sullivan's until he's getting around better. Maggie could probably do it," Kelly said, giving her father a little squeeze. "But you know what he says, 'As long as this place is called Sullivan's—' "

"There'd better be a Sullivan in charge," both Ryan and Nick finished for her.

Kelly took a few more orders, and then returned with his wings.

"Take a load off, honey," Ryan said.

Nick obligingly snagged a chair and pulled it up for Kelly to sit and then tucked into his wings. He would leave as soon as he was finished. No use in torturing himself sniffing around Kelly when there was nothing he could do about it.

But instead he found himself drawn into conversation with Kelly and Ryan, talking about everything—baseball, the ridiculous amount of building going on in the area, the challenges of ER medicine, even politics.

Kelly got up several times to get refills and take orders, and several customers interrupted them to welcome Ryan back. The next thing he knew, it was after ten and Ryan was practically dozing in his chair.

"Come on, Dad," Kelly said, giving him a little nudge. "Maggie, can you cover for fifteen minutes while I run Dad home?"

"Honey, don't bother coming back. There's no one here, and I can close up tonight," Maggie called back.

Kelly thanked her and helped Ryan stay steady as he pulled himself up, then left to pull the car around.

Nick stood up too. "I better get going." He started to pull out a twenty but was halted by Ryan's grumble.

"On me tonight, Nicky. Thanks for keeping me company."

Nick nodded in thanks. "Need any help, Ryan?"

Ryan waved him off. "Nah. I need to learn to get around by myself if I ever want to get back full time."

Nick followed the older man just in case.

"Shit!" Kelly's curse echoed across the parking lot, accompanied by the slam of a car door.

"Watch your language, young lady," Ryan yelled. "You're not too old for me to feed you soap."

Nick couldn't help laughing. He'd forgotten that Kelly could swear like a trucker if the mood hit her.

"Sorry, Dad," she replied in the least apologetic tone Nick had ever heard.

"What's the matter?"

She blew a stray strand of hair out of her face in an exasperated sigh. "My car won't start."

"Pop the hood. I'll take a look."

"Umm, I doubt it's anything you can fix," Kelly muttered. It was hard to tell in the dimly lit lot, but he swore she blushed. "I, um, ran out of gas." She looked at her watch, swore again. "And the gas station's already closed."

Nick threw back his head and laughed. "I can't believe you. IQ of over two hundred and you still can't remember to fill your tank."

"I had other things on my mind." She shoved her hands in the pockets of her skirt. "No big deal. I'll borrow Maggie's car and take care of it in the morning."

She started back to the bar, but Nick grabbed her elbow. "Let me give you a ride."

She couldn't hide the relief in her face. "Are you sure? It's really not a problem to borrow Maggie's car and just get a ride home after we close."

Nick smiled, squeezing her upper arm reassuringly. His thumb traced little circles against the skin of the inner curve of her elbow. Was she this soft everywhere? He swallowed heavily and released her arm.

"Kelly, it's five minutes out of my way."

Apparently satisfied that she wasn't inconveniencing him, Kelly went back to wait with her father as Nick pulled his extended cab Dodge around.

It was a short ride to Ryan's condo complex, and ten minutes later Nick helped Ryan down from the truck and waited while Kelly walked him to the door.

The atmosphere changed as soon as they were alone. Suddenly the cab was thick with the tension of two people intensely aware of one another but trying to pretend they weren't.

Before, conversation had flowed easily. Now, Nick couldn't think of a damn thing to say. Kelly wasn't any help. She stared silently out the window, hands clasped in her lap in a pose that belied her earlier vibes of sexual interest.

Nick cleared his throat nervously. "So are you still living in Boston? Jake mentioned he'd run into you a couple of times."

Her smile was tight. "Yeah, I saw him and Kit a couple of weeks ago. How funny that they ended up together." Silence filled the car, along with tension so thick he could practically see it. Finally Kelly broke it. "I was getting ready to move to Manhattan when Dad got hurt. Unfortunately they couldn't hold the position open, and now I'll have to find something else."

Nick could tell by the grim set of her mouth she regretted the lost opportunity.

"It must suck for you to have to give that up."

Kelly shrugged. "He's my Dad, and I wasn't always there for him."

Nick could only assume she referred to the aftermath of her mother's death but didn't want to pry. "He's lucky to have you."

He could barely make out her smile in the flickering light of the street lamps, slightly sad. She was silent for several moments, looking out the window.

He imagined how small and backwater the redwood-lined streets and rustic country houses must look to her. "This place must seem so boring to you now after living in the city."

She turned to face him. "The city's great, but this town has its charm. There was a time when I couldn't wait to get out of here." Then, licking her lips nervously or provocatively, he couldn't tell, she said, "But now I realize it has some things worth coming home to."

Kelly mentally slapped herself upside the head. Her big chance to put the moves on Nick, and she sat like an uptight schoolgirl, saying inane things like "it has some things worth coming home to."

What was it about Nick that made her cool competence disappear? It wasn't as though she was a complete social reject anymore. She'd made friends at work, had a respectable run at relationships.

And now, presented with the perfect opportunity to put the moves on him, she turned into a blithering idiot.

Clearly Nick felt the same, because he didn't bother to make conversation for the rest of the drive.

When they pulled up to the small two-bedroom house she was renting, she scrambled for the door handle. But Nick had already alit from the cab and was at the passenger door. He opened it and cupped her elbow as he helped her down.

"Thanks so much for the ride, Nick," she said once her feet were firmly on the ground. "I'll see you around sometime." She started up the walk but was stopped when Nick grabbed her arm again. She shivered, and not merely from the cool autumn breeze against her bare arms.

"Hold on, let me walk you to the door."

Kelly laughed softly. "It's not as though this is the crime capital of the world. I'm sure I can make it twenty feet safely."

He smiled, his teeth white in the dim streetlights. "No way. My mama always told me, you walk a lady to the door."

She found herself oddly touched by the chivalrous gesture. "Jeez, I practically had to pay the guys I dated in Boston to walk me home."

She could feel Nick's disapproval in the subtle tightening of his fingers around her arm. Underneath his easy-going exterior she knew that Nick was a man who would protect and care for his woman.

Kelly murmured a silent apology to all of her feminist values and let herself fantasize, for just a moment, about how it would feel to have Nick Donovan protecting her and seeing to her every need.

She pulled her key out of her purse, only to have him take it from her hand and unlock her door. Her stomach quivered. Chivalry again.

She tilted her head up at him, her mouth open to say good

night, but stopped dead. In the glow of her porch light, Nick's eyes glowed amber, seeming to devour the curves of her face and mouth.

Anticipation washed through her. He wanted her. She was nearly certain of it. Hadn't she vowed to do something about it the next chance she got?

Nick started to push away from the open doorway, his expression once again one of polite friendliness.

Oh no, he was leaving!

"Do—do you want to come in?" Kelly blurted. She mentally slapped herself again. Smooth, Kelly, real smooth.

Again, the heat of awareness flared in his eyes.

Maybe she hadn't completely blown it.

But then Nick started to shake his head. "I really should—"

It was now or never. Before he could utter the word *go*, she cupped his face in her hands, pulling his mouth down to hers. For a full second, his mouth was unresponsive, slack with surprise. Her stomach fell somewhere near her knees. *Stupid, stupid, stupid!* She'd known she'd make a complete fool of herself!

But then Nick was kissing her back, his tongue thrusting eagerly into her mouth, his hands sliding down her back. One hand slid into the waistband of her skirt, gliding roughly over the cheeks of her ass, while his other arm wrapped around her waist.

Kelly found herself pinned against the front door, Nick's denim-clad thigh wedged between her legs. She was on her tiptoes, moaning into his mouth as he surrounded her with his big, muscular body. Her breasts were deliciously crushed against his chest, her mouth filled with the slick, hot taste of his tongue.

Moisture rushed between her legs, and all he had done was kiss her. What would she do when he touched her breasts, her clit? The mere thought made her moan again, louder, and grind her throbbing mound against his thigh.

Then suddenly, he pulled away, chest heaving as though he'd

just run a fast mile. Without his support, Kelly staggered a little and reached out to grasp his shoulders. "What—why?" she gasped. "How can you possibly stop now?"

Nick groaned, leaned down, and ran his tongue across her bottom lip. To Kelly's dismay, he backed away before she could suck it back into her mouth.

"Kelly, I don't think this is a very good idea." Even as he said it, his palm curved around the back of her neck.

Now that she'd touched him she couldn't stop. She ran her fingers up the corded muscles of his forearms, explored his biceps, pushing her hands underneath the short sleeves of his T-shirt. "Oh, I have to disagree with you." She leaned up to lick at the salty sweet skin of his neck, gratified by the way his hips involuntarily yearned closer to hers.

"I'm not interested in anything serious," he said, settling his hands around her waist.

"And you think I am?" Kelly sighed as his mouth came down to explore her neck.

"You're a nice girl, Kelly," he murmured between soft sucking kisses that were turning Kelly's knees to liquid.

"How do you know? You haven't seen me for a long time." She tunneled her fingers into his hair. "Maybe I've turned into a big tramp." His soft chuckle told her he didn't believe that for a second. "What's the big deal? I'm leaving town in a few weeks, and I'm not looking for any great romance."

He lifted his head and looked at her, as though trying to decide whether she was telling the truth. "What exactly is it you want?"

She tilted her head up and gave him what she hoped was an enticing smile. "I've always had a crush on you, Nick. Back in high school I used to listen to what the girls said about you, how good you were." She reached down, slid one hand up his inner thigh to cup him through his jeans. "How big you were."

His hand came down over hers, pressing it even more firmly against the rock-hard column of flesh.

"I want to find out for myself if what they said is true." Kelly wrapped her other hand around his neck, pulling him down for her kiss. "I want to have the high school fling I never got to have. I want you, Nick."

Nick slammed his mouth down across hers, his dick hardening another inch at the eager way Kelly sucked his tongue into her mouth.

Grown-up Kelly, with her deliciously hot body and dirty mouth, was hotter than any fantasy he'd ever conjured in his own mind.

A high school fling. Kissing, touching, groping. Teasing a girl until she was so crazy horny that she was willing to go all the way. All of the ways he'd ever dreamed of touching Kelly with his fingers, lips, cock, rushed through his head, and for a terrifying second he was afraid he was going to come in his pants.

Something he hadn't ever done, even when he *was* in high school.

He slid his hands up the backs of her legs, under her skirt so he could cup her ass through the thin satin of her panties. She was perfect in his hands, firm but soft, overflowing his broad palms. Kelly had exactly the kind of body he liked. Athletic but womanly. Curved in all the right places, tall and strong enough that he wouldn't have to worry about going easy on her.

Kelly wrapped one long, strong leg around his hip, grinding her crotch against the bulge of his fly. Even through the heavy fabric her damp heat scorched him. No question, Kelly Sullivan could take everything he had to give.

She reached behind her, fumbling for the doorknob, but Nick stopped her as a fantasy he'd harbored for a long, long time took root in his brain.

He grabbed her hand and pulled her back down the walk.

Dazed, she followed him for a few steps, but then started tugging at his hand. "What are you doing?"

He didn't answer, just yanked the truck door open and practically threw her inside.

"Where are we going?" Her tone was sharp with creeping impatience.

He revved the truck engine and turned to grin at her. "You said you wanted your high school fling, right?"

She nodded, but a tiny frown knit her eyebrows together.

"Ever been parking?"

Her frown melted into a naughty grin as she slid across the bench seat and glued herself to his side.

The quiet of the truck cab hummed with anticipation. Nick's hand gripped her thigh, his fingers teasing the soft inner curve. She nuzzled her face into the crook of his neck, inhaling his masculine, spicy scent as she struggled to keep her breathing even. Her belly clenched as he pulled off the road, ignoring NO TRESPASSING signs as he followed a dirt driveway into a clearing several hundred yards off the road.

She bit her lip, feeling as nervous as the high school girl she was pretending to be. "What if someone comes up here?"

Nick turned off the ignition and leaned toward her. "This is a building site we're working on. No one's gonna bother us." Moonlight glowed through the sunroof, highlighting the sharp angles of his cheekbones and jaw. His lips parted as he bent his dark head, but instead of taking her mouth as she expected, Nick curved his hand around the nape of her neck and trailed soft kisses across her temple, down her cheek, to the corner of her mouth.

"What's your curfew?" he whispered, fingers trailing down her arm.

Kelly smiled, playing along. "I don't have one. My mom's not around, and my dad works nights."

"Mmm, no parental supervision," he murmured, flicking the seam of her lips lightly with his tongue.

"That's right," she whispered against his mouth, "I can stay out all night if I want to."

His lips slid against hers, his tongue licking inside her mouth in a caress that made her toes curl inside her Keds.

"Move over," he whispered, pushing her across the bench seat as he climbed over the gearshift to the passenger side. She awkwardly twisted until she sat sideways across his lap, her arm squeezed against his chest and her back against the door. With a little grunting and twisting, she found herself straddled on Nick's lap, her skirt up around her waist. He reached down alongside the seat, and with an abrupt jerk the seat slid back several inches.

"Now that's better." His hands settled around her waist, the heat of his palms radiating through the thin cotton of her shirt. He kissed her, long, slow, wet kisses that sent jolts of sensation pulsing between her legs. It wasn't enough. She wanted to feel his skin, see if it was as hot and smooth as she'd always imagined. She tugged his shirt out of his waistband and shoved it up his chest. A soft, satisfied murmur escaped her at the feel of his hot, silky skin against her palms.

He obligingly hooked an arm around to yank it over his head. "I want to take your shirt off, Kelly," he said. "Will you let me?"

Her nails combed through the crisp hair on his chest as she pretended to consider it. "I don't know. I've never gone that far with a boy," she whispered. "Are you sure you won't think I'm a slut?"

He slid his hand up her rib cage, cupping one heavy globe,

his thumb barely teasing her through the fabric of her T-shirt. He tasted her soft gasp in his mouth as he raked his thumb again, harder this time. "I promise I won't think you're a slut." He kissed her again. "And it'll feel so good, I promise."

Kelly leaned back and lifted her arms so he could pull her shirt up and over her head. Her dark curls drifted around her shoulders as she leaned back against the dashboard, clad only in a white lace bra.

"God, I wish I could see you better," he whispered as he traced her plump breasts spilling over the lacy cups. Beneath his fingers her skin was smooth and perfect as silk.

One hand slipped inside a cup to fondle her breast, testing the heavy weight. There was nothing he loved more than the feel of a woman's breast in his hand. The weight, the bounce, the softness. And hers were amazing, full, soft, her nipple like a hard little bullet pressing into his palm.

Her hands were hot against his back as she held him against her, leaning in to kiss him as he fondled and played with her glorious tits.

Sliding her hands up between them, Kelly reached and unhooked the front clasp of her bra. Her breasts sprang free exuberantly, as though eager to escape the confines of her lingerie.

Nick leaned back against the seat, cupping her breasts, loving the way the abundant flesh more than filled his big hands. "I've dreamed about your tits," he whispered. The brush of his fingers on her large nipples made her sigh and jerk against his lap.

Nick could feel her smile against his cheek. She rocked against his fly in a way that made him groan and lift his hips tighter against her. "Really?"

"Yeah. I used to think about how they would feel, how they would taste," he whispered, getting back into the role of teenage seducer. "When you come over to help me study, I dream about unbuttoning your shirt, pushing the books out of the way, and spreading you out on my mom's kitchen table." He loved the way her breath hitched at his words.

"I had no idea you even noticed," she gasped.

"Oh, I noticed all right. I wish I could see you," he repeated. "I want to see your nipples. What color are they, Kelly? Pink? Red? I can feel how hard they are, like they're begging me to suck them," he whispered, leaning his head forward so he could taste the soft skin, pearly in the dim light of the truck. Her breath rose in harsh pants in the steamy confines of the cab as his tongue teased her skin. He could smell the fresh, flowery scent of her soap, and under that, the heady smell of her arousal. She was so wet, so responsive, and they'd barely even gotten started.

His lips hovered above one nipple, his hot breath wafting over the ripe tip, but he didn't close his lips over it. Kelly tugged his head impatiently, the most adorable sounds of frustration emitting from her throat. "Do you want me to suck your nipples?" he teased. "I can't tell if you'll like that or not." He trapped the nipple between two fingers, applying the slightest pressure.

She let out a strangled cry. "Dammit, Nick, suck me." Her demand was accompanied by a sharp tug on his hair as she arched her back and pressed one hard bud against his lips.

"For someone who's never let a boy touch her like this, you're pretty demanding," he whispered around the swollen peak. Kelly's eager response and demands for pleasure drove him out of his mind. He was so turned on it was a wonder he could even speak. .

She let out a serrated moan as his lips closed over her nipple, sucking hard. Her fingers dug into his shoulders, and she squirmed in his lap. "Please, Nick, no more games, just touch me." Dimly Nick heard her moans as he was consumed by the delicious taste of her skin, the feel of her hard, swollen flesh against his lips and tongue. He released one nipple with an audible pop, only to fasten his lips on the other pleading tip.

The cab grew humid from their overheated bodies, and beads of condensation trickled down the inside of the windows.

"When we fuck I want you on top, so I can suck your tits while my cock is inside you," he whispered harshly, his fingers squeezing and pulling at the bud made slick and damp from his mouth. He heard her gasp, knew his words were making her hotter. He'd never been a big talker during sex, didn't even know where the words were coming from. But her obvious arousal inspired him. "What do you think of that? You think you're ready to go all the way with me?" He squeezed her breasts together, licking and sucking first at one nipple, then the other. "Maybe someday I'll fuck your tits," he rasped. "Would you like that?"

Her only answer was a sharp cry as she shuddered against him. A faint sheen of sweat gleamed on her chest, and she fell forward against his chest.

He stared at her, stunned. "Did you just—"

"I'm sorry," she whispered shakily. "I couldn't wait, I'm so sorry—"

Nick groaned and thrust his tongue between her lips, effectively shutting her up. His cock throbbed and twitched, and his balls tightened inside the suddenly torturous confines of his jeans. "You are so fucking hot," he murmured, trailing soft kisses across her cheeks and lips. "If I don't get inside you soon I'm gonna lose my mind."

Every muscle in her body tensed against him as she buried her face against his shoulder.

"What's wrong, honey?" His fingers stroked the damp curls around her hairline. This shy hesitation was so at odds with her earlier demands, Nick was afraid he had pushed too hard, too soon.

"I came too soon. I couldn't hold out, and now I'm already finished."

His laugh burst from his chest. "Premature ejaculation in a car. It doesn't get much more high school than that."

"This was a terrible idea." Obviously embarrassed, she crossed her arms over her breasts and tried to move off his lap, managing to pin herself with one knee on the floor and her head against the dashboard.

"Hey, come on now," Nick lifted her up and resettled her, gripping her thighs firmly to keep her in place. She reluctantly uncrossed her arms as his head bent to nuzzle against her breasts.

"Do you have any idea how sexy you are? The fact that you can come with nothing more than my mouth on your tits makes me harder than I've ever been in my life." He licked each of the now-soft nipples in turn as his hands squeezed the ripe curves of her ass.

"But I'm usually . . ." She paused, licked her lips, started again. "I'm usually only good for one a night. And I wanted it to be with you . . ." She hesitated.

Shy Kelly was back, and he nuzzled her neck encouragingly. "I wanted it to be with you inside me."

"You will," he whispered, one hand sliding around to cup her sex through the silky fabric of her panties. His fingers pressed against her drenched slit, and the heel of his hand ground against her mound. "Trust me."

3

"It's not that I don't trust you," Kelly murmured, grinding herself against the firm pressure of Nick's palm. "But I know myself, and I don't come more than once."

The air in the truck was close, echoing with the sound of their labored breath. Her soft moan filled the space as she surged against him, surprised when, in spite of her protests, the faintest tingles of renewed desire blossomed in her belly.

It wasn't that she had a problem having an orgasm during sex. As with everything in her life, Kelly was self-sufficient and took personal responsibility for her own sexual enjoyment. If it meant giving her lovers step-by-step instructions, or even taking matters into her own hands, she made sure she always got off.

But once she was done, she was done.

Even so, she let out a little moan as Nick's hand stole inside her panties. Two long, thick fingers pressed against her cleft, and his thumb traced firm circles around her slowly—unbelievably—

awakening clit. Nick captured the sound with his mouth, sweeping his tongue against her soft inner cheeks.

She spread her knees wider against the bench seat and leaned back against the dash, emitting a little sigh of frustration. She hated it when this happened, when she got turned on again, just enough to leave her really frustrated but never enough to reach another peak.

"Come inside me, Nick," she whispered, moving her hand between their bodies, her palm pressing firmly against the hard bulge in his fly. She wanted to feel him there, she really did. But she also wanted him to stop his futile teasing and just get on with it.

Her mouth went dry at the feel of his impressive length all but burning through the fabric of his jeans, and again she scolded herself. How could she have possibly lost control and come with just his mouth on her breasts? How could she have ruined her first time with Nick?

"Just relax," he whispered. "Trust me to make it good for you."

Her eyes snapped open. His amber gaze seemed to glow, even in the dim light. He captured her hand, preventing its further explorations, and raised it to his lips. He kissed her, pulling her flush against him so her breasts were crushed, his hot, hair-roughened skin burning her. "You have such beautiful skin," he said as he bent his head to kiss the smoothness of her shoulder, the curve of her neck. His hands splayed across her back, the faint calluses abrading the smooth expanse. "So soft and sweet." His tongue flicked out to taste her. "I wonder if you're this sweet everywhere."

He slid a hand under her skirt and hooked it in the waistband of her panties. Obligingly she rose up and leaned back against the dash so he could pull the miniscule scrap of fabric down her legs. His groan echoed hers as he slipped one blunt, long finger inside her, testing her, teasing her with what was to come. "Next time I'm gonna make you come in my mouth," he said harshly. "But now I can't wait anymore."

He pulled her hand back down to his fly. "Take me out."

Kelly obeyed with shaky fingers, and he impatiently lifted his hips and shoved his pants and underwear down around his thighs. She couldn't see him clearly, but she reached down to grasp him, silky hot skin over granite hardness pressing urgently into her hand. She circled him with her fist, realizing with a bit of trepidation that her fingers barely met.

She giggled nervously.

"I'm sure you realize," he said, his hand settling over hers, guiding her into a firm, pumping rhythm that brought a sheen of sweat to his skin, "that laughter is not an appropriate response when a guy takes his dick out."

"I'm sorry," she said, her voice quavering. "It's just—Vicki Jenkins was right. You're huge."

And he was. Certainly bigger than any other man Kelly had known.

"Vicki Jenkins told you I was huge?" he managed to choke out. Even in the dim light she could see his jaw clench. His hands clenched and unclenched in the soft flesh of her hips.

Kelly kissed him hard and felt an answering rush of moisture flood between her thighs. "I heard her on the bus." Kelly almost didn't recognize the husky throb of her own voice. Following his guide, she stroked him up and down in a firm squeezing motion, tracing the thick ridge beneath the head, circling the smooth, plump tip with her thumb until it was slick with his own fluids. "She was talking to a friend." She sucked at the salty flesh of his neck. "She said you were so big, she could barely walk afterward. Thinking about that used to scare me, but then . . ."

Nick's hands rubbed up and down her arms, over her breasts, her waist, in an aimless, arousing exploration. "But then?"

She sucked his tongue into her mouth, stroking it with her own until a deep moan rumbled from his chest. "But then I started to wonder how you would feel inside me, if I could take it."

His eyes gleamed wickedly as he shoved her skirt up around her waist, thrusting himself into her fist. "Oh, you can take it. I have no doubt."

All traces of teasing vanished as Nick captured one nipple in his teeth. Pleasure danced on the edge of pain as his tongue lashed at the sensitized flesh.

She guided his cock to the throbbing wetness of her sex, circling the head against her pulsing clit. Was it possible she could come again? Elated at the possibility, Kelly pushed her breasts against his face, begged him to suck her harder as she rocked against his huge erection.

She grunted in protest as he pushed her back against the dashboard. He reached down between them, fumbling. "Condom," he muttered. She rose up on her knees as he rolled it on in one quick, smooth motion.

One strong hand cupped her ass as the other positioned the head of his cock at her dripping entrance. Blunt, insistent, he squeezed inside. She let out a little moan as she felt her inner muscles clench in resistance. Her body was protesting. Not in fear, or in pain, but in self-preservation. This was supposed to be fun, a fulfillment of a fantasy, nothing more, but Kelly couldn't escape the sensation that if she let Nick inside she would never be the same.

"Take it slow, honey," he murmured, his fingers gripping the resilient flesh of her ass, "as slow as you need."

She braced her hands on his shoulders, moaning as she felt the thick, heavy slide of him inside her. She was wet and slick around him, relaxing now to take him deep. Surrendering. Surrendering to this exquisite fullness, the throbbing of him deep inside. Deeper than anyone had ever been before.

She began moving, faster now, spreading her knees wide to take him deeper with every downstroke of her hips.

He let out a low string of curses. "You feel so good, you have no idea," Nick whispered. He braced his big, booted feet on the floor and thrust up hard against her, sucking her nipples hard into his mouth.

The pressure built as her body grasped his cock, trying to hug it inside her. She ground her clit against his pubic bone, frantically working herself to another peak.

As though he read her mind, Nick slipped his hand between them. His thumb settled against her clit, the firm strokes perfectly matching the rhythm of their thrusts. Heat blossomed at the base of her spine, trickling through her limbs, tingling in her fingers and toes. "Come, Kelly, come again. With me inside you," he growled, swirling his thumb against her throbbing flesh.

At his command, she shattered, throwing her head back as her stunned cries echoed in the close confines of the truck. She slumped against him, dazed for a moment until she realized he was still rock hard inside her.

He shifted their position, pushing her onto her back so her head was wedged against the driver's side door. He was on top of her, one foot on the floor and one knee on the seat. He either didn't mind or didn't notice the gearshift bumping against his thigh as he seated himself more firmly inside her.

She closed her eyes, drifting. Heaved a contented sigh. Now Nick could take his turn.

"Hey, Kelly."

Her eyes snapped open at his commanding tone.

"Focus. Don't think just because you came you get to roll over and fall asleep."

She couldn't very well roll over with his cock pinning her to the seat, but it was probably best not to mention that.

"Come on, honey, I want you with me. All the way to the end." He emphasized this with a firm thrust that had the head of his cock bumping against her cervix.

She inhaled with a sharp gasp as, incredibly, her body responded to his heavy thrusts, tightening around him as he increased his tempo. Her tissues were swollen, sensitive almost to the point of pain, and still he pounded against her. It was too much, too overwhelming. "Oh, God, Nick, I can't take anymore," she whimpered. She, who was always in control of her own orgasm, forced to endure more pleasure than she'd ever experienced in her life.

Her previous languor vanished, bringing everything into sharp, bright focus. The hot feel of Nick's skin as her palms pressed against his back. The harsh sound of his breath as he struggled to hold back his release. The sheen of sweat that slicked his muscles, their ripples gleaming in dim light.

She smelled the heavy scent of sex in the air, the sharp tang of their mingled sweat. It pulled at something primitive inside of her, and she hooked her leg around his waist to draw him closer.

He grabbed her left ankle and propped her sneaker-clad foot on his shoulder. The other he hooked over the steering wheel, and Kelly braced her foot on the dashboard. They groaned in unison as he slid even deeper inside her slick, yielding softness. "That's it, honey, take me, take all of me."

She was spread wide open, helpless against the surging invasion of his cock. Vaguely Kelly felt her head bump against the door, but she didn't care, overwhelmed as she was by her own gut-wrenching response.

"Jesus Christ, you're killing me," he groaned, his hips pistoning harder, faster, his balls slapping the soft flesh of her ass with every stroke. One last thrust and he froze, shaking over her. His cock throbbed and twitched, sending her spiraling to another release.

If the first two orgasms had been like waves of pleasure washing through her, this one was like a tsunami, crashing over her, overwhelming her, seizing her in spasms so intense she feared for a moment her heart would stop.

She could see the headlines now: "Doctor fucked to death. Morticians unable to remove smile from her face."

He collapsed on top of her, his heavy weight pleasantly crushing her into the seat. His heart thudded heavily, echoing her own. As her breath and heartbeat returned to a seminormal level, she ran her hands up and down the sleek muscles of his back. Her soft tissues protested as his slowly softening erection slipped from her body.

Odd, that she should be so bereft to have him leave her. Usually once a lover was finished, she couldn't wait for him to pull out and get off her. But even in the cramped quarters of the truck, she wanted to stay under Nick forever, with him inside her. Eventually he would get hard again . . .

He levered himself off her, pausing to press a tender kiss against her mouth. He quickly divested himself of the condom and pulled up his pants.

Kelly felt around for her clothes. Suddenly she felt not just naked, but exposed. Half-naked in a truck with her body aching from vigorous sex was not a familiar situation. Now without the filter of passion, she wasn't quite sure how to act.

The man had just brought her to three—count 'em, three—screaming orgasms, and she had no idea what to say to him.

Now she remembered exactly why she didn't do one-night stands, especially with guys who completely outmatched her sexually.

What was she supposed to say? *Thanks, that was great? The rumors were true, you could go pro with that thing?*

Nick handed over her bra, chuckling.

"What?" she snapped, convinced he was laughing at her.

"We didn't even get our shoes off."

She looked down. Sure enough, her red Keds were still on her feet, and his work boots were tightly laced.

He hauled her against him, and her doubts momentarily fled as she was distracted by the luscious feel of his bare chest against hers. He cupped her face, licked inside her mouth, and against her thigh she felt the faint stirring of his penis where it peeked out from his open fly. *The man is a machine*, she thought as her womb gave an answering tug.

"Next time, I want you naked with the lights on," he growled.

She kissed him back with greater enthusiasm. "Next time?"

He lifted his head, cupped her cheeks in his hands. "You didn't really think one time would be enough?"

"I was prepared to let it be."

Nick's hands slid down her back to the waistband of her skirt. "No way. I've got over a decade of fantasies stored up, and I plan to get to every one of them."

He handed over her discarded garments—all except for her panties, which seemed to have vaporized. She dressed, trying not to read too much into the idea that Nick wanted to see her again. Just like her, all he wanted was sex.

But the thought that he'd enjoyed himself enough to want more thrilled her nonetheless.

They drove in companionable silence, and when they got to the tiny two-bedroom bungalow, he again walked her to the door. The way he tucked her hand into his was frighteningly soothing.

The universe was making it very difficult for her to keep her distance.

He leaned in and kissed her, and before she knew it Kelly had her leg hitched up over his hip again. He tore his mouth away and whispered, "I only had the one condom, and unless you're stocked up we better cool it."

"Nope. Unfortunately I don't generally equate coming home with getting action." She fought the urge to invite him in to spend the night anyway. That the idea of falling asleep with him tucked around her was so appealing was enough for her to keep her mouth shut.

"Now maybe you will," he said with a teasing nip at her bottom lip.

"When will I see you?" She hoped that didn't come out sounding as pathetically needy as she feared.

"Soon." He tilted her chin up for one last kiss. "I'll pass you a note in study hall."

She leaned back against the door, slightly dazed, as she watched him walk away. A very uncomfortable thought occurred to her. "Nick," she called, and rushed down the walk after him.

He turned to her, expectant.

"Can you do me a favor?" She stopped inches away, arms wrapped around herself to ward off the late fall chill. She told herself it wasn't especially sweet when Nick pulled her close and chafed her arms and buried his face in her hair.

"Anything, babe."

Kelly was momentarily speechless. No man had ever called her babe, and until this moment, she'd been certain she'd gut-punch any man who tried.

Then she remembered her purpose. "Can we keep this quiet? I mean, not tell your brothers or anything?"

His hands on her arms stilled, and he pulled away to look at her.

She rushed on. "You know our parents. If your mom or my dad gets wind of this, they'll misunderstand—start planning the wedding or nonsense like that. I'm leaving town in a few weeks, and we both know this can't turn into anything serious." Even as she said it a tiny voice in the back of her brain wondered why the hell not. She dismissed it as an overload of hormones from all the orgasms.

Funny, she thought he'd be relieved. But from what she could see of his expression in the dimness of the streetlights, he looked annoyed.

Nick's grip tightened around her upper arms for a split second. Then all tension faded from his hands and his face, and his lips quirked up into a half smile. "You're right. It's best if nobody knows."

"Including Mike and Tony," she pressed, knowing full well how close he was to his brothers.

"Including Mike and Tony."

Kelly smiled in relief, and in the next second her breath left her as he kissed her hard, turned, and walked to his truck. She raised her arms and stretched, feeling gloriously fatigued in every sinew. As she tracked the glow of taillights down the block, she ignored the little voice warning her that her feelings for Nick were anything but casual.

4

I am a lucky, lucky man, Nick mused on the short drive back to his house. It was almost too good to be true, Kelly proposing a secret, no-strings fling, with no hard feelings once it was time for her to go. It was just the thing, as his brothers put it, to get him back into the saddle.

He watched for familiar cars, but this time of night, the streets were deserted so there was little risk of anyone seeing him out this late and asking questions. And if anyone did he could just tell them he was over in Truckee getting a piece of ass.

He snapped on the kitchen light and winced at the clock. Twelve-thirty. He had to be up in less than six hours. The sacrifices a man had to make for good sex.

No, not just good sex, he thought as he undressed and slipped into his king-size bed. Awesome, unbelievable, soul-shaking sex. The mere memory of it made him hard as a spike, when by rights his cock should be wrung out like an old washrag.

Never in his wildest fantasies about Kelly—and he'd had

quite a few over the years—had he ever imagined she'd be so hot, so responsive. He'd never had a woman come just from having him suck her tits.

Funny how a woman so responsive could think she was only good for one a night. The men in her past must have been completely inept. His lips curled in a rueful smile. He had no doubt he was not nearly as smart and sophisticated as the men Kelly had dated, but he had a few special talents of his own.

He closed his eyes, revisiting the memory of Kelly clenched tight and wet around him. It had felt so good at the end, not having to hold back, not worrying that it was too much, too rough. Knowing that he could pound into her with abandon and still have her begging for more.

He groaned and squeezed his now-throbbing hard-on. Shit. He wished for the thousandth time that he'd stayed at Kelly's. Even without a condom there was a lot of stuff they could do that would relieve his current state. But spending the night was out of the question. There was something about sleeping with a woman, holding her while she slept, that felt too intimate, more intimate even than sex, and that level of intimacy wasn't part of their agreement.

But that didn't stop him from thinking about delving under the covers with Kelly. Burying his head between her thighs and licking her clit until she came against his mouth. Of waking up in the morning to the soft suction of her mouth on his cock.

He pumped himself furiously now, on the edge. His back arched off the mattress as he exploded, wishing it were Kelly's warm mouth receiving his come instead of his hand.

He went to the bathroom and cleaned himself up, hoping that now he could relax enough to sleep. Returning to bed, he flopped over on his stomach and stuffed a down pillow under his head. He couldn't afford to let this thing with Kelly get out of control. As far as he could tell, sex was the only area in

which they were compatible, and he couldn't allow it to interfere with other, more important areas of his life.

It was bad enough that he was breaking his vow not to date
anyone from town. But, he reasoned, since Kelly was only here
for a short time, she didn't really count.

This was just sex, nothing more. Even though Kelly was
everything he wanted in a woman—funny, beautiful, not to
mention wickedly smart—he'd learned the hard way not to expect more from a woman so far out of his league. But he could
have a hell of a lot of fun with her while it lasted.

Kelly hummed softly to herself as she stepped out of the
shower the following night. She hoped her shampoo was pow-
erful enough to eradicate the scent of frying oil that no doubt
clung to her hair. She rubbed lotion on her legs and pulled her
robe around her, pondering what to wear.

Her body hummed in anticipation. She had been more excited than she wanted to admit earlier that evening when Nick
had stopped by Sullivan's for a quick beer and actually passed
her a note along with his bar tab. "I haven't stopped thinking
about you," it read. "I'll be over tonight after you close. Wear
something that's easy to tear off."

The last part made her chuckle even as it sent heat pooling in
her belly. Even though Nick was so good humored and easy-
going, there was a darker, more commanding side that she had
glimpsed for the first time last night. She could easily imagine
Nick tearing off her clothes before throwing her down on the
bed and ravishing her like some pirate in a romance novel.

Hmmmm. A pirate and his lusty wench. That might be a fun
game . . .

She stood in front of her closet. Since her wardrobe leaned
more toward the practical rather than sexy and tearable, her
choices were limited.

In the end, she slid into a pair of cream-colored, lace-trimmed bikini panties and a matching bra, which she covered with her blue terry cloth robe. The robe wasn't sexy by a long shot, but it had the advantage of being easy to get out of.

She barely heard the ring of the phone over the roar of her hair dryer. She glanced at the clock. After midnight. Her stomach clenched as the phone rang for a third time. She prayed it wasn't Nick calling to cancel.

But who else would it be? Bracing herself, she snatched up the phone on her dresser.

"Kelly? It's me, Karen."

Kelly sighed. The only thing worse than Nick canceling on her. Her sister calling to harass her.

"Dad's fine, Karen," Kelly said abruptly.

"Have you even been over to see him today?"

Typical. No pretense of civility. As usual her sister launched directly into attack mode.

"Yes. I went with him to his physical therapist and spoke to his doctor. Then we had lunch and played cards. After that, I went to Sully's and managed to run the place without burning it down. And now I'm really tired and want to go to bed."

"You only stayed for three hours," Karen accused.

"I had an appointment with the head of the ER at Tahoe Forest. Once Dad is a little more mobile I'd like to do a few shifts a week if I can."

"I know that you think taking care of Dad is beneath you," Karen snapped, "but just because you're some big important doctor doesn't mean you don't have an obligation to your family."

Kelly closed her eyes and felt her shoulders knot, the way they did every time she spoke to her sister. "Karen, helping out at the hospital isn't going to interfere with running Sullivan's. Besides, Dad's going crazy having me underfoot all the time."

"I can't believe you're thinking of working at the hospital while you're there. Don't you ever think about anyone but yourself and your precious career? I don't know why I'm even surprised. You always got to do whatever you wanted, always got everything handed to you."

Kelly had heard this all before and didn't bother defending herself. It did no good to remind Karen that she'd had no interest in going to college or that their parents had happily financed cosmetology school, which had helped launch Karen into her very lucrative career as a hairstylist.

"Not to mention that you couldn't be bothered to come home when Mom was sick. It was up to me and Dad then to take care of her and watch her die."

That cut Kelly to the core. "When Mom got sick I was in the second year of my residency!"

"Cold comfort for a woman dying of cancer, not to mention Dad."

The well of guilt Kelly held in her gut threatened to overflow and consume her. It was that, as much as her love for her father, that had compelled her to come back to Donner Lake and help her dad.

It had meant giving up an incomparable opportunity in New York City, but Karen would never acknowledge Kelly's sacrifice. Kelly clenched the phone in her hand as Karen's last barb hung in the air. "Is there something you wanted, or did you just call to remind me of what a horrible daughter I am?"

"Actually, I need you to call the insurance company to let them know you're handling everything. I wasted an hour trying to deal with them today."

"And God knows you have more important things to do. Like give a spiral perm." Kelly winced at her own bitchy tone. But she'd learned a long time ago that if she didn't fight back, Karen would keep clawing until Kelly was all but eviscerated.

"Fuck you, Kelly. Other people have important lives, too, even if you don't think so."

"Love you too, Sis." Kelly slammed the phone down in its cradle, wondering why, after all these years, her sister still had the power to get under her skin. Maybe because somewhere in the far reaches of her memory, Kelly remembered a time when they'd gotten along, a time that existed before Karen had inexplicably decided her younger sister was the enemy. Why couldn't they, just once, have a normal, civilized—friendly even— conversation like other sisters?

A heavy knock sounded at her door, and Kelly couldn't mask her foul mood as she flung it open.

Misinterpreting her glare, Nick stepped back. "We don't have to do this if you don't want."

Kelly shook her head and pulled him into her house. "I do want this," she said, and truly meant it.

She let him in and slammed the door to let off some steam. Nick pulled her into a kiss, and Kelly felt her tension abate marginally at the feel of his tongue pressing sweetly against hers.

She commanded herself to relax as she twined her fingers into the hair at the nape of his neck. Forced herself to focus on the thick, silky strands against her fingers, on the mint-tinged taste of his tongue in her mouth. But even the skillful strokes of his tongue weren't enough to erase the awful guilt and frustration her sister's words had conjured.

Abruptly he pulled away. "What's wrong? Do you want me to go?"

Kelly blew out a sigh, clutching the lapels of his leather jacket as she beat her head against his chest a few times. "I'm sorry," she mumbled into the fabric of his denim work shirt. She took three deep breaths, inhaling the fresh scent of laundry soap and Nick's own spicy sandalwood-scented skin. "I don't want you to go, I'm just having a hard time relaxing," she confessed.

"Well there goes the football player and cheerleader fantasy I had planned," he said.

Kelly's head snapped up. "Are you serious?" Until last night, she'd never been much into role playing, but she had to admit it had been pretty fun.

One big hand came up to encircle the back of her neck, and Kelly arched in pleasure as broad callused fingers stroked and kneaded the rigid tendons. "I think you need something a little different tonight." He continued unraveling the tension in her neck with firm strokes. "Why don't you tell me what's up?"

He paused in his massage therapy to take off his jacket, depositing it onto a chair as he led her over to the couch. She bit back her protest at the loss of his warm hands on her skin. He turned her away from him and brought both hands to her shoulders, kneading the stiffly set muscles.

"I talked to my sister right before you got here," she said, her head falling forward to give him better access to the stiff muscles of her shoulders and neck.

"How is Karen?"

"Still as big a bitch as ever." Her spine went rigid as she remembered their conversation. "Really, in the scheme of it, it's no big deal. But she just makes me feel so, so—"

"Shitty?" Nick offered.

"Exactly. She says awful things that I know are unfair, but every time I revert to that stupid thirteen-year-old dying for her sister to like her."

"I remember she was pretty hard on you."

Kelly had a flash of being a high school sophomore. Her sister, four years older, was a junior. Kelly remembered, on more than one occasion, sitting alone in the cafeteria while Karen and her posse of friends sat at another table laughing and snickering. "Karen always hated that I got attention because I was smart." She told Nick what Karen said about Kelly's attitude and about their mother. As her anger rekindled, she did her best to blink back her tears of guilt and frustration. He pulled her back against his chest, and she leaned into him, savoring the feeling of comfort. "Do people think I'm really like that? That self-centered and elitist?"

"Come on, Kelly," he murmured, pressing a soft kiss against her cheek, "it's like you said. Karen is insecure, not to mention a bitch by nature. You were special, and she resented that. Your brains made her feel stupid, not you. All of us feel stupid next to someone like you. We can't help it."

"I hate that!" she exploded. "Resenting me for making you feel stupid is like me hating Heidi Klum because I'd never be chosen for the *Sports Illustrated* swimsuit issue. We're both freaks of nature."

"Hey, I never said I resented you. I just feel dumb next to you. But then, I'm pretty sure no one's ever going to get me confused with Einstein."

She turned and smacked him on the shoulder. "You're dyslexic, not dumb, and I hate it when you talk like that."

"Hey, we're talking about your baggage, not mine." Nick's voice had a new edge she hadn't heard before.

"Okay, fine. Then maybe we should talk about how I haven't been there for my family when they needed me. My mom—"

He gave her a hard look. "You think your mom would have wanted you to risk your career to come home and watch her die?"

Kelly just shrugged. She'd always felt, and Karen had eagerly fostered the belief, that her mom had never forgiven Kelly for not coming home in time to say good-bye.

"Nobody knew she was going to go so fast. We all thought

she had more time. Your mom was so proud of you when you got into med school, there's no way she wanted you to jeopardize that."

This was a surprise to Kelly. She'd always had the impression that her mom had regarded her as something of a genetic anomaly. "I never thought she really cared one way or the other," she murmured.

Nick kissed her forehead. "She used to brag about you all the time. But I already knew how great you were. If it wasn't for you, I would have never graduated from high school."

Her mom had been proud of her. She was going to have to tuck that piece of information away in her heart and reexamine it later.

Right now she was focused on Nick, who had managed, with his warm hands and reassuring words, to talk her out of her sour mood and make her tension disappear. She felt relaxed, safe, content. As his fingers dipped under the lapel of her robe the first faint twinges of arousal pulsed between her thighs.

"Sorry to dump on you like that," she murmured into the scented skin of his neck. "I know you didn't come over here to listen to me bitch."

"I'm still your friend, Kelly," he said, pressing a kiss to the corner of her mouth. "Besides," he said with a grin, "what I came over for works much better when you're not so uptight."

"I'm not uptight," she protested, pulling his shirttail from his waistband, eager to feel his hot skin against her palms. She jumped about a foot when his fingers grazed a ticklish spot on her rib cage. "Okay, maybe I'm a little uptight," she conceded.

"I have just the thing to calm you down." Nick took her hand and pulled her into the bedroom.

She did her best to relax as he led her down the short hallway to the bedroom. Earlier that day she'd bought some candles and flowers. The house came furnished, but barely, and

Kelly had done what she could to make her room look less like a cheap hotel room.

She stood quietly as he pushed her robe off her shoulders and draped it carefully over the back of a chair. He quickly rid her of her bra and panties and pulled her against him. The heat of arousal licked its way through her belly, between her thighs, along the tips of her breasts rasping against the soft cotton of his shirt.

"Lay down," he whispered huskily.

Kelly obliged, stretching against the soft cotton of her own six hundred thread count sheets. Furnished or no, some luxuries a girl just didn't give up.

She watched him through slitted eyes as he moved around the room, lighting candles and stripping off his clothes. She hadn't been able to see him very well last night, and now she drank her fill. The wide chest rippling with muscle, the burnished skin glowing in the candlelight.

The room quickly filled with the scent of green tea and cranberry candles. She breathed deep, the knot of tension in her belly finally starting to unravel.

Putting all thoughts of Karen aside, Kelly focused on Nick, magnificently naked in her bedroom. His eyes were dark and mysterious as they swept over her breasts and belly, finally coming to rest on the juncture of her thighs. She felt that look like a caress, felt her body dampening, softening. It was almost scary how easily he could turn her on.

Apparently the feeling was mutual, judging by the mammoth erection he was sporting. She leaned back against the pillows and parted her legs, certain that any second now he would climb on top of her and sink deep inside her already-wet sex.

But instead he just smiled at her and went into the bathroom.

"What are you looking for?" she called out when she heard him rustling around. "I put some condoms in the bedside table."

"I found it," he said. He appeared in the doorway, waving a bottle in a triumphant little shake. "Roll over."

She obeyed, looking over her shoulder to watch him. He uncapped the bottle and squeezed a generous amount of something—the fragrance hit her—her lavender-scented body oil.

"Put your head down," he chided.

"What are you—" Her question ended in a low groan as he spread the oil over her feet, up her calves and thighs. Pressing his fingers into the muscles of her legs, he moved his hands back down and captured her right foot in his hands.

Running the pub kept her on her feet, and the press of Nick's thumb against the ball of her foot was absolutely luxurious. He gave her other foot the same treatment, then worked his way up her Achilles tendons, her calves, her thighs, until her legs were like limp noodles and she was melting into a puddle of oil.

He lightly ran his palms over the curve of her ass, then knelt over her, knees bracketing her hips as his hands slid along the muscles beside her spine. With each stroke, his cock brushed against her ass. Her skin was slick with oil, and his hard flesh sliding against her slowly drove her insane.

Her languor diminished as she began to move in time, raising her hips slightly so his cock slid against her dripping cleft. Maybe if she got the angle right he could slip inside . . .

Nick splayed his hand against the small of her back. "I'm not done yet, Kelly," he whispered, bending down to nip her neck. The slight punishment sent a shiver down her back. "Just hold still and let me take care of you."

She obediently stilled her movements and blew a frustrated breath into the pillow. "You're torturing me."

His low chuckle surrounded her. "When I torture you, Kelly, I promise you'll know it."

She grumbled but let him continue his ministrations. She sighed in relief when he finally flipped her onto her back. Hard, oil-slicked palms captured her breasts, kneading and stroking her soft flesh. His eyes gleamed with a predatory light as he watched her nipples harden into gleaming red points. He leaned down to tease one, then the other with just the tip of his tongue.

She arched off the bed and threaded her fingers through his hair, trying to hold his head in place. "I want you inside me now," she said.

His face lit with a wicked smile. "Not yet," he said firmly. His mouth left her breasts, his tongue tracing under each before sliding down her belly. His tongue dipped inside her navel, traced the shallow dip.

Then his mouth, open and wet, grazed the flesh of her inner thigh. His hands pushed her knees up, opening, spreading her to his gaze, to his touch.

Her belly tensed as his mouth nuzzled into her mound, his tongue rimming her soft inner lips. Oral sex was always tricky for her. While she enjoyed it, she always had niggling doubts in the back of her mind. Was he enjoying it? Was she taking too long to come?

As though reading her thoughts, Nick stroked her with a long, slow lick of his tongue. "You taste so good," he murmured.

She let out a low moan as his tongue swirled around her clit, flicking against the firm flesh in a rhythm that had her writhing against the sheets.

"So sweet, juicy." His tongue slid down, slipping in and out in a delicious tongue fuck.

Oh God, that is it, she thought as his lips fastened on her clit again. She could feel her orgasm building as her hands moved up to pinch and rub her nipples, every sinew tightening as she pressed herself into his mouth.

"Oh, just like that," she moaned, "don't stop." Oh thank God, this wasn't going to take long at all. She shouldn't have worried. She was already going to come, just one more lick of her clit, that's all she needed . . .

And then he stopped.

She nearly howled in frustration as he slid his mouth down to the flesh of her inner thighs. One big hand moved up to cover her own where it rested on her ultrasensitive breast.

"What are you doing?" Kelly couldn't help the sharpness of her tone. "I was close, really fucking close!"

Nick chuckled, which only made her angrier.

"Why are you stopping?" she practically shrieked.

"I'm not stopping," he said, his tongue sliding against her slit. "I'm just slowing you down a little bit."

She let out a frustrated whimper as he slid one long, thick finger inside her. Her muscles clamped down around him as she tried to force him to finish what he started. But he withdrew, executing a swirl at the end that had her arching off the bed.

"You know what your problem is?"

Another slow lick.

"No, but I'm sure you'll tell me." She felt his hands on her ankles, drawing her calves up over his shoulders. She was spread out before him like a feast.

He made a low sound of appreciation as he bent his head to her. "Your problem"—he tasted her clit—"is that you're too goal oriented." One finger slid inside her as his tongue continued to tease.

She struggled to breathe. "Is that so?"

"It's like you're afraid if you lose focus, you're not going to get there," he continued. "But you have to trust me to get you there."

How could he sound so calm and matter-of-fact while he was slowly turning her into one giant, exposed nerve ending?

A second finger joined the first as his lips sucked at her. She gave a hoarse cry.

"I could do this all night and never get tired," he murmured. "Would you like that? Imagine me, licking and sucking you for hours." Mimicking his words, he licked and sucked, fingers slowly sliding and thrusting. "I'm getting so turned on," he rumbled, and Kelly could feel the vibration throughout her body. "It's all I can do not to come against the sheets."

He groaned and buried his face against her. She imagined how she felt to him, wet and slick and pulsing against his fingers, the throbbing bud of her clit against his stroking tongue and suckling lips. Her orgasm hit her almost without warning, sending her arching off the bed with a wild cry that sounded foreign to her ears.

He stayed with her all the way through it, his tongue circling her until finally her tremors stopped. He gave her one last, loving lick and withdrew his fingers.

He retrieved a condom from the bedside table and sheathed himself. Before she even had a chance to recover he was over her, gripping her hips in his hands as he slid inside her still-trembling sheath.

He held himself still for several moments, buried deep inside. His hands cupped her face as he leaned down to kiss her. His kiss was both tender and carnal, the slow strokes of his tongue matching the thrust of him inside her.

Kelly moaned into his mouth, twining her arms and legs around him as though, if she held him tight enough, she could keep him inside her this way forever. Her hands slid down to the hard muscles of his ass, loving the way they flexed and rippled with each pumping stroke.

She loved the helpless groans that tore from his chest as he drove inside her, reveled in the power of her own body to give him pleasure.

Their bodies slid against each other, skin slick with the mixture of sweat and oil. The rasp of his chest hair against her nipples, the unbearably erotic sound of flesh meeting flesh, the salty sweet taste of Nick's skin all combined to drive Kelly to yet another peak. She arched up, grinding against him as he pounded inside her. She milked him hard as she came, biting down on his shoulder to muffle her cries.

Nick watched Kelly come back to reality as he held himself still hard and throbbing inside of her. His shoulder stung where her sharp little teeth had marked him. He wanted to come, felt his climax building in the base of his spine. But his urge for release warred with his desire to get her off again. Watching Kelly come was the sexiest thing he'd ever seen. It was like she was launched into another world when she came, and he wanted to send her there again and again.

"I want to feel you come, Nick," she whispered.

He nearly lost control at that, but managed to hold back. "Not yet. I want to watch you get off again." He punctuated this by withdrawing almost completely, then working himself back in, millimeter by millimeter, until he wasn't sure which one of them he was tormenting.

Kelly gazed up at him through heavy-lidded eyes, her body going unnaturally still. Placing her hands around his hips, she blew out all of her breath. Then suddenly her lower abs started moving—undulating, really—in a slow, steady rhythm. His eyes involuntarily closed at the sensation. It was like nothing he'd ever felt before, like a firm, slick fist was kneading him from inside her body. Her hand came down to cup his testicles, cradling them gently in her fingers.

In seconds he was coming, his body jerking helplessly against her. He was wrung out, sucked dry as he collapsed on the mattress beside her.

"What the hell was that?" he gasped when he could finally breathe again. He forced his eyes open through sheer willpower.

Her full lips formed a sly cat-that-ate-the-cream smile. "Yoga," she said matter-of-factly. "I always wondered if that would work."

"Work? It almost fucking killed me."

She tucked her hands behind her head in exaggerated triumph. Her smile was an adorable combination of shyness and smug satisfaction. He rolled over on his back and pulled her against him, tucking her head snugly under his chin.

"Feel better now?" he murmured, dropping a kiss to the top of her head.

"I feel like a million bucks," she sighed. "From now on I know exactly who to come to when I'm in a bad mood."

"At your service." His fingers toyed with her hair, combing through the thick strands. The fresh smell of her shampoo teased his nose, and he buried his nose and inhaled deeply.

"I probably smell like French fries," she laughed.

"You smell great," he insisted. "All fresh and girly."

"Somehow I doubt it. That was the one thing I always hated about working at the pub." Her fingers idly played in his chest hair as she spoke. "At the end of my shift I could never seem to get the grease smell off my skin and hair, no matter how hard I scrubbed." She pulled a hank of hair to her nose. "Some things never change."

They were silent a few minutes. He should leave. But it felt so great just to hold her in the near darkness, their hands idly exploring naked skin, that he couldn't remember why it was so imperative to go home. "It must be pretty boring being back here, after living in a big city for so long."

"You'd think," she said, propping herself up on his chest so she could see his face. "It's strange. When I graduated from high school, I couldn't wait to go to college somewhere where I wasn't such a freak." Her brows drew together in a frown that Nick couldn't resist tracing with a finger. "But then I got to Yale, and I was still the freak. Except now I was a freak in a dirty, ugly city where I didn't know anyone. I actually missed this place."

"Do you still miss it?"

"Sometimes. But in a big city, even if I strike people as unusual, I'm not as conspicuous as I was here."

"So people still treat you like you're different?"

"Occasionally. Sometimes patients are surprised when they realize I'm the attending when I barely look old enough to have graduated." One side of her mouth curled in a rueful smile. "But since it's the ER and they're usually freaking out about something else, they tend to overlook my age."

"It must have been hard, being on your own so young." Had she really only been fifteen when she left? Even as he'd always been conscious of how much younger she'd been, in some ways she'd also seemed mature beyond her years. But still, it was difficult to imagine any fifteen-year-old being able to handle moving across the country to live on her own.

"I was used to being alone by then. It's not like I had hordes of friends. But I missed my dad a lot."

Nick felt a funny little catch in his heart as he remembered Kelly in high school. Looking back, he couldn't remember one time when he'd seen Kelly hanging out with friends. He and his brothers had been protective of her, to be sure, and he'd enjoyed her wry sense of humor when she'd tutored him. But he'd never counted her among his friends. And neither, it appeared, had anyone else.

He pulled her close, residual guilt and an urge to comfort

forming a strange lump in his throat. What was it about Kelly that made him want to take care of her, even when it was more than obvious that she could take care of herself?

Kelly snuggled her face into Nick's chest, breathing in the warm, musky scent of his skin. His hands stroking her back and the slow, steady beat of his heart lulled her into a peaceful half sleep.

She turned her head slightly to kiss the smooth skin of his shoulder. Such beautiful, strong shoulders. Shoulders that could help a girl carry her burdens. She tried to remember the last time someone had taken care of her and tried to make her feel better when she got stressed.

Mentally she snorted. How about never. Since she mostly dated other doctors, any complaint became an invitation to play "my day was so much worse than yours and here's why." No sympathy was extended, just a verbal kick in the ass and silent command to stop whining.

Not Nick. No, sweet, gorgeous Nick had soothed her, pampered her, and made love to her until her bad mood was forgotten. She sighed. What would it be like to come home every night to Nick and his big, dependable shoulders? To know that if she had a hard day he would be waiting there with his big smile and warm amber eyes?

What would those eyes look like if they were filled with love for her, full of determination to care for her and make her happy?

She could really fall in love with a guy like him if she weren't careful.

Her arms tightened around him even as she scolded herself to stop thinking along those lines. She was not going to fall in love with Nick, and that was that.

And more to the point, Nick was not going to fall in love with her.

With that firmly in mind, she slid her hand down his belly. She traced her fingers up the length of his penis, which was making a valiant effort to rally for another round.

"I'm still a little cranky," she whispered, and smiled as Nick tucked her underneath him and proceeded to lift her spirits.

An hour later, Kelly felt Nick inch his way out of the bed. She wished she could call him back under the covers, wished she could fall asleep in his arms and feel him snuggled up against her while she slept.

But it was obvious he was uncomfortable with spending the night, and she didn't want to make an issue of it. She kept her breathing slow and even so he wouldn't know she was still awake as he paused by the side of the bed, but she couldn't suppress a sigh as his fingers tangled gently in her hair. His hot breath smoothed over her cheek as he bent to kiss her softly one last time.

For all that this was a casual fling, it was the thought of that last sweet kiss, and not the memory of Nick's sexual prowess, that kept Kelly awake for a long, long time.

5

"Nick! Yo, Nicky!"

Nick jerked his head up and realized he'd been staring at his sandwich for a full minute without taking a bite.

"What, Tony? You don't have to yell," he grouched.

"I've been trying to get your attention for an hour," Tony said. "I asked if we're on for Sully's tonight."

"Yeah, of course we're on." Nick blinked, yawned, took a bite of his sandwich. Yawned again around the bite.

Jesus, he was tired. The past two and a half weeks were catching up with him with a vengeance. He'd been over to Kelly's every night except one, last Saturday. Mike and Tony had roped him into a night in Truckee. They'd been appalled when Nick hadn't partaken of the local fare. "Just not my type," Nick had asserted. Luckily they'd taken separate cars so Nick was able to make it home that night. And as much as he'd wanted to go over to Kelly's it didn't seem right to wake her up at three a.m.

But he had wanted to. Even now, after showing up at her

house night after night, he resented the one he'd missed. It scared him a little to think of how much he craved her. Not just in bed, but her company too.

Kelly only had to hint at a problem in her ramshackle little rental and Nick showed up, toolbox in hand, to fix it. Somehow they managed to resist making love during the day or Nick doubted he would ever get any work done. But the admiring glint in her eyes and the way she said, "You're amazing. You can fix anything," after he repaired her dishwasher or changed a fuse made him feel about ten feet tall. Each time he'd had to force himself to leave, consoling himself with the knowledge that he'd see her later that night.

At least every other night on his way home he'd found himself at Sully's. He came under the premise of playing a quick card game with Ryan Sullivan. But really he just wanted to watch her, talk with her over the bar about his day and hers.

Ryan had started working a little bit during the early evenings, and Kelly had used the extra time to take a couple of shifts at the hospital. She never failed to amuse him with stories about her patients. So far she'd seen a clueless hiker who didn't realize she couldn't complete a twelve-mile hike with only a Coke for hydration and a four-year-old who'd tried to break the world record for number of crayons shoved up his nose.

"At least," she'd laughed as she told him the story, "it's not like Boston where worse things are shoved up other holes."

Nick had leered at her and asked her if that had given her any ideas she'd like to share.

But no matter how much he enjoyed her company, he always forced himself to leave after one drink so that no one would get the wrong idea about them. Or the right idea, as it were.

He polished off his sandwich and washed it down with the remains of his soda.

Tony was staring at him, hard. They were working on a deck expansion on a vacation home in nearby Lakeview Estates while Mike was back at the office putting together bids on major remodels for two homes in the area.

"You look terrible, man," Tony said.

"I'm fine, just a little tired."

"Yeah, well you better suck it up, because if we don't get this deck done by tomorrow, Mike's gonna kick our asses." Tony paused to take a last, huge bite of his sandwich. "And then we have to start prepping for the tile work at that huge place out on Viewpoint."

Nick didn't respond. They had more work than they could handle, and all he wanted to do was crawl into bed with Kelly and fuck them both senseless, followed by a long nap.

But he couldn't tell Tony any of this. What could he say? That he was exhausted from staying up into the wee hours making love to Kelly Sullivan until they were both too tired to move? Even after she'd given him a key so that he could get into her house and take a nap before she got home, he was still only averaging four hours of sleep a night.

He sighed and pulled his gloves back on. Tony was right. He needed to get his act together and stop screwing around. He and his brothers had worked their asses off to expand their dad's business after they took over, and no way was his sex life going to interfere in his success. This thing with Kelly was all fun, but he couldn't allow it to interfere with his real life.

But he mused how the hell could he possibly stop seeing her, or even cut back? He'd never been addicted to anything, but this must be how it felt. Like when he drove by Sully's telling himself he was going home, it was like his truck had a mind of its own. And every day, like today, he told himself firmly that tonight was the night he was going to get some sleep, goddammit.

But like an alcoholic who can't resist just one more drink, he knew that if he showed up at Sully's tonight and saw Kelly, there was no way in hell he could resist her.

And he had to go tonight. Who was he to disappoint his brothers?

Kelly set a platter of fish and chips down in front of Molly Baxter and her husband, Craig, both of whom she remembered from high school. Both were surprisingly friendly, considering in high school they'd never given her the time of day.

Suddenly the hairs on the nape of her neck stood up and her gaze was drawn to the front door.

The Donovans were here. Nick glanced over, quickly enough so that no one caught him looking but long enough that she read the heat in his gaze.

Her pulse pounded in her head, in rhythm with the sudden beat between her legs. Molly had to ask four times before Kelly heard her request for a refill on her water.

Kelly smoothed her hands down the front of her denim skirt and made her way as calmly as possible to the table where Nick, Mike, and Tony sat, long legs and broad shoulders practically spilling out of their chairs.

All three turned to smile up at her, and Kelly felt her insides melt at Nick's knowing look. So far no one seemed to know about their affair. It had actually been kind of fun, the past two and a half weeks. Sneaking around, pretending there wasn't anything between them while sharing their own illicit secret.

She forced herself to greet Nick with the casual friendliness they always used in public. As she watched, Nick reached into his water glass and fished out an ice cube. He ran it suggestively around his lips, drew it into his mouth, released it. Just like last night, when he'd taken a cherry Popsicle and teased it around her nipples, chasing drops of juice with his tongue . . .

She felt heat rise in her face as she trained her gaze on Mike and Tony, for all appearances oblivious to the sexual currents vibrating across the table. How could everyone possibly be so ignorant? Kelly felt like she was oozing sex from every pore, like she was walking around with a WELL FUCKED sign across her chest.

But Mike and Tony only smiled up at her and ordered the usual. Nick, the rat, was rolling the ice cube around in his mouth in a way that could only remind her of his other oral skills.

Mumbling something that she hoped sounded like "Be right back," she hurried away.

She surreptitiously watched Nick and his brothers as she put in their order and waited on several other tables. Everything about him fascinated her—his long fingers as they wrapped around his water glass. Strong, skilled fingers that could as easily repair her light switch as they could bring her to ecstasy.

It never failed to amaze her how Nick could fix anything. He'd shown up at her house four times this week to fix minor glitches at her little rental. Even in high school, on the occasions when her tutoring sessions had happened at her house, she'd leave the room only to find Nick tinkering with something. One time it was the kitchen faucet, another time the disposal, and still another the refrigerator fan.

It got to the point that Kelly's mom would conspicuously leave any broken appliance for Nick to find.

Now, as then, he brushed off her compliments, insisting that his repair skills were no big deal. But to a woman who still could barely figure out how to check her voice mail on her cell phone, his ability to revive her toaster was pretty damn spectacular.

He just didn't give himself credit for how smart he really was. Her face pulled into a frown as she watched him laugh at something Mike said. Nick's dyslexia hadn't been diagnosed until Kelly started to tutor him his senior year. By that time, everyone had given up on Nick's intellectual abilities. Especially, it seemed, Nick himself.

"Kelly, your order's up." Maggie's call startled her, and she quickly grabbed the food.

As she carried the platters of fried fish, French fries, and wings to the table, she was struck by the easy camaraderie the brothers shared. She felt an odd tightness in her chest. *It must be nice*, she thought with just the barest twinge of envy, *to have siblings you can always count on for friendship and support.*

Any sentiment she was harboring vanished as she caught a snippet of their conversation, punctuated by raucous belly laughs.

"You should have seen what Carrie—" Tony was saying.

"Candy," Mike broke in, "Carrie was with me."

"Carrie, Candy, whatever—she could put her legs all the way over her head! You ever been with a chick who could put her legs over her head, Nick?"

Nick looked uneasily up at Kelly as she set the food on the table. "Can't say that I have, Tony."

Kelly had been doing yoga for four years now, so she was pretty close. But she knew better than to say anything. She went back to the bar, returning quickly with the pitcher of Bass they'd ordered.

"I still can't believe you went home, Nicky," Tony said around a mouthful of chicken wing. "That blonde was all over you, and she was hot. Her cans—"

"Were fake—"

"Like that ever stopped you—" Mike rolled his eyes.

"—just like the rest of her." Nick finished tightly.

"Sounds like you guys had a wild night." Kelly did her best

to keep her tone light even as jealously coiled like a viper in her gut.

Mike at least had the grace to look chagrined, but Tony was completely unabashed.

"Yeah, last Saturday we went out for a little fun," Tony said with a wink.

Saturday, huh? The one night since they'd started this thing that Nick didn't show up. She'd forced herself not to ask where he'd been, knowing it was none of her business.

But that hadn't stopped her from imagining exactly what he was up to. Apparently she hadn't been too far off the mark. She could easily picture it. A stacked blonde whose bra size outmatched her IQ, giggling as she crawled all over Nick.

She poured their beers, setting Nick's down with a force that sent suds sloshing into his lap.

"Sorry," she muttered, shoving a handful of napkins at him.

Keep your mouth shut, she told herself. The urge to launch into a scathing tirade about bimbos and STDs nearly overwhelmed her.

As far as the Donovans were concerned, why should she care about what they'd done last Saturday, or who they'd done it with? Their reputations were well established, and their behavior should come as no surprise.

Kelly retreated to the stockroom under the pretense of finding more ketchup. Maybe a few moments alone would cool her temper.

She jumped as a hand closed around her right bicep and spun her around. She whipped around to face Nick, bracing her palms against his chest as though to fend off an attack.

"What are you doing back here?"

"Kelly, nothing happened last Saturday," Nick said, placing his hands on her shoulders.

"I don't care if it did," she lied. She turned, pretending to search through boxes so she wouldn't have to look at him. "Honestly, we never made any promises except not to tell any- one that we're fucking." The crude word tasted bad in her mouth. She picked up a bottle of ketchup and stuck it in her apron pocket. "And I can only hope you're not telling your brothers about any of my specialties."

It was foolish, naïve, ridiculous to be hurt by the idea of Nick talking about her like Tony and Mike had talked about Carrie–Candy, whatever her name.

But it did hurt, dammit. Because like it or not, what she had with Nick was special. At least to her.

"I haven't told them anything, just like we agreed," he snapped.

"Good. Anyway, we never agreed not to see other people, not that this town has much else to offer." Kelly turned to face Nick, keeping her expression deliberately bland. His jaw was set in tense lines, his thumbs hooked aggressively in his belt loops.

"Except . . ." A little voice in the back of her head told her to shut up, but she barreled on, "except your brothers, of course. Now there's a thought. Karen dated Mike in high school and was very impressed even then, if I recall. I've never been much for threesomes. But—"

Nick's mouth slammed down on hers. She felt her lips grind against her teeth. She opened her mouth to protest, and Nick seized the opportunity to thrust his tongue inside.

Her arms twined around his neck, even as she knew she should push him away. She whimpered into his mouth, one leg lifting to twine around his waist as she ground her sex against the mammoth bulge at his crotch.

Nick tore his mouth away so abruptly Kelly stumbled back against a box of napkins.

His face was flushed with fury, his eyes burning with rage and arousal. He closed his hands around her shoulders and lifted her off the ground until she was at eye level. "I don't fucking share."

One last, brutal kiss, and he was gone.

It was just past midnight, and Nick stood outside of Sullivan's. He lurked in the doorway of the shoe store next door, waiting for Maggie to leave for the night. Everyone else had gone except for Kelly.

He was too restless to wait at her house tonight. After mauling her in the storeroom, he'd left with his brothers. Too keyed to read the mystery novel he'd started, and too impatient with the nonsense offered on TV, he'd gone for a walk.

But even as he'd wandered aimlessly for the past several hours, he couldn't shake the frustration, the anger—face it—the jealousy that had nearly overwhelmed him earlier that evening.

It was an emotion he hadn't felt in a very long time. Not even with Ann, his last girlfriend. But Kelly's snide joke about his brother made him want to grab her by the hair and pull her caveman style back to his lair.

He couldn't deny it anymore. Whatever he and Kelly had together had gone way beyond the bounds of a casual affair. He wanted to be with her all the time. Wanted to know that he was going to be with her every night. Parade with her down Main Street and say, "See this woman? This beautiful, smart, amazing woman? She's mine!"

Unwilling to examine his uncharacteristically territorial urges, he didn't question his gut-deep need to see her tonight, to put his mark on her in any way he could.

That was what had him lurking outside the pub, waiting for Maggie to leave so he could sneak inside and show Kelly that in some way, at least, she belonged to him.

Finally Maggie left through the front door. Nick waited until she got in her car and was all the way down the block before he slipped in. He took a moment to study Kelly. The muscles in her arms stood out in soft relief as she wiped down the bar. The cotton of her T-shirt puckered as her breasts strained the fabric.

A few coffee-colored curls had slipped from the clip holding her hair back from her face, teasing her high cheekbones and fine line of her jaw.

She turned away, bending to drop the rag below the sink. He felt his cock stiffen against his zipper. Even though he couldn't see her, he could imagine her skirt riding up the backs of her thighs. Her skin there was pale over firm muscles, leading up to a lush ass that begged to be squeezed and stroked.

"Take off your panties," he said, his voice sounding sharp in the silence of the bar.

Kelly gasped and whirled around, one hand to her chest, eyes wide with fear. "Jesus Christ! You scared the crap out of me." She took a couple of deep breaths, watching him warily as he approached the bar.

Nick didn't say anything. He took in the slight tremor of her hands, the nervous darting of her tongue over her bottom lip.

Her nervousness excited him. She didn't know what to expect from him. Hell, with all of the unfamiliar emotions roiling inside him, he didn't know what to expect either. Good. They were even.

"Didn't you hear what I said?" He shed his jacket as he walked, dropping it on the floor. His shirt followed.

She stood frozen, watching him as he lifted the partition and walked behind the bar.

"Take off your panties," he repeated.

Her chin tilted up, and her eyes narrowed. "Are you trying to intimidate me?"

Her hands went to her hips, but for all her bravado, he could see the telltale flush creeping up from the neckline of her shirt. He'd bet his stake in Donovan Brothers that under the T-shirt her nipples were hard and under the skirt she was already wet.

"I want to get something straight between us, Kelly." Now only an inch separated them, close enough for him to see the subtle flare of her nostrils, the nervous awareness in her wide blue eyes. "I don't sleep around. I only sleep with one woman at a time, and I expect her to do the same. I didn't like you talking about my brother—"

"It was just a joke," Kelly interrupted, her voice shrill.

"Even if you're joking. When you're with me, I don't even want the idea of another man to enter your head." He leaned down and kissed her, a hot, hard caress that bruised both their mouths.

"I don't—it didn't—" Kelly stuttered.

"Then prove it, Kelly. Prove that I'm the only one you want to fuck, the only one you want to be with."

"How?" she whispered. Her hands grasped his wrists as he cupped her face.

"By doing exactly what I want."

Kelly stared up at Nick, more than a little nervous. And more than a little turned on. This was a side of Nick she'd never seen before. Angry. Demanding. Domineering. Overpowering.

And he wanted her to prove he was the only one she wanted. God knew he was. He consumed nearly every waking thought, invaded her dreams. He'd reduced her to a lovesick, sex-crazed idiot who did little more than count the minutes until she could see him again.

But this made her nervous. He was calling the shots, he was in control. And he was demanding something from her that she wasn't sure he was willing to give himself.

Could she take the risk and surrender?

His hot amber eyes bored into hers. His breathing was unsteady, a faint sheen of sweat already glowing on the olive skin of his chest. She could only nod in mute assent.

Suddenly he was everywhere, overwhelming her. His tongue thrust lustily into her mouth, his hands tangled in her hair, and he pushed her back until the hard edge of the bar dug into her back. One big hand reached unceremoniously under her skirt and shoved her panties down to her knees. His big, booted foot came up to step in the crotch and pushed them the rest of the way down.

She looked around uneasily. "Don't you want to go back to my place?" she panted.

"Anything I want," Nick said harshly as he shoved her shirt up, stripping her like a child. "And I want you right here, right now."

Lust curled in her belly despite her misgivings.

"And you want it too." He slid his hand up her skirt, grunting in satisfaction when his fingers found her already wet and eager.

She flushed with arousal and embarrassment. Since when had she become so goddamn easy? Helplessly she ground herself against his fingers, urging him to slip deep inside.

"Uh, uh, uh," he scolded. "There's something I want first."

She felt the pressure of his hands on her shoulders, urging her down to her knees. Following his mute command, she unfastened his jeans and pushed them along with his briefs down his hips. His cock twitched as she cupped him in her hand, and she felt an answering pull in her womb.

"Suck my cock." His deliberately crude demand sent another rush of moisture between her thighs.

Her lips tingled, her tongue anticipating his salty, musky taste as she leaned forward. Her lips fastened over the tip, her tongue lashing the head in a teasing caress. She felt a surge of triumph at his quick inhale and sucked more of him into her mouth.

She closed her eyes, focusing on the taste, the thickness of him in her mouth. His fingers tangled in her hair, and his groan of satisfaction vibrated through his entire body. Everything about him seduced her, enchanted her. His scent, the feel of his hair-roughened thighs under her fingers, the contrast of the smooth skin of his butt as she palmed the firm cheeks.

Her entire being focused on him, on the pleasure she gave as she sucked him as deeply in her throat as she could take him.

Back and forth, take and release, she sucked him into her mouth and slid her lips back to tease the tip. One hand came up to cradle his sac, exploring the wrinkled skin, his heavy balls drawn tight and hard against his body.

She squeezed her thighs against an answering throb in her sex, let out a little cry around his cock.

He groaned, murmuring nonsensical words and phrases about how good she was, how good she felt. She felt him swell even bigger, the head of his cock throbbing against her tongue as she laved it in a swirling caress. He was close, she thrilled, and she relaxed her throat to take him deeper. Her sex was full and achy, and she realized suddenly that she was nearly as close as he was.

She tasted the hot salty drops of pre-come, and she wrapped her fist around his shaft. But before she could pump him to release he abruptly pulled free of her mouth.

Before Kelly could say a word Nick hauled her to her feet

and spun her around. She braced her hands on the back bar, startled by their reflection in the mirror. Her face was flushed and dazed looking, her mouth swollen red, slick, and wet. He was behind her, shoving her skirt up around her waist with one hand while he donned a condom with the other.

It was so raw, so carnal, she started to close her eyes against the harsh reality. But Nick would have none of it. His hand tangled in her hair, pulling her head up even as he tipped her forward with a firm hand at the small of her back.

"No you don't," he said harshly. He took his cock in one hand and teased her swollen slit. "I want you to watch me fuck you."

She saw her lips part in a low moan at his words, at the sensation of his thick head squeezing its way inside. She parted her legs to accommodate him as he slid home with one abandoned thrust. His hands gripped her hips as he pumped hard. Tonight there were no sweet words or soft caresses. Tonight he was taking her, using her.

And she loved it. She loved the way his abs ripped with every thrust, loved the way her breasts bounced and strained as she worked herself hard against him. Loved the harsh sounds that erupted from both their throats to mingle with the sound of flesh meeting flesh.

"You feel so good around me, so tight," he murmured. "I can feel you clenching around my cock."

She could see his chest heaving, felt his hot breath on her back. The glasses that lined the bar tinkled and shimmied as he increased the pace. Vaguely she heard something shatter but couldn't care as she watched Nick's hand leave her hip to disappear under her skirt. His fingers pressed hard against her clit. She whimpered and pushed back against him. Even now, taking her in the most primitive way she could imagine, he ensured her pleasure.

He thrust hard enough to lift her to her toes. Her eyes met his eyes in the mirror, saw the moment his face contorted and felt the spasms of his release inside her.

It was enough to send her flying over the edge, clenching around him, her sheath undulating around his rock-hard flesh as her moans echoed up to the ceiling.

Nick collapsed forward, catching his weight on the bar before he fell on Kelly's trembling form. His hands rested just beside hers, and against his chest he could feel Kelly's shaking back, the pounding of her heart, the rapid expansion and contraction of her rib cage.

His own lungs were heaving like a bellows, and his heart pounded hard enough to crack a rib. He nuzzled his face into the side of her neck, wanting to breathe her in, absorb a little bit more of her into himself.

Her expression was dazed and a little freaked out as he met it in the mirror. He could relate. He'd never taken a woman this way, with such a primitive urge to dominate her, to own her.

Now he wanted to comfort her, soothe her, put that happy, well-satisfied look back on her face.

He tried to think of what he could say. He didn't want to apologize. He wasn't sorry for what happened. He wasn't sorry for showing that she was his, even if she didn't yet realize it.

But he did want to reassure her that the considerate lover was still there, even if tonight he had acted like a Neanderthal.

He levered himself up so she could straighten. She turned on unsteady legs and groped for her T-shirt and shoved her skirt back in place. But before she could flee, Nick pulled her into his arms and held her against his chest, stroking her back until the tension left her shoulders and her arms wrapped around his waist. It felt good, just holding her like this, enjoying a little moment of peace when they seemed to spend most of their time together caught in a sexual maelstrom.

"That was, ahh . . . intense," Kelly finally said against his chest.

Nick pulled her tighter against him. "That's all you can come up with?"

"Give me a minute," she murmured, "I think I just lost half of my brain cells while my blood fled for other parts."

Nick cupped her face in his hands, tilting her head back. An uncertain smile teased her full lips. Her blue eyes were still wary.

I could spend my whole life trying to put a smile on this woman's face, he thought.

He loved her. It hit him with such force that for a minute he couldn't catch his breath. He was in love with Kelly Sullivan.

The thought thrilled and terrified him in equal measure. He'd tried this before, loving a woman completely out of his league, a woman whose intelligence and dedication to a high-powered career had dictated her life. And he'd crashed, hard. But as he gazed into Kelly's eyes he saw something that made him think that just maybe this time it would all work out.

He pulled her back against him and buried his face in her hair. He'd take it slow, ease her into a more public relationship. Make her see that he could make her happy, even if he wasn't some big-brained, big city hotshot.

He silenced the doubt seething in his mind, the voices that warned him that once again he was out of his league and should stick to small-town girls who shared his same small-town aspirations.

The warm, soft reality of Kelly in his arms told him differently, reassured him that Kelly wasn't like Ann. She was a small-town girl at heart, still humble even if she was smarter than most of the world.

And he'd never felt like this about Ann.

When they were kids, Kelly had touched a part of him few people could ever reach. Even when he'd felt like the world's biggest idiot, Kelly had had faith in him, had made him feel like more than just a big, dumb, pretty boy.

He smiled and hugged her so tight she grunted in protest. But mostly, she made him happy, content to simply be there sharing the same space.

It would work out. It had to.

"C'mon, I'll take you home."

6
_____

They took Nick's truck. Kelly barely spared a thought for her little Honda, figuring she'd pick up her car on her morning run.

"My house is that way," she said when Nick turned left instead of right down Maple.

"We're not going to your house."

"You said you were taking me home."

"My home."

Curiosity warred with uneasiness during the five-minute ride. On one hand, she was dying to see Nick's house. She knew he'd built it just two years ago after Donovan Brothers had enjoyed a particularly good year. You could tell a lot about a person by their home, and Kelly was hungry to know everything about Nick.

Which made her uneasy. As long as they kept their sexual escapades limited to the impersonal venue of her short-term rental, it was easy to keep in mind that this was all just temporary, just for fun until she got back to her real life. A life that included a full-time position at a prestigious medical center where she would continue to build her career. A life of long hours and hard work in a major metropolitan center.

In short, a life that did not include Nick.

An involuntary heavy sigh escaped her just as they pulled up to a two-story log and stone house at the end of a long driveway.

"What do you think?" Nick asked. Kelly thought she detected a little anxiousness in his tone, as though he needed her approval.

And how could she do anything but give it? The house, or at least what she could see of it in the porch light, was a stunning example of what a mountain retreat should be. Rough-hewn logs and natural stone blended seamlessly in rustic elegance. The expansive front porch wrapped around—maybe all the way to the back, offering views of the mountains.

The inside was just as impressive. The large great room was dominated by a leather sectional couch and, of course, a huge television and entertainment center. Bookshelves lined two of the walls up to the ceiling, and Kelly could see titles that ranged from architecture reference books to history to the latest bestsellers.

"Before you ask, yes, I have read them all," Nick said, his tone deliberately light.

"I never doubted it." She smiled.

"I still remember you helping me through *The Catcher in the Rye.* After that I read everything I could get my hands on— it just took me a little longer than some people."

A surge of pride washed through her. It had been a personal triumph when Nick had finished and written a paper on *The Catcher in the Rye* that had earned him an A. He'd been so discouraged at first, so convinced he wouldn't be able to do it.

"It's nice to know I've inspired you in some way."

His smile transformed to an exaggerated leer. "Oh, you inspire me all right, baby."

She shrieked as he grabbed her around the waist and flung her over his shoulder, fireman style. He took the stairs two at a time and entered a bedroom at the end of the hall. Kelly bounced a few times on the huge king-size bed.

He stood at the foot of the bed, kicked off his boots, and stripped off his shirt. A single lamp glowed from the dresser across the room, casting a dim golden glow across the rippling muscles of his torso.

He smiled slowly and crawled up the bed like a jungle cat, and Kelly felt herself go hot and achy between her thighs. She marveled anew at her relentless response to this man. She'd come, what, twenty minutes ago? Still her body reacted as though anticipating the end of a long dry spell. Nick surrounded her with his heat, his scent, and once again Kelly was dying to feel him inside of her.

How could she ever get enough of this man? How could she possibly give him up?

"Now," he whispered, bending down to kiss her neck, "I'm going to show you all the ways you inspire me."

"Wow," Kelly said, "I never realized my capacity as a muse."

Nick chuckled tiredly and ran his hand lazily down the slope of her back. His hands lingered at her ass, tracing soft circles on each cheek before sliding back up, a steady stroking that had Kelly halfway to a trancelike state.

Kelly nuzzled her face against Nick's chest, still trying to regain her equilibrium after this evening's events. Whereas in the pub Nick had been all macho force and domination, what had just passed between them had been almost unbearably tender. He had worshipped her, tasting and touching every bare patch of skin. Sliding against each other like otters, slick with sweat, they'd made love to each other with their whole bodies. In the end Kelly had wrapped her arms and legs around him, pulling him close and hiding her face in the hollow of Nick's shoulder so he couldn't see her tears as she came.

She should leave, she knew. But not yet. For now she let herself be soothed by the tender stroking of Nick's hands on her back, the steady beat of his heart in her ear, the soft ruffle of his breath across her hair. She closed her eyes and indulged herself in her forbidden fantasy. One in which she lived with Nick in this perfect house, woke up with him every day, went to sleep with him every night. A life where she was a small-town doctor with patients who knew and liked her, a woman with a normal marriage and a normal life with a good, loving man.

"What are you thinking about?" he whispered. "I can hear your gears turning."

Startled, Kelly said the first thing that came to her. "I'm wondering why a guy like you—successful, gorgeous, nice house—hasn't settled down with a nice girl yet." Kelly winced even as the words flew out of her mouth. Did she really want to know this?

"Right girl hasn't come along yet," he answered. His hand came up to tickle her scalp, raising goosebumps on her skin.

"But you thought she had for a while?" Danger! Danger! Do not ask about exes while in bed with a man! She wasn't terribly experienced, but even she knew that.

Nick made a sound, half sigh, half chuckle. "So you heard about Ann?"

Kelly propped herself up on his chest so she could see him. Fortunately, he didn't look pissed. Just resigned. "I've heard some stuff."

"Yeah it's hard to keep 'stuff' from the people in this town."

"So what happened?"

"You know, the usual. I was thinking about rings and she just wanted a good fuck and a nice place to stay."

His tone was casual, but the subtle stiffening of his muscles conveyed the hurt that still festered.

Kelly was trying to imagine a woman who would give up Nick, and couldn't. "I don't get it," she said simply.

"It's not that complicated," he said. "She was smart, ambitious. Kind of like you." he smiled a funny half smile down at her. "She wanted to do her time here and get the hell out and go on to bigger and better places, bigger and better things."

Kelly tucked her head back under his chin and thought about what he said. *I would have stayed for you, Nick*, she thought.

But instead she leaned up and kissed him, first his chin, then his mouth. "I don't know how smart she is Nick, if she didn't see what she had in you."

He smiled and kissed her back, and his next words cracked her heart in two. "You're a good friend, Kelly. You always know what to say to make me feel better."

Swallowing the hurt, Kelly pasted a brazen smile on her lips and rubbed herself sinuously against him, gratified when she felt his penis stir with renewed interest. In this aspect of their relationship, at least, she could be honest. "And I also know," she said, teasing his chest with the hard buds of her nipples, "exactly what to *do* to make you feel better."

Something is weird, Nick thought when he woke up Thursday morning. Light poured into his bedroom through the skylight above his bed. Whoa, he must have slept in, judging from the sun.

But there was something else too. He smiled as he rolled over. Right. There was the warm, sleeping presence of another body in his bed. And not just any body. Kelly.

Her face was half-buried in a huge down pillow as she was sprawled on her stomach, turned slightly toward him. Her arms and shoulders were bare above the covers, and he could see the creamy plumpness of her breast as it pressed against the mattress. He reached out and traced the dark feather of lashes against her cheekbones, laughing when she squinched up her face and rolled over in her sleep.

She didn't see what she had in you. Her words echoed in his mind. Was it possible that Kelly was falling for him, just as he had fallen for her? He tried not to get his hopes up, reminded himself to take it slow as he eased her into the idea of a real relationship.

He felt his usual morning wood grow an extra inch as he drank her in. Her back was to him now, the clean lines and fine-grained skin taunting him to trace it with his fingers. She had kicked the covers off and one leg was bent up, affording Nick a tempting view of her perfect round ass and the soft folds of her sex peeking out.

He could easily imagine waking up like this every morning for the rest of his life.

Inching himself closer, he slid his arm around her, cupping and teasing her breasts. With his other hand he positioned his cock between her legs, sliding, teasing through her folds, rubbing against her clit until he was bathed in her wetness. He grabbed a condom from the bedside table and rolled her to her back. She murmured something and reached for him, still not quite awake.

Carefully he eased inside of her. She woke with a soft gasp, her look of surprise immediately melting into a sleepy smile. She whispered his name and reached her hands up to touch his face, his temples, his lips.

He didn't think he'd ever seen anything as beautiful as Kelly, half-asleep and aroused, moving sweetly under him. He wanted to stay inside her for hours, for days, crawl inside her body and never come out. He couldn't stop the words from tumbling from his mouth, how beautiful, how sexy she was, how good it felt to be inside of her.

Kelly clutched him now, arching against his long, slow thrusts, her throaty moans matching his rhythm. He felt her orgasm coiling up inside her, reveled in the sharp, soft cry she gave before she hugged him close to her heart. He let himself go, and when he came he heard his heartbeat thundering in his head.

"Oh my god, someone's here!" Kelly was pushing at his shoulders, trying to squirm out from underneath him.

He shook his head and realized it wasn't his heartbeat he heard, but someone pounding at his front door.

"Nick! Hey, Nick, you awake?"

Shit. It was Mike. Kelly scrambled out from under him and rushed into the attached bathroom.

"Nick, what the fuck are you doing? You were supposed to be over at the Williams' an hour ago!"

Nick glanced at the alarm clock on his bedside table. Nine-thirty. He was over an hour and a half late.

And the funny thing was, he didn't even care.

"Just a sec, Mike." Nick grabbed his jeans from the floor and spared a glance at the bathroom door. Kelly didn't make a sound.

As Nick trotted downstairs, he half wished she would turn on the shower and take the decision out of his hands. Then he could tell Mike, tell Tony, hell, the entire world that Kelly was his.

"Sorry, man," Nick said sheepishly. "I must've turned off my alarm by mistake."

"What the hell is up with you lately? This is the third time you've been late this week." Mike cast a suspicious glance upstairs.

Nick did his best to paste a bland, nonchalant look on his face. "Nothing. I've been tired, and I overslept."

Mike's expression said he didn't believe him. "There's something going on with you, Nick, something you're not telling me."

Nick hated keeping things from his brother. He had no problem keeping secrets from the rest of the world, but he and his brothers shared everything. It was on the tip of his tongue to spill his guts, tell him all about Kelly and his newly discovered love for her.

But he didn't want to out them without talking to her first. It wouldn't be fair, since she agreed with him about keeping their relationship quiet. No, they would go public in a more subtle way. He'd take her out to a movie, or better yet, ask her to come to his folks' house for Sunday dinner this week.

That, more than anything, would be a strong declaration that he was serious. But he had to keep it quiet just a little longer.

"Trust me, Mike, there's nothing going on."

Mike didn't entirely believe him. "Look, Nick, I don't give a shit what you do in your free time. But we have too much to do before ski season starts for you to be fucking around."

Nick hated to disappoint his brother who had so capably taken over the business when their father retired. But at the same time he was glad Mike hadn't pressed for more answers.

Nick apologized and sent Mike on his way with assurances that he'd be at the building site in no more than half an hour. He whistled a little as he started the coffee brewing. Maybe they were different, but he knew in his soul that Kelly was right for him. And making their relationship public was the first step in convincing her.

* * *

Kelly held her breath as she listened through the barely cracked bedroom door. *Just tell him*, she silently willed. Just tell Mike that you're seeing me so that I know that what I'm feeling isn't all one sided.

The crack in her heart widened when she heard him assure Mike there was nothing going on. Nothing. That's exactly what she meant to Nick. Nothing more than the fulfillment of a silly high school fantasy. Nothing but a little on-the-sly nookie to keep them both occupied until she left town. At which point he would no doubt immediately find another playmate. Someone from the next town, or a little ski bunny once the snow started.

Slowly she pulled on her clothes, silently berating herself as she dressed. God, for a supposedly brilliant woman, she was colossally stupid. Stupid to think the torch she'd always carried for Nick wouldn't flame out of control. Stupid to think he would change his mind and his attitude toward relationships just because they had great sex together.

She had to end this now. Not only for the sake of her heart, but the sake of her life. She'd allowed this thing with Nick to distract her. Instead of pursuing real job opportunities, she was muddling along, biding her time at the county ER between shifts at Sullivan's. Based on his recovery rate, her father would be back at work full time in a couple of weeks, and Kelly needed to get her career back on track after this unplanned hiatus.

She had school loans to pay off and a reputation to build. Having to turn down the position in New York was a blow, but she was confident that she could find something comparable, but only if she got off her butt and focused.

It had been fun to indulge in a little hanky-panky with Nick. Her brain had dominated her whole life, and it was nice to be reminded that there were other interesting parts of her body.

But she hadn't counted on falling in love. Now the only

thing to do was to get out of this situation, and get out of town, as quickly as possible before her heart hurt even more than it did now.

She finished dressing and checked herself in the mirror over the dresser. She grimaced at her messy hair and smeared mascara. Yet another reason why sleepovers were a bad idea.

Kelly repaired the damage as best she could with the hand lotion, concealer, and lipstick in her purse. She brushed out her hair and was pulling it back into a ponytail when Nick walked in wearing only jeans and a sheepish smile. He looked so gorgeous with his dark hair tousled from sleep and his beard shading his jaw, she nearly forgot she had something important to tell him.

Oh, right. Tell him she couldn't see him anymore. Her mouth pulled into a frown.

"Sorry about that," he said. "I'm late for work, and I think we knocked the phone off the hook."

Kelly glanced at the bedside table, and sure enough, the handset had been knocked askew at some point during the night.

Nick handed her a cup of coffee, and she took a sip. She was stalling, she knew. What was so wrong with continuing this for a little longer, until she left town?

Her eyes met his over the rim of her cup and her heart did a triple salchow. *That's what's wrong*, she reminded herself sternly. She loved him, idiot that she was, and every moment she spent with him would only make that feeling grow, and she didn't have time to deal with heartbreak on top of everything else in her life.

But the words wouldn't come. How was it that she was so outspoken at work and yet she couldn't for the life of her think of the right thing to say?

This has been fun, Nick, but I can't see you anymore.

Easy, right?

She opened her mouth, but before she could speak, Nick said, "Look, Kelly, I've been thinking about what we're doing here. This morning was a really close call. This sneaking around thing has been fun but . . ."

Kelly closed her eyes. He was saying it for her. *I'm relieved*, she told herself sternly even as a basketball-sized knot formed in her stomach. "I know exactly what you mean," she interrupted. "I've been thinking too. This has been great, but I really don't think we should do this anymore."

Nick jerked his head back, looking startled. "What?"

"I agree with you. Today was too close, and it just emphasized how silly this whole situation is. It's been really great, don't get me wrong," she said. "But I need to figure out what I'm going to do next, and you—you need to stop being late for work. We both need to get back to our real lives, without this, this . . . distraction."

There, that wasn't so hard, was it? Kelly kept her gaze down as she pretended to search for something in her purse. If she didn't blink for long enough, her eyeballs would dry out and he wouldn't see the tears that threatened to choke her.

He didn't say anything, and the overpowering silence became too much for her to bear. "Don't worry, Nick, there's no hard feelings on my part. I knew this couldn't go anywhere. It was all just fun, right?"

"Right," he said tightly. "I'm going to get dressed, and I'll drop you at your car."

He didn't say anything on the ride to her car, didn't comment when she asked him to drop her off in an alley around the corner so it wouldn't be so obvious. He seemed upset. But why would he be?

"Are you angry about something?" Kelly asked as she got out of his truck.

"Nope," he said. "I'm just surprised you want to stop now. I was thinking we had at least a couple of weeks left."

She toyed with the clasp on her purse, confused. She'd been so convinced he'd been about to call things off himself. But even if he hadn't, surely his irritation at losing a sex partner was outweighed by his relief at how easily she'd let him off the hook. "Come on, Nick, it's not like you'll be hard up for long."

"No, I guess I won't."

Kelly felt like someone had sliced her chest with a scalpel. "So I guess I'll see you around?" She winced at the pitiful way her voice arced up at the end, like she was pleading with him. She was taking control, dammit, taking charge of the situation before she got too hurt. It didn't matter if she saw him again.

"I suppose."

Kelly slammed the door of the truck and walked the block to where her car was parked.

She prayed no one saw her, hunched over her steering wheel sobbing.

Nick's foul humor simmered all through Thursday, heated to a boil by Saturday, and was damn near combustible by Sunday.

"What's the matter, Nick, you on the rag?" Tony grumbled when Nick snapped at him for the fifth time in as many minutes.

"Tony, that's disgusting! Don't talk like that at my table." Maria Donovan ladled another serving of braciole on her eldest son's plate, her glare morphing into a beaming smile as Mike tucked into his meal.

Nick pushed his food around into piles, his appetite having virtually disappeared in the last four days. His last conversation with Kelly played over and over in his mind, and each time he got the same sick, hopeless feeling in his gut.

Stupid, dumb Nick. He'd done it again. Pinned his hopes on a woman who would never be interested in a guy like him for the long haul. Acting like it was nothing. No big deal. "It's been fun but . . ."

Fun. He'd felt like his soul was clawing out of his body every time he came, and she was just having fun.

"What is with you, Nick?" Mike asked around a mouthful of roast. "I hate to say it, but Tony's right. You're being a real bitch tonight."

"Michael!"

"Sorry, Ma."

As usual, Nick's father just ate and observed, more than happy to let his wife and children bear the brunt of conversation.

"I think he's having girl trouble," Tony said.

"Don't talk with your mouth full," Maria said automatically, but her gaze lit on Nick with an unholy light. "Girl trouble? Are you seeing someone, Nick? Is she nice? You should invite her over . . ."

"There's no girl, Mom," Nick said tightly.

They all stared at him expectantly, then dropped disappointed gazes to their plates. As pushy as they were, they all knew that when Nick didn't want to talk, bamboo shoots under his nails wouldn't pry it out of him.

"Speaking of nice girls," Maria said, "I ran into Kelly Sullivan again the other day. She's in town you know, looking after her father."

All three of the boys rolled their eyes, not bothering to remind their mother that they were the ones who told her she was back in town in the first place.

"I was thinking, Mike, you should ask her out," she said as she twirled spaghetti expertly against her spoon.

"Why Mike? Why not me or Tony?" Nick snapped.

"Nick, don't give her any ideas," Tony muttered.

If Maria was taken aback by his uncharacteristically harsh tone, she didn't show it. "Well if I could, I'd fix her up with Jake. He was always more intellectual than any of you," Maria said, "and Kelly's so smart."

"And I'm too stupid for her, is that it?" Nick said, throwing his napkin down across his plate.

"No, no," Maria backpedaled, "that's not what I meant. But you know how it went with Ann."

Nick stood so fast his chair toppled over backward, the clatter so loud even his father looked up in surprise. "Yeah, I know how it went with Ann. I wasn't good enough for her, and I'm not good enough for Kelly. Or any woman for that matter."

Without another word, he headed out the front door.

"What did I say?" His mother's words trailed after him.

7

Sullivan's was starting to clear out now that the Sunday game was over, but there was still a pretty decent crowd.

Kelly snuck a look at the clock above the jukebox. Seven twenty-two. Thank God they closed early tonight. She had to get up at the crack of dawn to be in Palo Alto by eleven, where she had an interview at Stanford. She needed to prepare and, God willing, get some sleep tonight. She hadn't slept more than three hours a night since Thursday.

Funny how all those late nights with Nick had left her tired yet strangely energized. But in the three days since she'd broken things off all she felt was exhaustion.

It was just as well that her father was recovering remarkably fast. If the position at Stanford worked out, she would be able to start within the month.

She set the pitchers down on the bar for her father to refill, fanning herself lightly. Despite the late fall chill in the air, the atmosphere inside Sullivan's was close and stuffy. "You look exhausted, Kelly," her father observed.

"I've been having trouble sleeping lately. I guess I'm a little nervous about tomorrow."

"You'll impress the hell out of them, like always," Ryan said as he plunked the first of her pitchers on the bar. "And the great thing is, you'll be only four hours away. Maybe I'll actually get to see you more than once every couple of years." Her father's tone was light, but Kelly sensed that he meant what he said.

"It never occurred to me that you missed me." It was true. As much as she'd loved her big, gruff father, she'd always felt like he'd appreciated her only because she followed directions and stayed out of trouble.

Her father looked taken aback, even a little hurt by her bluntness. "Of course I missed you. You were my little girl, and you left when you were practically still a baby."

"You had Karen," she pointed out, "And even now she's only a couple of hours away."

"Ah, your sister's a pain in the ass and you know it."

"How can you say that about one of your children?" Kelly said with a startled laugh. And here she'd always thought both her parents were so much closer to Karen.

"I always wondered if we did the right thing, sending you away so young." Ryan paused and cleared his throat. "Look, I know I'm not always so good at showing it, but having you here these past weeks has been great. And it would make me very happy if you ended up closer to home."

Pressure built at the back of her eyes. She'd also enjoyed her time with her father and the chance to share an adult friendship with him. She was surprised but touched to hear him voice it. On an abstract level, she always knew her father loved her, but the fact that he actually enjoyed her company warmed her heart. "Aw, Daddy," she said through a sniffle, and leaned over the bar to hug him.

He patted her back, and when he pulled away his blue eyes

were suspiciously bright. "So you have to promise if you get this thing at Stanford, you'll come visit on a weekend sometime."

She squeezed him again and kissed his cheek. "I promise." And she would, even if it meant she would risk running into Nick.

She retrieved the pitchers off the bar, grabbed a plate of nachos, and delivered both to one of the long trestle tables occupied by three couples. She tucked her tray under her arm, turned, and slammed into what felt like a brick wall.

The wall was Nick, and he looked . . . determined. And, she thought as she studied the slight tic in his jaw, pissed off. He wrapped his hand around her bicep and pulled her through the maze of tables and chairs.

"Nick, what are you doing? People are watching."

The expressions ranged from avid curiosity to mild confusion. She looked wildly at her father, who frowned but didn't try to stop Nick.

He pulled her into the storeroom, clicked on the overhead light, and slammed the door behind him.

Nick's hands shook a little as he grabbed Kelly around the waist and set her down on a stack of cardboard boxes. He was out of his mind coming here like this, but it was like someone or something had taken over his body.

He couldn't stop himself. He was so angry—at her for rejecting him, at himself for being so out of control he couldn't stop himself from coming here. From proving to her how good it could be between them.

He leaned in and kissed her, savoring the sweet taste of her tongue against his. He groaned in relief and desire as her arms wrapped around his neck.

But a second later she was pushing him away. "No, Nick, stop it! We can't do this anymore."

"Why not?" He sank his teeth into the tender skin of her neck, loving the hot shudder that coursed through her.

"Because . . ." her breath hitched, "because I don't want—"

"Don't tell me you don't want me, Kelly," he said fiercely, ducking until his forehead rested against hers. He palmed her roughly through her jeans. "Don't lie to me. I can already feel how hot you are." Her heat seeped through the denim fabric, and he ground the heel of his hand against her. "This is good between us, and I don't want to stop."

She grabbed his wrist in both her hands, shoving it away from her crotch. "Stop it! You can find another fuck buddy, Nick! I'm not going to do this anymore."

"I don't want another fuck buddy, as you so nicely put it." He stepped between her legs, planting his palms on her inner thighs to hold them open. "I only want you." He ground his erection against her crotch to prove how much.

His hands came up to hold her face still for his kiss. She tried to turn her face away, but he wouldn't let her. He squeezed her jaw, not hard enough to hurt, but enough that her mouth opened slightly, enough. "Let me in," he growled. He felt like an animal, all brutal lust. He couldn't let her get away from him. Not tonight.

Not ever.

Somehow he got her jeans and panties off, and she was standing before him in nothing but her red Sullivan's T-shirt. She was no longer trying to get away, but responding to his rough, carnal kisses as though she wanted it as bad as he did.

He slipped his fingers between her legs, parting the wet curls, feeling the thick moisture slicking her labia. Her clit was a plump little point nudging eagerly against his probing hand, and Nick was going to die if he couldn't taste her in his mouth.

He got down on his knees in front of her, pulling one thigh over his shoulder as he burrowed his face between her legs. She leaned back against the boxes as he licked and sucked, his tongue thrusting inside in a rough tongue fuck. Nothing tasted better than Kelly, nothing drove him crazy like the way she smelled when she was aroused, her hot juices pouring over his tongue.

He lashed at her clit and almost burst in his pants as she came against his face. Before her contractions stopped, he had his cock out and pushed her back against the boxes. He bent his knees and drove impossibly deep. "How can you tell me this is over," he muttered into her shoulder, burying his mouth in the crook of her neck. "How can we stop this when it feels so good?"

She clung to him, muffling her soft groans and pants against his shoulder. Her fingers clawed at his back, her fingers twisted in the fabric of the shirt he hadn't bothered to remove. He hooked his elbow under one of her knees, pushing her leg up so he could grind even deeper.

"Nick." Her voice was a frantic whisper as suddenly her head reared back and her mouth opened wide. But only faint sobs escaped her as she pulsed and throbbed around him, urging him to a climax that nearly made his knees buckle.

He clung to her, pinning her against the boxes as he tried to catch his breath. "Kelly," he whispered, bending his head to kiss her face, her lips. He tasted her skin, the warm spiciness of her mouth, the saltiness of . . . tears? It was then he realized that Kelly was trembling not only from the aftermath of orgasm but from the effort of holding back the sobs bubbling from her chest. Tears streamed down her face as she thrust herself away from him and frantically scrambled back into her panties and jeans.

A raw pit opened in his stomach. "Jesus, Kelly, did I hurt you?" He felt the back of his eyes burn as he realized he might have actually caused her pain. "I'm sorry, I don't know what to say—"

"You didn't h-hurt me, Nick," she sobbed, but she wouldn't look at him.

Before he could stop her she ran out of the storage room and slammed the door behind her. Nick pulled his pants up over his hips, realizing only as he tucked himself back in that he hadn't used a condom.

He buried his fists against his eyeballs, barely suppressing the scream of rage. Fuck! Not only had he just gone after her like an animal, he hadn't bothered to protect her against pregnancy.

He really was a goddamned idiot.

He needed to apologize.

He needed to stop acting like a caveman and tell her how he really felt about her. Her tears, while not exactly a positive response, were at least an indicator of some deeper emotion on her part, weren't they?

Clinging feebly to that hope, he gathered his car keys from the floor where he'd thrown them and let himself out of the storeroom. A quick detour to the men's room to wash the scent of sex from his hands and face and he was ready to face Kelly and beg for her forgiveness.

But when he got to the dining room, Kelly was nowhere to be found.

"She left—said she was sick," Kelly's father said.

Nick felt himself flushing under Ryan Sullivan's probing gaze. Now that was classy, he thought, doing a woman with her father in the next room. What woman wouldn't want that?

"Sick?" Nick knew he sounded like a moron, but the blood was taking its time getting back to his brain.

"Came running out and said she felt awful and was going home." Ryan wiped down the counter as though Kelly's sudden illness was of no great concern. "She looked like she was crying. Know anything about that?"

Nick shook his head, knowing Ryan didn't believe him but

unwilling to offer any other explanation. Somehow he didn't think Ryan would like the idea that he'd been secretly sleeping with his youngest daughter for the past few weeks, even if his intentions *had* recently become much more honorable.

Thud thud thud thud thud. Kelly jumped as a hard fist slammed repeatedly into her front door forcefully enough to rattle the windowpanes on either side.

She uncurled from the couch where she'd sat, head on her knees, crying for the last half hour.

Oh God, please don't let it be Nick, she thought, and felt another rush of tears. But if it wasn't Nick, it would be her father, and that would be even worse. How could she explain why his usually calm, cerebral daughter had so completely and publicly lost her cool?

"Kelly, I'm gonna use my key if you don't let me in," Nick's voice threatened through the heavy wood door before he resumed his pounding.

And if he didn't use his key, she thought as she shuffled to the door and wiped her eyes, the neighbors would have him busted for disturbing the peace.

"Go away, Nick," she said, opening the door a crack. "I don't want to see you anymore."

He ignored her, planting his palm against the door and shoving his way inside. Why had she never seen this pushy side of Nick before? She'd always thought he was so nice. Why couldn't he just leave well enough alone?

"Nick, please, I have work to do. I have to get up really early and drive to Palo Alto tomorrow." He blurred in front of her as tears threatened yet again. This was why she never cried. Once she started, she couldn't stem the flood.

He hugged her against him, which only made her want to cry more. "Kelly, honey, why are you crying? Did I hurt you?"

She shook her head mutely against his chest, wanting to cling to him, to let him hold her and comfort her and take care of her. But she was terrified that if she did, she was going to do something really embarrassing, like admit she was in love with him.

"I'm sorry about what happened," he was saying. "It's like I go kind of crazy when I get around you."

She sniffled and pushed away. "You didn't hurt me," she said, wiping her nose on her sleeve. "I'm sorry I freaked out. I've been stressed lately, and like I said, I have to get up really early tomorrow."

"Why?"

"I have an interview, at Stanford. And I really need to prepare, so . . ."

But instead of taking her hint, he made himself comfortable on her couch. "You're leaving, then?"

"As soon as I line up a new position, yes."

He leaned back against the cushions, his broad shoulders spanning nearly half of the couch. "Then I don't see why we can't keep seeing each other until you leave." His tone was casual, but his gaze was intense.

Kelly twisted her fingers in the hem of her shirt, wanting to scream in frustration at his thick-headedness. He should be grateful that she was cutting him loose without any complications, for Christ's sake! "If you're worried about a steady lay, I'm sure you won't have any trouble."

"I'm sure I won't," he said quietly.

Even though she knew she was expendable, that still stung.

"But like I said earlier, I don't want anyone else. And you seemed to enjoy it too up until recently. I don't get what changed."

He was up on his feet, moving toward her again, and Kelly fought the urge to run and lock herself in the bathroom. "I can't do this anymore. You're too much of a distraction for me, and I need to figure out what I'll be doing after I leave."

"Like move to Palo Alto?"

"Right. There's a staff position in their ER, and I'm a strong candidate."

"I don't see why you can't figure it out while still seeing me. I don't take up that much of your time."

"Look, I know you probably don't get rejected much, Nick, so I'll try to use small words so you can understand. I Do Not Want To See You Anymore."

"See, I could believe you if I hadn't made you come twice in the last hour."

"You're an asshole," she said, shoving him hard against his chest.

"And you're lying." He grabbed her by the shoulders, but gently. His grip held none of the brute force that he'd exhibited earlier.

The brute force that, though she hated to admit it, had excited her down to the tips of her red-painted toes.

His thumbs dipped beneath the crewneck of her T-shirt, sweeping against her collarbone in slow, seductive strokes. "Why can't you just accept the truth and leave me alone, Nick?" Her protest sounded feeble even to her own ears.

"Because I don't think that is the truth, Kelly." His hands slid down her arms to toy with her fingers that were clenched in tight fists at her sides. "The truth is that you still want me, but you're afraid of something and you're running away."

Something inside of her snapped. He wanted the truth? Fine, she'd give him the truth. The one thing guaranteed to send him running so fast he'd leave skid marks on her carpet.

"Fine. You win," she said. "I'm lying when I say I don't want to see you." She pulled her hands away from his, needing to put distance between them before she completely lost it. "The problem is that I'm falling in love with you, Nick. I thought I could do this, thought I could have fun, sleep with you, see what all the fuss was about." She laughed weakly. "But every time I'm with you, it just gets harder and harder to pretend it doesn't mean anything."

The words hung in the air and Kelly collapsed on the couch, deflated. She felt the cushions shift next to her. To her surprise, instead of running, Nick settled in beside her and gathered her tense form against his chest.

Why wouldn't he just leave? Typical Nick, she thought, always the nice guy, even when she wished, for once, he would just be a jerk and leave her to wallow.

She felt his arms close around her, felt the press of his lips against the crown of her head. She wrapped her arms around herself, cringing away as she felt her nose and eyes fill up again. She couldn't take comfort from him, not now.

Nick let the wave of joy wash through him as he wrapped his arms around her resisting body. He buried his nose in her dark hair, inhaling deeply, unable to speak for several moments. "Kelly, look at me," he whispered.

She shook her head, and Nick slid one hand to her jaw and forced the issue. Her blue eyes were red rimmed and puffy, her nose was bright red against her otherwise pale face, and her mouth had that soft blurred look that came from a hard crying jag.

"You are one of the most beautiful, amazing women I've ever known," he said, struggling to keep his voice from shaking. He'd never been exceptionally emotional, but right now he was afraid he'd start bawling like a chick.

Kelly loved him. Holy shit! Kelly Sullivan loved a stupid idiot goon like him. He better not fuck it up.

"But—" she said weakly, sniffling and blinking back tears.

He smiled, his own eyes stinging. "No 'but.' " He kissed her cheeks, her swollen damp eyes, her red nose. "I just never believed that a woman as great as you could ever love me back."

"What?" Her head snapped back, dislodging his hands from her face. She grabbed them hard in her chilled fingers.

"I love you, Kelly." This time he kissed her mouth, tasted the soft sob that escaped her chest. "But I didn't want to move too fast because I was afraid."

"Afraid of what?"

"I convinced myself that I could never be the right guy for you. I'm nothing like the braniacs you're used to, and I was afraid after the sex got old, you'd get bored."

She moaned and pulled him fiercely against her as though afraid he was going to slip away. "I think I've always been in love with you, Nick," she whispered. Her soft hands framed his cheeks. "I thought I could just be casual, but being with you—" She kissed him again, her tongue sliding against his, seeking out his taste. "No one's ever made me feel the way you do."

"How is that?" He pulled her hair from its elastic band and watched it fall around her shoulders.

"Safe. Cared for," she said, burrowing against his body as she slid one hand up the back of his shirt. "Like there's more to me than just a big brain." She paused to kiss his neck.

"That's not the only big part of you." Nick gazed meaningfully at her chest.

She laughed and swatted him on the shoulder, then hugged him hard. She sighed. "That's what I mean. You make me feel normal. And happy. And sexy," she purred, nestling those magnificent breasts against him.

He carried her to the bedroom and spent the next hour showing her just how sexy he found her.

* * *

"I'm sorry I doubted us," he said later as they lay in the dark. Their legs twined together beneath the sheets, Kelly's smooth thigh pressed against his groin.

"What do you mean?"

"I realized a week ago that I loved you, but I didn't want to say anything, because I didn't think there was any hope you'd feel the same way." He shifted and threaded his fingers through her hair.

"You thought I would be like Ann," she said simply.

Nick smiled in the darkness. That's what he liked about smart girls. They caught on real fast. "It took me awhile to get over myself, to get past my insecurities that she helped reinforce. But I know you're not like her. This is your hometown, and you're not the type to put yourself above your roots."

"No, but I don't really fit in here," she said uncertainly. "And I'm not sure what that means for us."

He smoothed the tension from her back with the flat of his palm. "You fit in here fine, you just don't see it." He sensed her frown. "But even if you don't want to stay here, we'll figure a way to make it work."

"How can you be so sure?"

"Because I know we'll both do whatever it takes."

Epilogue

The smell of fried fish hung heavily in the air. Sullivan's was packed with the usual Wednesday night crowd.

Nick took a swig of his Harp's and tucked Kelly's hand in his, pausing to run his thumb over the two-carat solitaire he'd recently placed there.

She squeezed his hand but didn't turn to him since his mom was sitting next to her and talking her ear off.

"I can't believe you're really moving, man." Mike shook his head. "First Jake, now you. What the hell is happening to us?"

Nick couldn't believe it himself. After living in this town for his entire life, it was hard to imagine living anywhere else. This would be his last Wednesday at Sully's for a good, long time.

But Kelly was at Stanford Hospital, and Nick was sick of the long-distance thing they'd been doing for the past few months. Besides, he was going to take a few business classes while he looked for work, and depending on how that went, he might enroll full time in the fall. As happy as he'd been here, he hadn't realized how much he'd limited himself before he was with Kelly. He'd miss his home, miss his family, but at the same time he felt like a whole new world had opened up to him.

He and his brothers had talked about eventually opening an office of Donovan Brothers in the Bay Area, and he and Kelly hadn't ruled out moving back here when they had kids.

"It's only four hours away," he heard Kelly say to his mother. He shook his head. As far as his mother was concerned, her baby boy was leaving and never coming back, and no reassurances could soothe her.

"At least she hasn't decided to blame Kelly for stealing you away," Tony said.

"She knows better than to alienate her this soon," his dad chuckled. "Besides, she's thrilled you're getting married."

Mike and Tony both squirmed in their seats. They knew that with both Nick and Jake engaged, their mother would redouble her efforts to marry them off.

"Lucky for us, you ran off with the best this town has to offer," Mike said, winking at Kelly across the table.

"You never know who's gonna walk through that door," Nick said. "Mark my words, you two are next."

Kiss Me Twice

1

Karen Sullivan slid onto a seat at the bar of Cleo's Lounge. The martini bar sported a decent crowd, but the bartender noticed her right away.

"What will you have?"

She crossed her leg so the slit up the side of her white mini slid open along her right leg, no doubt offering a nice glimpse of thigh, and she shifted her leg so it wasn't pressed too tightly against the vinyl, ensuring the flesh stayed smooth. It sucked that even the leanest thigh could look lumpy and cottage cheesy if the flesh was pressed too tight.

Karen smiled up at him through her lashes, leaning forward so he could appreciate the draped neckline of her coral and white flower-print sleeveless top. "How about a lemon drop. With extra sugar."

The bartender cast an appreciative smile. "Coming right up."

He made a big show of pouring the vodka, flipping the bottle and swirling it as he poured. Lemon juice and ice followed it into a shaker, which he shook with a vigor that would have done a paint mixer proud. He poured it into a sugar-rimmed martini glass with a flourish and set her drink in front of her.

"How is it?" he said, eyes riveted on her mouth.

Karen raised the glass and deliberately swiped her tongue along the rim and took a generous swig. "Delicious."

The bartender's eyes glazed over, and his mouth went slightly slack.

"Hey, dude, can we get some beers over here?" a deep voice boomed.

"I think you have some other customers," she said, gesturing her glass in the man's direction as she idly stroked her collarbone.

"Uh, right." He reluctantly backed away.

Karen rolled her eyes. Men. They were so freakin' easy. Another ten seconds and she would be drinking for free all night.

Mentally she scolded herself. Hadn't she vowed to stop using her looks to attract guys with no potential? Even if the guy was a potential source of free alcohol. Or, at the very least, focus her attentions on good men with good relationship potential instead of assholes who wanted nothing more than a hot piece of ass.

Not that her strategy had gotten her very far tonight. Here she was, drinking alone on a Saturday night in a lame club in Caesar's Lake Tahoe. Staying in her room definitely would have been the wiser choice, but she couldn't stand her own company. And call her shallow, but the admiring glances she'd received from the male patrons were a superficial balm for her badly bruised ego.

It could be worse. Caesar's definitely had its cheese factor, but it was a hell of a lot better than Circus Circus, where Brad had taken her.

Brad. What a dick. It should have been a tip-off when he'd

planned their weekend trip around gambling in Reno. He'd said he wanted to do something fun that was close to Sacramento, so she'd given him the benefit of the doubt.

At the end of the day, Brad had chosen the hotel because it had the cheapest rooms and a complimentary prime rib buffet.

Which wouldn't have been such a big deal if he'd been a typically clueless man and had honestly tried to plan a nice weekend for them.

But just like every man in her past, all he wanted was to get laid.

She took another gulp of her lemon drop, surprised to see it was already nearly gone. But the liquor did little to cool her fury as her conversation with Brad echoed through her head.

"Maybe next week we could have a barbecue and I could meet some of your family," she'd said. They'd been sitting on the lumpy love seat in their room. Brad had leaned in to kiss her, the smell of prime rib laced with beer almost enough to knock her over.

He had jerked back at her words. "Why would we want to do that?"

"We've been dating for over a month, and I just thought it would be good to meet your family since you spend so much time with them."

Warning bells had gone off in her head at the uncomfortable expression that crossed his face.

"Karen, come on, we're not exactly at the parent-meeting stage. It's not as though this is all that serious . . ." That last word had trailed off as he'd realized her elevated expectations.

"What do you mean?" She had a sinking feeling she already knew the answer.

"Well, you're, you—" he'd stammered.

"I'm what?"

"You're a, ah, a woman a guy has fun with, you know—"

"A slut?" She stood before him, hands on her hips. "Fast? Loose? Trashy?" All terms she had heard applied to her since high school.

Brad had held his hands up as if to ward off the anger radiating from every pore of her body. "No, not that. Just not . . ." He'd paused, hands dropping limply in his lap and head drooping forward. "Just not the kind of woman I could imagine bringing home to my mother."

"So you've just been biding your time for the last month and a half, wanting to fuck me for a while before you settle down with a nice girl?"

"Yeah, I guess," he had replied, his tone belligerent. "What do you expect? The way you dress, the way you act? We have mutual friends, Karen. I hear things. I know you're not exactly Snow White."

It had been on the tip of her tongue to tell him flat out that she hadn't been with a guy for almost two years, ever since she realized that she was never going to be happy if she didn't stop sleeping with guys who didn't even like her. But she'd be damned if she'd give Brad the satisfaction of knowing she'd chosen him as the best candidate to end her dry spell.

She snapped back to reality as the bartender whisked her empty glass away, replacing it with a full drink in one move. "This one's on me," he said with a wink.

He was sort of cute, she mused, in an overgrown, beefy frat boy sort of way. A little young for her, but she probably would have given him a toss a few years ago. If she hadn't had anything—or anyone—better to do.

But not now, she reminded herself firmly. Brad, the bartender, they were all the same.

Was it too much to ask for a guy who actually *liked* her for who she was and not just because she gave a good blow job?

So what if she dressed provocatively, used her beauty to get things she wanted? There was more to her than that. She wasn't Mother Teresa, but deep down she was a good person.

A fact she'd been trying to convince herself of for the past two years and was pretty close to believing.

She'd actually thought Brad was the guy who saw beyond the surface and really liked her.

What an idiot. She finished her second drink with an unlady-like slurp. Apparently she was so out of practice looking for nice guys she was no longer capable of identifying one.

Not that she'd *ever* been able to find one. The last time she'd thought she'd managed to snag a good, upstanding guy, he ended up worse than all the rest. And she'd been paying for it ever since.

Mike Donovan wound his way through the casino on his way back to Club Nero. The cavernous, smoky room echoed with the ringing of slot machines, groans of disappointment, and hoots of victory as patrons won or lost.

Too bad he hated gambling. A few hands at the blackjack table would be the perfect excuse to delay rejoining Day 2 of his brother's bachelor party in full swing at the biggest night-club Caesar's Lake Tahoe had to offer.

Mike politely brushed off a cocktail waitress dressed in a mini-toga and continued across the casino floor. As much as he dreaded going back to the noisy club full of drunken, sweaty bodies, he knew he couldn't avoid it. His baby brother was marrying Kelly Sullivan in two weeks. Pretending to enjoy the celebration of Nick's last few days of freedom was the least he could do.

As he passed the bars and restaurants on his way to the club, he heard the remarkably pleasant sound of a blues band spilling out of the hotel's martini bar. Mike paused and poked his head inside. Unlike at Club Nero, the crowd here was big but not overwhelming. The band played at a level that provided a nice backdrop but didn't eliminate all possibility of intelligible conversation.

And, he noticed as he looked at bottles lining the shelves of the back bar, he bet he could get a decent glass of cabernet here.

It was unlikely his brothers would miss him for one drink, he decided. When he'd left, Tony had been flirting with a stacked redhead and Jake was helping the groom-to-be fend off the advances of all the women Tony sent over to harass him.

Mike scanned the room. Though the crowd wasn't huge, all the tables were taken. The only empty seat was at the bar, next to a petite blonde.

Even though Mike tended to go for brunettes, he couldn't deny that, from what he could see, she was a hot piece of ass.

Her dark gold hair was tousled into one of those styles that was supposed to make a woman look like she just rolled out of bed, but it probably took an hour to achieve. He raked an admiring glance down the rest of her. Her body was sleek, tight, showcased nicely by her sleeveless top and a skirt so short it could be a belt. Long, tan legs begged him to trail his fingers up to where that slit ended to see if her skin could possibly feel as silky as it looked.

His gaze moved down to take in dainty feet encased in white stiletto sandals. Little white fuck-me shoes on her tiny little feet. Mike felt an immediate and surprising tightening in his groin as he imagined those feet, in those shoes, propped up on his shoulders.

I might be longer than one drink getting back to the party, he thought with a grin as he slid onto the stool beside her.

Mike leaned forward onto the bar and waved to get the bartender's attention. "Can I get a glass of that, please?" Mike said, indicating very good Sonoma Valley cabernet displayed on the wine shelf.

"You have great taste," the woman next to him said. Jesus, even her voice was sexy. Low and slightly raspy, like she had just woken up after a night of hard loving.

"Thanks," he said, smiling as he turned to face her fully. The smile morphed into a baring of teeth when he recognized the woman next to him.

Karen Sullivan.

For a split second, her expression mirrored his shock, but she recovered quickly. Her deceptively angelic blue eyes widened, then crinkled at the corners as her full, pink lips slid into a smile. Jesus, no wonder he'd gotten so turned on so quickly. He tried to ignore the surge of heat that shot through him as she placed a hand on his forearm, bare where he'd rolled up the sleeve of his button-front shirt.

"Mike, how funny seeing you here," she said. Though her tone was friendly he detected a slight strain underneath. Good. He made her nervous. Small payback for the way she'd twisted him into knots and tossed him away eleven years ago.

"Funny's one word you could use," he said as he accepted his glass of wine, his cool tone in direct contrast to the heat coursing through his veins. What the hell was it about this woman? One whiff and he was like a dog after a bitch in heat, any shred of common sense overcome by the need to rut until his dick was limp and his balls wrung dry.

She must have picked up on his tension, because her tone was more mocking than teasing as she said, "Wine? Isn't that a sissy drink for a big, macho man like you?"

His eyes narrowed to slits and his lips tightened in a feral smile. "You, of all people, should know how much of a sissy I'm not."

She sat back a little and leaned one elbow on the bar as she twisted on her seat to fully face him. Her index finger traced the rim of her martini glass, and her lips tilted up in a sly half smile.

She appeared unfazed and unruffled by his simmering hostility. But Mike detected her pulse beating frantically against the fragile skin of her throat and knew she felt the throbbing, seething tension that coiled and hissed around them.

She had her game face on, no doubt. But Mike knew all of her games, and he knew better than to play. *Which was why he should just get up and walk away right now.*

Instead he took a sip of his drink, savoring the rich flavor of the wine as it washed over his tongue. Leaning his right elbow on the bar in a mimic of Karen's pseudocasual pose, he said, "You look good, Karen."

She looked a little surprised at the compliment, as though fully prepared for a barb. It was true though. She looked fantastic, as always. Sure, she looked a little older than when he'd last seen her at her mother's funeral. A few tiny smile lines decorated the corners of her eyes. But the blond hair suited her as well as her own natural chestnut brown shade had, giving her a sassy, party girl look. Her body was no longer girlishly slim, but tightly toned in the manner of a woman who worked very hard at maintaining her appearance.

"Thanks, you do too," she said, deliberately sliding her gaze down his chest, lingering for a moment in his lap before sliding back up again.

Mike's hand tightened around the stem of his glass. Some things, however, hadn't changed. Karen was still the seductive little bitch who used her considerable assets to turn men into slobbering idiots who would do whatever she wanted. He held it as a point of pride that he had never completely fallen under her spell, though he'd come frighteningly close. Then again, when they had gone out, Karen had only been eighteen. Still an amateur. Now she was clearly a pro.

He pitied the poor schmuck who was dangling on her line. "What are you doing here, Karen?"

"I could ask you the same. This doesn't seem like your kind of place, Mike."

"You're right. I'm here with my brothers and some friends. Nick's bachelor party."

Her brow knit into a frown. "Oh yes, the wedding."

"What, not happy for your baby sister?" he mocked. Karen's long-standing resentment of her sister was well known by anyone who had gone to high school with the Sullivan girls.

"Sure I am. She's marrying a great guy."

Though her voice lacked enthusiasm, Mike was surprised that she wasn't insincere. "Yep, he's the best."

"Kelly did always get everything," Karen said, sounding like a sullen thirteen-year-old. That was more like it.

"What about you?" he asked.

She shifted uncomfortably on her stool. "A little fight with my boyfriend. I decided I'd be better off on my own tonight."

"So now you're going to fuck some poor unsuspecting schmuck to get revenge on him?" He'd meant the comment to be casually mocking, but eleven years' worth of resentment underscored his words.

If it were anyone else, Mike would have thought it was vulnerability that flashed in Karen's eyes. Instead he chalked it up to a flicker of the candle next to them being jostled by the bartender.

Her glossy, cupid's bow mouth curved in a feline smile as her hand dropped to trail seductively up his thigh. "Why, Mike, what a good idea. Lucky for me you came along."

2

Oh crap, I am in for it now. But even as Karen cursed her big, fat mouth, she felt a flash of triumph at the raw lust that ignited in Mike's hazel eyes.

Of all the cheesy bars in Reno, she thought, paraphrasing *Casablanca, why the hell did Mike Donovan have to walk into Cleo's?*

One look at his face, and all the pain, all the resentment at the way he'd turned his back on her came rushing back, along with all the gut-wrenching regret that she'd ever lost him.

Worse, even through her own anger and his obvious contempt, her body still erupted with lust at the mere sight of him. Everything about him drove her crazy. His big, long-fingered workman's hands. She could still remember the way they felt on her skin, sliding inside her. His wide, full-lipped mouth. Oh God, she knew how good he was with that mouth.

Just as she knew that beneath his white cotton button-front shirt and khaki trousers she'd find a wealth of tanned skin and rippling muscles. Her fingers tingled at the remembered feel of

skimming them up and down the sleekness of his back, sometimes digging her fingernails into the flesh as he brought her to
orgasm after orgasm.

And his eyes, she thought as she dragged her gaze back up to
his face. Thickly lashed, gleaming hazel, framed by heavy dark
brows. Eyes that used to smile down on her as he called her
"Tiny" with such sweetness, she'd almost had herself convinced he really loved her.

What a dumb bitch she'd been.

Now his eyes were cold, greenish gold slits that looked at
her with mingled lust and derision.

Which was why she should get up and leave, right now.

The sane, well-adjusted voice she'd worked so hard to cultivate over the last two years screamed at her to get out of there
RIGHT NOW, but her body was clearly not listening. Her
right hand slid farther up Mike's thigh. A smile curved her lips
as she felt the muscles tighten. Through her own sexual awareness came the rush, the familiar surge of power she always got
when she knew a man was helpless to resist her.

That this man was helpless to resist her.

Mike inched his body marginally closer to hers and took another sip of his wine. "What do you think you're doing,
Karen?" His voice was calm, but she could see the tiny beads of
perspiration form along his hairline. A good sign, considering
the bar was very well air-conditioned.

She leaned closer, keeping her right hand on his thigh and
shifting so her own knees were between his spread ones. "I'm
just following your advice, Mike. Brad has to learn he needs to
treat me right or I'm going to go find someone else to play
with."

Part of her, the sane, rational part, felt like she was watching
herself from across the room. *I can't believe you! What the hell
are you thinking?* sane Karen demanded. *The fact that Brad*

turned out to be such a colossal dick is not a free pass to do something stupid. You've been so good! No messing around for almost two years. You've worked so hard not to fall into your old bad habits, and the first glimpse of your high school boyfriend and you completely regress!

Karen moved one foot forward and rested it on the rung of Mike's stool, bringing her bare thigh into brushing contact with the soft cotton of his slacks.

He wasn't just my high school boyfriend, Karen responded bitterly to her sane self. *He was my first love. My only love. A girl can't be held responsible under these circumstances.*

In that case, I'm out of here. And with that, her inner voice of sanity departed for the night.

Mike, oblivious to her heated internal dialogue, said, "I wasn't volunteering to be your playmate."

And yet he didn't move away.

"But Mike," she said in her best Marilyn Monroe whisper, "you're the only one I want to play with." Though rusty, her little girl voice paired with the sidelong glance through her eyelashes had always been one of her best moves.

Strong fingers wrapped around her biceps and he practically lifted her off her stool as he pulled her face to his. "Don't fuck around with me, Karen," he said through clenched teeth. "I dealt with enough of your bullshit to last me a lifetime, so don't think you can play me like you used to."

Karen opened her mouth to protest, but her breath froze as she saw the lust in his eyes. He still wanted her. He might hate her, but he still wanted her. She had accomplished that. And sick puppy that she was, the knowledge fueled her rapidly mounting desire.

"Just be straight with me, Karen. Do you want to fuck me or not?" How very Mike, to lay it out in such basic, no-nonsense terms.

And God help her, she did. Wanted to feel him on her, in her, taste his smooth dark skin with her lips and tongue just one more time. Almost as much as she wanted to prove to Mike that she could still make him feel things no other woman could make him feel. That was her skill, her gift, her weapon. This was her chance to use it on him again.

Before she could whisper "Yes," his mouth came down hard on hers in punishing, forceful contact that could barely be called a kiss. Even if she'd wanted to, there was no way she could have pulled away with his hand tangled tightly in her hair.

Lust and heat poured through her veins. It had been so long, but the still familiar taste and feel of Mike brought her to swift and almost painful arousal. A creamy throbbing erupted between her thighs as she opened her lips, sucking his tongue eagerly into her mouth. Fisting her hand in his thick black hair, she nearly fell off her stool in her eagerness to get close.

The near fall brought her partially back to her senses. She needed to regain control of this situation, and fast. This was her seduction, her chance to teach Mike the lesson that no matter what he thought about her, she still had the power to make him crazed with lust.

But damn, it was hard to concentrate when he eased the pressure on her mouth and teased her with the slick, hot slide of his tongue against hers.

She uttered a low moan against his mouth and slid her hand up his thigh, not stopping until she felt the heaviness of his balls against her palm. She gave them a gentle squeeze, then moved her hand up and to the right, and pressed her palm against a skyscraper of an erection. Mike groaned into her mouth and grabbed her hand, pressing it even more firmly against his cock.

This was what I wanted, she thought as she sucked and bit at his mouth. Mike helpless, incapacitated with need and completely under her control.

Her self-congratulations were cut off as Mike countered her move by lifting her off her bar stool and setting her astride one of his thighs. Her wet, aching mound was pressed against him, and through the wispy silk of her damp panties his firm muscles flexed against her swollen clit. Splaying one big hand across her back, he lifted his thigh against her as she ground against him like a stripper giving the lap dance of her career.

A tight knot built low in her belly, a sensation so long forgotten she almost didn't recognize it. But holy shit, she was about to come right there, with nothing but his leg between hers and his tongue in her mouth. In retaliation she squeezed his erection and found the tip of his dick through the fabric of his pants, circling and squeezing it until he shuddered and clamped his hand around her wrist.

Her moment of triumph was short lived as Mike gripped the stretchy neckline of her top and shoved it down, and his mouth came down to latch firmly on her nipple, hard and pointy beneath the lacy cup of her bra.

Her back arched to give him better access, her hands gripping his head to press his mouth even more firmly to her breast. She shuddered at the hot slide of his hand up her thigh, at his thumb sliding against the leg opening of her panties. *Just a few more inches*, she thought desperately, *maybe just a few centimeters . . .*

"Hey!" Someone was yelling very near them. "HEY!" The voice grew more insistent.

Suddenly they were doused with icy cold liquid.

"What the fuck!" Mike roared, and both he and Karen looked into the angry face of the bartender.

"We don't have live sex shows in this club," he said, still waving the water hose threateningly. "Take it up to your room."

Karen looked around, dazed, and vaguely felt Mike pull her blouse back up over her shoulder. Indeed, they were still seated at the bar at Cleo's. Instead of looking at the band or each other, most of the patrons were staring right at them. Most looked completely scandalized, but a few obviously hoped for an invitation to join in.

She slid off her bar stool and wished fervently that she could melt into a puddle on the floor. She fumbled with her bag, but her hands shook so hard she couldn't even grip her wallet.

Oh God, she had nearly had sex with him right there in the bar. She hadn't done anything that outrageous in ... had she ever done anything that outrageous? A quickie in a bathroom or closet was one thing, but having a guy nearly finger her at a bar ...

Mike clamped his hand firmly around her wrist, threw several bills on the bar, and pulled her out of the club. Karen focused on keeping her balance in her four-inch stilettos as he propelled her across the lobby.

The next thing she knew he was pushing her into an elevator.

"What room?" he asked.

Karen blinked at him.

"What room?" he said, harsher now.

"Uh, 1165," she said, and watched him punch the floor number in so hard she marveled that he didn't crack the panel.

Then he was on her again, shoving her up against one of the mirrored sides of the elevator. He lifted her up by the waist, pinning her against the wall until her head was a few inches above his, using his hips to anchor her above the floor. He didn't even pause, just went straight for her breasts, tugging at her blouse and bra until both were bare. "Jesus Christ, how is it possible that you're still this hot?" He sucked a nipple in his mouth and captured the other in his fingers, pinching and rolling the hot, aching bud until she wanted to scream.

Karen opened her eyes, and their reflection in the opposite

mirror was enough to nearly send her over the edge. His dark head pressed against her gold-hued flesh, and his long-fingered hand all but swallowed up her other breast. Her own expression was dazed, eyes half-closed, mouth slack with lust.

She arched her pelvis against him until her mons came into contact with his rock-hard abs. Her moan was unnaturally loud in the close chamber as his mouth licked, sucked, and nipped at her breasts.

She had a fleeting thought that they were giving the security monitors one hell of a show. But even that thought couldn't stop her from grinding herself harder against Mike as she strove to satisfy the pounding ache between her thighs.

She almost sobbed when he abruptly pulled away and set her on her feet.

"This is your floor," he said.

Indeed, the elevator doors were open, and a middle-age couple stared at them with eyes the size of dinner plates.

Pulling her blouse up in what she hoped was a nonchalant manner, she followed Mike from the elevator.

Mike was looking at the room signs, trying to find the hallway to her room. He glanced over and met her gaze, an unmistakable glint of amusement in his eyes.

"I think those poor people thought they were getting on the elevator straight to Sodom and Gomorrah," she said shakily. Then it all struck her as too funny, and she started to laugh. And once she started, she couldn't stop. Mike started laughing too, and pretty soon they were holding each other up as they leaned against the wall.

Then before she knew it Mike was kissing her again, and she reached for his fly as his hand slid up her skirt. She gasped as he cupped her firmly through her panties, straining against the heel of his palm.

Abruptly he removed his hand. "Jesus Christ," he said

somewhat shakily. "At this rate we're going to get arrested." He stared down at her, all traces of amusement gone. "And I don't want you to come until you're begging me for it."

The verbal slap in the face served as a sharp reminder of what she was about. Her? Beg? She didn't think so.

Karen pushed herself away from the wall and sauntered down the hall toward her room. As long as he didn't touch her, she could maintain a modicum of control.

When he didn't immediately follow, she cast a glance over her bare shoulder. "Aren't you coming?" He didn't hurry, but there was a noticeable urgency about his stride.

Good, she thought, smirking to herself. Someone was going to plead for mercy, but it sure as hell wouldn't be her.

Despite her lapse in the bar, Karen was determined to maintain control of this encounter. Whether he realized it or not, she was calling the shots.

As he followed her down the hall, mesmerized by the swing of her perfect, firm ass, Mike asked himself for the hundredth time what the hell he thought he was doing. This was Karen Sullivan, for fuck's sake, the woman who had ripped his guts out and humiliated him with his so-called friend. Eleven years, and the thought of it still made him angry enough to put his fist through a wall.

She was a man killer, a scheming bitch who had learned at a very young age how to chew men up and spit them out.

He was a smart, level-headed guy who knew better than to fall victim to her. But he couldn't deny the rush he got from knowing she was as hot for him as he was for her. Just as a man couldn't fake a hard-on, Karen couldn't fake the dripping hot moisture he'd felt soaking the crotch of her panties.

As much as he knew he should leave now, leave her high and

dry, he knew he wouldn't rest if he didn't get to feel her clenching silky wet around his cock.

He couldn't resist her, but he could keep the upper hand.
He'd fuck her so good he would obliterate the memory of all
the other guys she'd been with since him, and she'd realize once
and for all that he wasn't just another dumb schmuck she could
fuck with for her own amusement.

He stood behind her as she opened the door with her key
card, inhaling the soft, sexy scent that surrounded her. A spicy,
vanilla-scented perfume mingled with the fresh smell of shampoo, and underneath was the smell of bare smooth skin, the
scent of Karen herself. He could barely resist the urge to hold
her close and breathe in the sweet, intoxicating essence of her.

He'd barely stepped into the suite before she launched herself at him, her hands unbuttoning his shirt in record time. Her
mouth, hot and slick, pressed against each patch of newly exposed flesh until she was sliding kisses along his waistband as
she nimbly unfastened his belt. He forgot all about teaching her
a lesson as the fiercest erection he could ever remember sprung
eagerly into her waiting grasp.

"I always thought I was exaggerating things in my memory," she murmured as she stared down at his throbbing cock.
Mike thrust against her fist as she measured him with an exquisite pressure that brought a thick drop of pre-come oozing
out of the tip. Karen whisked it away, using it to lubricate the
pad of her thumb as she swirled it around the unbearably sensitive head.

His knees nearly buckled and he swore softly. He'd forgotten how good she was at hand jobs. Unlike most women, who
could never seem to find the right rhythm and pressure, Karen
was so good it was almost like masturbating himself. Except
when it was just him, he didn't have the agonizingly erotic vi-

sion of his throbbing shaft squeezed in Karen's small, perfectly manicured hand.

Mike closed his eyes against the sight, afraid he would embarrass himself by exploding all over her. He tried to steady himself, leaning his back against the wall, and then his eyes flew open when he felt a puff of hot breath on the head of his cock.

Her tongue stole out, lapping at him and tracing wet circles around the ridge below the head. Her eyes were open, staring at him, challenging him even as she knelt before him in false submission, his cock firmly in her hand as she tormented him. He quaked with barely restrained hunger as the pink tip of her tongue traced the vein that ran along his length. Another thick spurt of liquid coated the head, and she lapped it up, licking her lips like it was sweet cream.

Shit. He was in serious danger of losing it, and they'd barely even started. He struggled for control, tried to pull away from her mouth. "Karen, I—"

His protest died in his throat as her soft, full lips closed over his cock and slid down almost to the base. A helpless moan he barely recognized as his own echoed up to the ceiling, and he leaned against the wall for support. The sight of her plump lips sliding up and down his thick, glistening shaft was too much. His mind frantically conjured building plans, bid numbers, materials costs—anything to distract him from the feel of her throat swallowing, her tongue lapping and swirling as she sucked him in and out of her mouth.

This wasn't how it was supposed to go! He didn't want to come yet, dammit! He wanted to get inside her, feel her rippling around his cock as she begged him to fuck her, to make her come.

Then he had no choice as Karen's hand came up to cup his balls, sucking him deep as one finger traced the seam and pressed firmly against the one spot guaranteed to make him go off like Mt. Vesuvius.

She sucked him dry, milking him with her lips and hand as he came in thick spurts against the back of her throat.

When his heart had slowed to merely beating double time, he looked down. Karen gazed up at him with an indisputably victorious look in her eyes. With a smirk, she straightened and sashayed into the sitting room of the suite. "I see the years haven't done much for your staying power," she tossed over her shoulder.

Mike pushed away from the wall and followed her, cursing his weakness and his ever susceptible dick. He *never* let himself get carried away with a woman, *never* lost control. Only Karen had ever been able to do that to him, and he had vowed a long time ago he would never let it happen again.

His eyes narrowed at her cocky little swagger. The night wasn't over yet, and now that she'd so graciously taken the edge off, he could keep a firmer hold on himself. She may have won the battle, but she sure as shit hadn't won the war.

3

"Would you like a drink?" Karen asked, bending over the minibar as casual as you pleased. As though he wasn't standing there with his dick damp and half-hard after she'd given him a blow job that had slain him inside of ninety seconds.

Mike shrugged out of his shirt as he walked across the room and then toed off his loafers. Karen straightened and regarded him with that same nonchalant expression as he stripped off his pants, boxers, and socks. "I don't think so," he said.

Her gaze dropped to his groin, and she smirked as his cock made a swift and complete recovery. "How flattering," she cooed, placing the vodka and tonic bottles she'd taken from the minibar on top of the refrigerator. For all her bravado, there was no mistaking the tremble in her hands.

He quickly closed the distance between them and wrapped one arm around her waist and shoved the other up her skirt as he half-dragged, half-carried her into the bedroom. Her mouth was a wide surprised "O" as he shoved her back onto the king-size bed so hard she bounced.

She struggled to sit up, but he easily restrained her with one big hand on her chest as he flicked on the light mounted to the wall beside the bed. No way was he doing this in the dark.

She struggled against his hold. "Mike, let go a second."

"Uh-uh. You don't get to call all the shots."

She exploded in a flurry of motion, slapping at his arms and kicking at him with those lethally sexy stilettos. She just managed to crawl to the edge of the bed before he tackled her, pinning her to the bed with his weight. To emphasize his point, he closed his teeth on the delicate skin between her neck and shoulder, not enough to hurt but hard enough to warn her to stop struggling.

"My turn," he whispered, licking at the faint tooth marks that marred her tawny skin. He felt as well as heard the hungry sound that escaped the back of her throat, and his cock strained against the smooth flesh of her thigh.

He flipped her back over, undressing her with an efficiency that belied the faint tremor in his hands. "Thank God you still don't wear many clothes," he muttered as she helped him strip off her blouse.

Within seconds she was completely naked except for her shoes. When she leaned down to unbuckle the straps, he stopped her with a firm hand clamped around her wrist. "No way. Leave these on."

"Kinky." She cocked an eyebrow at him and laid back against the pillows, back arched and legs slightly parted in an obviously well-practiced pose.

He bracketed her hips with his knees and braced his weight on his hands, effectively caging her in. Very deliberately, he stroked the tip of his erection against the soft skin of her belly, loving the way the muscles jumped and shuddered as though shocked by a live wire. Her tongue came out to moisten her lips—another choreographed move, no doubt, but it nonetheless sent another surge of heat to his cock. He leaned down and licked her lips with his own tongue, teasing her until her lips parted.

Nothing, he thought smugly, was feigned about her eager response to his liquid, carnal kiss. He savored the sweet, tangy, vodka-tinged taste of her. In a rush, he remembered how much he had loved to kiss her, how he had once craved the taste of her mouth like a junkie craves heroin.

Echoing his thoughts, she whispered, "I love feeling your mouth on me, Mike. I'd forgotten how good it feels just to have you kiss me."

He yanked his mouth away, ignoring her protesting tug on the hair at his nape. He wasn't about to let this turn into a walk down memory lane. He was already in dangerous territory as it was.

Mike pushed back, resting on his knees above her and seizing the opportunity to take a good, long look. She still had one of the hottest bodies he'd ever seen. Though petite, she was long limbed, her arms and legs sleekly muscled. Her breasts weren't especially large, but just looking at their pink uptilted nipples made him want to howl at the moon. Her belly was flat and tanned, and his mouth went dry as he took in the tan lines at her hips. What was it about tan lines that made a woman look even more naked?

A small tattoo spanned the tan line on her left hip, a tiny frog of some sort. He didn't have time to study it because he was immediately and completely distracted by what lay between her thighs.

He wondered if he'd ever seen anything sexier than her nearly bald pussy. Almost completely denuded of hair, it offered him an unobstructed view of plump lips, saturated with the slickness of her desire. Her clit, red and engorged, peaked through her juicy labia as though begging for attention. *She looks like a porn queen,* he thought as he slid one hand to her belly, inexorably drawn to that wet slit, barely decorated by a downy strip of *blond* curls.

Startled, he looked up into her face, eyebrow raised. She smirked back.

"Don't worry. It's a professional dye job."

A smile tugged at the corners of his mouth, and for God only knew what reason, the thought of Karen, legs spread while applying potentially toxic chemicals to her nether regions, suddenly struck him as devastatingly erotic. Unable to resist the lure, he slid his hand down her belly, over the gleaming flesh, spreading her creamy moisture over the plump lips, finally stopping to rest his thumb over the throbbing pulsebeat of her clit.

She inhaled sharply at the contact, the soft hiss unnaturally loud in the room. He captured her mouth again and pushed two fingers against her slick folds, his thumb moving in teasing circles as he came down over her, resting his weight on one elbow. His fingers dipped just inside the entrance of her body, tormenting her with light thrusts of his fingertips until her hips lifted off the bed and she was moaning into his mouth.

"Mmmm, deeper," she whispered, moving her hand down over his to show him what she wanted.

He tugged out of her grasp and moved his hand up to cup and squeeze her breasts, painting the beaded flesh of her nipples with her own moisture. He licked each nipple in turn, then sucked hard, savoring every last bit of her spicy essence. Karen let out a choked cry, and he swore his cock gained another inch. "God, you taste good." A lick, a suck. Her rich scent teased him, flooded his brain, and he shook with the need to sink his tongue into her slick, hot core. "But I have to have the real thing."

He slid down her body, palms spread on her inner thighs to

pin them open. Her hot, wet sex slid against his belly and chest, and the rich scent of her arousal clouded his brain and drowned out everything but the need to possess.

He hooked his elbows under her knees, spreading her wide, and swallowed convulsively at the sight before him. Pink, slick, shiny with her own juices. He wanted to feast on her all night, but the exquisite friction of the sheets against his cock warned him he might not have much time.

Pausing a moment, he took a deep breath and wrestled his libido back to a manageable level. He had Karen Sullivan writhing under him, completely at his mercy, and he wasn't going to blow it by losing control of himself again.

"Oh God, Mike," she whispered, arching her hips up off the bed.

She wasn't begging yet, but she would soon. He wanted to torture her more, but he couldn't resist the lure of those plump, juicy lips. His head bent, his tongue snaking out to flick the sensitive flesh, and he smiled as she nearly jumped off the bed. She let out a frustrated whine as he softly blew on her clit, her hands fisting into the fabric of the bedspread.

Mike chuckled and grazed his tongue against her clit, running it up one side of the engorged nub and down the other, finally capturing it between his lips to suckle it with a gentle but firm pressure.

She wriggled beneath him, striving for deeper contact, but he stilled her with big hands that nearly spanned her hips. This was his show, they'd move at his speed. His head was full of her, her scent, her taste, her cries, and he grasped for the control threatening to slip away. The heels of those fuck-me shoes dug into his shoulders as she strove to lever herself off the mattress, the pain sending little pulses of sensation to his aching cock.

He warned himself to slow down, intending to torment her further until she was begging him to let her come. But all it took was another thrust of his tongue and her belly tightened, her thighs clamped around his head, and she shuddered, hot juices pouring into his mouth as she came.

He indulged in one last, deep taste, felt her jerk as though electrocuted. He pushed himself up, pleased by the slightly shell-shocked look in her glassy blue eyes.

Christ, he hoped she had condoms on her because he seriously thought he might die if he didn't fuck her right now.

But as soon as his weight eased off her Karen scrambled out from under him and made a beeline for the bathroom. Cursing his slow reflexes, he watched her half-run, half-stagger on her ridiculous heels.

Maybe she'd read his mind and was going to get a condom.

He quickly quashed that notion as the door slammed and the click of the lock being engaged registered in his blood-deprived brain.

"What the fuck?" He pushed himself off the bed and marched determinedly to the bathroom. He heard the shower start. She thought she could come against his mouth and shower off without a word?

No fucking way, he thought as he reached for the doorknob. They weren't done until he said they were done.

Karen managed to unbuckle the flimsy straps of her shoes with shaky hands. After kicking them into a corner with a carelessness that belied their hefty price tag, she turned the shower on full blast, not bothering to wait for the water to heat up before she jumped in.

"What am I doing?" she said. She braced her hands against the tiled wall, shuddering both from the cold and the intensity of the climax she'd just experienced. She thought she had things under control when she'd gone down on him. Men were weak like that, and Karen had learned to exploit that weakness very early in life. But unlike most men, Mike hadn't missed a beat and had instead dragged her off to the bedroom like a caveman bent on ravaging her.

Despite everything that had happened, she'd loved every second of it. No matter how forceful and demanding he got, she knew Mike would never, ever hurt her. Not physically anyway.

She shook her head, sending droplets of water against the wall. Oh Christ, how could she be so stupid? After two years of hard work and therapy, one look at Mike and she was right back where she started. Except with Mike it was worse, because he held a power over her body that no man ever could match.

She was stunned at how quickly she'd come. Tempting though it was, she couldn't use her two-year sexual hiatus as an excuse. For years she'd faked it with her lovers, putting on Academy Award–worthy performances guaranteed to get her lovers off and get them off of her.

With Mike, damn him, there was no need to fake. Things were no different from the first time he'd ever touched her, back when she was eighteen. She still went off like a goddamn rocket and he barely even had to try.

"Get a grip, Karen." She had to salvage this situation. She'd come once, and that had to be a fluke. She would cool off, walk out there like it was no big deal, and . . . *fuck his brains out!* an eager voice all but shouted in her head. *No, you'll kick his ass out, now that you've gotten what you wanted,* the sly, manipulative voice she'd been trying to subdue for the past two years commanded.

Oh, but what she wouldn't give to have his hands on her, feel his amazing cock driving inside her, impossibly hard, impossibly deep.

That's what got you into trouble in the first place, a voice warned. *Wanting Mike too much, losing control and doing stupid, dangerous things.*

But I'm not a stupid teenager anymore. I can handle myself now, keep control of the situation . . .

And tonight is a good example?

The sound of wood cracking and the door banging against the wall startled Karen from her internal debate. Seconds later the shower curtain whipped open, and she couldn't stop herself from trying to hide from Mike's glower.

He smirked as he took in her pose, forearm over her breasts, her other palm pressed protectively between her legs.

"I think we're a little past that, don't you?" He stepped into the stall, dropping a foil packet in the soap dish.

The shower, which was actually quite spacious, suddenly felt cramped. Naked, with water running over the soft mat of dark hair that furred his chest, down the ripples of his abs, and over the jutting hardness of his erection, Mike was pure sex and intimidation.

"I don't know what you were thinking, locking yourself in the bathroom, Karen," he said, pressing her back against the wall and leaning into her. His head bent to capture her earlobe between his teeth. "We're nowhere near finished."

She couldn't keep from rubbing against him as he bent his knees to align their pelvises. Her arms wound up around his neck and she threw herself into the kiss, stroking her tongue into his mouth, enjoying for a moment the sheer pleasure of mouth on mouth, tongue on tongue, skin on skin. Her nails dug into the resilient muscles of his back, and she moaned as his hand slid between her legs, cupping her sex and thrusting a finger deep inside.

"Jesus, you're tight," he murmured.

She tried not to be hurt by the faint note of surprise in his voice. If he only knew how long it had been.

"I know you want to fuck me." His words thrummed through her, in perfect concert with the intoxicating thrust of his thick finger, the gentle grind of his palm against her mound.

She didn't want to tell him yes, didn't want to give him the satisfaction, but she couldn't stop a strangled sound erupting from her throat.

Thankfully, that seemed to be enough, because in seconds he'd sheathed himself and she felt herself being lifted off the floor, the broad head of his cock pressing just inside her soft folds.

And then all she could do was hang on to his shoulders as he slid her down his thick shaft. Her flesh stretched around him, yielding even as she gasped at the sharp pinch of pain. As though sensing her discomfort, he held back, kissing her softly as he stilled, allowing her to adjust before sliding her all the way down until she'd swallowed every inch of him.

She hung there, impaled, pinned against the wall, breath coming in harsh pants as long-unused muscles and tissues struggled to accommodate his massive length. Nerve endings awakened and danced as pain inevitably gave way to excruciating pleasure. Then he was moving, slow and so deep, and she was dying, pressing her clit against the base of his shaft, moaning at the delicious friction of every stroke. Her legs wrapped around his waist and she tried to drive him faster, but to her increasing frustration she couldn't get any leverage.

Suddenly he stilled, leaning into her and holding her immobile against the wall. She thrashed and struggled against him but couldn't dislodge his much-greater weight. Sick bastard that he was, he wouldn't move, just held her there, tormenting her with light kisses on her neck and shoulders and an occasional hard suck on a nipple.

Karen clenched around him as he nipped the beaded flesh, kneading him with her body, trying to seduce him back into the rhythm she needed.

But instead of moving like she craved, Mike pulled out, lifting her up and turning her so she faced away from him. She shivered in anticipation as he tipped her forward to brace her hands against the slick tiles that lined the shower.

Her cry echoed off the tiles when she felt him slide in from behind, filling her almost to bursting as he drove home.

Still he didn't move.

Seething with frustration, Karen tried to work herself against his cock, determined to reach the orgasm that hovered just beyond her reach.

He stopped her with a broad hand against her sacrum. She felt his hot, moist breath in her ear as he bent to whisper, "You be a good girl and hold still, Karen, or I'm not going to let you come."

She stiffened at that, hackles rising at his domineering attitude.

She turned her head to tell him to fuck off, but the words stuck in her throat. His face was set in savage lines, jaw clenched, full lips tight in an expression of pure sexual dominance. Then she saw the removable showerhead in his hand.

A helpless little moan sounded from her lips as he trailed the spray up her leg. Oh, just a few more inches . . .

With an evil chuckle, he bypassed the juncture of her thighs and instead moved the nozzle over her back, around to her belly, and ground himself just a little deeper inside her . . .

Karen held her breath as he allowed just the very edge of the spray to hit her nipple, bringing the already-aroused flesh to screaming awareness. She thrust back against him as her other nipple received the same treatment.

Her back arched and she was literally vibrating around his

cock as the spray slid down her belly and Mike's other hand came up to play with her breasts.

"Mike—"

"Tell me what you want." The spray moved down until it just barely touched her stripe of blond hair.

Karen stood up on tiptoes as she tried to get the water to hit her where she most needed it.

"Tell me," he repeated, running the water across the tops of her thighs, barely skimming her clit. It was just enough to make her clench and shudder around him.

"I need—" The words died at another pass of the spray, and this time he lingered for a split second. "Oh God, I need to come."

"That's it. You want to come so bad you can taste it."

Her only response was another moan as his fingers parted her labia, exposing her clit to the firm pressure of the shower for just a nanosecond before he whipped it away. "But you can't come until I let you." He moved the shower down her leg, then up, over her ass, around to her belly. "Now beg me. Beg me to let you come." His command was matched by a swift withdrawal and thrust, another pass of the spray.

Karen quivered on the edge, looking into the abyss of an orgasm more intense than anything she'd ever experienced. She cursed him silently as her words echoed, firm and clear as she pleaded for release. "Please, Mike," she said, beyond pride, beyond caring, "please make me come. Please."

Her voice cracked as he finally gave her what she wanted. The spray hit her clit and release rippled through her as the tremors started at her core, pulsing through each limb as she shuddered and jerked around his mercifully thrusting cock.

Abruptly he dropped the showerhead and, no longer holding back, pumped inside her with a force that lifted her onto her toes. Her muscles undulated and clenched around his shaft.

She gloried in his deep moan as she felt him swell even bigger inside her.

Sounds of flesh slapping flesh filled the shower as he pounded against her, hands clenched around her hips. "Oh Christ," he moaned, and she felt his thick cock twitch and jerk inside her. He collapsed forward, his hands coming to rest beside hers against the wall.

His heart beat like a trip hammer against her back, and his breath sounded harsh in her ear. She closed her eyes, savoring the sensation of him softening inside her, reveling for a moment in the knowledge that she'd given him an orgasm at least as intense as her own.

He pressed a kiss to her shoulder, a soft, gentle touch that belied his earlier predatory attitude. It was stupid, but suddenly Karen wanted to retreat to the bed with Mike and indulge in the kind of postcoital snugglefest she'd always scorned.

He slipped from her body and exited the shower without a word, and Karen took the opportunity to try to pull herself together.

She toweled herself dry and started a quick repair job on her makeup while she tried to formulate a game plan. *I'm going to walk right out there, fix Mike a drink, and see if he is up for another round*, she thought as she rubbed on moisturizer.

Or maybe she should tell him thanks for the good time, and he should get back to his party.

Or maybe, she thought in a moment of insanity, she could tell him the truth about what had happened that night eleven years ago. Maybe he would believe that she wasn't the awful, amoral person he thought she was.

The way he'd kissed her shoulder there at the end—maybe he did still harbor tender feelings toward her.

She opened the bathroom door and, telling herself she wasn't disappointed that he wasn't stretched out on the bed, moved into the sitting room.

Mike was fully dressed and stepping into his shoes. Her stomach sank even as she painted a bright "I don't give a shit" smile on her face.

"Leaving so soon?"

His smile didn't reach his eyes. "It's been fun reminiscing with you, Karen, but my brothers are going to wonder where I am."

"Don't let me keep you. As far as I'm concerned your work here is done." Her voice sounded huskier than usual around the lump in her throat.

He laughed softly, and for the first time since she'd first seen him at Cleo's, a real smile creased his face. "Ah, Karen, you're such a bitch." He walked over and tipped her chin up, kissing her with a force just this side of brutal. His hazel eyes were glowing when his mouth released hers. "But you're still a great fuck." He paused before he shut the door behind him. "See you at the wedding."

Karen stared at the door for several long moments, his parting words ringing in her ears.

She'd had lots of men tell her she was a great fuck, that she did amazing things with her hands and mouth. She couldn't remember a time that she hadn't used it as an advantage, a time when those words hadn't given her at least a little boost to her ego.

Ever since she'd given Josh Thompson a hand job her sophomore year and realized he'd do anything she wanted if she hinted she might go a little farther, she'd embraced her power over the male of the species. Of course, Josh had gone and told everyone that she had gone all the way, and pretty soon most of the boys at North Tahoe High School nearly rang her phone off the hook. She never went all the way with any of them either, and she soon discovered that they were all just as satisfied to get off in her hand or her mouth as they were in her body.

No one ever wanted to come forward and admit that *he* was the one guy Karen wouldn't have sex with, so as far as the school was concerned, if you went on a date with Karen, you fucked her.

She didn't bother dispelling the rumors, because it meant she was able to distinguish herself dramatically from her sister, the town genius. In her own screwed-up teenage logic she had been happier to be known as a slut than the geek's dumber sister.

In the meantime, she'd enjoyed the attention and waited for someone who really curled her toes.

Mike.

With other boys, she'd kept a certain objective distance, took pride in her ability to lead them around by their dicks. But not Mike. She'd never been able to lead him anywhere, and things now were clearly no different.

Tears poured down her cheeks, and Karen tried to wipe them away, but they flowed as though from a faucet.

Oh, you showed him who was in charge, all right. So much for her plan to bring him to his knees, prove how much he wanted her even if he didn't like her. All she'd managed to do was prove to herself that a man didn't have to like her to fuck her senseless. And that Mike still had the power to make her weak. To make her beg.

Her stomach squirmed as she heard her own voice echoing in the shower. "Please, Mike . . ."

Please, Mike . . .

Just like that night, eleven years ago, when she'd begged for his love, his understanding. Then, as now, he'd turned away, the look in his eyes telling her she was dirt.

Woodenly she pulled on a T-shirt and sweats, wincing a bit at the unfamiliar pull of muscles that hadn't seen action for a good long time. It was so quiet, and she was so alone; if not for the physical reminders she could almost pretend this had never happened.

She sighed and flopped back onto the bed. *I am a complete fucking idiot.*

Mike had always been in charge of every situation, and that hadn't changed even if she was older and more experienced. Even at the age of twenty-one, he'd seemed ages ahead of her eighteen. His strength, his maturity, on top of his outrageously macho good looks, had compelled her to chase him down in the first place.

She'd known him practically her entire life, but it wasn't until he'd showed up at her eighteenth birthday party with his brother Tony that she'd really noticed him. Home from UC Davis on summer vacation, he'd looked bored, as though he thought himself superior to the mostly just-graduated-from-high-school crowd. Like his brothers, he was big and dark, all rippling muscles and dark olive skin. Karen had viewed it as her personal mission to make sure he had a good time.

Much to the dismay of her date, Karen had ridden off that night in the passenger seat of Mike's Bronco, where she'd experienced her first orgasm at the tip of his tongue.

He'd been surprised to find her a virgin. She couldn't fault him since everyone knew everything in their small town, but for the first time, she'd felt the faintest twinge of regret over her reputation.

She'd fallen in love with him almost instantly. She never knew if it was because he was the first guy she couldn't manipulate, the first guy to make her come, or thanks to the influence of the romance novels she loved to read, but she'd formed an unreasonable attachment to the first guy she'd ever gone all the way with.

Or maybe it was because he was the first guy who, even after he'd gotten what he wanted from her, actually seemed interested in something other than sex.

He hadn't been ashamed about making their relationship known, hadn't cared that the other guys might be whispering about what *they'd* done with her. Mike didn't give a shit. Besides, of all of them, he'd known the truth.

She'd been crazy that summer, chasing him around, barely willing to let him out of her sight. She still cringed at the memory of how desperate she'd been for his touch. And his love.

She'd thrown herself headlong into their relationship, telling him she loved him after about a week, and after that several times a day. Each time he'd looked touched, tender, and on a couple of occasions she could have sworn it was on the tip of his tongue to say it back to her.

As the summer wore on, she'd grown more desperate, willing to do anything to capture and hold his attention. When they were alone, she'd tried to be the hottest, most obliging lover he'd ever had. When they were out, she'd amped up her already sexually charged image to make sure that all attention, especially Mike's, was on her.

Yet, instead of drawing him out and getting him to say what she needed to hear—that he loved her too and saw this as more than just a summer fling—he'd grown distant.

It was as she always feared. A guy had finally taken the time to get to know her and in the end realized he didn't like her at all.

Suddenly he'd become like all the other guys. He hadn't wanted to talk, hadn't wanted to discuss what would happen when he returned to Davis. All he'd wanted was sex. Oddly, it hadn't been selfish sex, like he'd just wanted to get off. Instead, he'd delighted in lingering over her for hours, as though her orgasms were more satisfying than his own. Almost, anyway. He was, after all, a guy.

He made her beg then, as he had tonight.

Then it had all gone to hell. Memories bombarded Karen's brain. Memories she didn't want to relive, images that made her hate herself, hate Mike, hate the world with such keen intensity it was as though no time had passed.

It was August, and Mike had announced he was leaving a week early for school. The only explanation he'd offered was "There's a problem with our apartment, and we have to get back early."

Karen was already irritated that Mike had invited his roommate from school, Jeremy, up for a visit. Now Mike was leaving a week earlier than planned. Worse, when she'd asked Jeremy about the apartment, he hadn't known what she was talking about.

That night Mike had told her he and Jeremy were going to hit the bars in Truckee, and it was clear she wasn't invited. She had decided to go to a party on the lake with her friend Kit. No way would she sit home alone waiting for Mike to sneak into her bedroom.

Karen felt a fresh, sharp pain as she remembered seeing Mike at the party. He'd been smiling down at some brunette, teeth white against his tan face, biceps bulging out of the cotton sleeves of his T-shirt.

In her jealous fury, it hadn't even occurred to her to talk to him. All she'd wanted was to get back at him. To make him feel some tiny bit of the pain she was feeling, even if it was only his pride that was hurt.

So she'd made a big entrance, greeting everyone loudly, doing a little bump and grind on the dance floor until she was sure Mike had seen her. Then she'd found Jeremy and proceeded to get her revenge.

Except she'd chosen poorly. She'd only meant to flirt a little, bat her eyelashes, maybe a dirty dance or two, just enough to incite Mike's jealousy so he'd whisk her away.

But it was Jeremy who had whisked her away. Or dragged her off to one of the bedrooms was more like it. Jeremy didn't like to be teased, and he didn't like girls messing around with his friends. And he'd viewed it as his duty to teach Karen a lesson.

Jeremy wasn't as big as Mike, but at 5'3" and not much over a hundred and ten pounds, she hadn't been able to put up much of a fight.

Bile rose in Karen's throat as she remembered the reek of beer on his breath, his stubby fingers with their chewed-up nails pawing at her breasts and shoving inside of her. Her skin still crawled, and she rolled over on the bed, remembering the tearing, the burning pain of him forcing himself inside her, his sweaty palm over her mouth to muffle her screams.

Then Mike's face as she'd stumbled out of the room, the look of disgust that had made her want to die on the spot.

"Mike, please," she said.

Jeremy had been right behind her, Karen's bra dangling from his fingertips. "Sorry, man, she couldn't keep her hands off me."

"Mike, please," she said again. "You have to listen. He—"

"I should have known," he cut her off. "I should have listened to what everyone said about you."

She remembered staggering toward him, hand out as she clutched at his arm like a lifeline.

He'd shaken her off like a gnat. The expression on his face said she was lower than an insect. She was filth. She was dirt.

Without another word, he'd turned his back on her sobbing pleas.

At that moment everything had shattered inside her. To this day, she still didn't know what had scarred her more, the horrific feeling of powerlessness and violation or the knowledge that Mike had never loved her. That he'd thought so little of her, he wouldn't even entertain her explanations. As far as he was concerned, she was the slut everyone called her.

The worst part was that she had believed it herself.

4

Eleven years later, the unclean feeling had finally ebbed, but now renewed anger and guilt were sharp in her chest. Fury at Jeremy for thinking he had the right to hurt her, to teach her a lesson. Anger at Mike for not even bothering to listen, for having so little faith in her that he hadn't realized how badly she was hurt.

And guilt that she'd let her feelings of insecurity drive her to put herself in such a vulnerable position.

She'd thought she was over it, that with the endless hours of therapy she'd finally managed to put the past where it belonged and forgive the stupid, naïve teenager she'd been. Thought herself ready to move on and develop a happy, healthy relationship with a nice guy who really would love her for the wonderful person she was.

She shouldn't care what Mike thought of her. It shouldn't matter that he thought of her as a slut, the kind of woman who slept with one guy to get back at another. The kind of woman who would cheat.

Even though he'd ultimately taken over tonight, as far as he was concerned, she'd used him in her revenge on some poor unsuspecting sap who had fallen prey to her wiles.

It shouldn't matter, but it did. Obviously, dealing with issues in the therapist's office was one thing. Facing them and the people involved head on was quite another. Instead of trying to have a constructive conversation with Mike, she'd slipped right back into her old habits the minute she sensed a threat.

She remembered her mother's words on her deathbed, telling Karen how much she loved her, and in the same breath how disappointed she was in the person Karen had become.

Manipulative. Cold. "Not a nice girl," as her mother had put it. And that wasn't even a critique on her sex life.

Karen had made a lot of mistakes. A lot of bad choices. Her mother's death had finally forced her to confront and own up to them. Now she had to face the fact that a lot of people—herself, Mike, and her family included—had fallen victim to her bone-deep belief that no one would ever really love her. Making things right with them was going to be even harder than she'd feared.

Long-suppressed sobs tore from her chest as she ground the heels of her hands against her eyes. She hated feeling like this, hated knowing that Mike couldn't stand her.

If only he'd been a little nicer to her.

No, this was her fault. She'd chosen to counter Mike's barbs with her super-seductress routine. She'd had the opportunity to act different, to be different, and instead she'd slipped right back into her old tricks the moment she felt threatened.

Now she mentally castigated herself for not making the slightest effort to tell the truth that was now burning a hole in her gut.

She picked up the phone.

Kit answered on the third ring. "'Lo?"

"It's me."

"Kar? It's—"

Karen looked at the clock and winced. "One-thirty. Shit, I'm sorry."

"No, it's cool. I was up late working anyway since Jake's in Reno for the bachelor party."

Karen smiled. Kit, her best friend from high school, had such a different life from her own. Last year she got engaged to Jake Donovan and had moved to Boston, and her first book was coming out early next year.

"Oh yeah, I forgot he was here too," Karen said.

Kit was absolutely silent for several seconds, then, "What do you mean , 'too?' Where are you?"

Karen picked nervously at a chip in her nail polish. "Kit, I did something really dumb."

"You slept with Brad?"

"No," she replied. "But why would that be stupid? You knew I was going away with him."

"Yeah, but a girl can hope. Brad always sounded like a total tool. Where are you?" she repeated.

"Brad and I had a fight, and I'm staying here—look, Brad has nothing to do with this."

"Then what?

"I ran into Mike Donovan tonight."

"Oh no."

"Oh yes."

"Did you *talk* to him?" Kit asked hopefully.

"Not really. I slept with him."

"You dumb bitch."

Karen winced. Kit's direct, no-nonsense manner was what she had loved about her from the first day they met. Kit had moved to Donner Lake their sophomore year and had started dating Rick Crawford over the summer. Apparently she'd heard about Karen's reputation, because the first day of school when they met in the bathroom, she'd introduced herself to Karen in the most pleasant manner, then calmly informed her that if she went anywhere near her boyfriend, Kit would cut her tits off.

Karen had believed her, and in that moment developed an intense same-sex crush that had grown into a friendship that had lasted nearly fifteen years. Karen had nursed Kit through her own traumatic encounter with a Donovan brother. Karen was struck again by the difference in their circumstances. While Kit's long-ago disastrous fling with Jake had resulted in a happily ever after twelve years later, somehow Karen didn't think Mike was going to show up on her doorstep with a ring anytime soon.

But sometimes she wished Kit's softer, more nurturing side was a little closer to the surface. Still, she had a point.

"Yeah, I know."

"How could you let this happen?"

"I don't know. He was there, and he's so gorgeous, but he's still so angry, and I—"

"You wanted to prove that even if you couldn't make him like you, you could make him want you?"

Ah, the blessing and the curse of having a best friend who knew her so well.

"Bingo."

"I hope it was good," Kit said.

"It was . . . intense." Gushing warmth flooded her belly as she remembered just how intense it was. She wasn't about to divulge the details to Kit. Her stomach clenched at his last words. *You're still such a bitch.* "But he still thinks I'm scum, and I hate it." Her voice broke on a sob.

"Karen, honey." Kit's voice immediately softened. "We've talked about this. You have to come clean with him. It's eating you up inside." Karen nodded, even though Kit couldn't see her.

Kit was right, of course. Just as her therapist was right. She couldn't change the past. She could only control how she behaved going forward. But to move past it she needed to set the record straight and give the people she'd hurt the chance to forgive her.

"Here's the deal," Kit said. "Kelly's wedding is in two weeks. Mike will be there. You can talk to him then. And talk to Kelly while you're at it."

"I don't even know if she wants me there. She only invited me because it would look weird if she didn't," Karen said sullenly. She cursed as she picked another chunk of polish off her toenail. Now she'd have to redo her pedicure.

Kit sighed, and Karen could practically hear her roll her eyes. "Now that's a very evolved and enlightened attitude. And you're probably right. I bet Kelly doesn't give a shit if you show up or not."

"Don't pull any punches," Karen snapped.

"Karen, we both know the truth. But we also know that avoiding Kelly's wedding will not get you off to a good start if you want to salvage your relationship with her. Just like you're going to keep feeling like shit as long as you know that Mike is out there thinking you cheated on him."

"What if he doesn't believe me?"

"He may not. Just like Kelly might not accept your belated overtures of sisterly love. But you can't control that. You can only control what you do. Just be honest and direct and hope it works out."

"But what if it's not enough?"

"It has to be enough for you that you tried."

"Thanks, Dr. Phil," Karen said. "You're right. But old habits die hard."

"Yeah, but your old habits didn't bring you much happiness, did they?"

"This better not end up in your next column," Karen sniffed. In addition to her upcoming book, Kit wrote a sex and lifestyle advice column for *Bella* magazine, and she wasn't above looking to her own life for inspiration.

Kit laughed softly. "You and Jake are so paranoid!"

"Yeah, only because we appear like every other month."

"Don't worry. If I write about you, I'll be sure to make you completely unrecognizable."

Karen said good night and flopped back on the bed.

No, her old habits hadn't brought her much happiness. She'd learned to use her looks to get almost anything in life, but she never believed that anyone—except maybe Kit—ever really liked her. For a long time she hadn't even liked herself.

Mike—she thought—for a brief time, he had liked her. She was sure of it.

Two weeks, she thought, wrapping her arms around her knees and rocking a little on the king-size bed. Two weeks to figure out how to apologize to Kelly for a lifetime of being a terrible sister. Two weeks to muster up the courage to tell Mike the truth about what happened that night. And pray that in that time she would grow a thick-enough hide to survive their likely rejection.

"Lauren, what the fuck are you doing here? You're supposed to be over at the Hillside place finishing the railing," Mike yelled as he got out of the truck. He slammed the door and stomped over to Lauren MacLean, the carpenter they'd hired after Nick moved to San Francisco.

Lauren froze, nail gun in hand, as she prepared to attach siding to the house Donovan Brothers was building in an exclusive gated community.

Mike glared down into Lauren's sweat-streaked face. "I told you we need to get that railing done by the end of the day today so we can start working on the deck!"

Before Lauren could answer, a big hand gripped hard on his right shoulder. "Mike, lay off her, okay?" Mike turned to meet his younger brother Tony's glare.

"Look, I told her to get over to Hillside and—"

"And I left you a message that the materials weren't going to be in until Monday so I called her over here."

Mike looked down at his cell phone. Sure enough, the screen indicated he had a new voice mail. Shit.

"I think you owe Lauren an apology," Tony said.

Tony's condescending tone set him off again. He thumped Tony hard with two fingers to the chest. "From now on, don't reassign people. You may be my brother but I'm the boss, and I decide how to prioritize our schedule."

"Is that so? Last time I looked the name was Donovan *Brothers*—"

Mike pushed Tony's shoulder, hard. "Don't start with me, Tony—"

Tony pushed him back, sending Mike back a couple of steps. "You don't want me to start? Don't come out here yelling at Lauren like she doesn't know her ass from her hammer—"

That was it. Mike charged Tony. The tension, the fury that had been boiling in his gut finally erupted. He'd been wanting to pound his fists into someone for two weeks, and now he had his chance.

They grappled like Greco-Roman wrestlers, staggering around the work site as each tried to knock the other down and get the upper hand.

Suddenly Mike felt something—or someone—attach to his back, accompanied by a harsh female voice blasting in his right ear. "CUT IT OUT." Arms wrapped around his neck, a feminine hand splayed against Tony's face, and a foot lodged against his chest as Lauren tried to pry them apart. "Stop it right now, you two."

Tony broke free first and stepped back. But his stance was still poised, aggressive, as though ready to charge at the first provocation.

"You can get off me, Lauren," Mike said. Or rather croaked, as Lauren's strong forearm was still clamped across his throat.

"Not until you promise to ease off."

"I will if he will." Mike indicated Tony with his chin.

Tony threw up his hands. "I will if he stops being an asshole."

Lauren slid off Mike's back and came around to stand between them. "I don't know what's up with you two lately. You," she whirled on Mike, "have been acting like you never got over the hangover from Nick's bachelor party."

"Yeah," Tony said. "You've been acting like a dick."

"And you," Lauren said, a virago in a tank top and jeans as she turned on Tony, "have been baiting him at every opportunity. Now I know it's hard for you, being men and all," she said with a derisive sneer, "but why don't you two work this out like adults so the rest of us can get some work done."

She picked up her nail gun and went back to work. Thankfully, the rest of the crew followed her example.

"She's right," Tony spoke first. "You've been totally wacked ever since Nick's bachelor party, and that's just not like you."

Mike looked sheepishly at Tony. He'd been an unreasonable prick ever since that night with Karen. No question, they had a lot to get done as this was the busiest part of the year. But that didn't excuse how hard he'd been riding Tony, Lauren, and the rest of his crew.

He, who prided himself on being unemotional, who always kept his cool and rarely let anything get to him, was a tangled mess inside for the second time in his life.

And once again it was because of Karen Sullivan.

If he could have beaten the crap out of himself, he would have. That was how pissed he was for not just walking out of that bar and running like a vampire from garlic.

He couldn't get her out of his head. Her scent. Her taste. How it felt to be buried to the hilt inside her slick, tight pussy. The sounds she made when she came, shuddering and completely out of control.

He wanted to scrub his mind clean of her.

He wanted to savor every vivid memory.

He was as shaken now as he'd been that night when he'd left her with nothing but harsh words and a harsher kiss.

She was driving him crazy. Again.

"Come on, man, why don't you tell me what's going on?" Tony said in a much calmer tone. That was Tony. Quick on the trigger but equally quick to calm down.

Mike and Tony walked back to his truck and Mike pulled two sodas out of the cooler he kept in the cab.

Mike unlatched the tailgate so they could sit. "You know that night at Caesar's?"

"When you went AWOL?"

"Yeah." Mike paused, took a sip. "I ran into Karen Sullivan on the way back to the club."

"You didn't—"

Mike nodded, mouth set in a tight line.

Tony shook his head as though trying to make it not so. "Oh man. She is bad news."

Like he needed Tony to tell him that. Mike was silent, staring off into the grove of redwoods that abutted the property. "I don't know what it is about her," he said finally. "It's like I get close to her and I can't control myself."

"She always led guys around by their dicks," Tony pointed out, "even back when you dated her."

"Yeah, I know. But I fooled myself into thinking I was different." He shook his head ruefully.

"Why would you ever think that?" Tony scoffed.

"She was different around me. She had a really warm, funny side she didn't show much. And in spite of all the rumors, she was a virgin when we started dating." He couldn't believe he was defending her.

Tony's eyes opened wide in surprise.

"I know, I was shocked too." He still remembered that first night. The look of surprised delight on her face when she came all over his hand. How hot and impossibly tight she'd felt around him, and the sharp cry of pain he couldn't mistake. "It's okay," she'd whispered against his lips as he'd frozen, mid-thrust, his shock palpable. "I want this, I want it with you."

"I managed to convince myself that the bitch goddess seductress thing was just an act."

"I guess the bitch goddess was the real thing. After all, she did cheat on you with your best friend."

Even after all this time, the memory of that speared him straight in the gut.

He'd fallen hard, convinced himself he knew the real Karen. The sweet, surprisingly smart, wickedly funny girl he spent two blissful months with. Not the manipulative, flashy sexpot the rest of the world saw.

He'd loved her so much it had scared the shit out of him. So much so that when she told him she loved him, he'd never let himself say it back. Never in his life had he thought himself a coward, but he'd been one with her. At twenty-one, he hadn't been prepared for love, for what it meant. He hadn't been ready to commit to one person for the rest of his life. Shit, at the beginning of that summer, before he and Karen had hooked up, he hadn't been ready to commit to someone for more than a couple of weeks. As much as he'd loved her, he hadn't been able to override the fear that drove him to push her away.

Mingled with the fear had been unease. As much as he had loved her, Mike wasn't one to be ruled by his heart or his dick, and he'd known Karen had a reputation. She may have been a virgin, but she'd known her way around a guy's body. He'd seen how she worked, seen how she had tried to work him. Even though he knew it was insecurity that drove her, it was so ingrained it had become instinct. And Mike hated to be manipulated.

His friend, Jeremy, had summed up Mike's fears perfectly that night at the bar in Truckee. "Mike, when you get back to school, you're going to have pussy coming out of your pockets. Do you really want to give that up for someone like her? No offense, man, but as soon as you're gone, she'll be on someone else faster than shit through a goose."

Jeremy. The bastard had decided to prove his own point later that night by going off to a bedroom and fucking Karen. Images and emotions from that night assaulted him. The joy he'd felt when he saw her across the room, followed almost immediately by the panic he'd come to feel every time he looked into her gorgeous blue eyes so full of love and expectations he wasn't sure he was ready to meet.

Then anger when she'd started to flirt with Jeremy. Mike had refused to take the bait, knowing she just wanted to make him jealous. She'd been insecure about him, and she'd had every right to be, given his distant behavior. He'd vowed to take her out the next day, really talk to her for the first time in what felt like weeks, straighten everything out.

Despite what Jeremy said, despite his own fear, he hadn't wanted to lose Karen. He'd loved her. And scared shitless or not, he'd known he needed to stop running from it.

But then he'd gone to get a beer, and when he came back, both Karen and Jeremy were gone. When he asked, he was told they went upstairs.

"I still can't believe they did that," Mike said, trying to force the distasteful images from his mind. Tony laid a comforting hand on his shoulder. His stomach clenched, just as it had then as he'd walked down the hall. He'd heard the unmistakable sounds—bedsprings creaking, muted grunts—coming through the slightly ajar door to one of the bedrooms. He'd peeked through the cracks. All he'd seen was Jeremy's torso, a woman's long, tan legs spread under him. Tiny feet with the ridiculous platform shoes he'd teased Karen about that very afternoon.

The rest of that night was a blur. He remembered Jeremy's face, smug and self-congratulatory. Karen's a mask of guilt as she grabbed his arm and begged him to listen. As though she could possibly explain.

"At least you beat the crap out of him," Tony said. "Did he ever manage to get his teeth fixed?"

Mike smiled grimly. He could still remember the satisfaction of Jeremy's face crunching under his fist, the primal pleasure he'd received at Jeremy's new snaggle-toothed smile. "I think so. I didn't keep in touch after that."

He smashed his empty soda can. "I can't believe she still gets to me like she does," he ground out, slamming his fist against the tailgate. "You'd think after all this time I would be over it. Goddamn her, she's still fucking with my head after eleven years."

Tony was quiet, knowing that Mike's tirade didn't require commentary. Mike didn't often lose his cool, and his brothers had long ago learned to listen quietly as he got it all out. After several moments Tony said, "You know she's probably going to be at the wedding tomorrow. What are you going to do?"

Mike laughed humorlessly. "Avoid her like the plague."
Right. As though that would be possible.

"Smart move," Tony nodded soberly.

"Or drag her off and fuck her out of my system." But that
might take another twenty years.

Tony laughed. "I know what I'd do."

Mike snorted. "Yeah, I know what you'd do. But then, you're
a freakin' menace." Tony's idea of a long-term relationship was
having sex with the same woman more than once. He didn't
allow his feelings to get so complicated.

As a rule, Mike didn't either. Sex was something he enjoyed
a lot, and he liked having it regularly. His usual pattern was to
date a woman for a while, always clear about his intentions or
lack thereof. Within a few weeks, sometimes a couple months,
inevitably whomever he was seeing would want to take their
relationship to "the next level." Mike never had any problems
cutting it off, had never been emotionally engaged enough to
even be tempted to move to any level beyond friends who fuck.
And he never, ever, let his dick overrule his brain when he
sensed a woman might be more trouble than she was worth.

His sharp laugh caught Tony's attention. "It figures," he
said. "The only woman who can twist me in knots is the one I
let screw me over."

"Yeah. Too bad Nick got the nice Sullivan sister."

5

Karen paced outside of Kelly's dressing room as she waited for the last of the bridesmaids to leave. Given their relationship, Karen wasn't surprised when Kelly didn't ask her to be a bridesmaid. Still, she was a little sad. She knew her mother would have wanted them to resolve their differences before now and would have wanted the sisters to play bigger roles in each other's lives.

It was on Karen's shoulders to make the first move, and here she was. Better late than never.

The ceremony was in ten minutes, and this was supposed to be Kelly's time alone to compose herself. Karen didn't want to intrude, but she didn't have much choice. She had tried to schedule drinks Thursday night, here at the Plumpjack resort, but Kelly had too many last-minute details to handle. Breakfast and lunch yesterday were booked, and of course last night was the rehearsal dinner.

Even if Karen had been able to get Kelly alone, she'd been so distracted by Mike she wouldn't have been able to focus enough to say what she needed to say.

Karen couldn't blame Kelly for avoiding her. She couldn't remember a single conversation in their lives that hadn't ended in an argument.

Kit suddenly appeared by her side and grabbed her in a quick hug. "It's all going to be fine. Just get in there and say what you need to say." Karen returned her friend's embrace and stepped back and looked into Kit's encouraging gray eyes. Jake stood next to her, looking hunky in his tuxedo, demonstrating yet again that all the Donovans were put on this earth to be ogled. He regarded Karen with wary friendliness, which was a nice break from the hostility Karen had expected. As far as she knew, all of the Donovans still saw her as that little bitch who had screwed Mike over.

An unpleasant thought reared its ugly head, and she tugged Kit out of Jake's hearing range. "You didn't tell Jake, did you? About what really happened?" She wasn't ashamed or embarrassed, exactly, but she wanted to tell Mike first, in her own time, before his brothers found out.

"No," Kit said. "I only told him that it didn't exactly happen the way he heard and he should cut you some slack."

Karen let out a sigh of relief and squeezed Kit's hand gratefully. Kit leaned down and brushed a kiss across her cheek. "Remember, you can only control what you do." Kit and Jake left Karen standing outside Kelly's room.

Karen squared her shoulders, waiting for Kelly's attendants to leave. She squeezed her fist, the diamond pendant she held pressing into her palm.

Finally the last of the bridesmaids three—Jenna, Jenny?—something like that—emerged. Even as Karen allowed herself the faintest regret that she wasn't in her sister's wedding, she consoled herself with the fact that she looked putrid in that particular shade of lilac.

Mike and Tony came around the corner just as she reached for the doorknob. Both eyed her warily.

Mike looked delicious in his tux, immediately reminding Karen of how good he looked out of it. His suspicious glare was the only thing that prevented her from melting into a puddle right there on the hardwood floor. She glared back. "Don't worry, I'm not going to splash red paint on her dress or anything." God, was it too much to ask that someone had a little faith in her better nature?

"If you do anything to upset her, Karen, I swear—" Mike let his threat trail off.

"Or what, you'll spank me?" She couldn't help taunting him.

Tony glared at her, arms folded over his massive chest like an angry bouncer.

She shook her head and let out an exasperated sigh. "Look you two, I want to give Karen my mom's necklace, that's it."

"Let me see it," Mike said.

"You want to frisk me too?" Karen snapped, gratified at the involuntary glint of interest in Mike's hazel gaze. Karen thrust the necklace into his face.

Tony observed them warily, as though scenting tension and attraction.

"If you hear any screams, you have my permission to raid the premises."

She turned her back and opened the door before they could stop her.

Kelly turned.

Karen gasped. "Kelly, you look gorgeous," she breathed.

Kelly stared at her as though she'd grown a third boob.

Not surprising, since Karen hadn't said anything that nice to Kelly . . . well, ever.

"I mean it, Kel, you're a groom's wet dream." Kelly's sleeveless dress hugged her torso like a glove, playing up her enviably full bust and narrow waist before falling into a simple A-line skirt that just brushed the floor. "You look so elegant and sexy." She ran her gaze up and down again, pausing at Kelly's deep cleavage framed by the sweetheart neckline. "I can't believe you got all the brains *and* all the boobs."

Kelly started to laugh, then caught herself, eyeing Karen warily, poised for the customary attack. "What are you doing here, Karen? I'm getting married in ten minutes, and I really don't want to get into it with you right now."

Karen held up a palm. "I know, and that's not what I'm here for. I have something to give you, and I promise I'll leave." She held out the hand with the necklace where Kelly could see.

"Mom's necklace," Kelly said, unconsciously touching the matching bracelet already clasped around her right wrist.

"Here, let me," Karen said, reaching up and around Kelly's neck, careful not to mess up Kelly's veil as she fastened the two-carat solitaire pendant around her neck. "You probably already have something borrowed, but I know Mom would want you to wear it."

From behind her, Karen caught their reflection in the full-length mirror. Tears shimmered in Kelly's eyes. "I don't know what to say. Thank you."

Karen closed her eyes as warmth rushed through her. Amazing, she thought wryly, how good being nice felt. But she wasn't finished yet. She licked dry lips and tried to remember what she'd planned to say. "Look, Kelly," she began, stomach clenched in knots. *How come no one ever said how hard it was to apologize?* "I know I haven't been the best sister." She saw Kelly's eyes widen in the mirror. The wary look was back as Kelly turned to face her. "Okay, I've been a really shitty sister." Her palms were sweaty, and she fought the urge to wipe them on the chiffon fabric of her dress. "I know this is too little, too late, but I just want you to know that I love you, Kelly."

Kelly shook her head and actually glanced behind her shoulder, as though waiting for Ashton Kutcher to tell her she was being punk'd.

"I mean it. I love you, and I'm really happy for you. Nick is a great guy, and I know he'll treat you well."

"Karen, are you okay? You're not, like, sick or anything? Stanford's a great hospital and we have top specialists—"

Karen laughed. "It's okay, Doctor, I'm not terminal. Someday I'll tell you all about Mom, therapy, and figuring out what's important, but today you have to get married."

"I'm going to hold you to that," Kelly said, still completely weirded out. She glanced up at the clock again. "Guess I better get out there."

Karen smiled. "Guess you better."

Karen held the door as Kelly walked out of the dressing room and chuckled to see Mike and Tony still out there on security detail. "Your guard dogs," she muttered to Kelly. "See guys? All in one piece. No tears, scratches, or mussed hairdo." She turned back to Kelly. "Be happy."

Kelly reached out to hug her, but Karen held her away. "I don't want to muss you," she quickly reassured her when she saw the flash of rejection in Kelly's face. Karen leaned up on tiptoe and pressed a kiss to her sister's cheek, and turned to find her father standing with Mike and Tony. After shaking Ryan Sullivan's hand, Tony left to take his place beside Nick, but Mike lingered.

"Ready to go?" her father asked Kelly. She nodded and took his proffered arm. As they walked down the hall, both looked back, pleasantly bewildered.

Karen started to follow them so she could take her seat before the ceremony began but was stopped by Mike's firm grip on her forearm. She could practically hear her skin sizzle at the contact, sending heat spiraling through her limbs. Memories, hot and vibrant, sprang into her head.

Mike, hard and thick against her tongue as she sucked him. His lips and tongue buried between her thighs, savoring her wet, juicy sex and making her come like no one ever could. Her eyes drifted shut at the remembered feel of him driving, thrusting, so deep inside her, taunting her, making her beg.

She shook her head, forcing down the temptation to pull him into the dressing room. She could not give in to him—or herself—again. Couldn't fall back into that trap, no matter how much she wanted him.

For two weeks, she'd tried to put their encounter out of her head, instead focusing on the best way to approach Mike and get him to listen to the truth. But all it took was one touch and she was about to fall apart. Again.

"What are you up to, Karen?"

"Let go of me please," she said quietly.

He didn't. "Your entire life you've been nothing but mean to your sister, and suddenly you're friends? I don't buy it."

She wrenched her arm from his grip. A snappy remark was on the tip of her tongue. Instead she said, "People change, Mike. Even me."

His scornful gaze raked her from the top of her tousled curls to the tips of her pink polished toes. "Two weeks ago being an example?"

Heat bloomed in her cheeks and hurt clenched in her chest, followed quickly by anger. "Fuck you, Mike."

He opened his mouth, but before he could reply, Nick poked his head around the corner and indicated with an impatient gesture for Mike to get his ass out to the altar.

Karen followed them out onto the lawn and took her seat next to Kit. Nick and his brothers stood waiting at the altar, the all of them looking like an advertisement for gorgeous male escorts. The harpist plucked out the first bars of the wedding march, and everyone stood to watch Kelly walk down the aisle.

She really does look like an angel, Karen thought, surprised at the sentimental turn of her thoughts. Behind the gossamer-thin veil Kelly's blue eyes sparkled with happiness and her lips trembled even as she smiled.

Never in her wildest dreams had Karen imagined that her best friend and her little sister would end up with Jake and Nick Donovan. The world was so strange.

Karen looked up at the altar and sucked in her breath when she saw Nick. He fairly glowed as he looked at Kelly, all the love in the universe right there on his face.

Karen closed her eyes. What would it feel like to have a man look at her like that?

She looked at Mike, her gaze drawn like a magnet to steel. He stared at her, but there was no love in his expression.

She watched him, her building anger distracting her from the beauty of the ceremony.

She hadn't been alone in that suite two weeks ago, and for Mike to try to make her feel trashy about it was completely unfair.

So much for her plans for an amicable discussion. Karen was almost tempted to abandon her plan to tell Mike the truth.

No, she thought. She needed to. She knew, deep in her bones, that she would feel better to have the secret out, have it purged from her system. For eleven years she'd carried this burden of shame and self-disgust, and Mike's abandonment of her had only compounded it. He shouldn't be allowed to bask in self-righteous anger over her perceived sins. It was time he knew the truth, so she could finally move on.

She focused again on Mike to find him still staring at her. His expression certainly wasn't loving, but it wasn't hostile either. He seemed to be studying her, trying to figure her out. She stared him down. She confused him. Good. She hoped he was thrown off by what happened two weeks ago and befuddled by her behavior today. About time someone challenged his assumptions. Maybe he would finally realize how wrong he'd been about her all along.

Five minutes after Karen got to the reception, she was ready to leave. She'd been grateful that she'd only been required to stand for three quick photos, especially when the photographer stood her in front of Mike.

"Hey, big guy, put your hand on the little blonde's shoulder. You're all family here. Make it look friendly."

She glanced down at her shoulder, bare except for the thin spaghetti strap holding her dress up. Shockingly, no brand or burn mark had appeared. She could still feel the imprint of Mike's hand on her bare skin, the gentle stroke of his callused thumb making circles along her shoulder blade. She'd turned to look at him but he stared straight ahead, as though unaware of his caresses.

Anxious to get away and numb her nerves with some champagne, Karen made a beeline for the bar.

She took her glass, drank a hefty swallow, and looked around.

Objectively, she readily admitted that they had put together a gorgeous party. But then, it *was* Plumpjack, one of the nicest resorts in Squaw Valley. Tables were set around the pool deck. Waiters passed hors d'oeuvres like prosciutto-wrapped figs and smoked trout canapés, while a lavish seafood buffet awaited the arrival of the bride and groom.

No, the party itself wasn't the problem. Rather, it was the guest list. Karen hadn't looked around much at the ceremony, focused as she was on Mike, but now she recognized several faces, male and female, from her high school.

She scanned the crowd for Kit and saw her talking to Maria

Donovan. No way was she going to bust in on that conversation. Earlier, when Karen had tried to congratulate her on her son's marriage, Maria had looked through Karen as though she didn't exist.

Karen straightened her shoulders and walked over to the nearest empty table. At least Kelly had foregone assigned seats so Karen wouldn't be forced to share a table with, say, Katie Hossford, who glared at Karen and clenched a chicken skewer in a manner that had Karen worried for her eyesight.

She sat for several minutes watching the guests with feigned casualness. Used to being the life of any party, Karen's pride was pricked when no one sat with her even as the tables began to fill up. After a bit, she couldn't help but be amused. Several men, some she knew and some she didn't, smiled at her and made as though to come join her. All were quickly herded away by wives and girlfriends nipping at their heels.

She would stay through the first dance, and then she was getting the hell out of there.

"Not too popular, I see."

Karen twisted in her chair and glared up at Mike. She still hadn't forgiven his earlier remarks. "Can't say I really blame them," she said, glancing at their former classmates. "Most of their boyfriends cheated with me at one time or another."

Mike sat down, surprising her. "At least you're honest with yourself."

"I try."

She studied him as he ordered a glass of wine from the waiter.

"What's with the wine?"

Mike quirked a questioning brow.

"I never figured you for a wine kind of guy. It seems so refined."

Mike's lips quirked in the barest suggestion of a smile, and

Karen restrained herself from launching into his lap and taking that curved bottom lip between her teeth.

"Just because I'm not a yuppie like Jake," he said and grinned, "doesn't mean I don't appreciate nice things. We have a client, a developer who's built a ton of high-end homes in the area. He's a big wine aficionado and got me into it." He paused as the waiter brought his glass. The look of pleasure at his first sip brought Karen's senses sharply to awareness.

Though he came off as practical and no-nonsense, underneath Mike was a closet sensualist. He savored the pleasures in life. Good food, good wine. Good sex.

Karen's thighs clenched beneath the table, and she mentally kicked herself. What kind of masochist was she, to be so turned on by a guy who seized every opportunity to insult her?

They sat in silence for several moments. Tension hummed between them as Karen prepared for another verbal assault. But he said nothing. She relaxed marginally, grateful to have him sitting at her table so she didn't look like such a loser.

Then everyone was called to stand and welcome the new Mr. and Mrs. Nicholas Donovan. Karen clapped as hard as anyone.

"Jealous?" Mike said softly.

"Of course," she admitted. "But I'm happy for her."

"I don't get you. For as long as I've known you, you couldn't stand Kelly, and now all of a sudden you're supportive big sister?"

Karen's hackles raised and she started to reply, but was cut off.

"Michael, what are you doing sitting over here?"

Karen barely stifled a groan and forced a smile up at Mike's mother.

Maria Donovan had a look on her face like she'd just eaten a turd.

"Mom, you remember Kelly's sister, Karen?" Mike said.

"Yes, I do." Clearly she remembered *everything* anyone had ever said about Karen.

"You must be very happy for Nick," Karen said in her most charming voice.

"*Kelly* is a wonderful young woman. Any mother would be happy to have *her* become part of the family."

Unlike you, you little tramp. Karen heard her loud and clear but kept her smile pasted on her face. Their past aside, if there ever was a reason she and Mike could never be together, Maria Donovan was it. "Kelly's very lucky too, to have found Nick."

Maria turned to Mike, clearly having maxed out her ability to be civil to a woman who had messed with one of her sons. "Mike, why don't you go sit with Tony and Lauren? Your father and I are just at the next table over." She indicated a table near the buffet, clear on the opposite side of the deck.

Karen stared at her glass of champagne, hoping her humiliation didn't show. His fucking mommy was escorting him away. She shouldn't have bothered coming. She could change all she wanted, but everyone's attitude would stay the same.

She nearly fell off her chair when Mike said, "I'm okay here, Mom. Don't worry."

Maria looked like she wanted to argue, but Mike's expression was firm, warning her not to make a scene.

"You don't have to babysit me, Mike." Karen said.

But he stayed, and Karen took that as a positive sign. She grabbed another glass of champagne and gulped it down for liquid courage. The time had come to tell him the truth.

What the hell was he doing? He should be avoiding her like the plague, not sitting there making chitchat while his dick got so hard it practically thumped against the table.

But she'd looked so sad, sitting by herself. Vulnerable. *Yeah right*, he snorted silently to himself. She was about as vulnerable as a barracuda.

Yet he couldn't leave her alone. She drew him as surely as if she had a leash around his balls. Arousal had exploded in his veins the moment he touched the silky skin of her shoulder during the picture. Thank God his tux jacket was long enough to cover his crotch.

Now, with the breeze teasing her soft curls and bringing her sweet, sexy scent to his nostrils, he was afraid he was going to do something inappropriate. He watched her sip her champagne and lick her lips nervously. He couldn't remember ever seeing her so ill at ease.

A drop of champagne beaded on her glossy lower lip and he didn't even think, just reached out and brushed it off with the pad of his thumb. Her lips parted in surprise, and the sight of his blunt, thick thumb against her plump bottom lip brought a sudden, painfully vivid image to mind. One of those lush lips closing over the tip of his cock, her tongue snaking out to lap up drops of thick fluid oozing from the tip.

He was done playing around. He stood and seized her wrist, pulling her to her feet. "Come on."

Karen stumbled a few steps after him, then stopped short, tugging at his grip. "Where are we going?"

"Your room."

"Why?"

"Don't be obtuse." He barely noted the stares they attracted as he maneuvered her through the tables. Let them look. For two weeks he'd been tortured by images of her. Naked, water running in rivulets down her smooth spine as she arched her back to take him deeper. Her legs wrapped around his shoulders as he licked and sucked her beautiful, smooth pussy lips. He had to have her again, and to hell with what anyone else thought.

6

Halfway back to the lodge, Karen dug her heels into the cobblestone path.

"Let go of me," she yelled when Mike pulled her off the path and pushed her up against the trunk of a tree. "What do you want?"

"I want to take you upstairs," he said, leaning in so he could rub his straining erection against the softness of her belly, "strip you naked, and spend the rest of the night fucking you senseless."

She braced her palms against his chest, but didn't push. "Don't do this, Mike," she whispered brokenly. "I don't want this."

He bent his head to kiss her, but she turned her head at the last minute. Mike settled his mouth on the silky curve of her neck.

"We need to talk," she half whispered, half moaned. Maybe she should take him up to her room, where they could talk in private.

294 / Jami Alden

"I can think of better ways to use your mouth."

The hot, wet feel of his mouth on her throat momentarily paralyzed her. Against all sense, her hands crept up around his neck, and she turned and buried her nose in his hair. Her womb clenched as she inhaled the clean scent of his shampoo combined with his own unique masculine smell.

No, if they went to her room, there would be no conversation.

Even knowing how he felt about her, she was so very, very tempted to give in.

"Don't," she said again, pushing feebly against his brick wall of a chest. "I don't want this," as though by repeating the words she could convince her body.

"Bullshit," he said, and roughly shoved a hand up her skirt. "You're so hot you're dripping," he said, teeth sinking into her shoulder as he roughly palmed her sex. "I can't get you out of my head," he said between soft sucking kisses. "All I can think about is getting inside you again." He slipped a finger inside the leg of her panties, pressing firmly against her creamy slit.

She moaned, using every last bit of resolve to keep from grinding herself against his hand. Oh God, it would be so easy to give him what he wanted. What she wanted too.

"Maybe if I stop fighting this I can finally fuck you out of my system."

She froze, pain shooting in icy trickles down her back as his words registered. "So you can finally forget about me once and for all?" she whispered.

He didn't have to answer. The truth was in his eyes. He hated himself for wanting her.

She reached down, grabbed his wrist, and tugged it from between her thighs, digging her nails in when he didn't immediately respond. "I said STOP," she said firmly, her resolve strengthening by the second. She was so done having sex with men who wanted her only for her body. Finished with letting them take whatever they wanted regardless of her feelings.

"Why are you jerking me around? It's not complicated. I want you, I know you want me." His breath came in angry pants, and his hazel eyes glittered as desire warred with frustration.

"I'm tired of being used like a brainless vessel that guys can fuck and forget," she snapped, ducking out from under his arms and pushing away from the tree. She whirled to face him. "You're all the same. You don't even like me, you won't even listen to what I have to say, but you expect me to spread my legs and give it up so you can get off."

"You get off too," Mike said.

Only with you, she thought. "That's not the point. I want someone to see me as a whole person, to actually like me before they fuck me."

Her stomach clenched at Mike's cold smirk. "Isn't it a little late for that? Ever since I've known you, you've played guys, using their lust to get what you want. Why change now?"

"I never played you, Mike," she said softly.

His eyes narrowed and his lips curled in disgust. "Baby, I was the biggest fool of all." He took two menacing steps and grasped her by the shoulders, bending several inches until his angry gaze was level with hers. His voice was a menacing whisper as he said, "I actually had myself half convinced that I loved you, before you went off and fucked ol' Jeremy."

A raw sound of pain ripped from her throat. She didn't know what hurt worse, the ugly memory of Jeremy or hearing Mike mention love in the most scathing tone she'd ever heard. Her forearms came up, knocking his grip loose. "I didn't fuck Jeremy!" she yelled, loud enough that the wedding guests probably heard her over the band.

"Bullshit! I saw you, Karen! I saw him on top of you—"

"You saw him rape me!"

Mike froze, his mouth hanging open. He shook his head back and forth, denying the truth.

Her stomach seized, and she thought she might throw up. He didn't believe her. She'd tried to convince herself that it didn't matter, but his incredulity sliced at her heart with surgical precision.

"He raped me," she repeated as Mike stayed silent, still shaking his head. "You don't believe me now, just like you wouldn't believe me then, but that's the truth."

"But I saw—"

"You don't know what you saw," she spat. She willed Mike to say something, anything. He said nothing, his face blank, expressionless as his fists clenched and unclenched at his sides as he shook his head in denial.

Mike barely heard Karen over the roaring in his ears. Rape? Jeremy? Could he possibly have been wrong all of these years?

He looked at Karen, at the devastation and fury in her face. She could be a manipulative bitch, but she wasn't a liar. And if she wanted to make him feel like shit she had thousands of other ways to humiliate him.

She wouldn't lie to him about this. Somehow every fiber of his body knew it.

She stared, waiting for him to say something, but he couldn't force any words past his lips. She whirled on her spike heel and ran down the path.

He knew he should stop her, but her news rendered him numb. Snapshots of what he'd seen that night flashed in his mind, and suddenly small details snapped into focus. The way Jeremy's body heaved over Karen's much smaller frame. His arm, partly hidden by his torso, angled across her chest. As though he was pinning her down. From that position he could have easily covered her mouth, stifled her screams.

Oh Jesus, he had seen it happening and done nothing to help her. He stood outside the bedroom and waited for Jeremy to finish . . . to finish raping her.

And then he had pushed her away, treated her like she was filth when she'd been reaching out, begging for help.

His legs were suddenly too wobbly to support him, and he staggered over to a bench. He hung his head between his knees, gasping for oxygen.

"Mike, where the hell have you been? It's time for the toast."

Mike looked up at his irritated youngest brother and new sister-in-law. Jake and Kit followed close behind. Kelly's scowl immediately morphed into a look of concern when she saw Mike's face.

"Mike, are you okay? You look gray!" Lifting her skirt, Kelly rushed over and grabbed his wrist to feel his pulse and tilted Mike's head back to look in his eyes. "Are you on something?"

"She finally told you, didn't she?" Kit said quietly.

Mike looked at Kit, her eyes wide and serious, her full mouth bracketed by lines of tension.

"Tell me it's not true." He could barely force the question past the lump in his throat.

"What?" Kelly said, bewildered.

Kit shook her head, ignoring the others' confusion. "I wish I could. But I'm the one who took her to the emergency room."

"What are you talking about?" Nick asked.

Mike struggled to keep his self-loathing from spinning out of control. "About Karen. About Jeremy, about how he—" He stopped himself. This was Karen's secret. If and when she chose to share it with Kelly was her business. "I have to go. I have to find her." He pushed himself off the bench and ran to the lodge, determined to find Karen.

Mike paused outside of her door. What could he possibly say to her? Guilt and shame flayed him. If only he hadn't been so scared at the prospect of falling in love with her, she wouldn't have been alone. Hell, he would have never invited Jeremy down in the first place but instead would have followed his gut and savored every moment he had with her.

He knocked on the door, three short raps. Nothing. He knocked again, pressed his ear to the door, and heard muffled footsteps. She had the chain engaged so the door only opened a few inches. Through the crack she peered at him with one big tear-swollen eye.

He swallowed convulsively, uncharacteristically close to tears himself. "Can I come in?"

She closed the door, and Mike heard the scrape of the chain lock being unfastened. The door opened and he stepped in, following her out onto the veranda. An open bottle of chardonnay sat on the table next to a glass.

Karen had changed from her dress into a peach terry cloth shorts set with a zip-up sweatshirt and shorts that showed off her long, tan legs. Barefoot, she came up to the middle of his chest, and he was struck again by how small she was.

Too small to defend herself against most men. His hands shook at the thought.

He fought the urge to pull her into his arms and beg for her forgiveness.

Without asking, Karen poured him a glass of wine and settled into one of the wrought iron chairs.

He sat next to her and took a fortifying sip. He studied her profile, the small straight nose, full lips set in a tight line over her small upraised chin. He willed her to look at him, but she kept her gaze averted, staring instead at the view of Squaw Valley below.

Never had he so completely loathed himself. "Karen, I owe you an apology," he began. Christ that sounded so lame and inadequate.

"I was trying to make you jealous," she said softly, still staring off into the horizon. "I was so angry that you were leaving early and that you'd lied to me about the apartment. I finally realized you were never going to love me back, and I wanted to hurt you." She turned to face him, her gaze oddly blank. "I thought I could make you jealous enough to take me home with you at the very least."

Mike didn't say anything, sensing she needed to purge herself of the memory and knowing that he deserved every bit of pain and regret her words conjured.

"He told me he was teaching me a lesson, not to mess around with his friend. Like he was protecting you," she said with a short, humorless laugh. She refilled both empty wineglasses.

Mike pressed his thumbs into his eyeballs, as if that could stem the flow of horrific images in his brain. Looking back, it didn't surprise him that Jeremy was capable of such brutality. He was crazy, the kind of guy you love to party with but a borderline sociopath. Women were nothing but objects to him. Guilt flooded Mike's chest as he realized the kind of person he had brought into their lives, how oblivious he'd been to Jeremy's true nature. He wondered how many other women Jeremy had hurt.

"Why didn't you go to the police?" He regretted the words the second they passed his lips.

Karen finally focused on him, anger and disbelief crackling in her eyes. "My own boyfriend wouldn't believe me. Why would the police?"

He winced, ashamed. "Kit said something about the hospital," he heard himself say. Part of him couldn't bear to hear it, but he needed to, as though by experiencing his own pain, he could absorb some of hers.

Karen sipped at her wine and looked away. "I had some bleeding afterward and I wanted to get checked it out, not to mention make sure he hadn't given me anything."

Rage and guilt nearly overwhelmed him, and he wanted to smash Jeremy's face in all over again. But this time he wouldn't stop at knocking out his teeth. No, he'd bash in his skull and rip off his balls so he could never, ever hurt another woman. "Oh God."

"I'm okay now. No permanent damage," she said matter-of-factly.

"I'm so fucking sorry," he said, reaching out to grab her hand but stopping before he made contact. He was the last person she'd want touching him. "I would give anything to go back and change what happened. Anything."

Karen leaned back in her chair and propped her feet on the railing, turning to face him once again. "I know, but you can't."

She was so beautiful. The rays of the evening sun burnished her tawny skin and made her golden highlights in her hair glow. Even puffy eyed and red nosed, she was more beautiful than any woman he'd ever known.

For eleven years he'd pushed every thought of her from his mind, unable to think of her and the time they'd spent without anger and bitterness. Now that was gone, and he was left with nothing but a deep, aching regret and a conviction that he had forsaken something very, very important.

"I'm sorry," he repeated. As though that could make it all better.

"Do you know how awful I felt, what it's like to have someone you love turn their back on you like that?" She choked.

Pain and guilt ravaged his face, but she didn't let that stop her. For eleven years she'd swallowed her pain and borne this burden alone. He wasn't getting off the hook with a simple apology. "You didn't care about me at all, or you wouldn't have ever treated me like that. Like I was a piece of shit you'd scraped off your shoe."

He winced like he'd taken a blow, and his lips pressed together in a tight line. But not before Karen saw their telltale tremble. "I did care," he said, voice choked. "I cared so much that it scared the shit out of me, made me run from you instead of being honest like I should have." He closed his eyes, and a big, fat tear rolled under his thick lashes. He angrily scrubbed at his eyes. He took a deep, shuddering breath, and Karen tried to ignore the unmistakable sensation of her heart softening.

His beautiful hazel eyes were a more vivid green when he cried. "But that's no excuse. I should have trusted you, trusted how I felt. I would never ask for your forgiveness," he said shakily, "but I would do anything to take it all back."

Part of her wanted to launch herself into his lap while the other told her to twist the knife a little deeper.

But with her initial surge of anger spent, she felt deflated. Strangely empty.

She observed Mike, so obviously consumed by guilt. When she'd imagined this scene, she thought she'd revel in it, that she'd seize the chance to rub his face in how wrong he'd been about everything. She finished her second glass of wine.

"Funny, I thought it would be good to make you feel bad, but it's not," she said, words slightly slurred. "But I needed to tell you, just the same. I didn't realize how much I cared what you thought of me until I saw you at Caesar's. The way you looked at me . . ."

He winced as though the memory of that night pained him.

His hand rested on the glass and wrought iron table between

them. Long fingered, tan and strong looking, with neatly trimmed nails. He had a scab on his thumb, and the index fingernail was slightly bruised. Without thinking, she laid her palm over the back, noting that with their wrists aligned, her fingertips didn't even make it to his first knuckles.

He turned his hand over, capturing hers and interlacing their fingers. Warmth spread from her palm, up her arm, and pooled low in her belly.

For several long moments they stared at each other, saying nothing. It would be so easy to nurture a grudge or to use his guilt to manipulate him. But it felt so good just to hold his hand, to take and give comfort now that the truth was out.

"I wish I could make it up to you," he said, "that night at Caesar's—all of it."

"That night at Caesar's was a relapse," she said.

"How do you mean?"

"After my mom died I took a hard look at my life, particularly my relationships with men, and realized I needed to make a change."

He squeezed her hand in encouragement.

"I never really believed that anyone would ever love me, you know? And so I acted in a way that basically guaranteed that." She took another drink of wine. "With guys, I knew none of them ever really cared about me, but at least I could use sex to get them to do what I wanted." She smiled humorlessly. "At least most of the time I could. I remember the first time you and I had sex," she said. "I never wanted to do it before you. I never really enjoyed fooling around until you, and when you made me come that first time . . ." She closed her eyes, savoring the memory like she would a piece of rich, dark chocolate. "I knew you were the one, and I knew I wanted you to be the first. But then after Jeremy"—her mouth tightened—"I slept with just about every guy who asked, because I figured, hey, at least if it's my choice, I'm in control, right? I thought on some level it would help erase the memory of what happened. And I got some nice dinners and even a vacation or two out of most of them. But then they'd roll off and go home and I always felt . . . empty." She looked at him then, challenging. Mike didn't tolerate weakness of character, and she was surprised at the lack of censure in his expression.

"Two years ago I went into therapy, and I decided I needed to clean up my act, find a nice guy, make peace with my family—all the stuff I'd been running from for so long."

"I still don't understand why what we did was a relapse," Mike said gently.

"I hadn't had sex for two years before that night," she said, a slightly crazed laugh erupting from her chest at his look of surprise. "I took a year off dating entirely, and then I was holding out for a nice guy. A guy with potential, you know?" She shook her head at her own stupidity.

"So what happened?"

"It's so stupid—I'm so stupid. I went to Reno with this guy, Brad. I should have seen it coming. I mentioned meeting his family, and he told me I wasn't the kind of woman a guy took home to his mother. Turns out he just wanted a hot chick to fuck for a while."

"When you saw me," she continued, "I was having a drink, planning to go back to my room. I honestly wasn't planning to, how did you put it, 'fuck some poor schmuck for revenge'?"

Mike winced. "Karen—"

"It's okay. I didn't exactly behave in a way that would make you think otherwise," she said, starting to disentangle her fingers from his. "I thought I was going to show you—you know, teach you a lesson. You acted so superior, but you were just another guy who could be led around by his dick." She pulled her hand from his and drew her feet up, wrapping herself in a tight ball on the chair. "I don't know why I thought I could handle it. I've never been able to control myself around you."

Mike swung his chair around to her side of the table so he sat facing her, his knees close enough to brush the edge of her chair. "If it's any consolation, you do the same to me. I kept telling myself I should get up and leave, but I couldn't. It pissed me off that after all this time I couldn't resist you, even though I knew being with you would only tear me up."

"Did it tear you up?"

"Ask Tony. I haven't slept in the past two weeks, and I almost beat the crap out of him yesterday over something stupid."

She couldn't help it. The thought of reserved, controlled Mike losing his cool all because of her brought a satisfied smirk to her face.

"You don't have to look so happy about it."

"Misery loves company."

"I'm sorry for the way I treated you that night, and earlier today," he said, his tone somber and sincere.

She shook her head. "I hated myself for falling back into my old patterns, for not being able to stand up to you and try to talk to you like a sensible person."

"Sensible is the last word I would use to describe our behavior around each other," he said ruefully.

She nodded. "We're really bad for each other's peace of mind."

"Uh-huh," he said, moving infinitesimally closer.

"We should probably avoid each other like the plague."

"Probably," he agreed.

She studied his mouth, the full lips pulled into a line of regret. She knew he would leave if she asked. Maybe she was a masochistic fool, but she wanted him to stay. Needed him to wash away the memory of the last time they were together.

Wanted to indulge in her uncontrollable desire without the wounds of the past intruding. Maybe this one night could wash her clean, help her recapture a brief time when sex was about pleasure instead of a complicated exchange of power.

Crazy as it seemed, Mike was the only one who could set her free.

"I don't want you to leave." She put her hands on his knees. "I don't want to."

Decision made, she closed the distance between them. Her hand wrapped around his neck, drawing his face toward hers. She kissed his cheeks. Her tongue flicked delicately along the seam of his lips, and he groaned, but didn't increase the contact.

She kissed him more firmly, encouraging his lips to part with tiny flicks of her tongue. Heat exploded between her thighs as he finally opened to her, his tongue tangling with hers in a kiss that tasted of regret and barely restrained desire.

He pulled her from her chair, and she found herself in a cocoon of muscles and chest. He lifted her legs across his lap and tipped her head back against his arm. One big hand came up to cradle her face as he sucked and licked at her mouth with increasing urgency. Each fervent caress was an apology, a plea for forgiveness. He didn't bother to hide his need, letting her feel everything in his all-consuming kiss.

She couldn't help but respond and squirmed against the hard bulge of his cock pressing eagerly against the backs of her thighs. She wanted him inside her with a fierceness that bordered on desperation. Her moan was part pleasure, part distress. As always with Mike, her need overwhelmed her, terrifying in its intensity.

7

Mike recognized her hesitation and gentled the pressure of his mouth. He pressed soft kisses to her cheeks and chin, and whispered, "We don't have to do anything you don't want to do, sweetheart." His cock twitched against her ass in vehement protest. He ignored it.

Apparently Karen noticed because she cast a questioning glance at their laps.

"Just because I'm hard as a spike doesn't mean we have to do anything about it."

"I don't want you to leave," she said, her voice shaky, with a vulnerability he'd never heard before. He looked into her face. The guarded, cautious look he'd always seen in her eyes was gone. Her fear of rejection was front and center for all the world to see.

His throat closed up and several seconds went by before he could speak. "I'm not going anywhere, Tiny. I'll stay here all night and talk, or we can watch TV." He wrapped her in his arms and tucked her against his chest. "I just want to be with you," he said, and realized it was true.

She stiffened in his arms and looked at him with patent disbelief.

Tender, unfamiliar emotions filled his chest as the wall around his heart developed a hairline crack. Warmth steadily seeped through to the rest of his body. For eleven years he'd refused to let himself get close to a woman. Like Karen, he'd feared the vulnerability and loss of control that came with being in love.

Right here, with her warm and soft in his arms, his fear slid away, and all he wanted was to make up for every hurt he'd ever caused her. Even if it meant keeping his hands off her to prove he wanted Karen herself and not just her body.

He squeezed her and kissed the top of her head. "You know what I wish?"

"Hmm?" She traced lazy circles around the patch of skin exposed by his open collar.

He sighed in contentment at the soft press of her lips. "I wish I hadn't had my head up my ass back when we were dating."

She chuckled and slid her hand farther inside his shirt. "That makes two of us." Her tongue stole out and flicked the hollow of his throat. He slid one hand over her ass and squeezed in warning.

"You're making it hard for me to behave myself."

"I'm sorry," she said, pulling his shirt down to nibble on his collarbone. "It's been a long time since I've had the opportunity to be this close to a guy for more than two seconds before he started pawing."

Mike stiffened, then banished the thought of her with any other man from his brain. If he had anything to say about it, he was going to be the only man in her life from now on.

KISS ME TWICE / 309

A conviction that should have scared the shit out of him, but didn't.

"So you're trying to test my limits?" he asked as his hand slid up the back of her sweatshirt. The skin of her back was satiny beneath his callused palm.

"No." He felt her smile against his skin and bent his neck to the side so she had better access to his earlobe. "Just enjoying the buildup." His balls tightened at her nipping caress, and he shifted under her. She lifted her head and met his eyes, her expression serious. "It's been a very long time since I've actually anticipated sex, and I want to savor it."

He groaned and licked his tongue inside her mouth. "Take as long as you want, Tiny."

She smiled even as she kissed him back, tangling her tongue with his and turning so her legs straddled him. "I want you so much, Mike," she whispered shakily. "You're the only one who makes me feel this way." Her hands trailed down his shirtfront, trembling a little as she struggled to unfasten the studs. "It scares the hell out of me."

"I know. Me too," he confessed.

That seemed to hearten her, and her mouth devoured his. The taste and feel of her consumed him. His hand slid up to capture a breast, pinching her tight nipple through the soft fabric. She moaned and squirmed in his lap, her moist heat penetrating the layers of their clothing. His cock throbbed in protest against the prison of his trousers.

He wanted inside of her more than he wanted to breathe, but he waited for her cue. This was her show, and he was determined to give her everything she wanted. Her mound pressed against the iron rigidity of his cock and he caught her hips, grinding up against her in a motion that quickly had her flushed and panting.

"I want to feel you come," he whispered, his tongue snaking out to lap at her ear. "You're so sexy when you let go."

"No." She stiffened in his lap, and Mike immediately froze. "I want you inside me the first time."

Mike stood up with her in his arms and carried her inside. His hands shook as he unzipped her sweatshirt. She was bare beneath it, and his mouth watered at the remembered taste of her perfect tits in his mouth. He took a deep breath, forced himself to calm down. By some miracle she had given him a second chance. No way was he going to blow it by losing control. He needed to make this perfect for her, to make up in some infinitesimal way for all the other times he hadn't given her the love and affection she deserved.

She stripped her shorts and panties down her legs and sprawled naked on the bed as she watched him strip. "You're so gorgeous," she said, her eyes traveling over his chest, abs, and legs. Last time they'd both been so focused on getting the upper hand, they hadn't taken the time to really look at each other.

For a moment, they simply admired one another, savoring the anticipation. Mike quickly got rid of his shirt and pushed his pants and boxers down his legs. He nearly purred in relief as his cock sprang out, finally free of restriction.

Under her unabashed admiration, his erection hardened another inch, straining eagerly toward her luscious sex as he knelt between her thighs.

"And you're beautiful." He kissed her with barely restrained control, his tongue thrusting in a lusty rhythm that quickly had her writhing. "You're the sexiest woman I've ever known," he whispered, "and I can't believe how lucky I am to be with you again."

She wrapped her legs around his thighs and levered herself

up so the tip of his cock slipped inside her slick folds. She moaned, grinding against him. She slid up and down his shaft, slicking him with her juices, wrenching a moan from his chest.

"Wait," he groaned. He was dying, his dick so hard he was ready to burst through his skin. He wanted to make this good for her, give her everything she ever wanted, but the feel of that hot, smooth pussy against him was more than any mortal man could be expected to handle. "Slow down, honey, or I'm gonna lose it."

"I don't want to slow down," she said, her voice harsh with need, her heels digging into his ass as she urged him closer. She wrapped her hand around his cock and rubbed the bulbous head against her pulsing clit. A sheen of sweat bloomed on her skin, and her breath grew choppy. "I want you inside me, now," she said, staring straight into his eyes. "Don't make me beg."

He groaned and squeezed his eyes shut. "If you don't stop, I'm gonna be begging your forgiveness when I come two seconds after I get inside you." Beads of sweat popped out on his forehead as the head of his penis slipped inside her melting core. It took all his strength to resist the hot kiss of her body, to not let go and mindlessly thrust until he came hard and deep inside her.

"I want it to be different this time," he panted, arms trembling as he braced himself above her. "I want it to be perfect for you." She was so fucking gorgeous, lean and golden and spread out beneath him. He couldn't resist; he slid inside her a few more inches, gasping at the firm clasp of muscles around him.

She was hotter, wetter, tighter than anything he'd ever experienced. It felt so good that the top of his head nearly blew off. "Oh fuck," he said, and pulled out.

"What?"

"Condom!"

"It's okay. I'm on the pill," she said, and guided him almost roughly back inside.

"Jesus, you feel so good," he murmured, teasing them both with shallow thrusts. He looked down to where they were joined, and almost lost it. Her tiny patch of gold ringlets was dark with moisture, and her beautiful plump labia were flushed pink, stretched around his thick shaft. Her clit was shiny wet, peeking through the folds, begging to be stroked. He swept his thumb across the engorged bud and felt the answering jolt along his cock as she squeezed him like a fist.

She squirmed under him, and the sting of her nails in his back sent a shiver through his body. "Deeper," she demanded. "I want you to fuck me deeper."

He set his jaw and closed his eyes against the unbearably erotic vision she presented. "I want to make it last. I don't want to lose control," he said, all the while sliding incrementally deeper.

"I want you to lose control," she said fiercely. "I don't want to do this alone."

He looked into her face and saw the savage desire that couldn't quite disguise another emotion. Fear.

Understanding dawned on him, along with relief. She didn't need long, drawn out foreplay. She needed him out of control, needed to know that she had the same effect on him as he had on her.

With a grateful groan he slid all the way in, and the low sound of pleasure that escaped her throat made his toes curl. He eased in, then out, feeling her stretch and yield around him as she arched up to take all of him.

He leaned down to kiss her, moaning around the sweet thrust of her tongue and at the feel of her smooth breasts against his chest. His head ducked and he tongued a nipple into his mouth, sucking hard enough to make her yell.

His hips pumped in a firm, steady rhythm. High, keening sounds erupted from her throat as she ground her pelvis against him, urging him harder, faster, deeper, with every pounding thrust.

"Oh Christ, honey," he moaned as he felt his balls tighten in warning. She writhed underneath him, straining as she fought against her body's desperate need to climax. "It's okay, baby," he whispered. Droplets of sweat dripped from his face onto her chest, and he imagined he heard them sizzle across the tawny expanse. "Let go. It's okay, I'm with you." He captured her hands, pinning her wrists to the bed and twining his fingers with hers. His back arched as she wrung him dry, her body sucking him deeper as she fought for control. Suddenly she arched and jerked against him, her hands clenching his in a grip that should have hurt.

She called his name in a high thready voice, and tears squeezed from her eyes as her orgasm tore through her.

He pounded her relentlessly as his own orgasm hit him with the force of a Mack truck. He trembled above her, fingers digging into the soft flesh of her hips as he shot thick jets of come as deep inside her as he could possibly get.

Karen wrapped her arms around Mike as he collapsed on top of her, burying her nose in the damp skin of his neck. He smelled glorious, like salt and sex and Mike. She wanted to bottle the scent so that after tonight she could rub it on herself and remember how unbelievably perfect she felt right now. Her fingers tangled in the damp hair at his nape, and she shivered as his lips trailed lazy kisses along her shoulder.

Their hearts hammered against each other, and harsh breathing pressed breasts to chest. She wanted to keep him in this bed forever and never let go.

Reality crept in as she came back down to earth, and the enormity of what she'd just experienced started to sink in. Her wildness scared her, and she was overwhelmed by the intensity of her reaction.

Nervous tension coiled in her gut. Now what? Even though she didn't dare hope for more than one night, she was terrified he would get up and leave.

He levered himself up on one elbow. "You are so fucking amazing," he whispered, and leaned down to taste her lips.

As love talk went, it wasn't much, but the look that accompanied his words was so unbearably tender that it hit her like a fist to her belly.

To her absolute horror, she burst into tears.

Jesus Christ, Karen, why don't you guarantee that he leaves fast enough to put a Mike-shaped cutout in the wall?

But to her shock Mike didn't flee as though the hounds of hell were chasing him. Instead he rolled to his back and tucked her against his chest. Strong arms wrapped around her back, and one big hand stroked her hair. "Oh, Tiny, it's okay," he whispered, and pressed his lips to her hair. "I've got you, go ahead and cry."

She sobbed harder while he held her and whispered words of comfort. Released pain and newfound relief combined and rushed out in a flood of acidic tears, and it took several minutes for her crying jag to run its course.

Once the sobs subsided to sniffles, Mike disentangled himself from her and got out of bed and went to the bathroom. She stiffened, humiliated, convinced he was about to make a run for it. She buried her head in a pillow to stifle a fresh wash of tears.

Mike emerged from the bathroom seconds later with a big glass of water in one hand and a handful of tissues in the other. She was momentarily stunned by the unbelievably gorgeous site of him naked. Someone needed to pass a law making it illegal for him to wear clothes.

Which reminded her of how very attractive *she* must look.

He climbed back in bed and propped himself against the headboard, pulling her up to snuggle against him. "Here," he said, handing her both the water and the tissues.

She took a big gulp, washing the salty, sticky taste of tears away, and blew her nose as delicately as possible. "Sorry about that," she mumbled. "I don't ever cry," she sniffed.

To his credit, he looked only marginally freaked out. "Normally my ego would be wounded, but I think tonight there are special circumstances."

She nuzzled her face against the firm muscle of his pec and settled her palm across his lean abdomen. "I think I've cried more tonight than I have in the last decade."

He tipped her chin up to kiss her. "Get it all out then, 'cause I want only smiles from here on out."

She obliged, albeit a little shakily.

The red numbers of the clock radio caught her eye, and she was shocked to see it was only a little after eight. The reception would no doubt still be going strong.

Sudden guilt washed through her. Ditching Kelly's wedding and taking the best man with her was not the best way to build up the shaky foundation she'd laid this afternoon.

"I'm sorry I made you miss the reception," she said. "It's still early if you want to go back."

"Not unless you want to." He shifted against the pillows. "I'm enjoying myself right here." He stretched his legs out and crossed one ankle over the other.

Even his feet were sexy. Big, high arched, with just enough hair to be appropriately masculine.

Oh boy. She was in serious trouble when even the guy's feet turned her on.

316 / Jami Alden

"Kelly's probably pissed," she sighed. "And you're Nick's best man—maybe you should go back."

"I saw her and Nick before I came up here." His eyes got dark and serious. "She understands."

Tension knotted in her belly. She still had a lot to discuss with her sister. She hoped Mike was right. Aside from what Kelly thought, she was starting to get really nervous about what spending more time with Mike would do to her own emotional well-being.

On one hand, she was grateful beyond words that he didn't jump at the chance to leave, but on the other, having him stay here and be so damned nice encouraged some very unrealistic scenarios. Like one where Mike told her he'd never stopped loving her and wanted a second chance.

Yeah, like that would ever happen.

"Ouch!" Mike's hand closed over hers. She looked down and realized she'd inadvertently yanked out a tuft of chest hair.

"Sorry." She grimaced and pushed herself up. As casually as possible she leaned over and picked her shorts and sweatshirt up off the floor and pulled them on. She scooted away from Mike and tried to ignore the delicious picture he made stretched out on her bed, hands folded beneath his head as he looked up at her in puzzlement.

"Really, Mike, you don't have to stay here with me."

His thick black brows snapped together over the bridge of his nose. "Karen, if you want to be alone, I understand, but I'd much rather be here with you than dance bad disco."

She hung her head, scared and vulnerable and hating it. "I don't want to be alone," she whispered finally.

He pulled her down and kissed her so tenderly she almost started bawling again. "Thank fucking god for that," he said, kissing her more fiercely this time. "For a minute I was afraid you were going to try to kick me out again."

Happiness and renewed desire surged through her, and she firmly pushed her misgivings aside, determined not to let her doubts get in the way of her enjoyment of this night. "I'm not done with you yet." She grinned and slid her hand down between them. The thick club of his sex surged in her palm, and she teased him with a swirl of her thumb across the tip.

"I live to serve," he said. He took a rough–tender nip at her bottom lip and ran his tongue along the sleek inside. "I've spent the past two weeks thinking up ways to make you come."

"Yeah? Did you come up with anything original?" She sucked in a breath as he unzipped her sweatshirt and pushed it off her shoulders. Her shorts followed, and he followed their progress down her legs, lingering at her feet. She jumped when he tongued the sensitive arch. Mike managed to turn every square inch of skin into an erogenous zone.

"Probably nothing that hasn't been done before, but there's something to be said for tradition." His lips slid up her shin, and he stopped to bite into the firm muscle of her calf.

Her knees drew up to allow him better access to the tender flesh of her inner thighs as he worked his way up.

Warmth seeped between her legs as his lips continued their journey up, until she could feel his hot breath against her sex.

"This, for example, is an oldie but goodie," he said as he draped her knees over his shoulders. Her hips jumped off the bed at the first touch of his tongue in the crease of her thigh.

"Mike, I—" Her throat closed on a moan as his thumbs spread her apart and his finger flicked at her clit. "I—we—I need a shower!" she gasped. Sure, she'd had a lot of sex in her life, but nothing quite this . . . earthy.

But Mike resisted her squirms and held her easily, hands spread wide on her inner thighs.

He chuckled softly. "It turns me on to taste myself on you," he rumbled, sliding his tongue along her juicy folds. One thick, broad finger slid inside, and her sensitive tissues trembled around the invasion. "I loved coming inside you," he whispered, "knowing there was nothing between us." His finger thrust in and out lightly, just enough to stretch her swollen passage and make her arch with renewed need. "I want to fill you up until you don't remember what it's like not to have part of me inside you."

The words and the remembered feel of him pulsing inside made her womb shudder and sent another rush of moisture over his tongue. Perhaps she had a kinky side she'd never acknowledged.

His lips closed over her clit, suckling ravenously. She mewled at the now-familiar sensation of her orgasm building. Streaks of vibrant crimson flashed behind her eyelids as she twitched and shuddered. His tongue lashed at her in firm, unrelenting licks, and every sinew tightened until her entire existence centered on his greedy mouth and her aching sex.

She yelled his name and arched up off the bed as her orgasm roared through her, but he didn't stop. His tongue continued stroking, drawing out her orgasm until she finally twisted away from the almost painful pleasure.

"Stop," she whispered, turning her face into the pillow. She pulled her legs closed and rolled to her side. "I'm afraid if I keep coming like that, I'm going to rupture an artery or something."

Mike chuckled and scooted up the bed, hands and lips teasing her ultrasensitive skin.

"I mean, it, cut it out," she said around a yawn, slapping back feebly at his hands. "I need some personal space for a minute."

He evaded her protesting hands and managed to land a smacking kiss on her cheek. Karen felt the bed dip as he got up.

She dozed off, and the next thing she knew Mike was carrying her into the bathroom. "What are you doing?" Even though part of her wanted to protest that she needed a rest if this was going to keep up, it wasn't so bad being naked in Mike Donovan's arms.

"We can't waste this," he said, nodding toward the gigantic Jacuzzi tub, filled nearly to the brim. Patches of bubbles floated at the top, and curls of scented steam swirled around them. Karen sighed in hedonistic pleasure as she sank into the tub, the warm water rapidly soothing the aches and twinges she had already developed.

"Besides," he continued, "I thought maybe you could use a soak."

She heard a splash and opened her eyes to see Mike climbing in the other end. He was still hugely aroused, and for a half second, Karen felt a pang of guilt. She really ought to help him out with that. Common courtesy and all that.

But lassitude quickly set in, and Karen didn't think she could move a muscle if the hotel caught on fire.

They lay there, heads leaning back against opposite ends of the tub, legs sliding and tangling in water slippery with bath oil.

"Make sure I don't fall asleep and drown, okay?"

"Don't worry, Tiny, I'll take care of you."

The words were innocuous, said in such a teasing way, but they clutched at her heart nonetheless. She opened her eyes and found him staring at her, as though he knew exactly what she was thinking.

The intensity was too much, and she strove to lighten the atmosphere. "I can't believe my baby sister married your baby brother. Who would have ever imagined?"

Mike smiled, a flash of white teeth through the mist. "Not me. I thought she'd marry some professor or another doctor or something."

"Still," she said, savoring the feel of Mike's ropy calf against the sole of her foot, "I'm glad for her. He's better for her. Balances her out."

He quirked a brow. His lips pressed together, then relaxed, as though he wanted to ask something but wasn't sure he should. Finally, "Since when do you care if Kelly's happy? No offense, but as I recall—"

"I was a complete and heinous bitch to her our entire lives? I know."

"I was going to say I recall an intense case of sibling rivalry, at least on your part, but if the shoe fits . . ."

She sighed and gathered quickly dissolving bubbles in her cupped hands. So much for lightening the mood.

Every way she could think of to explain it sounded like new-age therapy-speak. How could she explain so Mike would believe her? He, as much as anyone, knew the deep-seeded jealousy that had defined her relationship with her sister. Next to Kelly, she had felt invisible and ordinary. That, in conjunction with her own shaky self-esteem, had prevented her from ever trying to develop any kind of friendship with her only sibling.

Mike prodded her hip with his toes. She sensed her explanation was important to him.

"I know you believe people don't change," she started.

"I'm beginning to think the world's not quite that black and white."

"When my mom died, I went through a really rough time. I spent her last two weeks with her, watched her die, watched my dad watch her die," she said, a lump plugging up her throat as she remembered the sight of her father weeping as he held his wife's pale, bony hand. "He loved her so much, and it's sick, I know, but I was actually jealous of them right then." She rolled her eyes, sniffed, and caught a tear with the edge of her thumb. "I know, ridiculous, to be jealous of a woman dying of cancer and her husband watching her die. But they had that love, that connection, and I realized I had never, ever found that, and probably never would if I kept going the way I was. I had a lot of sex," she said bluntly, relieved when his face remained impassive. "But I never got close to anyone—before or after you. My therapist said I used my sexuality to keep people at a distance." She laughed ruefully. "Which is also ridiculous but also true."

"I still don't get what that has to do with Kelly," Mike said.

"I'm getting to that. Anyway, so as I was thinking about this, considering my future as a washed-up, once-hot old maid, Mom said something very hurtful but very true. She said out of me and Kelly, she knew I was the one who most needed her love and attention but that I made it almost impossible for someone to love me."

She closed her eyes and clenched her jaw to stop the trembling of her lips. "Pretty bad, huh? When your own mother says you're unlovable?"

Mike's hand cupped her calf in a reassuring squeeze and didn't say anything.

"She was right though. I'd pushed everyone away to the point where even my family didn't like me much. And they're *supposed* to love you." Water sloshed around as Mike shifted position, pulling her feet up into his lap. "It took a lot of therapy to get me to realize that if I don't love myself, no one else can either." She flicked water at him. "And don't I just sound like a self-help book?"

"So do you? Love yourself I mean," he said with a sweet, crooked smile.

She let her hand trail up his hair-roughened calf. "Most days I like myself pretty well."

"Sounds like you figured stuff out."

"Yeah, but I couldn't work up the courage to do anything about it until recently. I kept putting off that phone call to

Kelly. What was I going to say? Sorry I was such a bitch to you, I always loved you underneath?"

Mike laughed. "She seemed to respond well. But it sounds like you two have a lot more to talk about."

Karen smiled. "I hope that after her honeymoon she'll be willing to give me another chance. Kelly's a nice sort, unlike her bitchy sister."

"Watch it. I happen to like the bitchy sister." Mike squeezed her foot in warning. The warm, teasing expression on his face was enough to make her melt into the bathwater. "You just have to know how to bring out her sweeter side," he said in a low, sexy voice. He caught her right foot in his hands and pressed his thumb into the arch in a caress that had her purring in pleasure. "See what I mean?"

"Did I tell you to stop?" she said, raising her head to find him contemplating her foot, tucked inside his palm.

"You have the smallest feet I've ever seen," he said. Indeed, her foot fit easily in his hand with enough room for his fingers to curl over her toes.

"You don't," she said, pulling Mike's foot over to rest against her stomach. With his heel just above the juncture of her thighs, his toes brushed the undersides of her breasts. "You also have unnaturally large hands."

He waggled his brows in an exaggerated leer. "Big hands, big feet—"

"Big gloves, big shoes?" Her left foot stole between his legs and pressed gently against his testicles. "Hmm, big balls?"

"Careful there," he warned.

She slid her foot up until it rested against the thick column of his penis. "Big, beautiful cock," she said, and slid the sole of her foot up, then down his hard length.

Hazel eyes darkened and he leaned forward to wrap his big

hands around her thighs. "Get over here, sweet thing," he murmured, and pulled her up over his lap.

On some level she was shocked at how the mood had gone from somber, to playful, to sexually charged in a matter of minutes. But that was the incredible thing about Mike, she realized. She could show everything to him, her dirty little secrets and her not so noble tendencies, and he still wanted her. He listened to her pour out her heart and held her and called her sweet while she cried.

A sudden, dreadful realization blindsided her. She loved him. Had never stopped. She chased away the voice that whispered that nothing could ever come of it. Instead she grabbed his face and kissed him, pouring every tender and primal emotion into that kiss, moaning around his tongue when he gave it all back. The bathroom echoed with the soft smacking of lips, the splash of water, and the rapidly increasing harshness of their breath.

His cock pressed insistently against her belly, and she slid her hand down between their bodies, closing her hand around him. His throat arched as she pumped him with her fist, the oily water easing the way for her firm strokes. She loved the fierce cast that arousal gave his face, loved the rasp of his beard against her lips and fingertips, loved the salty taste of his neck against her tongue.

With a rough groan he grabbed her hand. "I need to get inside you again, feel you around me when I come."

A shuddery breath escaped her as he lifted her up until the blunt head of his erection nestled against her folds. His hand slid down and parted her labia, and her breath hissed out as he eased inside.

"God, it feels so good inside you, nothing between us," he murmured. "So hot and tight."

Karen's only response was a whimper as she worked herself up and down in tiny little strokes, working him in inch by inch. Finally he was fully embedded, so deep she could feel him against her spine. "You feel amazing inside me," she whispered, arms looping around his neck. She wriggled experimentally and gasped as the thick press of his cock brushed against her G-spot. His hair-roughened thighs brushed against her back as he shifted to get better leverage.

She sucked greedily at his mouth and ground her pelvis down to meet every upward thrust. She'd never experienced such unrestrained pleasure, never so wanted to give someone ecstasy in return. She clenched her muscles around him, and his groan sent an answering current through her body as though she felt that hot clasp of flesh herself. He wrapped his arms around her back, pulling her close until they were all but glued together.

With every downstroke her clit ground against his pubic bone and his cock filled her to bursting. She consumed him, was consumed in return, as he thrust and heaved under her. She opened her eyes and met his.

The look of unadulterated need on his face sent her over the edge. The moment she convulsed around him he let out a bellow and pumped hard inside her, his cock jerking as hot jets of liquid bathed her. His orgasm sparked hers until they slumped, panting into the now-tepid bathwater.

Mike gathered her slippery-wet body close and nuzzled his face in her hair. Wet curls tickled his nose as he inhaled the fresh fragrance of her shampoo, and through that, her own unique scent. He slid his hands up and down her back, luxuriating in the silky texture of her skin. He tried to remember a time when he'd ever felt this kind of bone-deep contentment.

"I could stay like this forever," he murmured.

"Me too, but my knees are going numb," she mumbled into his chest.

He laughed and pulled her, wobbly kneed, to her feet. Served him right for getting all romantic and mushy on her. Mike, as a rule, did not do romantic and mushy.

Still he couldn't keep from taking the towel from her hands to dry her, chasing any stray droplets of water with his tongue.

"You'll spoil me," she said.

"That's the plan." If she wanted him to carry her around on his shoulder and feed her grapes, he'd probably do it.

"You know, I never really enjoyed bathroom sex until you," he said, wrapping his arms around her from behind and propping his chin on her head. He studied their reflection, she, golden and feline, tucked against his dark brawniness. The princess and the barbarian. They looked awesome together.

"I never enjoyed any sex until you," she quipped.

He couldn't suppress a surge of masculine pride. "Does it make me a total asshole if I say that's a complete turn-on?"

She turned in his arms, tipping her head back so she could see his face. "You enjoy having power over me?"

He shook his head. "I won't say it's not an ego boost, but it's more than that." He struggled for the right words. "To know that you want me half as much as I want you . . ." He bent to kiss her and felt his cock make a feeble attempt to rouse. "To know you trusted me enough on some level, even that night at Caesar's, to let yourself go." He didn't have words. "I'm a prick, aren't I?"

She shook her head against his chest.

He swallowed hard, suddenly afraid *he* was going to burst into tears this time. "I just want to make you happy, Karen, in bed and out." He grinned, looking down into her moist eyes. "Or in the bath, or wherever."

She threaded her fingers through his hair and nestled close.

"Multiple orgasms are great, but you know what would make me *really* happy?"

"Hmm?"

"A cheeseburger."

Mike carried her into the bedroom and they both donned spa robes while Karen ordered cheeseburgers, fries, chocolate sundaes, and a bottle of champagne.

An hour and a half later, Mike was licking the last of the whipped cream from a very satisfied Karen's breasts when he again noticed her tattoo.

His index finger traced the bright lines of green and yellow ink that graced her hip bone. "I like your tattoo," he said, softly kissing one of the frog's feet.

"I got it after my mom died," she said, settling herself against a pile of pillows. "Every time I pull down my pants, I'm reminded that I've kissed enough frogs," she smiled.

"Ribbit."

The smile faded from her face as she looked down at him. Her fingers traced his jaw, and he leaned into her caress like a dog seeking a pet. "You were the only prince in the bunch."

Had he been standing, the look on her face would have brought him to his knees. Her eyes were bright with love and joy, and the wary, guarded look that had always haunted them had disappeared.

And just like that, he knew. This tiny, smart-mouthed, hot-bodied woman had him by the balls, and he couldn't have been happier. He scooped her up and carried her into the shower where they rinsed off the bits of sundae their tongues had missed. She was half asleep by the time they were finished and snoring softly as soon as her head hit the pillow. He couldn't wait to wake up with her in the morning. His fingers grazed her cheek as he curled himself around her. He loved her. And this time he was never going to let her go.

8

Karen winced as the sound of her suitcase zipping roared through the dead-quiet room. She glanced at the bed, relieved to see Mike still blissfully asleep, and again fought the urge to jump back in and cuddle close.

No, this was the smartest move. Save herself the awkward morning-after scene and make a clean break. Leave with only the good memories of Mike and the incredible night they'd spend together. Now she could finally let go of the past and move on to a brighter future.

How bright do you think it will be without Mike? an inner voice scolded.

It's not as though I have a choice. Mike's a good guy and he wants to do the right thing, but just how far can guilt carry a relationship?

Because for all his tender care, she couldn't afford to hope that he loved her back. He hadn't loved her before, so what made her think that one more night of hot sex would be enough to make him start?

She ruthlessly squelched the sob that clawed at her throat. She'd cry later. Now she had to make her escape before Mike woke up, before she completely humiliated herself by blurting out how much she loved him.

She tiptoed to the door, ignoring the voice that called her a coward. For a long minute she drank him in, burning this last image in her brain. Someday she'd see him again, but never again like this. Naked, sheet tangled at his hips and exposing an expanse of dark skin and rippling muscles. His face was relaxed, lips faintly smiling as though he was having a very good dream. "I love you," she whispered inaudibly, almost wishing he would wake up and stop her. Finally she stepped out into the hall and closed the door behind her.

The click of the latch rang like a bullet through the room and sent Mike jerking upright, fully awake.

"Karen?" But he knew she was gone. "Goddamn you!" he howled, surging out of bed. *Maybe he should just let her go.* Clearly she wasn't interested in more than a one-night stand or she wouldn't have snuck out.

No, he couldn't let her go, not without a fight anyway. She needed to understand exactly how he felt, and if she still wanted to go, he'd deal with that rejection later.

He yanked on his tux pants, fastening them as he sprinted barefoot down the hall. He ignored the curious looks of other guests as he sped through the lobby and out into the parking lot.

He saw her across the lot, hefting her suitcase into the trunk of her cherry red Acura. He raced through the rows of cars and slammed his hands on the trunk just as she was backing out. She stomped on the breaks just short of hitting him.

"Get out of the car," he yelled.

She pulled back into the space and killed the ignition, and he waited, arms folded, for her to get out of the car. He became aware of several curious stares aimed in his direction.

"Where do you think you're going?"

Her chin tipped up and she glared at his tone. "Home. I do have a life there."

"And you were just going to leave without saying a word?" He braced his palms on either side of her shoulders and leaned in menacingly.

"You should be grateful. I'm saving you the awkward morning-after scene." Her wary blue gaze met his and just as swiftly shifted back to her red sandals.

He took a steadying breath. After everything she'd been through, bullying her was not the right approach. "Karen, I don't want you to just leave like this. I was hoping to spend the day with you, maybe—"

She cut him off. "Mike, last night was wonderful, but I don't expect anything more out of this. You don't have to go all romantic on me for the sake of your own conscience."

Damn gorgeous frustrating woman. She made him want to shake her in one breath and kiss the life out of her in the next. "What did you think last night was? A pity fuck?"

She shrugged, but her hunched shoulders and folded arms said that was exactly what she thought it was.

"Karen, believe me when I say nothing could be further from the truth."

She shook her head, and his gut clenched at the resigned look on her face. "Even so, Mike, we both know better than to try to make more of this than it is."

"So this is how you work now? Reject me before I can reject you?"

"That's not what this is about. What happened was amazing." She swallowed hard, willing her voice not to crack. "Wonderful, even. And now thanks to you I have closure and can move on. Let's not make it any more complicated by trying to turn this into something it's not."

Then it all became horribly clear. "You can't forgive me, can you. That's why you're leaving." Not that he blamed her, but still . . . Something cracked inside as he realized how stupid he was to think he'd ever really get a second chance. But how could he let her go without a fight?

The utter devastation on his face stunned her. "Mike." She reached up, but he shied away before her fingers reached his cheek.

"I know it's crazy," he said, "but I hoped . . ." his voice trailed off.

A pearl of hope blossomed in her belly. "Hoped what?"

"I hoped after last night you'd give me another chance. I want to get things right this time." He grasped her hands in both of his and squeezed his eyes shut. "I never stopped loving you, Karen. I don't know if you can ever forgive me, but you have to know that." He raised her hand to his mouth, his lips a hot brand against her palm.

Her mouth fell open. "You never stopped loving me? When did you start?" She got a strange floaty feeling, like she was watching herself from one of the puffy white clouds that decorated the vivid morning sky. Surely this could not really be happening.

"I never told you I loved you because I was scared shitless. It never occurred to me that I'd find the love of my life at age twenty-one."

Her fingers clutched his hand in a death grip.

"And you love me too, admit it." He pulled her against him and kissed her hard. She opened her mouth on a sigh and tasted his love and desperation.

"I love you," she said against his mouth. "But I'm afraid."

"Afraid of what?"

"That you'll realize you made a huge mistake and leave me," she said, knowing she sounded pitiful but unable to stop herself.

He pulled her against his chest, and for the first time she realized he was wearing only his tux pants. Smooth skin rippled under her palms, and she inhaled his spicy, masculine scent. Even if he left her in the end, how could she possibly say no to him?

Suddenly, he pulled away. "I'll prove it."

"Prove what?"

"How serious I am about you, about us." He took her suitcase out of the trunk and led her back to her room.

Her nipples tightened in anticipation as she thought of the many ways he might prove his love. To her surprise, he didn't put the moves on her. Instead he gathered up his clothes and kissed her with such love she could practically taste it.

"Meet me in the lobby in an hour," he said with a self-satisfied grin. "Wear the dress you had on yesterday."

Mike couldn't stop grinning. He'd been half-afraid she would take off after he left. But no, she'd met him in the lobby looking sexy and gorgeous in her flirty little sundress, hair tousled to perfection.

What he was about to do was by far the craziest, most impulsive thing he'd ever done in his life. And also by far the smartest. For once, his head and his heart were in total agreement.

"Where are we going?" she asked for the twentieth time.

"I told you, it's a surprise."

It took only thirty-five minutes to get to the Nevada border and only two to find a wedding chapel. "The Little Chapel of Love" advertised twenty-four-hour services.

Kit and Jake waited at the door, Kit wearing a smile that took up the bottom half of her face. Jake looked like he wanted to cart Mike off for a psychiatric evaluation.

Karen's jaw dropped open as he pulled up in front. "What are you doing?"

"Marrying you, if you'll have me."

"Isn't this a little sudden?" Her eyes were darting around frantically.

"I wouldn't call eleven years sudden."

"But we don't even know each other anymore. We have totally different lives, and—"

"And I love you." He leaned over and silenced her protests with his lips. "I love you," he repeated between kisses, "and I want to marry you."

She was silent for several moments, and his stomach knotted. Maybe she was right. This was too fast; he was scaring her away.

"Jeez, Karen, say yes already," Kit said, exasperated.

Karen looked dazedly at Kit, then back up at Mike. "Okay. Let's get married."

Five minutes later they stood in front of the minister and, with Jake and Kit as witnesses, Karen became Mrs. Mike Donovan.

When it came time to kiss, she clutched at his shirtfront and her mouth trembled underneath his. "I love you, sweetheart," he whispered soothingly.

"I love you too," she whispered shakily, "so much."

He pulled her to him, and he kissed her so fiercely she squealed in protest. Immediately he gentled his caress. "I'll spend the rest of my life trying to be worthy."

"It'll probably take you that long."

* * *

Marriage is full of compromise, or so Karen had always heard.

She received her first real-world lesson later that afternoon.

She remained dazed for about an hour after their quickie wedding, during which time Mike retrieved her suitcase from the hotel and drove her back to his house.

She'd snapped to attention as he carried her over the threshold and into the bedroom, where they wasted no time in consummating their union. The entire time the thought that Mike was now her husband gave their lovemaking an extra level of intensity. A few hours later he rolled her out of bed and took her on a hike. Though she would have been content to spend the day rolling around in bed with Mike, she supposed she needed the exercise to work the kinks out.

And, as Mike pointed out, the ten-mile hike was the perfect opportunity for them to fill in the gaps of the last eleven years.

She already knew that he took his work very seriously and was dedicated to maintaining and growing the business his father had started. By the time they arrived back at the car, she also knew that Mike liked to cook and was somewhat of a neat freak. Which was great since her culinary skills were limited to microwaving and she hated mess and clutter.

They still hadn't resolved whether they would have two kids like she wanted, or four, like he did, but they had time to figure that out.

To her horror, Mike still listened to Van Halen, but she figured she could get used to that.

Mike learned that she kept herself in very good shape, as evidenced by her ability to keep up with him on the trail even with the increased altitude. He also knew she took her own career very seriously and that she still devoured romance novels.

All in all, nothing pointed to any major incompatibilities.

334 / *Jami Alden*

Until now.

"We're going where?"

They had gone back to his house to clean up for dinner. Somewhere special, he said. Sneaky bastard, he'd waited until she was in the car and buckled in before he told her where they were going.

"My folks' house."

Karen swallowed hard and looked over at the speedometer. Damn, at this speed she would be seriously injured if she bailed out. "Mike, your mom hates me. I can't possibly have dinner with you."

"Karen, you married me this morning, remember? You'll have to deal with her sooner or later."

Karen snorted. "I still don't see why we have to ruin a perfect day by having dinner with your parents."

"Trust me. It's better to get it over with. The sooner she realizes this is forever, the sooner she'll settle down and accept it."

A panicky thrill shot through her at the thought of forever. Forever with Mike sounded pretty damn good to her.

Forever under the disdainful eye of his mother, however, was another thing entirely. "Why did Kit have to leave after the wedding?" she groaned. "At least if she were there I'd have an ally." She was silent for a moment. "You realize, of course, that your mother will probably have a stroke." Mike laughed but didn't deny it. "This is really important to you, isn't it?" she sighed, slumping against the passenger door.

Mike reached across the seat and grabbed her hand, the warmth of his caress penetrating her anxiety. "I love you for understanding."

Every time he said that, she practically melted into a puddle. She supposed she could put up with his mother for a few hours if it meant he would tell her he loved her for the rest of her life.

They pulled up to the Donovans' house within a few seconds of Nick and Kelly. They stopped short when they saw Mike and Karen on the front stoop, hands clasped.

"What are *you* doing here?" Nick asked bluntly.

"I should ask you the same," Karen replied. "Shouldn't you be on your honeymoon?"

"We're leaving tomorrow," Kelly said, squeezing Nick's arm and gazing up at him adoringly. Karen wondered if she got that same dopey expression when she looked at Mike. Probably. Kelly leaned in close to Karen and said in a low voice, "I'm taking Maria's baby away. This is the least I can do to keep the peace."

"Don't worry. She'll be so horrified when she finds out what we've done she'll forget your transgressions."

Kelly's eyes bulged and her hand flew to her mouth when she spotted the simple gold band adorning Karen's finger. She looked wildly at Mike. "You didn't—"

Mike flashed a matching band. "We sure as hell did."

Kelly let out a horrified laugh and hugged them both. "She's going to have a kitten."

Mike kept a firm grip on her forearm as they walked inside, sensing her overwhelming urge to flee.

"Oh, are the newlyweds here?" Maria called as she bustled into the entryway. She froze when she saw Karen, and Karen felt her glare like a laser beam. Somehow Maria managed to loom over her even though Karen's platform sandals afforded her a two-inch height advantage.

"Michael, I didn't know you were bringing a guest."

Mike laced his fingers through hers even as he bent to kiss his mother's cheek. "There's plenty to eat, right?"

Maria didn't reply and walked stiffly back to the dining room.

"The real question," Karen muttered, "is if there's enough to drink."

"It'll be okay," he whispered, tipping her chin up for a kiss. The brief contact managed to banish thoughts of angry mothers, at least for a second.

They pulled apart and Karen caught Nick's gaze. A look passed between the brothers. To Karen's surprise, Nick gave her shoulder a reassuring squeeze. "Shall we?" he asked.

Tony was already there, sitting on the couch and talking to their father, Frank. Unlike the others, Tony didn't look shocked at Karen's arrival but instead wore an oddly satisfied smirk on his face.

"Guess you figured out a solution to your problem," Tony said, looking pointedly at Mike's left hand.

Mike only smiled and nodded.

"Dad, you remember Karen Sullivan, Kelly's sister," Mike said. Karen shook the older man's big, work-roughened hand. A loud clatter sounded from the kitchen as Maria slammed down a ladle with unnecessary force.

Frank's chocolate brown eyes twinkled. "Don't mind my wife. She'll come around."

Karen smiled stiffly, not at all convinced.

They sat down around the table, and Karen was relieved to find herself between Mike and Kelly. The tomato and fresh mozzarella salad looked delicious, but Karen's stomach curdled under Maria's incessant glare.

"So, Karen, when are you heading back to Sacramento?" Kelly asked, to break the awkward silence.

"Tomorrow," she replied. "I have the day off, so I'll leave sometime tomorrow."

"We could have lunch before you go," Mike said.

"Aren't you working?" Maria asked sharply.

"Mom, I can take time for lunch," Mike said firmly.

Maria focused her attention on Karen. "So what do you do in Sacramento, Karen?"

"I'm a hairdresser." The statement came out sounding like a question.

"A *hairdresser*?" She may as well have been saying "prostitute."

Karen's shoulders hunched. For the life of her, she couldn't remember why the idea of being brought home to Mom was ever appealing. "Yes. And I'm good at it too."

"With you in Sacramento, you and Mike won't be able to see much of each other." Maria didn't bother to disguise the relief in her voice.

Karen didn't have a ready retort since she and Mike hadn't discussed the matter themselves.

"There's a new spa opening over on the Lake. I'm sure they'd love to hire someone with Karen's skill," Mike said.

Karen's frustration with Maria was momentarily derailed. "So you think I'll be moving back here?" she asked with a grin. "I guess we never got around to discussing that detail."

Heat bloomed in her stomach at his grin. "My house is too big for just me. I was going to get a dog, but I suppose you'll do," he teased.

She punched him in the shoulder.

Maria wasn't ready to admit defeat. She cocked her head to the side. "Didn't you and Michael date while he was in college?" she asked, even though she damn well knew the answer. No doubt she knew the circumstances under which it ended, and probably Karen's high school reputation too. "I seem to remember you splitting up under rather bad circumstances."

She didn't have to take this shit! Her palms hit the table, and she was just about to push back when she felt a feminine hand on her right thigh. She was marginally comforted by Kelly's sympathetic smile.

*   *   *

Mike knew Karen was close to her limit. She was so tense she practically vibrated. He threaded his fingers through hers, wincing at the iciness of her hands.

"Mom," Mike said warningly, "that was a long time ago."

"All I'm saying is it didn't work then, what makes you think it would work now?" His mom forked a bite of tomato into her mouth and chewed deliberately.

Shit. Maybe thrusting Karen into the bosom of his family wasn't the best idea he'd ever had.

"Because I'm a lot smarter than I was back then. Now I know a good thing when I see it," Mike said. Then he shocked everyone by leaning over and kissing the hell out of Karen, right there at the dinner table. "And because this morning, Karen and I got married."

Tony's chuckle rumbled through the room, only to be cut short by his father. "Do you girls have a cousin or something for Tony here?"

"Screw that," he said. "These two want to get nailed down, that's their business."

Maria slammed down her fork and excused herself to fetch the main course. Mike followed.

"How could you do this, Michael? To marry such a woman . . ." She shook her head as she retrieved the pot roast from the oven.

Mike clenched his jaw. "I love her, Ma, I really do. And she loves me too."

"But she—"

He held up his hand. "Whatever you heard about Karen, and what happened between us, forget it. It was my fault. I screwed up, and now I have a chance to fix it."

She didn't ask for details, for which he was thankful. She studied him closely. Finally she said, "You think this will make you happy?"

"I know it."

Maria rolled her eyes. "What do I know, I'm just your mother." Despite her sarcasm she looked slightly more accepting.

Mike breathed a sigh of relief.

Karen looked up warily as his mother placed the pot roast platter on the table.

"You know," Maria said, looking pointedly at Karen's barely touched salad, "all of my boys were huge babies."

Karen looked confused at the turn of conversation.

"Mike was almost ten pounds."

Karen looked at him, horrified, then back at his mother, whose petite stature was a match for Karen's.

Maria continued. "I'll be expecting several grandchildren. You're going to need to keep your strength up," she said, forking a huge slab of pot roast onto Karen's plate.

Karen looked at him very pointedly and stuffed such a huge bite in her mouth Mike was surprised she didn't choke.

He grinned at her look of smug determination. That was his Tiny, all right, feisty as ever. This time, he knew, he was up to the challenge.

Here's a sneak peek at Devyn Quinn's scorching
FLESH AND THE DEVIL,
available now from Aphrodisia . . .

To distract herself a bit, Líadán swirled the last of the wine in her glass, drinking it down. "Some of us are meant to walk alone," she murmured when her glass was empty.

He lifted her fingertips gently to his lips. "I want to do something about that." The arousal blooming so softly when they'd danced body to body suddenly exploded into roaring flames. His eyes found her face, studying her, waiting for her reaction. Sensual awareness pulsed between them.

Brenden sat up, taking the glass from her hand, setting it aside. He leaned forward, bringing his face within inches of hers.

Without thinking, Líadán tipped her head toward his. Their mouths brushed together, gentle, slow, and ever so exquisite, tasting each other in a kiss made all the more erotic because of its stealth in arriving. Neither planned it. It just happened. Beneath the gentleness was a longing neither could ignore. As a ribbon of desire curled through her breasts down to her nether regions, the need to make love to him overtook her.

"Wow," he breathed, when their kiss had ended. "I've never felt anything like this before."

Líadán drew in her own breath. In that instant she knew without doubt Brenden Wallace would follow her through hell and back, even if it meant he was destroyed himself. A man like Brenden didn't come along often. She would hold on to him, this lifeline unexpectedly having been tossed into the dark void of her life.

Silence followed, a silence in which nothing but the rain came between them. No more words were needed.

Climbing to his feet, Brenden pulled her to hers. Slipping off his shirt, he let it drop to the floor. Just as she reached up to undo the thin chain across her neck keeping the backless halter in place, he caught her hands. "Let me," he rumbled in a husky voice.

Líadán nodded. His hands slipped behind, expertly loosening the clasp. Freed, the silky folds drifted over her breasts, down her hips, falling around her feet in a soft hush. Dressed only in panties, garter, hose and heels, her bare breasts were proudly erect, the tips of her nipples hard little beads. At the sight of her, Brenden groaned, an earnest and besieged sound escaping his throat. When he reached for her, his hands trembled.

She watched as his eyes betrayed the effect her almost nude body was taking on him. The knowledge she could affect him so deeply almost brought tears to her eyes. While many men had gazed upon her body with admiration and desire, she had in turn despised them, knowing they were weak and could be manipulated by their sexual needs.

"You're so beautiful," he murmured. "So perfect."

The humbling, marveling tone in his voice almost brought tears of emotion to her eyes. Her mind screamed a volley of warnings and objections, but her senses screened them out. They were not what she wanted to hear. Instead she wanted to hear the sounds of love, the erotic sounds of his breathing, the soft feel of his hands as they moved over her skin. Mesmerized, she waited. Only when he drew her into his arms did she relax. She could feel his whole body trembling with anticipation, the fierce hardening of his erection under his slacks. She aroused him and he wanted her. Her heart fluttered with a ray of hope. He so clearly demonstrated physically what she was feeling.

"It's crazy, I know, but I need you so much." Brenden's hands touched her face, his fingertips skimming her cheeks before sliding to the nape of her neck, tangling his fingers in her long hair. His head dipped and his mouth captured hers.

Líadán opened her mouth to allow the invasion of his tongue. She pressed herself closer to him, sliding her arms around his shoulders. Brenden nipped at her lower lip, tracing it with his own tongue before sucking it gently. His hand found her breast, cupping its weight and squeezing lightly. His fingers began to tease, making slow circles. Her nipple came to instant attention under his fingers, the pebble-hard nubbin acutely sensitive. She sucked in a breath, her body arching against his. A small moan escaped her lips. "That feels so good."

His exploring tongue traveled the delicate whorl of one ear, tracing a warm, wet path along the delicate shell-like curve. Catching her dangling earring between his teeth, he gave it a gentle, teasing tug. "Only the beginning of what you're going to feel tonight." Kissing the soft pulse at the base of her throat, he worked his way lower, each teasing lap of his tongue setting goose pimples of excitement into action across her exposed skin. Her breath caught in her throat, hovering like a tiny hummingbird in flight, anxious, oh so anxious, when he flicked at one pink peak.

Stifling a cry of pleasure, Líadán curled her fingers through Brenden's thick hair. He seemed to take her anxious tugs as a sign she was enjoying the sensations. Tongue swirling in clever delicious ways that aimed blazing little darts straight at her vibrating core, his teeth raked the sensitive nub. His free hand covered her right breast, rolling the little pink nubbin between thumb and forefinger.

"That feels so good." A shiver ran through Líadán's body. Lust heated, then sizzled. The throb between her legs made it impossible to think about anything but gratifying this aching need.

"I want to please you this time." Brenden kissed the softness between her breasts. "Taste you . . ." His hand slid down to her flat belly, then between her legs to gently caress her softness. The feel of his fingers sliding against silky panties wet with her cream created a mesmerizing sensation. He slipped a finger beneath the elastic of her panties, maddening her with an erotic flick against her little button.

Tilting back her head, Líadán gasped aloud. Her body shuddered with tiny tremors when his finger found and stroked the slick softness between her labia. He added a second finger, searching for her depth. Finding her slit, he slid in, to work his magic.

"Oh, wow!" Jerking in surprise, she sagged against him. She needed to get a grip, control and pace herself or she'd lose herself to orgasm too quickly. She didn't want to. She wanted to wait, enjoy the moment just as he came to climax with her. *Steady . . . Take it slow.*

Brenden, however, wasn't giving her that chance.